Praise for
THE WRONG REFLECTION

"Noted historical novelist Bradshaw expands her repertoire to include an SF thriller laced with intrigue and a truly star-crossed love affair."   —*Library Journal*

"Versatile Bradshaw turns from historical fiction to ring the changes on star-crossed lovers who, in this case, are fresh, consistently entertaining, and head a cast much more empathic than usual for the thriller genre."   —*Kirkus Reviews*

Praise for the novels of
Gillian Bradshaw

CLEOPATRA'S HEIR

"Fascinating historical figures—Julius Caesar, Marcus Antonius, and Cleopatra—roam the ancient Egyptian desert and the glittering city of Alexandria in this latest from classics scholar Bradshaw . . . Bradshaw's attention to . . . convincing historical detail . . . gives the novel substance."
          —*Publishers Weekly*

continued . . .

THE WOLF HUNT

"A beautifully written, lyrical novel about an often brutal time. Each character is fully realized and the story, as embellished by Bradshaw, is both entertaining and historically accurate."
— *Historical Novel Society Review*

"Gillian Bradshaw takes an obscure historical footnote and embellishes it into an intricate, multi-layered tale."
— *Romantic Times*

"Her confident and intimate writing, her rich variety of characters and her refusal to use stock descriptions of the people and period make *The Wolf Hunt* an engaging experience . . . her descriptions of the lives of wolves would sit comfortably with some of the best nature writing."
— *BookPage*

"*The Wolf Hunt* is a captivating tale of a woman's journey through the twisted paths of the medieval forests where the everyday is overwhelmed by the supernatural, and where only love and loyalty can keep the darkness at bay . . . and the wolf from your throat. If you love the fables of the medieval world, then this book will enchant you."
— Sara Douglass, author of *The Wayfarer Redemption series*

THE SAND-RECKONER
Winner of the Alex Award

"Armed with just a few antique facts, Bradshaw ably recreates the extraordinary life of Archimedes, the great mathematician and engineer who built sophisticated we ___ during the first Punic War . . . Bradshaw is skilled ___ ing historical figures to life, and this intriguing ___ taining novel of the boyish dreamer who pos ___ the ancient world's most brilliant minds d ___ vivid imagination." —

ISLAND OF GHOSTS

"Despite the fiery turmoil of the climactic duel and intrigues involving legionaries, Druids, turncoats . . . *Island of Ghosts* hinges on character rather than plot. Although Ariantes is rewarded with Roman citizenship for his courage—the highest recognition the state bestows—can he ever really be Romanized? Gillian Bradshaw asks questions like this, ambiguities that lend the conventions of the historical novel a rare and unusual depth."   —*The Boston Globe*

"A vivid, atmospheric work . . . Fluidly written, well researched, and luxuriant with colorful authentic detail, this fact-based chronicle of a proud tribe of legendary horsemen and their gradual assimilation by the empire will engage readers with an interest in the history either of Rome or of its exotic outposts."   —*Publishers Weekly*

"Classics scholar Gillian Bradshaw has penned a historical novel of extraordinary depth and passion . . . A multi-layered drama that will appeal to fans of intelligent historical fiction."   —*Booklist*

"Bradshaw explores the demands of loyalty and honor amid political intrigue and rebellion. She deftly melds her expert knowledge of the period with her moving portrayal of a compassionate and honorable man adapting to a foreign culture. Both the setting and the riveting plot should appeal widely."   —*Library Journal*

DANGEROUS NOTES

"This surprising book unexpectedly grabs one's attention and won't let go, thanks to the intensity of the characters' feelings and the expertness of their portrayal . . . Bradshaw adds obstacles, changes situations with uncanny rapidity, and makes a not-unexpected ending still come as quite a shock."   —*Booklist*

THE
WRONG
REFLECTION

GILLIAN BRADSHAW

ACE BOOKS, NEW YORK

This is a work of fiction. Names, characters, places, and incidents either are the product of the author's imagination or are used fictitiously, and any resemblance to actual persons, living or dead, business establishments, events, or locales is entirely coincidental.

THE WRONG REFLECTION

An Ace Book / published by arrangement with
Severn House Publishers, Ltd.

PRINTING HISTORY
Severn House hardcover edition / 2000
Ace mass-market edition / September 2003

ISBN: 0-441-01097-0

ACE®
Ace Books are published by The Berkley Publishing Group,
a division of Penguin Group (USA) Inc.,
375 Hudson Street, New York, New York 10014.
ACE and the "A" design
are trademarks belonging to Penguin Group (USA) Inc.

PRINTED IN THE UNITED STATES OF AMERICA

10 9 8 7 6 5 4 3 2 1

ONE

SHE ALMOST KEPT ON DRIVING.

Sandra Murray was on her way back from an evening out with friends when she saw the break in the roadside fence—the black gash in the headlight-whitened blur. As she rounded a bend, her headlights transcribed an arc across a rough darkness of field and picked out something which stood out against a gleam of water. It was only when she had already passed it that she realised the shape in the water was a car.

For perhaps thirty seconds, she kept on driving. There was nothing to show that the accident wasn't hours old and long sorted out, the people involved all gone home to fill out forms for their insurance companies. But Sandra was meticulous and conscientious, and now a tiny uncertainty quavered in her gut: what if . . . ?

She stopped the car, backed it into a farm track, and resignedly turned around. It was quicker and easier to check that all was well than to go home and lie awake worrying about it.

She pulled into the break in the roadside fence and stopped so that her headlights shone over the field, the

water, and the half-submerged car. One sleek silver-grey
bumper thrust from the black stream of a small river showed
that the car was lying on its side but that most of the vehicle
was underwater, though near enough to the surface to make
the water above it eddy and glisten. Something red and
white was sticking up from the region of the back seat window. The field was full of wheat, its blades layered and
translucent in the white glare of the lights. The track which
the wrecked car had made crossing the field was plain and
raw—and so new that the bent grain at its edges was still
shaking itself slowly upright.

Sandra flicked on the hazard lights and climbed out of
her car. She felt short of breath and her throat was tight. Desperately afraid of what she might find, she hurriedly picked
her way down the torn slope to the water.

The red-and-white object thrust from the drowned window resolved itself into a human arm, limp fingers dangling
in the air.

"Oh God," whispered Sandra, under her breath. "Oh
God, oh God, oh God."

She hesitated stupidly among the rushes at the stream's
edge. The world lay still under the pale moon, and before
her the hand senselessly held the air its owner had not
reached. She was alone: the road behind her was silent, and
there was no one to bring help, except her. She took a deep
breath and waded in. Her sandalled feet sank, squelching
into the thick mud at the bottom of the stream, and the roots
of the rushes tangled her ankles. The water was cold and, at
the back door of the car, it came up to her waist. The awful
hand was covered in blood. She grabbed it—whether to reassure its owner or to haul him out, she couldn't have said.
The hand was warm but did not stir under her own, and her
uncertain jerk did not shift it at all. The current pressed
against her, pushing her thighs against the harsh, uneven
bottom of the car. She peered into the water, trying to see
what to do. The full brightness of the beams cast by her own
car's headlights fell short of her and cast bewildering shad-

ows through the reeds; the hazard lights blinked as if in panic. The arm was held upright by the broken edge of the window. The body beyond it was only an indistinct black shape. She groped under the water for the handle of the rear door; found it; dragged at it: it was jammed. She heaved at it with both hands, and it eventually gave. As Sandra wrenched the door upwards, the arm was dragged back through the window and fell with a splash into the stream.

She felt for the arm and found it again, then stooped to drape it over her shoulder. Now her eyes were adjusting to the half-dark, and she could see that the dark shape of the body twisted into the front of the car. She staggered backwards, pulling at an angle to free it, and the body came with her, its weight suddenly dragging at her shoulders, its wet head flopping against her side. It got stuck, then came free, legs trailing in the stream. It was a man. She dragged him towards the bank, panting and slipping in the mud, up through the reeds. He was very heavy, and horribly inert. She let go of him at the edge of the crushed wheat, and staggered back into the water.

She groped through the open door and once again peered into the murky water inside, but there did not seem to be anyone else in the car. She splashed back to the bank.

The man was lying as she'd left him, on his side with his face in the wheat and his heels in the river. In the glare of the headlights he was all black and white: water-darkened suit, water-darkened hair, white shirt, chalky skin. She heaved him on to his back, kneeling beside him with her ear against his mouth, and looked down the line of his body away from the dazzle of headlights. There was no lift of the chest, and no warmth against her cheek. He wasn't breathing. She felt under his jaw for the pulse: nothing. Desperate, she dug her fingers deeper: still nothing. She struggled to remember the first aid class she'd taken once: perhaps she'd just done it wrong and made a mistake? She lowered her head and looked again, pressing and prodding once more. The man's flesh was warm, but no surge of blood met her fingers. She shook him, and heard the water gurgle in his lungs.

Too late. If she hadn't driven past at first, if she'd stopped instantly . . .

She set her teeth, pulled his head straight and pushed his jaw upward. Clear the airway. She felt in the slimy mouth and checked that the tongue wasn't blocking the throat; the teeth were hard against her fingers, like insects in mud. She pinched his nose shut, set her mouth against the slack wet lips, and breathed hard into the water-clogged lungs; once . . . and twice. Then she checked for the right spot at the base of the breast bone, and laced her hands together. *Heart massage.* She'd done it on the first aid dummy, she could do it now. *Push* hard. One, two, three, four, five. *Push*, and two, three . . . fifteen presses, and then two breaths. Now check the pulse again.

Nothing.

A voice called down to her, "Hey—uh—do you need help?"

She looked up and saw that another car had stopped. The figure of its driver stood black against the glare of a new set of headlights. Relief came with a rush that tried to weaken her, and she drove it back ferociously and started pressing again.

"Call an ambulance!" she howled. (*Push. One, two, three, four, five.*) "This guy was in an accident, he's drowned."

"Can I—" faltered the stranger.

"Do you know how to give CPR?" she demanded hopefully.

"I . . . uh, no."

"Then just call an ambulance, OK?"

"OK."

The new headlights swept off: she realised how deeply she must have been concentrating, not to have noticed them arrive. *Push.* One, two, three, four. *Push*, and up, and check the airway, and pinch the nose shut, and *blow*, and back, and *push* . . .

She was checking his pulse for the third time when the body underneath her gave a long shudder. All the short hair on her own body stood on end. In the hollow of his throat, her questioning fingers felt the weak, unsteady flutter of returning life.

"Oh God," she whispered again, and her eyes filled with tears. She hadn't expected it to work.

She leaned back on her heels. The man drew his first gasping breath and coughed feebly. She turned him over carefully into the recovery position—knee bent, head to the side, one arm drawn up—and sat beside him, crying quietly. Her every muscle was trembling, and she felt as weak as she would have done if the newly recovered life had been her own.

The ambulance arrived shortly afterward, together with a private car that proved to be the man who'd stopped before. The ambulance crew poured down the hill and checked over the accident victim. Sandra sat numbly in the crushed wheat, watching them. In the new lights, the man she'd pulled from the car looked like a corpse unearthed from a fresh grave, his still-chalky face smeared with mud from the field. The ambulance crew, backlit by headlights, moved about him like ghouls. But she knew he was alive.

The ambulance crew asked her about what she'd done; she told them. Some police appeared, and she told them, too. The driver of the private car, a pleasant middle-aged man, babbled loquaciously about how he'd seen hazard lights, and had stopped and found Sandra. "She was giving him heart massage!" he exclaimed admiringly. "Lucky for him she knew how!"

"Very lucky," agreed the police and the ambulance crew. They took one of the blankets they'd brought for the victim, and draped it over Sandra's shoulders. Now that the crisis was over and she could feel again, she was shivering from the chill of the stream and the night. Her arms were shaking, too, from the strain of pushing. She wondered what the injured man's chest would feel like when he woke up.

The unconscious man was loaded on to a stretcher and carried up the slope. Sandra tramped up behind him. A confusion of lights flashed and glared—headlights; blue police; blue ambulance; amber hazard. She watched as the man she'd rescued was strapped down in the back of the ambulance. The crew climbed in and the doors banged shut. One of the blue lights stopped flashing and the vehicle's red tail lights pulled into the pale moonlit ribbon of road and receded into the enveloping dark.

The police slapped an orange "POLICE AWARE" notice on the broken fence and sat in their own car, writing up the details of the accident. "You look all in," Sandra's fellow rescuer told her. "Can I drive you home?"

She shook her head. "I'll need my car," she said, coming back to earth, to the practical damp exhausted present. "I'll just go very slowly and carefully."

Her fellow rescuer smiled, and she smiled back. Suddenly reluctant to part as strangers, they exchanged names and shook hands. He told her that he'd felt useless when he'd had to admit that he didn't know how to give a heart massage, and Sandra confessed that she hadn't expected it to work. They agreed that it was really something else, hoped that the accident victim would make a full recovery, and wished each other a good-night. They climbed into their respective cars. Sandra started the engine, to make sure that the battery wasn't exhausted, then sat silent while the other car drove off. Something over her shoulders dragged as she shifted to turn on the interior light, and she realised that she was still wearing the ambulance blanket. She would have to give that back. The prospect of white hospital corridors and smiling receptionists seemed remote and improbable. She felt vaguely unreal, and looked in the rear-view mirror to see if it showed. Her hair hung in bedraggled tangles around her familiar freckled and bony face. There was a smear of blood along one cheek, and two or three smears of mud. But the eyes that met hers glowed. She realised why.

"Christ!" she said out loud. "I saved his life!"

And suddenly she was flooded with an enormous happiness. She, Sandra Murray, a twenty-four-year-old not-particularly-heroic plant pathologist, had fought death on another's behalf—and won. She didn't know who he was, but he'd looked old enough to have a wife who would not now be a widow, and children who would not now be fatherless. It was such a vast thing that it was hard to comprehend. All at once, she felt certain that when she was seventy she would remember sitting here, wet and exhausted and with aching arms—remember this moment as one of the high points of her life.

She hoped he was all right, the man she'd pulled from the river. She would have to phone the hospital in the morning. Carefully, she checked the time on her watch. She would have to tell the hospital the approximate time he was admitted, because she didn't know his name. Eleven forty-two. "Excuse me, I'd like to ask about a patient of yours, an accident victim who was admitted last night sometime between half-past eleven and midnight ..." That ought to find him. There was only one hospital he could be in.

She switched off the car's interior light, released the hand brake, and started very carefully, gently, slowly, on to the road home.

THE PATIENT HIMSELF SWAM IN AND OUT OF CON-sciousness for the first day after the accident. He was aware, on and off, that he was lying in a bed in a room with one window, and that people in white were pulling his arms about and shining lights in his eyes or sticking things in his mouth. But it was too much effort to decipher it all. He was only fully aware of the pain. He wasn't used to pain, and now it was everywhere: a savage flare across his chest that accompanied each slow breath; a dull gnawing ache in every

limb; a hot clammy nausea overall. It left him no space for
any other feeling but a kind of remote astonishment.

Gradually, though, the pain grew less and the periods of
awareness grew longer. Finally he struggled out of the fogs
and realised, with a sense of enormous triumph, that he was
alive.

He lay still in the bed, looking out the window. It was full
of dove-grey clouds. At first the clouds seemed motionless
but, as he continued to watch them, he saw that the whole
surface of the sky was in fact gliding toward him, driven by
a steady wind and glowing with diffuse light from a concealed sun. His sense of triumph grew. He was here, in this
place, *alive*. It was an immense victory.

He considered the place, and found that he knew he was
in a hospital. Some of the people in white had told him so
during his intervals of partial awareness. He'd had an accident and been taken to hospital, and now he'd be all right:
that was what they'd said. Nobody had seemed to expect
him to know about the accident, so he was not concerned to
find that he did not remember it. Hospital. Accident. It hurt.
He had not thought it would hurt so much. He closed his
eyes against the vast steady movement of the clouds.

"Mr Anderson?" said a voice beside him.

He turned his head, and saw that two of the white-clad
people were back. One was a man: pink-skinned, about
thirty, tall and thin with weak blue eyes behind panels of dis-
torting glass. A blue badge on his white coat read "Dr J.
Evans. Senior House Officer." Behind him stood a dark-
skinned woman in her mid-forties, with a badge that read
"Sylvia Brown. Staff Nurse." From his bed, he stared at
them in silent confusion. If the doctor's name was Anderson,
why did the badge say "J. Evans"?

The doctor smiled at him. "Nurse," he commanded over
his shoulder, "make a note that the patient responded to his
name." Turning back to face him, the doctor said, "Mr Anderson, I've come to check on how you are this evening."

The doctor pulled back the bed sheets, and hauled open

the front of a gown. The patient watched curiously. A body stretched away down the bed from him: a narrow chest sprinkled with coarse black hair and a lax stomach running down under the turned-back sheet. Arms lay limp beside the torso, both hands and one forearm wrapped in white. The right arm and most of the right side of the torso were black with bruising, and another great crimson and purple bruise glared from the base of the breastbone. The doctor listened to the chest with a tube-like instrument. He tapped it. He prodded the right side of the chest. It was only with the resulting stab of pain that the patient realised that this battered lump was himself. His curiosity vanished abruptly, and was replaced by a queasy horror. He looked away quickly.

"Well," said the doctor amiably. "Everything seems to be fine." He pulled the sheet up again. "Do you understand me, Mr Anderson? You're doing just fine."

The patient stared again. He manoeuvred an unwieldy tongue around swollen lips and whispered hoarsely, "Anderson?"

The doctor smiled at the patient. "Paul Anderson? That is your name, isn't it?"

"No," said the patient.

The doctor's smile faltered. He looked at the nurse. "That's what it said on his ID," said the nurse. She took some papers out of the folder she was holding and offered them to the doctor. "His place of work confirmed it. They were the only emergency contact number we had, and Admissions rang them this morning. They were in." She went to a table beside the bed, opened a drawer, and took out a damp leather wallet and a stack of plastic cards. "You see?" she said to the patient, speaking slowly and clearly as though he could not be expected to understand otherwise. "We put your things here, safe. Except your clothes. They were wet." She selected one of the cards and held it out so that the patient could see it.

The card was made of laminated plastic. It had a photograph of a dark-haired man of about thirty-five, who gazed from the tiny square with an expression of arrogant boredom. Beside the photograph was a tiny drawing: the sideways figure eight of infinity enclosed·in a stylised star, with the words "Stellar Research Ltd" wreathing it. Below the drawing were the words "Paul Anderson. Marketing Director."

"Not me," croaked the patient, though something about both photograph and drawing tugged at his memory.

The nurse was surprised. She looked from the patient to the card and back again.

"Who are you, then?" asked the doctor, blinking in bewilderment.

The patient opened his mouth and found that he could not answer. A wave of violent disorientation descended on him with a crash. He could feel his name, somewhere beyond an interior fault line, but it was as though the mental ground he stood on dragged, grating past it like the edge of an opposing continent. He struggled to reach across the divide, and the world spun sideways. The clammy nausea, which had never quite gone away, swelled up to choke him. He made an inarticulate noise of terror and pain and, with a strength he did not think he'd recovered, fought to sit up. The nurse hurriedly put down the card and grabbed his shoulders to steady him. He vomited bile and air, then bent over across his doubled knees. The bruises on his chest throbbed savagely. He could not remember his name. He set his bandaged hands against a face wet with tears.

"All right, all right," said the nurse, patting him on the shoulder. "Calm down. It's OK. Calm down."

He shook his head. Beneath his thighs, the bed was wet and warm. In his terror, his bladder had emptied itself. He revolted from the sick dirty ache of his body and reached still more desperately for his elusive name, but it was further away than ever. Panic began to give great shoves against his aching chest. He was trapped here. He was ill and in pain, and he didn't remember who he was. He gave a moan of anguished disbelief.

The doctor picked up the card and looked at it, then looked at the man in the bed. "It was natural to assume that it was his," he told the nurse defensively. "It was in his wallet. It looks like him."

The nurse was busy trying to soothe the patient and didn't reply.

"He must have stolen it," Dr Evans continued unhappily, to himself. "And the car he smashed up." He looked resentfully at the patient, who was now curled up with his face buried against his knees, panting. A stupid joyrider! And this one was no wild teenager, but a grown man who ought to have known better. Yet here he was wasting medical time and resources that could have been spent on those whose sufferings weren't their own fault. And to top it all, when faced with admitting what he'd done, the fellow had hysterics and wet the bed!

"Well?" demanded the doctor angrily. "What is your name?"

The patient looked up at him, face white under its bruises, eyes black and blind, mouth working. For the first time Evans realised the depth of the man's distress, and was taken aback by it. "What's the matter?" he asked in surprise.

The nurse was more perceptive. "Don't you remember your name?" she asked.

The patient shook his head. He drew a deep shuddering breath and tried to speak, but no words came out.

Dr Evans stared. He dealt with general medicine. Amnesia was outside his expertise, and he was uncomfortable with it. He tried to think what he should do. The patient's blank terrified gaze remained fixed on him. The man drew in another breath as though he meant to speak or scream, but he made no sound. The nurse began speaking to him quietly, trying to calm him. "Nurse," the doctor asked at last, "has he had a head X-ray?"

"He had several X-rays and a check-up on admission," she replied impatiently. "The results are in his notes. Everything looked normal, apart from the cracked ribs, the fin-

gers, and the bruises and contusions. But he needed CPR at
the accident site and he was unconscious for a long time.
He's confused, OK? Doctor, you're going to have to give
him something to calm him down."

The doctor nodded. He'd come equipped to administer a
painkiller, and he took out the syringe. He filled it with the
dosage he'd prepared before, then decided to use twice as
much. As he stepped up to the patient, who was still staring
in blank horror, he suddenly realised that the fellow probably wasn't a joyrider after all. Someone in this condition
might not recognise his own name. "Are you sure you're not
Paul Anderson?" he asked as he readied his swab.

The patient could not answer. His instinctive denial was
caught in another spasm of nausea. He made an inhuman
barking noise, and vomited an agonised heave of air from
his empty stomach. Evans was once again taken aback. "I'll
just give you this to calm you down," he stammered apologetically. "It will help the nausea and the pain from your
bruises, too."

He slid the needle into the rigid arm, then took Paul Anderson's ID and went off to check the patient's identity with
Admissions.

The drug took effect quickly. Not-Anderson relaxed, un-
coiled into the bed, and lay limply. The sick panic about his
lost identity was still there but it was on the other side of a
thick glass wall now, where it couldn't hurt him. He watched
it like a man watching a shark in an aquarium. The nurse
changed the sheets under him, moving him from one side of
the bed to the other, then matter-of-factly changed him into
a clean gown and settled him between the clean sheets. She
stroked his forehead gently, and he looked up at her, his
pupils dilated with shock and morphine so that they looked
like holes bored into his face.

"It's OK," she told him, years of practice combining with
her native compassion to produce the authoritative tone of
comfort. "Lots of people find they don't remember things
after an accident. But give 'em time, and mostly everything

comes back except the accident itself. Don't worry, man, it'll be OK. Go to sleep, and you'll feel better in the morning, I promise."

He felt stronger in the morning, but not better. His awareness of what he had lost only grew clearer as his strength crept back. He had no history. His own identity had become a blank, like an unknown n in a mathematical equation whose value he could not determine. Every effort to retrieve himself brought only a return of the nausea, and eventually the doctors had to give him another dose of morphine. But that was not the worst of it.

At some point in the middle of the morning, one of the nurses came in and suggested that he might like to shave. He did not remember what shaving was, but it seemed that he didn't need to: she intended to do it for him. She fetched a towel, a basin of water and a small electrical device, and set them on the table beside the bed. Then she went to a cupboard at the side of the room and came back with a small round mirror framed with stainless steel. "You can see you need a shave," she said smiling, and she held the mirror in front of him.

He looked into the glass and, in it, saw the face from the photograph. The dark hair that had been sleek in the picture was stiff and tangled, the region around the eyes and about the swollen nose was now one great bruise, the jaw was dark with stubble, but the narrow angular shape was undeniably the same. The bloodshot eyes widened as they met his own. The lips gaped. Something cold swept through his aching chest, as though he were being poured into a hole. He screamed desperately and pushed the reflection away. The mirror flew from the nurse's hands and rang on the floor.

"What's the matter?" asked the nurse in bewilderment. "It's only bruises."

He shook his head, once again covering the face with his bandaged hands. He could not bring himself to tell her that it was not his face.

When the puzzled nurse had gone, he lay awake, staring

at the curtains round the window. They were of a coarse
weave, the thick threads visibly forming a myriad tiny
squares. To stop himself from thinking about the face in the
mirror, he calculated the number of squares in the curtain,
then treated the squares as a graph and solved equations pro-
posed by the curves of the fabric's folds. He closed his eyes
and tested himself with complex problems in abstract logic.

Nurses came back periodically, to pull at his arm, put
straps around it and stick rods in his mouth, as they'd done
as far back as his memory started. They offered him food,
but the thought of eating revolted him. In the afternoon, an
unknown doctor came and gave him another dose of
painkiller.

He was dozing behind its protective wall of glass when a
nurse roused him with a touch on his shoulder. "Mr Anderson!" she said.

"I'm not," he insisted, opening his eyes with a shudder. It
was like opening a window in a stifling black room. He was
not Anderson. He didn't know who he was, but he knew
that, could assert it without thinking. His identity might be
n, but his amnesia had not altered its value and, in some part
of him, the knowledge of that value persisted.

The nurse smiled with the smug assurance of one who
knew better. "It's time for your supper," she said.

She pressed him so hard to eat—"just a little, to settle
your stomach"—that at last he agreed to try, simply to get
rid of her. When the food arrived, he refused her offer to
spoon-feed him and she finally left. He intended to ignore
the tray on the folding table. But the smell curled insidiously
into his nostrils and nudged at his distracted mind. Because
he'd been vomiting he'd been given only a light meal: a
bowl of tomato soup; a plate of toast; and a dish of pineapple chunks. He stared at them for a long time, absorbing the
warm orange of the soup, the dappled rectangles of the toast
and the pale geometric blocks of the pineapple. The smell
continued to tickle his senses, and at last he realised that he
was hungry. He picked up a piece of toast, his white-

wrapped fingers clumsy and hesitant, and cautiously inserted it in his mouth. The warm floury fullness of it seemed to flood him. He bit off a chunk, gulped it down, and started on the rest.

The soup came from a packet, the toast from a white-sliced loaf, and the pineapple from a tin, but he did not know that. It was the first meal he could remember, and it seemed wonderfully exotic: the soup velvety, with hints of unknown spice; the toast crisp, yet juicy with melted butter; the fruit succulent and cool and sweet. He ate it clumsily, picking up the bowls with unsteady hands and spilling juice down his chin and on to his gown. He ate it all. His depression began to lift. Even without identity, it was good to be alive.

The nurse was pleased with him for eating up his dinner, and suggested that an orderly help him to the toilet. It was hard to get to his feet, even with the help of the grinning orderly, and walking was worse. He could not balance: every attempt to take a step had him turning back to the bed in alarm. In the end, he had to shuffle over the slick floor with the orderly on one side of him and the nurse on the other. When he lay down again, though, he was filled with triumph at the accomplishment. He was recovering. His strength and balance would come back. Surely his past would come back, too?

He slept well that night and woke feeling better, as Sylvia Brown had promised he would. When Dr Evans returned after breakfast, not-Anderson felt much more able to face him—though the doctor, too, looked smug.

"How are you feeling today, Mr Anderson?" he asked, taking the folder of notes from the foot of the bed.

"I'm not," the patient whispered back.

"Not feeling well?"

"Not Anderson."

Evans smiled and sat down on the side of the bed. "Mr Anderson, the morning after you were brought here, the hospital phoned your office and told your secretary that your car had crashed and you'd been found unconscious. We asked if she could send us something to confirm your identity. It seems that your company occasionally does defence work, and keeps very careful records of all its employees for security purposes. They faxed us everything, up to and including your fingerprints. You definitely are Paul Anderson."

Not-Anderson didn't respond. He had had a breakfast of toast and marmalade, the pain was receding, and the sun was shining through the window. He focused desperately on these things, refusing to think about his identity. He was determined not to panic again.

"How are you feeling today?" Dr Evans asked again after the silence, appearing less smug than he had a moment before. He almost regretted the absence of another panic-stricken outburst. There was something unsettling about the patient's dark, evaluating stare. "I see you've been up to the lavatory," he went on brightly, checking the notes. "And you've been eating. The nausea's better?"

A nod.

"Is your memory coming back at all?"

A shake of the head. "The fingerprints," whispered not-Anderson, then cleared his throat with a cough and tried again. His tongue was still clumsy, and the effort he needed to produce his words made them feel strange, as though he were trying to recite a speech he had memorised imperfectly. "The fingerprints came from . . ." he paused to get it right, "Stellar Research?"

The name and the emblem of the star-enclosed infinity had tugged his memory before, and they tugged it again now. He did know something about Stellar. He disliked it, distrusted it, feared it. But he could not remember why.

"That's right," agreed the doctor.

"My fingers . . ." Not-Anderson held out one hand. The bandages were stained now with tomato soup, pineapple juice, and marmalade, but they still covered the whole hand. The fingers underneath had started to hurt more as the bruises on his chest hurt less. "No prints," not-Anderson concluded triumphantly.

The doctor made an embarrassed noise. "We didn't actually *use* the fingerprints. There was enough else in what they sent us. Height, weight, distinguishing markings—that sort of thing. You definitely are Paul Anderson."

"Stellar Research knows I'm here?" whispered not-Anderson.

"Of course," answered the doctor, surprised. "I understand they were very concerned to hear about your accident." He riffled through the notes and glanced over a sheet. "The hospital hasn't, er, notified anyone else yet. Apparently you only moved to this area recently. The only name you gave Stellar to contact in emergencies was that of your ex-wife in London. Do you want us to tell her you're ill?"

Despite his resolve, not-Anderson almost panicked again. He turned his head away from the doctor's pink bespectacled face, and stared desperately out of the window. His room was high up in the building: from where he lay he could see only sky, with a few white clouds drifting in it. He estimated their height, then calculated the speed of the wind from the clouds' motion. The surge of nausea receded. He looked back at the doctor. "Wife?" he whispered.

"Ex-wife," Dr Evans corrected. "Christine Anderson Barlow. You were divorced two years ago. Do you want us to get in contact with her?"

"No," not-Anderson said fervently. Contact some perfectly unknown woman who knew herself to be on intimate terms with him? The image of an emotional meeting—of tears and embraces he could not respond to—overpowered him. He was so shaken by it that he could not focus on the rest of what Dr Evans said, though he strove to register it carefully in his mind.

Evans had arranged for not-Anderson to have some neurological tests that day, to determine whether his amnesia had any physical cause. Evans had also arranged for a hospital psychiatrist to see him within the next couple of days, to give him counselling. Evans was pleased to tell him that as far as he, Evans, could make out, Anderson was making an excellent recovery, physically at least. Evans issued reassurances and left.

Not-Anderson lay still and looked out the window. The clouds swirled, high up and far off, shifting in the turbulence of the winds. They were no distraction, no relief: the terror he had determined to avoid continued to judder through him. He cast a horrified inward glance over his situation, then rammed down the rising panic and forced himself to steadiness. He had to consider this abstractly, logically. He was not insane, whatever Evans meant by his talk of psychiatric counselling. He could still reason coherently—or, if he couldn't any longer, if his logic was already corrupted by some maggot of unreason, he could not perceive it. Since it was therefore no help to question his sanity, he must assume himself sane.

Either he was Anderson, or he was not. Those were the first two propositions he had to decide between, and they were mutually exclusive.

As he struggled to find his way to reason, his mind moved from a jumble of words, emotions and half-formed images to the cool purity of symbolic logic, and at this conclusion he felt the terror drop away behind him. He took a deep breath of relief and continued, framing his arguments now in a wordless succession of concepts that no batterings of the self could confuse.

Was he Anderson?

The evidence for the proposition (A), that he was Anderson, was the ID card, which he had apparently been carrying at the time of the accident, and the material—nature undefined—sent from Anderson's place of work.

The evidence for (not-A) was his own conviction that it was true.

Neither proposition was self-contradictory.

An argument for (not-A) would have to explain why he'd been carrying another man's ID, and why the descriptive material from Anderson's office matched him well enough to satisfy the hospital. Further, it would have to explain where the real Anderson was. If the man had been in his usual place of work, Stellar Research would surely have said so.

An argument for (A) would have to explain why he was so certain of (not-A). He must *know*, somewhere, at some deep level, who he really was. His conviction on that point could not be lightly dismissed.

The conclusive proof for either proposition would be for him to remember his identity. But he flinched from the prospect of flinging himself again into that interior divide. He couldn't bear the panic and nausea, not now, not while he was still so weak, so (he admitted it) precariously balanced above his own terror. Very well, what could he say about the propositions in the absence of proof?

Proposition (A) depended entirely on evidence produced by Stellar Research. And he knew that he feared and distrusted Stellar Research. Conjecture: Stellar Research had deliberately—and falsely—identified him as Anderson, perhaps to protect the real Anderson.

His heart began to beat quicker, sending throbs of pain through his chest. He made himself stare out of the window and do calculations until his heartbeat slowed again. The conjecture might account for all the facts, but it still remained nothing more than conjecture.

There was another piece of evidence, which until now he had not considered. His reflection in the mirror (he fought back a surge of terror, and forced himself to reason on) had seemed alien to him. On the face of it, this supported (A), since the reflection did match the ID photograph. But if Stellar Research's evidence were false, then the reflection could match the ID and still not be Anderson.

He dragged back the sheets and swung his legs out of the bed. The orderly had taken him to the toilet again that morning, but he still couldn't balance on his own. He lowered himself cautiously to his feet and stood against the bed for a moment, clutching it with both hands. The floor seemed a long way down. Still facing the bed, he dropped to his knees. That was better.

He crawled across the smooth green floor to the cupboard, found the mirror, and crawled back. Lying on the bed again, he propped the mirror against his knees and stared into it.

A day recovering had not improved the face. The bruises had turned yellow at the edges, and the stubble was thicker on the jaw. The eyes slid guiltily from his own. He found the sight utterly repellant, and set the mirror down.

Query: did he only reject the face because its battered condition offended his image of himself?

Reluctantly, he lifted the mirror and stared at it again. This time he made himself examine the shape: the large nose and the strong bones about the eyes. Is that what it should look like? His heart began to pound again, and a wave of clammy heat swept over him. *No*. What should it look like? *No, no, no!*

He shoved the mirror away and bent over, taking deep breaths. The pounding and the nausea receded again.

Footsteps flapped against the floor, and he looked up to find Staff Nurse Sylvia Brown coming into the room. She was smiling and carrying a large bowl of red and yellow flowers. He was surprised by his own pleasure at seeing her again. He had not distinguished between the various nurses before, but now he found that her compassion had made her stand out for him.

"Look what's come for you!" she said cheerfully. She set the flowers down on the bedside table. They were fixed in green foam within a white ceramic basin. Their strong sweet scent filled the room. "From your friends at work," Sylvia Brown told him, handing him a card which had been propped up among the flowers.

He turned it so that he could read it. "To Paul Anderson, with best wishes for a speedy recovery, from all at Stellar Research." He dropped the card and put his hand in his lap, staring suspiciously at the flowers.

Sylvia Brown laughed. "Don't look like that! They don't bite." She bent over and sniffed a bloom appreciatively. "Gorgeous!" Then she trod upon the mirror, which had ended up on the floor again. She picked it up and raised her eyebrows at not-Anderson. He felt curiously ashamed, as though he'd been caught doing something disgraceful. But all the nurse said was, "You fetched this yourself? You must be feeling better! Did you like yourself any better this time?"

Relieved, he shook his head.

She surveyed him critically. "Well, you're not looking your best. Maybe you'll feel more at home with yourself when you've had a shave. I'll ask somebody to come and help you with that, if you like."

"I'm hideous," he whispered.

"No," she replied easily. "Just a bit bruised." She picked up his hand and set her fingers under his thumb, then took a shiny flattened circle from her pocket—an old-fashioned watch, he realised. All the nurses did this, whenever they came to check on him. He had never enquired why.

"Why do you do that?" he asked now.

He made her explain each step this time: pulse, temperature, blood pressure. She humoured him. When she took the bandages off his hands, he was interested in that, too, though he shied away from looking at the blood-marbled fingertips. "What happened to my hands?" he asked.

She hesitated, then answered seriously, "I don't know for sure, but it looks to me like you were trying to get out of that car you were in. That's probably something you *don't* want to remember."

"What car?" he asked, risking a glance at the hands.

She began to spray the fingers with something cold and then wrapped them in clean bandages, smaller than the wad of linen she had taken off them. The middle finger of the right hand was splinted. "The way I heard it, your car came off the road on a bend and rolled into a river. It had an airbag, so you weren't thrown into the windscreen when it

crashed. You must have been conscious after it went in the
water, but for some reason you couldn't get out. It looks like
you tried pretty hard."

He looked at the hands steadily for a few seconds, and a
strange knowledge crept into his mind of them scrabbling
frantically at the door of a water-filled car. It was not an
image from memory but an awareness, as though he had
once read an account of the hands' injuries listed line by line
in some register. He knew exactly when that finger-nail
broke and tore off, and at what point in the sequence those
strips of skin were ripped away. That splinted finger broke
dragging at the door handle; that bruise was where the fist
had pounded frantically at a window; that long stitched gash
on the right forearm came from the glass broken in the desperate struggle to claw through to the precious air outside.
He looked away, shuddering, wondering why it made him
feel guilty. Sylvia Brown went on bandaging.

"The bruises came then as well?" he asked her curiously,
when most of the lacerations were safely out of sight.

"Shouldn't think so," replied the nurse. "Most of the
bumps and bangs must be from the crash. It's a wonder you
didn't break anything major. You've got a classic pressure
bruise on your face, which must be from hitting the airbag.
Don't worry, man, it'll fade, and you'll get your looks back!
Then you have two cracked ribs and some nasty bruises on
the right side from being thrown against the door when the
car rolled down the bank: the ribs are from the arm-rest. The
bruise on your chest that's been bothering you so much is
from the heart massage."

"The what?" he asked helplessly. He seemed to know
nothing whatsoever about medical matters. He'd noticed
that she'd been surprised to find he didn't know what a pulse
was, and probably this was something just as commonplace.
He wondered if he'd known about such things before the accident.

Sylvia Brown laced her hands together and made a pressing gesture with them; she drew them back, then pressed

again. "When they finally got you out of the river, your heart had stopped and you weren't breathing. Lucky for you, the lady who pulled you out knew first aid. She push-started your heart and gave you mouth-to-mouth resuscitation. She pushed a bit hard, maybe, but that's better than not hard enough, isn't it?" The nurse grinned. "Incidentally, she's been phoning the hospital, asking how you were. She'd like to come in and see you. Would you be up to seeing her some evening?"

"Does she think I remember her?" whispered not-Anderson.

"She only ever saw you drowned," answered the nurse. "That's why she wants to see you now, I'm sure. She wants to see for herself that she really did save your life. I think you should see her. She won't expect you to remember her, so it won't upset her when you don't. And you ought to thank her."

TWO

THE ACCIDENT HAD HAPPENED ON A FRIDAY NIGHT.
Sandra Murray arrived at the hospital at about seven o'clock
Tuesday evening, an ambulance blanket tucked under one
arm. She got rid of the thing at reception, and in return was
given instructions for finding the man she'd come to see:
"Paul Anderson, Ward C-2, room 3—that's a private room."

"Why's that?" she asked, surprised.

The receptionist produced a meaningless formal smile.
"He had a medical insurance policy that demanded it."

The uneasiness Sandra had been feeling as the meeting
drew nearer abruptly doubled. The man she'd rescued must
be rich, or at least very well-off, to have the kind of medical
insurance that demanded a private room. His car, now she
came to think of it, had been of the sleek expensive kind.
Perhaps he thought that she'd asked to see him because she
wanted a reward. Perhaps the hospital thought the same. The
staff had certainly been extremely reluctant to tell her anything: when she first telephoned she'd been told that they
couldn't divulge information about patients, except to rela-
tives. She was only here now because the patient himself
had given his permission for the visit. And did she have any

right to thrust herself upon him? Even if he didn't think she was after a reward, wasn't there something sordid about turning up to demand gratitude? How could she explain, un-invited, that she wasn't demanding anything, that she'd only come because what she'd done had made his life important to her—that she wanted to be sure that the rescue was com-plete and worthwhile? She was afraid that they would end up being polite to one another.

A shop in the hospital foyer was selling flowers, and she paused and bought an African violet in a black plastic pot. It seemed better not to come empty-handed.

In spite of her reluctance, she got lost only once on her way to ward C-2. At the entrance to the main ward stood a nursing station, an L-shaped counter with a couple of chairs and a plastic rota board. The ward itself was busy. It was vis-iting time, and friends and families of patients were talking, presenting flowers, fetching coffee, and, in the case of a couple of younger children, running up and down the en-trance corridor shrieking. An extremely pretty young nurse was sitting at the counter writing, oblivious to the racket, but aware enough to look up when Sandra stopped before her. Sandra nervously identified herself, and the nurse dropped her pen and smiled broadly.

"Oh yes!" she exclaimed. "You're the one who saved him. I'm glad you've come. He hasn't had any other visi-tors, poor man, and he needs cheering up."

"Is he badly hurt?" asked Sandra. She was tired of that question even before she asked it. Every time she thought about the incident and remembered the corpse-like shape being strapped into the ambulance, the question had formed afresh, and it was always unanswerable.

The nurse hesitated unhappily. "Well, yes and no," she said at last. "At first we thought he was fine apart from shock and bruising. But it turns out he is suffering from total amnesia. We're still trying to understand how much of that is physical. I heard you gave him CPR; you don't know how long—"

"No," said Sandra abruptly, shocked. She had understood both the question and its implication. The brain begins to die four or five minutes after its supply of oxygen is cut off. If Anderson had been in the car longer than that, he had probably undergone permanent brain damage. The thought horrified her: the life she had fought to return to him might be a travesty of the one he'd had before, so much so that if he'd been given a choice he might have refused it. "I'm sorry, I don't know how long he was in there before I came by," she said more quietly. "He was still warm when I pulled him out, that's all I can say. Is . . . is he OK apart from the memory loss? I mean, can he understand what's going on? They told me he was willing to see me."

"Oh, yes!" replied the nurse. She seemed to understand perfectly what Sandra was thinking, and she assumed an obviously professional cheerfulness and a reassuring smile. It was, Sandra thought, nearly as bad as saying, "Don't worry if he dribbles a lot." What she actually went on to say was, "His understanding is perfectly normal. Don't worry! The only real question is whether the memory loss is physical or mainly psychological. His fine motor coordination and his sense of balance seem to have suffered too, but we're not sure whether that's brain damage or just general shock and trauma. He tore up his hands quite a lot, you know."

Sandra remembered the blood-smeared hand limply grasping the night air. She nodded.

"The main thing is," the nurse went on, "he's been a bit depressed over it all." Her professional cheerfulness wavered, the smile for a moment slipping, leaving her mouth fixed in a rictus of unease. The nurse found the patient unsettling. She was not sure why: he did not make endless demands, or complain. And he didn't lose his temper, or behave in a way that was obviously unbalanced. All he did was ask questions about his treatment which she could not answer. Yet the memory of his dark, evaluating stare made her uncomfortable. She had to recollect herself and pick her smile up again with a conscious effort, before she could go on. "I'm glad you've come to visit him," she said. "It will take his mind off it. It seems he's new to the area, and doesn't know many people here. We have the address of his ex-wife in London, but he doesn't want us to contact her because he can't remember her, poor man. Here, I'll show you to his room."

Room 3 was just up the corridor from the nursing station. The patient was sitting up in bed, staring at the yellow curtain that covered the window, but he looked round quickly as they entered. His face was bruised, but under the bruises it was a normal colour, and the eyes—dark and anxious— were so unquestionably aware that Sandra's heart skipped a beat with relief. He was younger than she'd expected—the half-corpse in the ambulance might have been ancient. He was also bigger than she remembered. She guessed that he'd be about six-feet tall when he stood up. However had she managed to drag him out of that car and up on to the bank? She stopped in the doorway, stiff with embarrassment. The nurse bustled over to the bed and adjusted the pillow.

"This is Ms Murray come to see you, Mr Anderson," the nurse told the patient. "She's the lady who saved your life."

Sandra smiled nervously. "Hi," she said. "I wanted to see how you were."

Not-Anderson looked at her in uncertain silence. He saw a tall, angular young woman, with pale skin, freckled across the nose, blue eyes and bright red hair. Not-Anderson didn't often notice hair, but Sandra Murray's was hard to ignore. There was a lot of it, and it fell in a wavy mass over her shoulders, held out of her face by a green headband. She was dressed in a green T-shirt and black skirt, and clutched a potted plant which not-Anderson, who couldn't remember any plant names, registered only as purple-flowering. Her speech had an accent which he noticed, but he did not remember enough to recognise it as Scots. He was surprised by his own pleasure at her visit, his relief at her un-medical appearance. He could not remember speaking to anyone who wasn't a member of the hospital staff, and by now he

was sick of all things medical. But he couldn't remember
how to negotiate the currents and eddies of ordinary conversation. What should he say?

His silent dark stare would have unnerved a visitor far
more confident than Sandra. She felt her smile wilting, and
struggled to maintain it. Then the man in the bed said—hesitantly, in a hoarse whisper—"Thank you. I am very glad
you saved my life."

It sounded so ridiculous that her false smile turned into a
genuine grin. "Thank *you*," she replied. "I don't doubt saving your life was the most satisfying thing I've ever done.
I've been six inches off the ground since I did it." There.
That ought to make her position clear.

The nurse excused herself. Sandra edged into the room,
holding the African violet as though it might explode. There
was a magnificent arrangement of red carnations and yellow
roses on the bedside table, a display that must have cost
thirty pounds if it cost a penny. Sandra set her inexpensive
pot plant defiantly down beside it and glanced about. Except
for a cupboard on the wall to the left of the door, the room
was bare. "Is there a chair?" she asked.

"No," croaked not-Anderson. "People sit on the bed."

Feeling uncomfortably intimate, she sat on the foot of the
bed. He had his knees drawn up, and there was space. "How
are you?" she asked.

Not-Anderson was unsure how to reply. Sylvia Brown
had told him that he ought to say thank you: he'd said it.
What now? Should he reassure his visitor, the way the
nurses tried to reassure him? Should he answer her question
with Dr Evan's medical report? He shook his head, deciding
that the only thing he could do was to explain his problem
honestly. "I do not know how to answer you," he told her. "I
have lost my memory. It makes it difficult to know what to
say."

She gave a matter-of-fact nod. "The nurse made that clear
to me when I arrived. I'm very sorry." She looked at his
sombre face, and thought of waking up with no memory, and

only a blank where your past should be. "It must be *terrifying*," she said, with a sudden burst of sympathy.

Since not-Anderson had first realised how serious his situation was, everyone had treated his feelings about it as a problem to drug or reassure away. ("You'll be all right. It will come back. Here, take this, and it will calm you down.") Nobody had admitted that he had any reason to be terrified. It was an enormous relief for someone to recognise that he had a right to be. "It is," he whispered to Sandra, all at once more grateful to her for her empathy than for saving his life.

"The nurse said they didn't know why?" Sandra asked, after a moment's silence. He nodded unenthusiastically. This was something he did not want to talk about. Over the preceding two days he had undergone a battery of tests. He had been poked and prodded and knocked with hammers to check his reflexes; lights had been shone in his eyes; he had had eye tests and hearing tests; tests for pattern recognition and speech, motor coordination and simple arithmetic. He had had a psychological evaluation, which had dismayed him by revealing even more things that he should have been able to remember—parents, childhood, places of residence—and could not. He had had another head X-ray. A brain scan had been cancelled when the outdated EEG machine blew a fuse. The medical staff had not explained much of what they were doing, but he had nonetheless grasped that they were trying to see whether his brain had been damaged in the accident. The image of his own brain battered and paralysed inside his skull made his skin crawl, though he tried not to think about it. One thing he did remember about brains was that they could not regenerate.

"Well," said Sandra, after another silence, "amnesia is terribly romantic. At the minute I'm sure it feels just plain terrible, but you'll be able to swank it at dinner parties after your memory comes back."

He let out his breath a little raggedly. "Will I?"

"Oh, definitely! It'll one-up everyone's appendectomy, no doubt about it."

He studied her intently. "The hospital staff keep telling me that my memory will come back. But they admit that they don't know why it has gone. It isn't clear to me that they have sufficient information to predict how it will behave in the future. I think that they say this to me simply to reassure me."

She made a face, realising that she'd been doing the same thing. As a woman with a scientific background, she'd had to endure a lot of ignorant and patronising reassurances about things she was perfectly capable of understanding, and she'd always detested it.

"Do you know anything about such things?" the patient asked.

The question was straightforward and hopeful, not sarcastic. "Not really," she admitted, then tried to supply the information anyway. "But I probably know more than the average layman. I studied biology at university, and I read books and periodicals that touch on the subject sometimes. If there are programmes about the brain on the box I generally watch them. As far as I can make out, nobody really understands how memory works, though I do remember that we have two different sorts of memory, long term and short term—do you know all this?"

He shook his head, the hopeful look sharpening. "I know almost nothing about medicine," he told her. "Perhaps I have forgotten it. Please, go on."

She told him what she knew about the workings of memory: its mysterious and complex mechanisms; its lack of fixed location in the brain; its selectivity and persistence. She recounted famous incidents of amnesia: an adulthood wiped out leaving a childhood intact; all knowledge of a language spoken for twenty years destroyed while one previously half-forgotten was retained; the recollection of persons entirely preserved though all knowledge of time spent with them was lost. She told him about cases where the mechanism of remembering seemed to have been damaged, and everything before an accident was remembered clearly, while new memories were formed only with difficulty or not at all. He listened avidly. This was hard information, information he needed to resolve the pressing torment of his identity.

It was only when she was explaining hysterical amnesia and retrograde amnesia, where the physically undamaged mind seeks to obliterate memories of events too painful to live with, that he began to feel any relevance to his own case. His mind evaluated what she was saying, compared it with what the doctors had said, and against his will came up with another conjecture: *my belief in (not-A) is the result of my desire to escape something that happened to me as Anderson.*

Like his first conjecture, this was internally consistent and accounted for all the facts, but it was far more complete and convincing. It explained what otherwise was unaccountable: his sense that the face he saw in a mirror was not his own. That he still could not believe he was Anderson might only be evidence that his rejection of the identity had never had a rational foundation.

He sat very still. The world was threatening to turn sideways again, and he could feel the familiar nausea surging into the back of his throat. He focused desperately on his visitor's face, watching concern slip over it, as her brow tightened and she drew in the sides of her mouth.

Sandra had been in full flow about hysteria when she noticed that her audience had gone white and was visibly sweating. She stopped. "Are you all right?" she asked anxiously.

He said nothing, only sat there motionless, his eyes watching her as though from a great distance. She rose unhappily to her feet.

"I'm sorry," she said guiltily. "I shouldn't have gone on about things like this. It was too much, wasn't it? I've worn you out. I'll go."

"No!" he whispered. "Please. It was only that I was trying to . . . to understand something that has been troubling

me. You have helped me very much. Is there somewhere I
could learn more about this?"

"I could lend you a couple of books," she said, uncer-
tainly. He still looked very ill, very frightened, and somehow very much alone. "Can I help at all?" she asked
impulsively.

He met her eyes. He had told the hospital nothing about
his conjectures. The staff were satisfied that he was Paul
Anderson and if he continued to dispute it he suspected that
they would regard this as evidence of mental disorder. He
didn't like being in the hospital, and he wanted to get out.
Showing evidence of mental disorder would make it more
difficult to achieve that. But he did want help. There were
things he needed to know, which he dared not ask about. His
rescuer had understood him—she had spoken facts to him,
not reassurances. He obeyed his impulse and decided to trust
her.

"I have been told that I am Paul Anderson, the marketing
director of an organisation called Stellar Research," he said
slowly. "I feel a strong conviction that I am not Anderson.
However, I was carrying an ID card in that name at the time
of the accident, and the hospital admissions office contacted
Stellar the following morning and was provided with evidence which satisfied them that the identification was correct. Either I am Paul Anderson—and for some reason I
wish to forget it—or I am not, and the material that was
given to the hospital was in some way misleading. I am certain that I do not like or trust Stellar Research, but I cannot
remember why. I need to know more about them. I would be
very grateful if you could tell me anything you may have
heard."

She stared at him for a long time. Two patches of red
glowed in the fair skin of her cheeks. What he had said was
so extraordinary, and the way in which he'd said it so matter-
of-fact, that she didn't know how to respond. She had heard
of Stellar Research. Not only was it a local company, it was
one of the Great British Successes of the decade: a research

and engineering firm that specialised in alternative power, and had risen from nowhere to multi-million pound turnovers and contracts all over the world. It had devised a new type of solar energy panel which now sprouted from every other roof-top, and a switching system for superconducting electricity cables, which every power company in the world seemed to want an option on. Its chairman, Sir Philip Lloyd, had been knighted for his "services to science and industry" and was a regular guest on television discussion panels. Sandra was not sure whether she was more amazed to think that she'd saved the life of one of Stellar's directors, or by the cool suggestion that the company would dishonestly identify somebody as one of its most exalted team players if it wasn't true.

"I have not discussed this with the hospital," not-Anderson added, after a minute. "Please don't repeat it. I believe it would be seen simply as a symptom, and not as a serious question."

"Why do you think Stellar Research would say you were their marketing director if you aren't?" she demanded, the flush abruptly spreading over her face.

"I don't know," he replied quietly. "To begin with, I don't know what material Stellar sent to the hospital. It may be that the hospital simply glanced over a few chance similarities between me and the real Paul Anderson, and made a false assumption. But perhaps the real Paul Anderson was in some kind of trouble, and Stellar wished to protect him . . ."

"So they tried to fake his death by murdering you?" Sandra asked incredulously. "That's . . . that's—you can't believe they'd be capable of something like that!"

Not-Anderson hesitated. But she saw at once that it was not the sort of hesitation that comes from realising that the accusation was outrageous: he was simply reevaluating the evidence. He seemed to find the possibility neither incredible nor even particularly distressing. "I don't remember enough to be able to judge," he concluded. "Perhaps . . . perhaps the real Paul Anderson was already dead from some other cause, and I was an enemy they could dispose of unobtrusively under his name. On the other hand, the simplest explanation that accounts for all the facts is that I am Paul Anderson and don't want to remember it. By the principle of Occam's razor—that's what it's called, isn't it?—that is the explanation most likely to be true."

She stared in consternation. "But I thought you said you were convinced that you aren't."

"I said I *feel* a strong conviction that I'm not Anderson," he corrected her. "But if it were something I didn't wish to remember, that's exactly how I would feel." There was a pause and then he added, with a touch of reproof at the very notion, "If the balance of probability inclines to a particular proposition, I would never adhere to a contrary proposition out of sentiment alone."

She realised that he meant it: he had faith in reason. So few people did that it came as a shock to Sandra. "Look," she said, after a moment. "Surely you must be able to prove to yourself who you are? You must have family, people who know you, who can tell you something about yourself? I think the nurse mentioned an ex-wife?"

He hesitated. "I was told Anderson had an ex-wife. I don't want to see her. I don't remember her, and she may . . ."

He stopped as the same realisation hit them both. Anderson's ex-wife would only recognise him if he were Anderson. He had been certain that she would recognise him. Therefore, at heart, he knew himself to be Anderson.

For a moment a crowd of memories hovered at the edge of his consciousness, and he snatched at them eagerly. Then the nausea swept up, more violently than ever, and battered him down again into a choking hole. He bent over with his forehead pressed against his knees, heaving with a clenched throat. He was afraid that he would be sick, now, in front of the visitor, and it seemed ridiculously important that he should not be. He tried to breathe evenly, and clenched his hands against his knees until the pain of doing this cut through even the waves of clammy heat.

Sandra watched him go white and fold up, and instinctively hurried to his side. She caught one of the clenched, bandaged hands in an unthinking gesture of comfort, and his head jerked up. For a moment he stared at her as though she were a strange and possibly dangerous animal. Shocked, she took her hand away. He continued to stare at her for a few endless moments, in a puzzled way now, and then slowly straightened and looked away.

"What happened?" she asked, shaken.

He wiped the cold sweat from his face. The nausea was receding again. "I began to remember something," he admitted. "When that happens, I feel very sick."

"Christ!" she said. "It's awful!"

He considered it. "It is very unpleasant," he concluded. "But I would rather endure it than not know the truth. Only it achieves nothing: I *can't* remember." He wiped his face again, then pressed the heels of his hands against his eyes for a moment before setting them back on his knees. "I think I will have to assume that I am Anderson," he continued thoughtfully. "Unless some contradictory evidence turns up."

"Oh Christ!" she exclaimed again, and laughed unsteadily. "Your memory may be playing tricks on you, but there's nothing wrong with your reason, is there?"

He looked back at her in confusion. "I hope that's true," he said seriously. "Do you know anything about Stellar Research?"

She told him what she knew and promised to find out what more she could, and he thanked her. It was only when she was leaving the hospital that she realised that they had both assumed that she would visit him again, soon.

SANDRA BEGAN HER INQUIRIES AT THE INSTITUTE OF Plant Pathology, where she worked as a research assistant. It was unlikely that her fellow workers would have any direct experience of a company that specialised in power generation. They were all biologists of one sort or another, and the

Institute's own task was to identify the diseases afflicting samples of crops sent to it by concerned farmers, and to research the illnesses of plants. She expected, though, that somebody would have a university friend who had joined Stellar, or thought of joining it, and had passed on all the gossip. On Wednesday morning, therefore, she parked her red Ford Sierra in the IPP lot and entered the building with a swinging step, eager to ask around. In fact, she barely needed to.

"How's the rescuee?" her colleague Robert Singer asked, as soon as Sandra walked into the lab. She had told him how her Friday evening had ended.

"Bruised and confused, but improving," replied Sandra, tossing her handbag into her desk drawer and picking up her white lab coat. "His name's Paul Anderson, and he's the marketing director of Stellar Research."

"Cor!" exclaimed Robert facetiously. "You couldn't save just anyone's life, could you? What's he like?"

"Tall, dark and handsome," Sandra replied at once.

Robert, who was average and ordinary with light-brown hair, made a jealous face. Sandra grinned back at him. They had been partnering each other to films and gatherings for some time, and had reached the stage where their relationship was sufficiently well-recognised for them to be invited to events as a pair. They hadn't gone to bed together, but that was because Sandra was cautious. Breaking up was painful and messy and she didn't know yet whether she and Robert had enough chance of sticking to make the risk worth taking. Robert was conventional enough to be boring sometimes—and what was worse, some peculiar desire for compensation had provided him with an unconventional hobby, UFOs, which Sandra's firm Scottish common sense found daft. She never dared tell him so, however, knowing beforehand the lengthy arguments which would inevitably follow.

"Married?" asked Robert, with an air of expecting the punchline "with three kids."

"Divorced," replied Sandra triumphantly. "He has an ex-wife in London who he doesn't want to contact because he can't remember her. He has amnesia—yes, really! I was worried when they told me that, because I thought it might mean brain damage. But if his brain is damaged now, I tremble to think what it must have been like before. He has a mind like a super-cooled CRAY."

"More like a calculator, I should think, if he's marketing director at Stellar," said Robert.

Sandra shook her head, though she was surprised at her own simile. Anderson had not said anything particularly intelligent to her, and his faith in the power of reason might have been no more than touching. Instead, she felt instinctively that in his case it was fully justified. She thought of him sitting in his room gazing at the yellow curtains, and the image of an enormously powerful, infinitely precise computer returned to her more forcefully. He was only waiting for enough information to run some inscrutable programme of his own. The impulse to tease and joke about him deserted her.

"Do you know anything about Stellar?" she asked Robert. "He asked me about it. It's another thing he's forgotten, and it bothers him."

It turned out that Robert knew quite a bit about Stellar. The company had developed a portable magnetometer which his group of UFO enthusiasts had just purchased at great expense, and he thought well of it. He told Sandra all about the magnetometer, and the importance of magnetic fields in detecting UFOs, until she had to bite her tongue to stop the sarcastic rebuttal. However, once UFOs were safely out of the way, he became more informative. He had a friend from university who had almost taken a job with Stellar, but thought better of it. The friend's reasons for turning down the job seemed extremely relevant to Sandra. She was pleased with her haul of information as she returned to the hospital that evening.

She knocked on the door of room 3, ward C-2, without

bothering to check in at the nursing station first. There was a scraping noise from inside, and then a voice that wasn't Anderson's called, "Come in!"

She thought he must have been moved, and she opened the door with an apology ready on her lips. But he was sitting up in bed just as he'd been when she left the evening before, bandaged hands on drawn-up knees, and when he saw her his serious dark face lit in a sudden smile, dazzling with unexpected warmth. There was another man with him, a trim short man in a beautifully cut grey suit and beautifully cut blond hair. The visitor had managed to acquire a chair, which scraped again as he turned it to look at her. He was about forty; his bright, keen-eyed face was familiar, but she couldn't think where she'd met him.

"Er—hello," said Sandra.

The other visitor shot an enquiring look at Anderson.

"This is Ms Murray," said Anderson. His voice was still hoarse and uncertain, but he was not whispering today. "She's the one who saved my life."

The visitor's eyebrows shot up, and he got to his feet and offered Sandra his hand. "I'm delighted to meet you, Ms Murray," he told her, smiling. "You've done us a tremendous service, and I'm very grateful to you."

Sandra smiled confusedly back and shook the man's hand. "I'm very glad I was able to help Mr Anderson," she said. "I'm sorry, Mr . . . er, I don't remember your name."

He smiled more widely. "Don't worry," he told her. "No reason why you should. It's Sir Philip Lloyd." Chairman and Managing Director of Stellar Research. His face was familiar not because she'd met him, but because she'd seen him on television. She swallowed, and glanced helplessly at Anderson, who was now looking remote again: it was impossible to tell what he thought of his boss's visit. It could be that his memory was starting to come back, and he regretted what he'd said to her the evening before. She'd thought at the time that he might do: it was the sort of jumbled nonsense that comes out in shock and is shamefacedly disowned afterwards. But whatever he thought, she couldn't possibly discuss Stellar with him in front of the company's smiling chairman.

"I, uh, brought the books you wanted," she said instead. She'd collected them from her house before coming over: two popular science books on the brain.

"Thank you," said Anderson, reaching out for them.

Sir Philip intercepted them, glanced at the covers, then handed them over. "Reading up on what's wrong with you, Paul?" he asked.

Anderson nodded and began looking over the books. His fingers fumbled the pages so clumsily it was painful to watch.

"Don't let them scare you," said Sir Philip. "Try not to worry about it too much, eh? And try to get better. We could use you back in harness by the first of the month."

Anderson looked up again at that. "How long is it until then?" he asked. "And why?"

Sir Philip gave another smile, but there was a certain wariness in his manner that had not been there a moment before. "It gives you nearly three weeks, Paul," he said. "If that scan's right, there's no reason why you shouldn't make it. As to why . . . well, you don't remember it, but when your memory comes back, you will. Our latest project." He turned the smile on Sandra. "You know we research power generation?"

"Yes, sir," said Sandra respectfully.

He nodded. He'd seen that she'd recognised him. "We've got a new project which we very much hope Paul will be able to be on the team for. Those look like interesting books: are you a psychologist, young lady?"

Sandra shook her head. "A plant pathologist," she said. "But I was telling Mr Anderson about these when I came to see him yesterday. He wanted to understand what's happened to him, and they were the best I could come up with."

Sir Philip showed a polite interest in plant pathology and discussed the IPP for a few minutes. He went on to ask her

about how she'd come to rescue Anderson, congratulated
her on it and, at last, just as she was wondering if she should
excuse herself and leave, he moved to the door.

"Well, I must be off," he told Anderson. "But do ring
Stellar if you need anything. You don't have to sit there in
that ghastly NHS gown, Paul. Your secretary can fetch you
some of your own clothes. Hang on, do you want to give me
the key to your house?"

"I don't know where it is," said Anderson.

Sir Philip gave a rueful snort. "Well, find out and let us
know what you want fetched. All of us at Stellar are your
team-mates, Paul, your working family, and we're happy
to help. And do remember—that fellow Jones has no right
to bother you."

"I'll remember," said Anderson.

"Goodbye, then, and get well soon! Young lady, nice to
meet you."

Sir Philip departed. Sandra looked at Anderson question-
ingly.

Anderson (he acknowledged that name for himself now,
but with an inward hesitation, as though it were set in quotation marks) put both hands over his face and dropped back
into the pillows. He was feeling weak and sick, as though he
had once again squeezed out from under the edge of death.
He had recognised Stellar's chairman instantly, and felt an
absolute certainty that this man was an enemy and that he
himself was in great danger. His position, trapped in a hospital bed, unable to remember and barely able to walk, had
appalled him. But he had struggled not to show this, afraid
that if he displayed his weakness the other would be encouraged to attack. It had made the visit a nightmare test of
endurance; and most nightmarish of all was the way Sir
Philip had treated him as a friend. He had smiled, asked Anderson how he was, expressed concern about the bruises and
relief that the injuries weren't worse. He'd suggested that
Anderson should leave "this depressing place" as soon as he
could, and have "a good rest at The Oaks." He did not ex-

plain what "The Oaks" was, and Anderson could not even remember that the name referred to trees: to him it sounded threatening. Sir Philip had been told about the amnesia, and he'd expressed sympathy, but with an arch look, as though he suspected that Anderson was shamming it as an excuse for something unspecified. Anderson had decided that it was safest to make it clear that it was genuine. If Sir Philip had indeed done the kind of thing that Anderson's instincts were screaming he'd done, the last thing his victim should do was make him fear exposure.

But when Sir Philip grasped this, he showed none of the relief Anderson had expected. Instead, he was shocked and concerned. He asked about doctors and tests. From his questions, it emerged that he already knew as much as Anderson himself: he'd seen the results of the CAT scan Anderson had had only that morning, and the inconclusive-but-hopeful psychological evaluation Anderson had endured that afternoon. That, Anderson thought now, was troubling. He'd gathered that the hospital had not been nearly so forthcoming to Sandra. Sir Philip must have some influence with the medics. It would be good to get away from the hospital as soon as possible.

Once Sir Philip had concluded that Anderson's condition was more confused than he'd expected but that it was likely to improve, he'd begun talking about somebody called Jones. Anderson was not to see Jones; Jones would have to understand that he could not expect to bully a man in Anderson's condition. Sir Philip would tell the hospital to explain as much, if Jones called. But it would be better if Anderson could move to The Oaks. Jones wouldn't be able to pull any tricks there. Stellar owned it and the staff would do as Sir Philip said. The Oaks was secure. Sir Philip would arrange it.

The thought of moving to some place secured by Sir Philip made Anderson feel faint with terror. But he had not dared give away his suspicions and, evaluating the meeting now, he was suddenly certain he'd been right not to. Sir

Philip had shown no sign of apprehending any danger from Anderson.

Anderson paused in his evaluation, startled, then he checked again. Everything Sir Philip had said and done was consistent with him believing that Anderson was . . .

He crashed into the tilted edge of his memory and was left grasping through the wrench of sickness after the completion of a thought so dislocated and strange. Sir Philip appeared to believe that Anderson was . . . what?

He could not reach it. His eyes stung. He drew several deep breaths, and waited for his stomach to stop heaving. Then he took his hands away from his eyes and looked at Sandra. His silent evaluation had been rapid: only seconds had passed since Sir Philip had left, and the questioning look in her eyes was still in the process of being replaced by one of anxiety. She was wearing a black tank top today and white trousers, and a gilt necklace called attention to the over-prominent ridge of her collar bone. The enormous relief he'd felt when she opened the door now returned: here was his rescuer, his rescuer for a second time.

"I am very glad you came," he told her gratefully.

She did not know what to make of it. "Are you all right?" she asked him.

He nodded. "I told you how it is when I start to remember."

"Oh," she said, staring. "And you remembered Sir Philip Lloyd?"

He nodded again. "I am very glad you came," he repeated. "I was afraid."

She had no idea what to say, so she occupied herself by rearranging Sir Philip's chair and sitting down in it. She had not liked Sir Philip, but that was only because she'd found his tone patronising, and she knew that she was overly sensitive and probably being unfair. She certainly couldn't see that the man had done anything to make Anderson afraid of him. "He seems to think highly of you," she said tentatively.

Anderson looked thoughtful: again she thought of a great

computer whirring through some enormous and obscure calculation. "I did not expect that," he said, after a minute. "When he first came in, I thought he was a danger to me. But it does seem that whatever reason I have to be afraid of him, he is unaware of it. Did you learn anything about Stellar?"

She sighed. It looked to her as though Anderson's calculations, like most attempts to apply pure reason to human affairs, could leave him stuck in thin air well beyond the limit of common sense. On the other hand, he *would* yield to a better argument even when he didn't like it, she'd seen that. He'd be OK.

"I only found out a little bit," she said. "But it might be enough to explain why you feel you don't like Stellar. A friend of mine says a friend of his was offered a job with Stellar once. The starting salary was good and the work sounded exciting, but the friend eventually decided to turn the job down. Apparently Stellar demands incredible dedication of all its employees. The people who run it think alternative power is the greatest thing going and that their company's the greatest thing in alternative power: they expect you to eat, breathe and sleep Stellar. When a new project's under way, you're expected to work all hours every day of the week." When Robert had told her this, it had answered a certain small niggling question in her mind: why had Anderson's secretary been in his office ready to fax his identification to the hospital on the Saturday morning after the accident? "The friend had a fiancèe who didn't much like the sound of that," she continued, smiling. "And then, Stellar is very secretive about its research. Alternative power is a very competitive field, and they want to protect their trade secrets. So they almost *never* let their researchers publish—and that's a fate worse than death to a good researcher! They also have a reputation for being jealous and grasping over other people's discoveries, always going to court to protect anything that could have been borrowed from them. They make it very difficult for workers to leave the firm once they've joined. They give all their employees a huge bonus on recruitment, but if you leave or are sacked within five years you have to pay it back—and in most cases that means you have to sell your house, because most people use the bonus for the downpayment on their mortgage. So nobody dares to quit or do anything that might get them sacked. And Stellar can sack you for breach of confidence, or for not putting in all the overtime, or for something called 'damage to company morale,' which means talking about your salary or complaining about anything. They can also sack you for something called 'disloyalty,' which means having anything to do with companies that could conceivably be rivals. They have a reputation for enforcing all this ruthlessly. It's legal because it's all set out in the contract, but it's fierce."

She paused. Anderson was watching her with a slight frown. "Don't you think that that could be why you feel you dislike Stellar so much?" she coaxed. "Because you were trapped in your job?"

Without the least hesitation, he shook his head.

"Are you certain?" she asked, disappointed. It had seemed to explain everything. She suspected that it still did.

"The reason I have for disliking Stellar," said Anderson levelly, "is something so terrible that I do not want to remember it. This is not."

"But it could have been devastating," she said. "Especially if . . . I mean, perhaps it was the cause of your divorce: you being stuck in the office all the time, doing a job you'd discovered you didn't like; your wife getting more and more angry and unhappy alone at home. Perhaps you could see your marriage falling to bits around you, and you couldn't do anything to—"

"That is simply ridiculous," he interrupted impatiently. "I would not stay in a job I didn't like if it was destroying a marriage I wished to preserve. I would sell my house and quit. To do anything else would be irrational."

She opened her mouth to argue, then closed it again. He was right. Other people might get tangled in webs of finance

or romance, but not Anderson. One touch of that super-
cooled mind, and all the clinging strands would go as brittle
as if they had been dipped in liquid nitrogen; they would
snap off and be brushed aside. For the first time, she tried to
imagine something so terrible that *he* would try to enclose it
in oblivion—and found it easily. She saw him in the
wrecked car, clawing at the doors as the water rose, desperately struggling into the back, drowning with his hand
through the smashed window. Where had he been going that
night, driving so fast that his car came off the bend? Why
hadn't he been able to open the doors? For the first time she
seriously considered the possibility that he was right to feel
suspicious and afraid of his employer. Stellar was a powerful company that demanded fanatical dedication from all its
staff and defended its secrets ferociously. If one of Stellar's
employees had defied it, perhaps by betraying one of those
secrets, was it inconceivable that Stellar might have lashed
out at him?

She stared at Anderson uncomfortably, feeling as though
she'd walked down a gently sloping beach, and plunged
over a drop-off. She was out of her depth here.

Then she told herself that she was being silly. The
chances were that Anderson's wild conjectures were wrong.
He might be brilliant but the fact remained that he did not
remember anything that had happened to him, and had forgotten great chunks of information about how the world
worked. He was like a man trying to work out what an animal had looked like from three or four pieces of bone. As
more bits turned up, the dragon of first conjecture was
bound to turn into something more ordinary. He simply
needed support while he sorted things out.

"You don't really know that your amnesia is anything to
do with Stellar," she told him.

"No," he agreed at once. "That is simply the explanation
that best accounts for all the facts known to me. Of course I
will revise it or reject it if it is contradicted, but for the mo-

ment I must assume that it is true. If I rejected it prematurely, it could . . ." he stopped.

Sandra completed the phrase for him silently, "it could kill me." But she realised that he didn't like to talk about that. She had used the word *murder*, to reprove him, but he had never uttered it. Abruptly she understood that he was not nearly as cool about this as he was pretending to be. His few sticks of logic were like a caveman's fire, a small defence against the terrible things that growled unseen in the darkness around him. She was swept by another wave of sympathy for him.

"Is there anything I can do to help?" she asked for a second time.

He hesitated, then said, in a lower voice, "I would like to leave here. Sir Philip Lloyd wants me to go to a place called The Oaks. He implied that he had some kind of control over it. And it's clear that he has some influence even in this hospital: he knew the results of the tests I had only today. I believe that it is of critical importance that I put myself as far as possible beyond his reach. Can you tell me how I could discharge myself from this hospital?"

THREE

ANDERSON WENT HOME FROM THE HOSPITAL THE FOL-
lowing evening. Sandra had not been keen to see him do so,
and the hospital had been very reluctant to let him go—but
it was impossible to keep him in. Once he'd grasped that the
hospital had no right to detain him—he had assumed previously that it had—he was perfectly adamant that he would
go. He no longer needed any medication apart from
painkillers, had never needed any life-support, and the battery of neurological tests he'd taken had culminated in a
CAT scan that showed no evidence of brain damage. His
doctors strongly recommended that he have physiotherapy
and psychiatric counselling—but there was no reason he
couldn't receive these as an outpatient. It was quite clear,
however, that he was not capable of managing on his own.
His best walk was a clumsy shuffle, he did not have the full
use of his hands, and the image of him trying to drive a car,
let alone navigate a supermarket, was pitiful. In the end,
Sandra found herself sorting out a care package for him with
the medical staff. It turned out that his extravagant insurance
would cover a paid care assistant or home help, and the hos-

pital volunteered to find one. Beyond that, he would be left to his GP—and Sandra.

"I've got to go and fetch some clothes for Paul Anderson after work this evening," she told Robert on Thursday morning. "He wants to go home, and he's got nothing to wear but a hospital gown. He gave me the keys to his house."

She did not mention the uneasy, conspiratorial feeling it had given her when Anderson fumbled out from the bedside table the ring of keys that he had coolly denied any knowledge of to Sir Philip. She did not want to repeat any of Anderson's suspicions: it made her feel as though she were condoning them. She told herself that to mention them would simply embarrass the man as he recovered and abandoned them.

Robert was unhappy. He had been proud of Sandra after the rescue, and had thought nothing of her wanting to visit her rescuee—but to have her running errands in and out of the man's private house was another matter. However, he could not begrudge help to an accident victim, even a tall, dark, handsome divorced one. "Do you want some help?" he offered instead. "I'll come with you if you like."

Sandra was about to refuse, then understood the reason for the offer and accepted. They set off on their joint errand in separate cars, since neither could afford to be without transport the next morning.

The IPP lay on the north side of a large East Anglian town; Anderson's house was on the east side. The address, 12 The Mays, had been obtained from his hospital file. Sandra, going first, wove through the rush hour traffic into the town. At first she got stuck in a jam on the high street, but then escaped on past shops, bay-windowed terrace houses and street lamps, and into the countryside. As fields of sugar beet opened around her, she realised she'd gone too far. She pulled over, consulted a map, and with difficulty turned back, cursing and cursed by the flood of homeward-bound commuters. This time she found the turn: a quiet street whose entrance was half-concealed by towering horse chestnuts. The houses were large and detached, set back from the road. She turned again, into The Mays, and the houses became even grander, rising elegantly from behind dark hedges. She found the number 12 set in gilt on a black gate post by a hedge of yew, and pulled into the drive. Robert's car was already parked there, waiting. He got out when she did, the two car doors slammed, and they stood looking at the house together.

"Rich, isn't he?" asked Robert.

The house reeked of money. It wasn't as large as some in the estate, but from the glassed-in spiral stairs at one side of it to the double garage on the other, it was clear that number 12 belonged to someone important. A vast lawn stretched smooth and immaculate in the soft June evening, the yew hedge was neatly clipped, but there were no flowerbeds. Sandra, who'd chosen her profession because she loved growing things, ached at the lost opportunities. Her own garden was lovely, but minute.

She squared her shoulders and walked up the drive to the front door. It had a deadlock and a Yale. There were more than two keys on the ring Anderson had given her, and it took her a while before she found the right ones.

"This is where we find the puppy dog that starved to death waiting for its master," said Robert, as the deadlock at last clunked back.

"Don't!" she ordered, pushing open the door.

No dead puppies, only a cold entrance hall with a few letters and a pile of uncancelled newspapers. Beyond it lay plush green wall-to-wall carpeting, and off-white walls studded with photographs and a few uninspired modern watercolours. The peculiar flat, breathless silence of an empty house weighed on them both, crushing any words they might have said. A huge television dominated one corner of the sitting room, and an equally huge music centre squatted in another. There was a glass-topped coffee table layered with old copies of *The Times*, and a fat off-white settee. There was one mahogany bookcase, not quite full. As they crossed the room to the spiral stairway they'd noticed from outside the house, Sandra couldn't help pausing to glance over the titles of Anderson's collection of books. A dozen or so books on marketing, half a dozen on alternative power, and the rest popular thrillers. She felt odd.

They climbed up the metal staircase, nervous of the loud clunking of their feet in the oppressive quiet. Upstairs, they found luxurious red carpeting and several closed doors. The first concealed a bathroom, the second contained an immense desk groaning under the burden of a first-rate personal computer, printer, photocopier, and fax machine. The third was a bedroom. Going in, Sandra caught a flash of movement to one side, and froze. Her heart thundered, and suddenly she was enormously glad of Robert's presence behind her. She edged forward—and found that the wall surrounding the door was totally covered with mirrors, and the flash of movement she'd seen had been nothing more than her own reflection. She made a face at her gawky dishevelled look. She'd never liked big mirrors: they made her self-conscious.

She took some socks and underclothes from the chest of drawers and put them on the bed ready for packing, then went to the wardrobe. Robert sat down on the bed, and picked up a magazine from the bedside table. With a twinge of disbelief, Sandra saw that it was a popular soft-porn title. She tried to imagine Anderson sitting on the rumpled white candlewick bedspread before his mirrored reflection, supercooled mind concentrated on a girlie mag. Her imagination rebelled.

"This is wrong," she said out loud.

"He asked you to fetch his things," replied Robert reasonably, tossing the magazine down again.

"Not that," she said. "This whole house. It's so . . . banal. He isn't like this at all."

Robert snorted. "You don't know him. You've only seen him in hospital."

"I suppose so," she said reluctantly. She told herself that

Robert was right, that she didn't know Anderson well, and that people might seem very different to their normal selves when they were recovering in hospital after a brush with death. But she still could not picture him living in this soulless and pretentious house. He ought to have somewhere . . . different. Carpets and walls in five different shades of white, Japanese futons and uncomfortable angular furniture, fearfully modern etchings that nobody else could make head nor tail of, books and bizarre Eastern music everywhere.

Then she remembered that he was new to the area. Perhaps his predecessor was to blame for the decor.

The wardrobe was full of suits, all of them expensive looking. She started to take one down, then thought of Anderson's bandaged hands on the buttons, and put it back. She chose a tennis shirt and jumper instead, and a pair of plain trousers. She picked up a pair of shoes, found an overnight bag in the back of the wardrobe, and packed Anderson's things.

"Right," she said, with a degree of resolution she did not feel. "Now we go to the hospital."

"What about supper?" asked Robert.

"We'll get it later."

"What about him?" Robert demanded reasonably. "Will he have had something, or will we need to pick up some food on the way back from the hospital? He'll want something for breakfast anyway, won't he? I bet all the things in the fridge have gone off."

"We'll talk to the home help at the hospital," said Sandra, after pausing to consider what Robert had just said. "See what she plans." She could only hope that a home help had been found. Otherwise, somebody was going to have to stay the night at Anderson's and make breakfast for him in the morning, and she didn't want to be the one who had to do it. She didn't want Robert to stay, either, even if he offered: it would be too embarrassing. The whole house made her obscurely ashamed.

They drove to the hospital in Sandra's car, leaving

Robert's in the drive. Robert spent the journey talking about Stellar and UFOs. One of his ufologist friends had told him that Sir Philip Lloyd was personally interested in the search for extraterrestrial intelligence, and had visited the UFO group some months earlier. "My friend said he was really keen to know all about it," Robert enthused. He was pleased, Sandra sensed, because Sir Philip's stature conveyed respectability to his own interest. "He didn't just ask about the magnetometer his company sold us, but he wanted to see everything—all our records and reports of encounters, everything. My friend said he talked to our president for *hours*, and photocopied a lot of papers."

Sandra remembered Sir Philip's bright false interest in plant pathology. She bit her tongue, made no comment on the credulity of UFO enthusiasts, and concentrated hard on her driving.

The home help was waiting in Anderson's room. However, at first, Sandra did not recognise him as such: she'd been expecting a grey-haired lady, and couldn't think what this young black man in a fluorescent purple, green and orange T-shirt, black shorts, and orange flip-flops was doing there. Anderson, who was sitting on the edge of the bed talking to the stranger, gave her the same brief illuminating smile that had greeted her the day before.

Anderson had only realised how much he hated being in the hospital when he had a real prospect of leaving, and his eagerness to go had been increasing with every minute of that endless day. It was partly because he disliked the tests and the condescending way some of the nurses spoke to him but, more importantly, he loathed the sense of being in the power of others. It was true that he had ignorantly believed the hospital's power to be greater than it was: he had not known, or had forgotten, that he could refuse treatment; had not realised even that he could ask to see his medical file. But even allowing for exaggeration, he had been subject to the orders of doctors long enough. He was glad to escape.

He was pleased with the home help, too. Malcolm Brown

was his own discovery, not obtained through the health authorities, nor provided by Stellar Research. Staff Nurse Sylvia Brown had come into his room at lunchtime and told him that her son would be available for the position.

"He's a student at the Royal College of Fine Arts," she'd said, with unconcealed pride, "but he's looking for a summer job. He's worked at the hospital as an orderly before, and he's very patient and gentle—I can get you references. And he passed his driving test last summer."

Sylvia Brown was the only member of the hospital staff Anderson really liked, and he trusted her recommendation. He was unaware that home helps were generally older, drabber, and female, and when the young man turned up that evening he could not understand why the nurse, who came with him to introduce them, kept giving her son's T-shirt and flip-flops despairing glares of maternal disapproval. Anderson and Malcolm Brown agreed on a salary and were discussing arrangements when Sandra Murray came in.

"This is Ms Murray, who saved my life," he told Malcolm Brown. "This is Mr Brown, who has agreed to help me at home until I've recovered," Anderson explained to Sandra.

"Call me Malcolm," he said grinning at Sandra and shaking hands. He looked inquiringly at Robert.

"Uh—this is my friend, Robert Singer," stammered Sandra, staring flabbergasted at the T-shirt. The more she stared, the weirder it looked. A spiderweb of black criss-crossed its explosion of lurid colours, like the strokes of letters which never quite formed words. "Uh—you're a home help, Mr . . . that is, Malcolm?"

"I guess I am this summer," replied Malcolm easily. "In real life I'm an art student—or maybe I should put that the other way round? How we gonna work the cars to take Mr Anderson home?"

They took a long time discussing cars and groceries, and then there was a wait while a nurse looked for Dr Evan's letter for Anderson's GP. The others went down the corridor to see what had become of this, and Anderson was left to dress himself. He made the humiliating discovery that he had no idea how to do so. When he got both legs stuck in his trousers, he had to give in and summon help. But at last he was clothed, put in a wheelchair, and pushed out of room 3, ward C-2, into the lift and along a corridor to the hospital foyer, and out into the bright strange bustle of the real world.

He rode to the house with Malcolm and Sylvia Brown in the nurse's ancient Citroen 2CV—Sandra and Robert were to go separately, and pick up some groceries on the way. Anderson sat silent in the front passenger seat, gazing out of the grimed window. It was about eight o'clock by now, a bright clear summer evening. Restaurants, and a few shops, were still open, and people hesitated on pavements by traffic lights. Anderson's exhilaration at his escape began to fade. So many people! Each with his or her own life, each the central point about which an interior world revolved. Watching them—the couple rushing laughing across the road; the young mother pushing her baby home in its pram; the old man threading a careful path on his bicycle—he felt that he had plunged into deep water without troubling to learn first whether or not he could swim. Whatever he might once have known about the world he had now forgotten. He was a stranger among all these people, blundering and ignorant. He had been safe in the hospital, under the guardianship of wiser men. Perhaps he should have stayed there.

Malcolm found the house without difficulty, and pulled the 2CV into the drive with a putter-putter-clonk. He jumped out and hurried round to help Anderson out. Anderson wavered to his feet, resolutely unassisted, and stared at the house before him. He did not remember it at all. He did not remember being in any house, ever, and this one was no more real to him than an architect's drawing. That he should be the owner of it seemed fantasy.

"Ring any bells?" asked Malcolm.

Anderson shook his head unhappily, and began his unsteady shuffle towards the door. Malcolm followed, close enough to catch him if he tripped, and Malcolm's mother followed watchfully behind. She was staying to take her son home that evening, since Malcolm had no car of his own. It was hoped that in the future he could use one of Anderson's—the file Stellar sent the hospital had revealed that Anderson possessed two—but they would have to arrange insurance cover for it first.

When Anderson reached the front door, Malcolm, who'd been given the keys by Sandra, came forward and unlocked it.

Stepping into the interior, Anderson felt a curious sense of guilt, as though he were disturbing a tomb. He stumbled through the hall into the sitting room and stood still, looking around. The photographs stared back at him. Looking at the nearest, he recognised the unfamiliar face that was his, smiling against the backdrop of a snow-covered mountain. He looked away, ashamed.

"Can I put on some coffee for you?" asked Sylvia Brown.

He nodded silently, and sat down heavily on the overstuffed sofa. Malcolm went to the CD player and began to examine the discs. Apparently he found nothing he liked, for he left the player switched off and went to help his mother with the coffee.

When the Browns came back into the sitting room with the coffee, they found Anderson on his feet again. He was staring at another of the photographs: a wedding party laughing over a bottle of champagne in the garden of a country house. The bride was a strikingly beautiful blonde girl; Anderson was the groom. His face, as he regarded the picture now, had the look of blank withdrawal that the nurse associated with bereavement: it was plain that he remembered nothing of the occasion. She had seen enough grief to know when and when not to offer comfort. "How do you like your coffee?" was all she said.

"White, with lots of sugar," replied Anderson absently. He did not really like the bitter taste of coffee, but he'd discovered in hospital that his body welcomed the drink. Malcolm put the mug in his hand, and he cradled its warmth as he shuffled over to the next picture. This one was a group of men in suits, standing in the drive of a different country house and, like the wedding guests, drinking champagne. He had no idea why, or who they were, apart from the second on the right, whose face he was beginning to pick out as his own.

After a while, Sandra and Robert arrived with a Chinese takeaway and a bag of assorted groceries. Laughing, they pulled a pack of chilled lager from among the milk and cereal. Sylvia Brown found glasses, cutlery and crockery in the kitchen cupboards, and the whole party sat down at the table in the dining area.

Anderson sat awkwardly silent, watching the others eat prawn crackers. He wondered about the young man with Sandra, whom he had barely even greeted. Her lover? She undoubtedly would have lovers. He imagined that men would find her very attractive, with her red hair and her freckled, mobile face, and the long angular body that folded itself so elegantly into the chair . . .

Query: did he himself find her sexually attractive?

He felt a sudden giddy wave of terror. He did. He also found the whole concept of sex alarming and repulsive. He pushed aside untouched the glass of lager Robert had poured for him, and rested his head in his hands.

"Are you OK?" Sandra asked him anxiously, noticing his distress while the others were still talking.

He shook his head, not so much in denial as in exasperation. "I'm tired," he said, in an unsteady whisper. "I can't remember this house. I want to lie down."

"I'll help you upstairs," Malcolm offered instantly.

He refused the offer, and crawled up the spiral staircase on his own. He found the bedroom, collapsed into a sitting position on the bed—and found himself staring at his own haggard reflection: a tall, dark-haired man in his midthirties, dressed in a tennis shirt and trousers, bruises fading on a strong-boned face. Passionate denial swept through him: it was not his face, it was Anderson's. The clothes he wore, the bed he sat on, the house he had invaded—they were all Anderson's. He was the survivor of some unknown catastrophe who had taken refuge in a stranger's tomb, and was now buried alive with the alien dead. He covered his eyes, fighting back a scream.

On the bedside table, the telephone rang.

He picked it up on the fifth ring, unable to endure its shrill demand.

"Paul?" asked Sir Philip Lloyd's voice.

He did not reply immediately: in that instant of pause he felt that to answer to Sir Philip would be to lose himself utterly. He struggled to arrange himself in order to answer his enemy with a mask of composure. "Who's speaking, please?" he croaked at last.

"Philip," came the answer. "Paul, I just phoned the hospital, and they told me you'd gone home. Are you sure you're well enough? I spoke to Maureen at The Oaks: she's happy to take you."

"I'd . . . rather be here," said Anderson breathlessly. "I have help."

"Are you sure?" came the doubtful reply. "You sound odd."

"I'm . . . tired," replied Anderson. "I'd rather be here than at The Oaks."

"Paul, you'd be better off with some medical help. The Oaks doesn't just do conferences, you know. They have all the health staff, too; a swimming pool, a jacuzzi and a first-rate chef. Stellar would pay."

"I'd rather be in my own house," said Anderson, more strongly now.

"Look," said the voice. "There's another reason I think you'd be better off at The Oaks. I'll come and discuss it with you tomorrow evening, shall I? Is your memory starting to come back?"

"Not yet."

"Well, maybe now you're home . . . remember, you don't have to talk to Jones. If he comes to see you, he's trespassing. You don't have to let him in. I'll see you tomorrow, Paul."

The line clicked off. Anderson set the phone down, missed the cradle, and pushed at it clumsily with the heels of his hands until it fell into place. His reflection made the same fumbling and incompetent gestures. He covered his face again, and began shaking.

"Who was it?" asked Sandra's voice from the doorway.

"Sir Philip Lloyd," he replied heavily. He lifted his head to look at her, and saw her standing framed in the doorway, with his reflection sitting beside her. The scream came back into his throat, and he bit his tongue to stop it from getting out.

"You look awful," she said anxiously. "What's the matter?"

"The mirror," he told her indistinctly.

She came and sat down on the bed beside him, one concerned hand resting on his shoulder. It sent a shudder through him, though whether from pleasure or disgust he could not have said. Her presence was deeply comforting, but he wished she'd go away. "You shouldn't have come home yet, should you?" she said. "You're not ready for it. Look, we can ring the hospital, and tell them you're coming back in. I'm sure they wouldn't mind."

He shook his head. "It's simply . . ." he said, choking on it, "it's simply that . . . I don't recognise this house. I don't recognise my face in the mirror. I don't belong here. It frightens me."

She did not know how to answer. She hadn't thought he belonged here, either, so how could she dispute it? But this was his house: his keys had opened the door.

Three other shapes darkened the doorway: Sylvia Brown, Malcolm, and Robert. The telephone had interrupted a concerned discussion about Anderson. "Are you OK, Mr Anderson?" asked Malcolm, coming into the room and bending over him.

"I don't like the mirrors," said Anderson, in an unexpected tone of slow deliberate hatred.

"OK," Malcolm replied, completely unperturbed. "I'll get your bed fixed up in a room without 'em. Till then, why don't you sit in the study?"

There was a guest bedroom on the other side of the corridor, and Malcolm found sheets and made the bed with effortless efficiency, then moved Anderson in and helped him to get his shoes off.

"I'll sleep in the other bedroom tonight, if that's OK," he said.

Sandra stared at the young man in the garish T-shirt in surprise. The arrangements made at the hospital had not included anyone staying for the night: Anderson had thought it unnecessary. Sylvia Brown had agreed to take her son home and drop him back at the house the next day on her way to the hospital for her morning shift. The nurse now gave a satisfied but unsurprised smile and said she would stop by in the morning with some clean clothes: she had clearly expected her son to stay as soon as saw that he was needed. Sandra began to feel somewhat happier about Malcolm. She hadn't objected to his colour or sex, but she'd distrusted his age and deplored his occupation. As a scientist, she'd left university full of contempt for arts students— feckless, self-indulgent layabouts who didn't know what *real* studying was—and she'd been seriously worried about entrusting Anderson to one. But maybe he'd be all right after all.

But she was still determined to come back the next evening, and check that her rescuee wasn't being neglected. She was surprised at her own protectiveness. She appeased the uneasiness she felt about it by telling herself that it was natural that she feel responsible for the man she'd rescued.

At least Robert was no longer worried about Anderson. Meeting the man had reassured him. The rescuee might be tall and dark, but Robert did not think he was particularly handsome, and the poor guy was obviously in a state of bat-

tered and helpless confusion. Robert could not believe that
any woman would find that sexy. He also told himself that it
was natural that Sandra take an interest in the life she'd
saved, and when she announced that she was going round to
check how Anderson was on Friday evening, Robert merely
shrugged and invited her out for Saturday.

On Friday the spell of fair weather broke with capricious
English unexpectedness. The morning was sunny and warm,
but the clouds gathered through the afternoon and, as Sandra left work, it began to rain. The green summer dress she'd
put on that morning was far too light for the wet chill, and
her bare arms came up in goose-pimples. When she reached
12 The Mays, she pulled as far up the drive as she could, and
made a dash for the front door.

Malcolm opened it for her, his T-shirt partially concealed
by a maroon-and-grey anorak, which she guessed must be
Anderson's because it wasn't flamboyant enough to be his
own. He grinned as he ushered her in.

"Good to see you," he said. "Mr Anderson's upstairs,
working on the computer. He's been a lot better today. His
GP came round a couple of hours ago and checked on him,
and the district nurse made a visit this morning. She thinks
he doesn't need any more bandages on his hands, but she put
them on in the end because it upsets him to see his fingers.
No other problems."

"Oh, good!" she exclaimed, chafing her cold arms in the
entrance hall. "Did you sort out the cars?"

Malcolm shook his head. "Not yet," he said. "We have to
go over to the insurance office in person, with lots of ID. A
note's no good because Mr Anderson can't sign it so you can
read the signature." Then he laughed. "I dunno that I'm
gonna *dare* drive that car anyway," he said. "Have you seen
it? It's a Jag. An XJS. All the driving I've done has been in
my Mum's tin snail: I dunno how to drive a real car. Besides,
from what I hear, any black guy driving a car like that's
gonna get pulled over by the police every five minutes. You

wanna see if you can borrow a jacket? You've got goose-
pimples."

"Er—yes," she said, disconcerted by his openness. She
went through into the sitting room. The old newspapers had
been put away, but one of the photographs had been taken
from the wall and was propped up on the coffee table. It was
facing one bathroom mirror and leaning back against another. Sandra looked at the odd arrangement in surprise,
then noticed a large sketching pad on the sofa. She gave
Malcolm an inquiring look.

He picked up the sketching pad, flipped a few pages, and
showed her a drawing. The bridal couple from the photograph were reflected in the first mirror as though the shapes
had been cut out with scissors, leaving a hole into darkness.
There was something wrong with the angle of the second
mirror: the black cut-out shapes were distorted in it, and reflected back into the corner of the first mirror only to be distorted again, so that they receded from mirror to mirror in a
blur of shadowy torment. The twisted angles and the missing images were profoundly disturbing, and after gazing for
a few seconds Sandra had to look away. She looked back to
Malcolm.

"I thought maybe I could work it up in oils later," he said.
"Call it *Amnesia*."

"It is *good*!" she said; then blushed at her own tone of astonishment.

Malcolm grinned. "I *am* good!" he announced, with all
the joy of a young man who has recently discovered this.
"I'm aiming to have a chapter in the art history books all to
myself." He flipped through the preceding pages of the
sketch pad, and she saw that it was full of earlier attempts at
the same image, most only half-complete. The angle of the
mirrors started off straightforward and became stranger and
more stomach-churning as the series progressed. "The trouble will be painting it," he confided. "I dunno how many
times I've had a dynamite sketch that ended up looking like
shit when I put the colours on it." He sighed. "And I don't

dare even try and paint here. Sketching I can pick up and put down again, but put a paintbrush in my hand and I'm gone. Mr Anderson could somersault down the stairs and pass out at my feet, and I wouldn't even notice. I'll have to get the camera."

She turned the pages back carefully to the first study he'd shown her. The newlyweds smiled into the tortured shadow. She shivered. "I don't know how you did this," she whispered. "I think it does feel like that for him."

Malcolm nodded. "Yeah. I saw that last night. He was looking at that photo. It's what gave me the idea."

"Have you shown him this?"

"Uh-*uh*!" said Malcolm emphatically. "The last thing he wants now is to have what he feels thrown back at him. I'll show him when he's got his memory back."

The confidence of that "when" gave Sandra a flush of warmth, despite her bare arms. She smiled at Malcolm. "I'm glad you took this job," she said. "You did it because you like helping people, right?"

Malcolm grinned back. "Nah. I took it because my Mum made me. She said I needed to do something to pay for the oil paints. But don't worry, I do like working with sick people. Your friend is in safe hands. You weren't too sure of that before, were you?"

"Well," she said, "I sort of expected you to be an old lady."

His eyebrows expressively rejected old ladyhood. "Sorry to disoblige."

They walked companionably to the foot of the stairs. "He's been on the computer most of the day," Malcolm said, glancing up the metal spiral staircase. "I couldn't make him stop even for lunch—had to take it up to him on a tray. See if you can get him to switch the thing off and come downstairs for supper. I was gonna make a stir-fry: you want some too?"

Sandra nodded, thanked him, and clattered up the stairs.

The door to the study was ajar. Anderson could certainly

have heard them talking in the sitting room, if he'd listened. But he was too focused on the screen in front of him to stir when Sandra opened the door and came into the room. "Hello," she said.

Anderson turned from the screen frowning and blinked at her as though trying to make her out through a telescope. Then he smiled—the brief intensity of welcome she'd seen twice now, an intensity that vanished before her own lips could do more than curl in response. "Hello," he replied, in his hoarse, hesitant way. She'd forgotten his initial fears about whether his voice would work. The reminder put a catch of uncertainty in her own throat.

"I've come to see how you are," she told him. She waved a hand at the computer. "What are you doing?"

He turned back to the screen. "There are a number of files here which are secured with a password. I've been trying to see what's in them." He typed something into the computer, using the unbandaged knuckles of his little fingers, and pressed the return key. The screen went blank, except for a clock symbol, and the machine whirred. "Since I don't know what password he used, I've had to bypass the directory and read them directly from the disc."

"He?" she asked. "Who do you mean?"

He looked down shame-facedly at the keyboard. "Anderson," he muttered. "It's easier to think of him as though he were distinct from myself. I accept that this is unlikely."

He did accept it. He believed in what his own reasoning had shown him—but the part of him which had rejected the identity before had being growing stronger since he arrived at the house. The decor was not to blame: unlike Sandra, he had no idea what it *should* look like. But he had spent the day wading through Anderson's work on the computer, trying to find a way into the locked files. He felt sure that they contained some clue to the thing that had happened to destroy his memory. The more he read, the more inaccessible the mind that had written the files became. Most of the files, locked or open, were irrelevant, but even the most irrelevant were disturbing. There was a crudity of expression and an imprecision of thought that was utterly foreign to him. Worst of all was a series of letters from Anderson to his ex-wife concerning alimony payments. It had shocked him profoundly. Firstly he was distressed by the bitter animosity the letters revealed towards the woman—he could not conceive of wasting so much emotion on what was lost—but secondly, he was astounded by the illogical approach, the self-contradiction, the total absence of rational analysis. He believed deeply and implicitly that to reject reason was to embrace a fatal corruption of the mind. Had the writer of those letters corrupted his own mind, and left his heir seeded with insanity? He was ashamed to admit the anxiety it caused him; ashamed, too, by the fact that he had not dared to go back into the bedroom to face the mirrors. But in his own mind he had ceased to be Anderson, even in quotation marks: he had become an identity without a name, waiting in darkness for his memory's return.

The screen filled with words. The man at the keyboard summoned up a window in a few keystrokes, checked some information on it, then began to scroll forward rapidly.

"Do you want to stop now and have some supper? Malcolm said you've been on this all day," asked Sandra, her eyes picking odd phrases out of the documents as they flooded past.

Re your letter of the 17th . . . sales of the Photolath panels to June . . . Consolidated Power reserves the right . . . current profits of the department . . . no benefit to Stellar . . . option on low-temperature geothermal . . . interest in the Astragen Project . . .

The flow of documents stopped. The man at the keyboard moved slightly forward, his strong nose and hunched shoulders giving him a sudden resemblence to a bird of prey. "This is part of one of the locked documents," he said.

"Part" it was: everything on the screen seemed to be par-

tial. A statement about investment by the Italians in geothermal power was broken without warning by the half-sentence
that had caught Sandra's eye: ". . . interest in the Astragen
Project." The document went on:

> *I told him this was totally unacceptable, and I've warned
> him that if he makes any attempt to publicise it we'll hit
> him with everything we've got. But he's got hold of some
> shit version of what happened at the trials in March, and
> he's going to keep digging until he finds out more. To get
> an injunction we'd have to go to court and if we do that
> we might as well hang banners out the windows saying,
> "We've got a secret!" Phil's very reluctant about apply-
> ing for a notice, though, because he's afraid it will affect
> sales. I tell him we could finesse it, but Denise thinks
> that . . . had a rival bid from Icelandic Power of 5.34
> m . . .*

Sandra blinked, and realised that the final phrase had come
from a different document. "Why's it so jumbled up?" she
asked.

"I told you. I've had to read it directly from the disc,
where the documents are interspersed." He moved the cursor with a fierce deliberate jab of the knuckle, then hit
delete. All the writing above the phrase about the Astragen
Project disappeared. The cursor jumped down to what
Denise thought, and the documents began to flow rapidly up
the screen again.

"Could you stop now?" Sandra asked again. "This is not
going to run away if you come downstairs for supper. And
can I borrow a jacket? I didn't take one to work this morning, and I'm cold."

He stopped scrolling and looked at her. Her arms were
pale and pimpled, and she stood with them wrapped about
herself. Something opened inside him like a rusty sluice
gate, letting out a swift eroding trickle of tenderness. He
started to imagine himself putting his arm around her to

warm her—but the image he had of himself was the fumbling shape he had seen in the mirror, and he thrust it fearfully away. He looked back at the screen. "Borrow whatever you want," he told her. "I'll save this, and come down."

He had been assembling the passworded files in a new file all day. He saved his latest fragment, and shut the machine down. Sandra came back in a much-too-large sports jacket, and he followed her down the stairs, ashamed of the way he had to shuffle after her backwards, one step at a time.

Malcolm enlisted them both in preparing the stir-fry, asking Sandra to chop onions and not-Anderson to put bread in the toaster and take toast out. Malcolm's own part of the task seemed to involve frozen turkey breast, frozen peas, curry powder, and *lots* of garlic.

"Royal College speciality!" Malcolm exclaimed, dishing out the sizzling assembly and setting the plates on the dining table with a flourish. "Better 'n hospital food, huh?"

Not-Anderson thoughtfully chewed a mouthful and swallowed. He could not remember curry, or garlic. They weren't exactly unpleasant, but they were certainly surprising. "It is much more highly spiced than hospital food," he equivocated.

Malcolm was amused. "You like it, Ms Murray?" he asked.

"It's delicious!" she said, through a tingling mouthful, "—and call me Sandra."

Not-Anderson was uncomfortably aware that he had invariably referred to her as Ms Murray. "Should I call you Sandra, too?" he asked.

She turned to him, smiling. She swallowed her mouthful of stir-fry and said, "Yes, of course! Can I call you Paul?"

He could not meet the smile, and looked away. "Please, no," he whispered. "I . . . am not comfortable with that name just now."

They both stared at him. The question in their eyes chafed his anxiety about his own sanity.

"I accept that it is overwhelmingly likely that I am Paul Anderson," he said defensively. "But I do not feel I understand the man at all. I would prefer not to use his name until I can . . . adjust."

The stares lasted another few seconds. Then Malcolm asked, "You don't want her to call you Paul? Do you mind me using 'Mr Anderson'?"

Not-Anderson gave an awkward, inconclusive twist of the body. "I accept that that is probably my name. Obviously I will have to use it for the bank and the insurance company. I do not want to cause confusion by rejecting it from old associates. But I would prefer it if . . . if *friends* avoided it."

"OK," said Malcolm, surprised but equable. "What do you wanna be called then?"

Not-Anderson saw what was coming even before the question was complete, and struggled frantically to divert his mind. It was useless: once again his thoughts tried to reach over the tilted edge of memory, and once more the nausea crashed upon him. Its horrible familiarity did not make it any easier to endure. He bent over, gritting his teeth, and calculated the percentage of passworded documents he had so far retrieved from the computer. He heard Malcolm exclaiming in concern. He took a few deep breaths of curry-and-garlic scented air and forced himself to straighten up. The two pairs of eyes still questioned him, but he was too embarrassed to meet them.

"I'm sorry," he whispered helplessly. "This seems to happen when I start to remember." He wiped his face. "Call me whatever you like, or don't call me anything. I suppose 'Paul Anderson' is as good a name as any. Only . . ."

Only he felt as though "Paul Anderson" was stamped on the lid of a metal box, and that he were being dismembered and crushed so that he could be jammed into it. But he was ashamed to admit it, and left his sentence hanging. There was a long and uncomfortable silence. Then the doorbell rang.

FOUR

NOT-ANDERSON HAD NOT ACTUALLY FORGOTTEN THAT
Sir Philip Lloyd had arranged to visit that evening, but he
had been far too preoccupied to relay the information or
make any mental preparations for the meeting. When Malcolm opened the door and the voice of Stellar's chairman
questioned him from the doorstep, Malcolm was surprised,
Sandra, shocked, and not-Anderson, guiltily alarmed. Sandra, sitting opposite, felt that he was folding a part of himself away, like a photographer packing up some delicate
piece of equipment so that it would not be damaged in a
jostling crowd.

"There you are, Paul," said Sir Philip, coming into the
dining area. A slim, dark-haired woman in a severely elegant
suit followed him, and Malcolm brought up the rear. It was
evident from his nervous expression that he knew who Sir
Philip was. He exchanged a what-do-we-do-with-a-televi-
sion-personality look with Sandra.

"I'm sorry I've caught you at dinner. Don't get up," Sir
Philip went on. "Hello, Ms . . . Murray, isn't it? Nice to meet
you again."

Malcolm glanced at not-Anderson, who sat silent and

withdrawn in his place at the dining table. Then he offered the newcomers a choice of drinks or coffee.

"I'll have a whisky and ginger ale, fairly weak," said Sir Philip. "Denise?" This was the name of the dark-haired woman.

"I'll have a dry sherry," said Denise. She had a low, creamy voice and a country-house accent. She might have been younger than Sir Philip or much older: she gleamed with so thick a layer of polish, buffed to so high a gloss, that it was impossible to tell.

"Er—right," said Malcolm, flustered. "You wouldn't happen to know where the drinks cupboard is, would you?"

Denise smiled at not-Anderson. "Paul, help the poor man out! Where's your drinks cupboard?"

"I don't remember," not-Anderson replied evenly.

Denise blinked.

"I think it's the other side of the music centre, in the sitting room," supplied Sir Philip.

Malcolm went off, and came back with bottles and glasses. Sandra decided that she ought to be helping, and jumped up and fetched ice. "You'll join us?" asked Sir Philip, smiling at her and at his host.

Not-Anderson said nothing. Sandra, embarrassed, helped herself to some of the sherry. Malcolm hesitated, then poured a whisky and ginger ale and hefted it suggestively at not-Anderson. When not-Anderson shook his head, Malcolm sipped the drink himself.

"Coffee for him," said Sir Philip, smiling. "Black, no sugar—right, Paul?"

Not-Anderson looked at him with interest, but said merely, "No, thank you."

Sir Philip was concerned. "Aren't you feeling well?"

"He gets bouts of nausea from time to time," said Sandra, feeling some explanation was called for. "He had one just before you came."

Sir Philip gave an exasperated snort. "You really are not well! I told you that you should have gone to The Oaks."

"I am recovering," said not-Anderson shortly. "Why did you want to see me this evening?"

Sandra expected Sir Philip to protest that he'd come out of goodwill, to visit his sick team-mate—but he didn't. "We need to talk to you about this man Jones," he said instead. He directed a smile at Sandra and Malcolm, and his next words were to them. "I hope you don't mind, but we badly need to discuss some very important confidential business with our friend. There's a muck-raking reporter who's making a documentary about Stellar, and he's been trying to get hold of some of our trade secrets to spice it up with, since he hasn't got much else in the way of mud to fling. We're worried that he might try to interview Paul while he's vulnerable and confused. Denise wants to brief Paul on what to do if the fellow does turn up—Denise Gresham here is Stellar's legal adviser." Denise gave a cold, self-satisfied twist of the lips. "But we need to talk privately," Sir Philip went on, apologetically now. "I'm sorry if I seem inhospitable, but would you two mind leaving the house for a bit?"

"I would mind their leaving," not-Anderson said sharply. "It is raining, and we were eating supper. They are my guests."

Sir Philip looked annoyed. Denise Gresham looked insulted. Sandra opened her mouth, then closed it again. It wasn't her house.

"If you think it essential to talk to me privately, we can go upstairs to the study," not-Anderson pointed out reasonably. "If you are concerned that we might be overheard, put some music on. Malcolm and Sandra can stay here and finish their meal."

Sir Philip sighed and nodded. Denise went to the CD player, rummaged through the discs with a grimace of distaste, then put on a collection of classic Beatles. Not-Anderson got to his feet and shuffled up the stairs. It took all his concentration to walk up, and he had to clutch the rail with both hands, but he was determined not to crawl in front of Sir Philip. The two visitors followed him.

Malcolm and Sandra stood at the foot of the stairs, watching the others disappear to the strains of "All You Need is Love." Then Malcolm gave Sandra a look of bewilderment. "What is going on?" he demanded.

"I have no idea," Sandra admitted. The uncomfortable out-of-her-depth feeling had returned.

"This muck-raking reporter called Jones," said Malcolm. "Do you suppose he meant Rodney Jones?"

"I don't rightly know," replied Sandra dispiritedly. "Who is he?"

"Oh, you must have seen his stuff!" exclaimed Malcolm. "He did that documentary on gypsies, and the one about the exploitation of AIDS victims, and the exposé of that county council that was selling planning permission."

"I saw the one about AIDS victims," said Sandra, feeling yet more dispirited. It had been a good documentary—not scientific enough for her taste, but hard-hitting and burning with a genuine moral indignation that made it stand out like a rock in the grey tide of synthetic emotions that ebbed and flowed each day over the television screens of Britain. Stellar didn't want the man she'd rescued to talk to the man who'd made that documentary. She did not like the pattern that was beginning to emerge.

She looked at Malcolm's puzzled face, and realised with relief that she could confide in him. Malcolm was involved now, as much as she was herself: she was not just spreading gossip. She could tell him all about Anderson's wild suspicions. She hoped that in turn he would tell her that they were symptomatic of a traumatised mind.

"Paul—" she began, then bit her lip. *Paul*. She shouldn't call him that. She didn't know what else to call him. It seemed that some part of her had started calling him that, even without his permission. "Paul has an idea that Stellar did something terrible to him," she tried again. "He thinks it's the reason he lost his memory. He feels as though he's someone else, too, not Paul Anderson—that's why he doesn't want us to call him that. He's not obsessive about it, and he's open to reason: he decided that there was so much evidence to prove that he is Paul Anderson that he'd have to accept it. But he doesn't like it, and he thinks the reason why he is so averse to it is because Stellar did something so dreadful that he can't bear to remember it. He says he woke up feeling he disliked and distrusted Stellar Research, and he's afraid of Sir Philip Lloyd. I thought—*think* it just means that he was unhappy in his job, but . . ."

But she had disliked the cold smirk on Denise's face when Sir Philip had tried to order them out of the house. She felt that there was something presumptuous about making such a demand. She didn't like the way Sir Philip had sketched a compliance with social mores—"Don't get up. Yes, I'd like a drink"—only to abandon them half-complete, like a bored actor tiring of his role. She mistrusted the urgency of this visit, the secrecy, the disturbing reference to a journalistic investigation of . . . what?

"I don't really know what to think," she told Malcolm.

Malcolm was now frowning. "I've always thought Stellar was one of the good guys—for a company," he said. "You know, alternative power, saving the earth, all that kinda thing."

"Yes," said Sandra unhappily. "But in the research community it has a reputation for being ruthless and secretive. I don't rightly know what to think." She was silent a moment, and then added reluctantly, "I don't like Sir Philip Lloyd."

She'd felt compelled to add that because the dislike weighed on her. It was more than Sir Philip's condescending nature. There was something hard and cold about him, something that his bright blonde pleasantness didn't quite conceal. But was that her own perception, or had she merely been infected by Paul's fear?

"You like the vampire?" asked Malcolm.

Sandra giggled half-heartedly. "Isn't she, then? No, I don't like her, either. But I only met her just now, and probably we're being unfair to both of them."

"I know I'm just the hired help," said Malcolm, "but I

don't like it when people look through me. I don't like either of 'em, and I'm not gonna apologise for it."

They drifted back to the dining table and sat picking at their portions of stir-fry. Sandra told Malcolm about Stellar's employment practices. The CD player sang its way through "Here Comes the Sun." They finished their stir-fry. Malcolm took the third plate into the kitchen and put it in the microwave. The disc played "I Get By with a Little Help from My Friends."

"This was the only half-way decent disc in the house," said Malcolm, after a long song-filled silence. "The rest are all 'All Time Favourites' and 'Greatest Hits' crap."

"I don't think Paul knows very much about music," replied Sandra, and bit her lip again.

The disc played "Nowhere Man." Sandra considered going home—but somehow couldn't bring herself to go while Anderson was trapped in the study with the two "Stellars." She felt a quiver in her stomach when she thought of it. She told herself not to be silly: they *wouldn't* hurt Paul. It was ridiculous to think that if she and Malcolm weren't here as witnesses, something . . . no, it was ridiculous.

At last feet clanged on the spiral, and Sir Philip and Denise Gresham descended to the sitting room. They looked puzzled and ill at ease. Sandra could not have explained why this made her heart skip a beat with relief.

"We must go now," said Sir Philip, eyeing the two of them. "But I hope you'll contact us if Paul needs help. He has the number." He was about to say something else, but stopped himself and politely issued Malcolm and Sandra with his regulation goodbye instead. He and Denise Gresham stepped out into the rainy green dusk.

Sandra shot up the stairs before the door had closed behind the visitors. Paul was sitting in the chair before the computer, staring blankly at the dark screen. "Are you all right?" she asked breathlessly.

He turned and gave her another vacant look. Then he

nodded and heaved himself stiffly to his feet. He was so unsteady that she caught his arm.

"Do you want your supper now?" she asked. "It's in the microwave, and we can heat it up in a minute."

"Thank you," he said hoarsely. He pulled his arm gently away from her, and wavered out on to the landing, bracing himself with one hand against the wall.

The talk with Sir Philip Lloyd and Denise Gresham had left him feeling battered. The more he found out about Paul Anderson, the less he liked the man. The effort of identifying himself with such a contemptible person made his mind throb and stretched his reason on the rack. The inaccessible continent of his memory heaved convulsively, sending splinters of nausea and unintelligible terrors into his consciousness. He wondered if this was what the onset of insanity felt like. He wished he were in the hospital, and that Dr Evans was standing over him with a syringe full of cool oblivious morphine.

He struggled on down the stairs, pondering whether it was wise to involve Sandra and Malcolm. He could not ask them to trust him or rely upon him; he could not trust or rely upon himself. But he needed advice, needed it desperately. Sir Philip and Denise had said too many things he had not understood, and he did not know where he could turn for explanation, if not to these two.

He stumbled back to the dining table and sat down. At last, the CD reached an end, leaving silence and the sound of rain on the roof. Sandra sat down opposite, watching him in freckled anxiety. Malcolm went into the kitchen and switched on the microwave, then came back and looked challengingly at not-Anderson.

"You gonna tell us what's going on?" he asked.

"I don't know what's going on," not-Anderson answered painfully. "All I can do is repeat what was said upstairs." He stopped and swallowed; something hard and angular seemed to be choking him. "I think perhaps I am going insane," he admitted. "Please, if I go insane, I want to die." He imagined insanity: imagined his reason disintegrating into gibberish, while his consciousness screamed ever more faintly, until it was gone. He covered his face and forced himself to construct a truth table according to the principles of symbolic logic.

"You're not insane!" exclaimed Sandra. She reached across the table and caught his hands. "Paul, you're not! You're perfectly coherent. Please, tell us what happened. We want to help." Then she realised that she had spoken for Malcolm as well as herself. She blushed, and shot the art student a look of entreaty. He nodded back.

Not-Anderson looked at her earnest face. He withdrew his hands from hers and took a deep breath. "Sir Philip," he began, "told me about the dealings of Paul Anderson with a man called Rodney Jones, who is a . . . freelance documentarist." (He pronounced the title with care. It was a term whose meaning he had guessed from the context in which it was mentioned, though he could not recall it.) "I find it impossible to believe that I would ever behave as Anderson did—I try to believe it, but I can't. I have a sense of who and what I am, and he violates it at every point of contact. And there was so much I simply didn't understand. I don't remember—I can't remember—enough to grasp what is happening, even when I'm told. What is an MP?"

Sandra and Malcolm both blinked and stared. Then Sandra blushed again, afraid that her astonishment might wound him. "Member of Parliament," she explained faintly.

"Anderson owns a villa at a place called Ischia, which he lent to an MP called Henry Ellis," not-Anderson went on. He was gaining control of himself now, and the anguish in his voice had given way to hoarse neutrality. "He paid for Ellis and his family to travel to it, as well. Jones was gathering information for a television documentary on links between business and government, and he found out about it. From the way that Sir Philip talked about it, I gather that the loan would be considered wrong, but I don't remember enough to know how seriously wrong. Was it in fact illegal?"

Sandra swallowed and shook her head. This was the stuff headlines were made of. To have it happen before her seemed unreal. To have it involve someone she cared about hurt and confused her.

Malcolm pursed his lips in a soundless whistle. "Umm—Ellis would definitely have to resign if it came out," he said. "He's Secretary of State for Energy. Yeah, he certainly *cannot* go around borrowing villas from the directors of energy engineering companies. But this isn't actually illegal, just against parliamentary regulations. *You* couldn't be punished for it."

Not-Anderson blinked, and Sandra again had the impression of a computer processing a crucial piece of information. "Thank you," he said. "What's a rottweiler?"

Malcolm's expressive eyebrows shot up. "A kind of dog that's famous for attacking people. Who's a rottweiler?"

"According to Sir Philip, Mr Rodney Jones is," replied not-Anderson, and his mouth tightened. "Though it could just as well be Anderson, who apparently resented bitterly what he regarded as Jones' interference. He wanted Stellar to take steps to muzzle Jones—what does that mean?"

Malcolm actually grinned. He seemed more able to take things in his stride than Sandra. "One field you've forgotten about is dogs," he said. "A muzzle is what you'd put on one to stop it biting."

"It was a metaphor, then?" asked not-Anderson. He looked so relieved that Sandra wondered what he'd thought it meant. "Stellar at any rate didn't agree to the muzzling. It regarded Jones as nothing more than a minor nuisance, and considered that to make moves against him would simply attract unwelcome attention. So the company ignored him, even when he decided to investigate it more thoroughly and looked into Stellar's working practices and acquisition of patents. What's a patent?"

He took them through the whole account, just as he had

heard it from Sir Philip Lloyd and Denise Gresham, requesting explanations for every other phrase. Jones had uncovered various practices of Stellar's which were sharp and unsavoury, but not actually illegal, and Anderson had fumed and fretted over each. He had done everything he could to put obstacles in the reporter's path. Potential sources of information were bullied or bribed into refusing to give interviews; archives were closed. Jones' office was raided by the police after a false tip-off about drugs. Television executives were induced to make anxious telephone calls about the undesirability of offending Stellar. But Jones persisted. In the end he even found out about Stellar's newest and most prized research programme, the Astragen Project—but this coup was his downfall, as it forced the company to take action. Stellar maintained the strictest imaginable secrecy about Astragen: Sir Philip had refused to answer any of not-Anderson's questions about it, and said that he never allowed the project to be discussed off-site. To protect Astragen, Stellar's board of directors agreed to take steps to silence Jones. Anderson went to a friend at the MoD. "— what is that?"

"Ministry of Defence," whispered Sandra, feeling more horribly out of her depth than ever.

"Anderson apparently had some link to them, and was able to have the Astragen Project 'classified,'" said not-Anderson. "Is 'classified' a conventional expression? Sir Philip never said what the classification was."

Sandra nodded: she could not speak.

"Classified secret," said Malcolm. "On the grounds of national security. It means Jones couldn't broadcast anything about it."

"I see."

Not-Anderson continued with the story. Jones' office was raided again, this time by MI5, and all the material relating to Stellar was removed "for examination." But even this was not enough for Anderson. He sent Jones a letter, threatening to sue him for damages and prosecute him for theft of intellectual property if he didn't stay away from Stellar Research henceforward. This was more than the board of directors had agreed on, more than he was legally entitled to do, and it backfired: Jones was fully aware that only the Crown can prosecute on criminal charges. This further evidence of collusion between Stellar and the government had merely provoked him. He went to his MP and complained; he demanded that MI5 return all the material they'd seized which was not directly relevant to Astragen and he threatened to turn to the newspapers and the courts. Denise Gresham had tried to calm him. She'd promised the reporter that the threat of prosecution was empty, and had no origin but Anderson's temper—and incidentally let out that Stellar's marketing director was the one who'd caused Jones all the trouble before. This left Jones eager to speak to Anderson. Anderson, however, refused to meet him. Jones, ever persistent, eventually followed Anderson from work and tried to question him in a pub. Anderson lost his temper, insulted Jones, punched him in the nose, and threatened him with unspecified disasters if he didn't go away. This incident had taken place on the Wednesday before the car accident.

Not-Anderson stopped and sat with his head bowed, staring at the space of table between his bandaged hands. This was the incident that appalled him most, the one that left his sense of himself and his own nature in an irreconcilable turmoil. The idea of committing an act of violence was distasteful enough, but the thing that left deep wounds was the senselessness of the violence. It had served no purpose. It was even contrary to Anderson's own interests, since it left him vulnerable to prosecution for assault and did Jones no lasting harm. It was an act as spontaneous and irrational as an animal's. It was almost insane! He could not believe that he would ever have indulged in it—and yet he must have.

He forced himself to go on, but his voice was now flat, almost mechanical, as though it came from some detached part of him which recorded and felt nothing. Stellar was still angry with Anderson about the violence, because it was bad publicity. Denise Gresham had been trying to find out if Jones would prosecute, but she'd been unable to contact him: his company consisted only of him and a cameraman, and no one seemed to be checking the answering machine. She thought, however, that Jones was unlikely to prosecute, as it wouldn't be good publicity for him, either. Any competent defence attorney could make a good case out of the respectable businessman driven to uncharacteristic violence by the persistent harrassment of a scurrilous reporter.

"But she says that Jones is likely to try to provoke me into losing my temper again," not-Anderson said, "on camera this time—and that is why she and Sir Philip came tonight."

Even without mentioning the Astragen Project, if Jones got his tapes back from MI5 he still had enough material to embarrass Stellar, particularly if that material included a sequence of a company director attacking the reporter. As a counter-measure, Sir Philip had decided that Jones should get his interview with Anderson while he was still obviously incapacitated by the accident. The sight of a bruised and bandaged director struggling with the reporter's bullying was bound to win the company some sympathy, and the amnesia was a cast-iron excuse for not answering any awkward questions. It was so convenient that Sir Philip had at first believed it was an act. Since it was genuine, however, Sir Philip wanted the interview to take place in a location where it could be controlled by Stellar. That way, if Anderson lost his temper, or, worse, began to talk about things which he was too confused to remember were secret, the proceedings could be halted. Sir Philip's plan was that Anderson should move into The Oaks, which proved to be a luxury health resort owned by Stellar and run by a friend of Sir Philip's. Jones would not know from the address that he was being set up, the ambience could be adjusted to the proper sickbed atmosphere, and the staff would make certain that Jones was admitted, but allowed to ask only such questions as Stellar was willing to have answered.

"So what are you gonna do?" asked Malcolm.

Not-Anderson looked up at him quickly, and when he answered his voice was normal again. "I told him that I would speak to Jones here, in this house, and I promised that I would not lose my temper. He yielded, eventually, when he saw that I would not, and now he wants to attend the interview himself. He wants to arrange it for early next week—Monday, if he can contact Jones in time."

Malcolm let out his breath slowly. "I don't understand," he said. "It looks like you went into that accident on one side and came out on the other."

"Don't you see? Paul Anderson must have been insane," not-Anderson demanded, with a sudden fierceness. "Why else would he have acted against his own interests at that pub?"

"That's not insanity!" protested Malcolm in surprise. "That's just stupid. Anybody can do something stupid like that if they lose their temper."

Not-Anderson stared at him in disbelief.

"It's true," said Sandra. "You may find it hard to understand, because you're so ultra-rational, but most people . . ."

"But I am Paul Anderson," not-Anderson said bitterly, "and I don't understand it. Therefore, I am not rational, but schizophrenic."

There was a cold embarrassed silence. Then Malcolm said hesitantly, "But Sandra told me that you don't feel as if you're Anderson."

Not-Anderson sighed. "In favour of the proposition that I am Paul Anderson are the following. I was driving his car and carrying his ID at the time of the accident. My face matches the ID photo, and also matches other photographs, in his hospital file—which I have now seen—and in this house. I am approximately his height and weight, I fit his clothing and his shoes, and I have the marks of an old break in the bones of my left leg, which match his medical records. I felt instinctively that his ex-wife would recognise me. There is no rival Paul Anderson to dispute me. None of these things can be accounted for if we assume I am not Anderson.

"In favour of the proposition that I am not Paul Anderson, I can say only that all along I have felt that I am not him, that I do not think I am inclined to lose my temper, and that I like coffee white with sugar while he liked it black without. These can all be accounted for as the result of physical and mental traumas. The evidence that I am Anderson is overwhelming. How could I have Anderson's face, if I were someone else?"

Malcolm shrugged. "I dunno. Plastic surgery?"

Not-Anderson stared. "What's that?"

Malcolm's explanation astonished him. He'd had no recollection that such a thing existed. Proposition (not-A), left behind at the hospital to die, suddenly revived, and he welcomed it with joy. The thought that he *must* be Anderson had been torment, and even the slight possibility that he might not be was refuge and relief.

"If I had had this plastic surgery," he asked eagerly, "how would I know?"

Malcolm was embarrassed. "Shit, I didn't really—I mean, you couldn't have had it. It takes time, and you'd have hair-line scars—pressure bruises . . ."

"I have a pressure bruise," said Not-Anderson, touching his face.

Malcolm's eyes widened. "You do. Shit, you could have had it! Everyone would think the marks came from the accident. And your hands—no one would check for fingerprints when they were so ripped up. It could've happened."

Sandra had been listening in growing alarm. She'd expected Malcolm to tell her that Paul's theories were completely wild. Instead, he was finding evidence to support one so extreme that Paul himself had rejected it. "This is silly," she now declared loudly. "You're saying that somebody kidnapped Paul, fixed him to look like Stellar's marketing director, and then dumped him in the car to drown under somebody else's name. Why bother? If you're going to murder somebody, why all the rigmarole? Why not just knock him on the head and drown him in his own car? Nobody'd know the difference, and you wouldn't have to bribe your kidnappers and find a corrupt plastic surgeon. Besides, Stellar may not have been behaving well, but we haven't heard anything to make us think they'd be *that* ruthless. You can't just throw accusations like that around as though they were frisbees! Come up with fantastic theories when none of the simple explanations work, not before!"

Malcolm subsided. After a moment, he nodded. Not-Anderson, however, was more tenacious. "I am not as certain as you that the simple explanations do work," he told Sandra. "I've made every effort to believe them, and I can't. That, surely, must in itself be evidence of a kind. The elaborate deception might very well have a rational motivation—to divert suspicion from a murderer who was known to have real motive. I agree, however, that the conjecture should at present be regarded as unsubstantiated, and that the balance of evidence still favours the proposition that I am Anderson."

His mind whirled eagerly through analyses and conjectures connected to proposition (not-A). Little things noted and dismissed before now formed patterns: the mirror; his own bewilderment when Sir Philip proved friendly; the alien patterns of thought and expression in Anderson's letters; the way Sir Philip and Denise Gresham had grown more and more puzzled during their conversation with him that evening. He now saw that their bewilderment had sprung from his failure to react and behave like Anderson. And he could finally complete the dislocated thought whose end had eluded him after first meeting Sir Philip at the hospital: *everything Sir Philip has said and done is consistent with him believing that I am Anderson.*

If this theory were correct, what was he to make of the fact that Sir Philip and his legal adviser believed he was Anderson? If he had been substituted for Anderson at some point, and if the chairman of Stellar didn't know about it, who had done the substitution?

The obvious target of suspicion was the real Anderson. He had plainly feared Jones' investigations more than his employers had. Did he have some guilty secret which he was afraid might come out? He seemed to have had contacts in government and army—people who might, perhaps, assist him in covering his tracks. Where was he now? And who was not-Anderson?

Conjecture: Anderson attempted to murder Jones because of something Jones had discovered in his investigations. He diverted suspicion from himself by faking his death, using his victim as his own corpse. I am not Anderson, but Jones.

The conjecture was consistent and accounted for all the facts, and felt right to not-Anderson.

He re-evaluated it. The name Jones seemed no more familiar to him than the name Anderson, and television documentaries were as unfamiliar and improbable a career as marketing. On the other hand, his sense of identity was by now so mauled, so set about with double checks and doubts, that it could no longer be used as evidence of anything.

"Do either of you know what Rodney Jones looks like?" he asked hopefully.

Malcolm stared, understanding what lay behind the question, and burst out laughing. "He's big, and he's got black hair and a big black beard. Hey, look, there was an article about him in *TV Times* a few weeks ago: I can get the picture, and show you what they'd have had to do to make him look like you. But Sandra's right, it's pretty far-fetched. Shit. This job is a lot more interesting than I thought it would be."

"I'd be grateful if you could check that picture tomorrow," said not-Anderson.

"TOMORROW," SATURDAY, WAS ALREADY SCHEDULED to be busy. Sylvia Brown had planned to take her son and his employer into town so that they could arrange insurance

cover for Anderson's car. They also needed to visit Anderson's bank to arrange for Malcolm's salary to be paid and to
collect cash for the household expenses. Sandra, however,
volunteered to take Mrs Brown's place as chauffeur. She
was not meeting Robert until the evening, and she felt that
any attempt to spend a quiet day at home was going to be ruined by worry. Malcolm phoned his mother to cancel the car
and request the *TV Times* and a few sundries of his own.
Sandra arranged to return to 12 The Mays at half-past nine
next morning.

She was reluctant to depart that night, and when she arrived back at her own house, it seemed different. She found
that she was examining it with a stranger's eye: she regretted the drab Victorian terrace it stood in the middle of but
admired the hanging basket of fuchsia and trailing lobelias,
and the bay tree in its pot by the front door. Then avoiding
the worn paint and the scruffy carpet inside, she settled instead with approval on the abundant greenery. She wandered
through the sitting room, picking up the scattered papers and
abandoned coffee cups, and stopped before the unwashed
breakfast things piled hastily in the sink. It was not a
stranger's eye, she realised sourly. It was Paul's eye she was
trying to mimic: subconsciously she'd been considering
whether to invite him and Malcolm back for lunch, and she
wanted to make a good impression.

She tipped the cold water from the washing-up bowl and
turned the hot tap on. OK, she told herself, mimic Paul: be
rational about it. What exactly are your feelings towards the
man?

She sighed: her feelings were a complete jumble. Pity,
certainly: the terror on his face when he said he thought he
must be going insane had torn at her heart. Responsibility:
she *had* saved his life. Curiosity, too: she could not simply
back out without first finding out what was going on,
whether (she admitted it) any of the wild theories were right.
But there was even more than that. She was intrigued by
him. He was unlike anyone she had ever met, and she was

instinctively certain that it was not just the drama of the rescue and his amnesia that made him seem that way. He was enormously intelligent, but innocent of preconceptions. Something in him seemed to strike the world at a tangent, and pierce through to dimensions previously unseen. She was hungry to understand him; she wanted to have, to be part of of him. Was that sexual desire? No. Yes. It was something more complicated, and yet it would end in desire: standing there before the sink she saw that it would end in desire, and in pain. He did not want her too close, did not want her to touch him, though he seemed to welcome her as a friend. Always he'd withdrawn his hand, pushed her arm gently away. Amnesia had left him emotionally shattered, she told herself sensibly: how could he fall in love when he didn't even know who he was? Then, more sensibly and more honest, she admitted to herself that he might not want to fall in love at all, not with her.

She looked up from the sink, and saw her own reflection in the dark glass of the window, a long bony face framed in bright red hair, and pale blue eyes looking small and weak because her eyelashes were too fair to show up. She'd never painted them: as a teenager she'd been superior to painting her face ("I'm a scientist, not a dolly-bird!" she'd say) and as an adult she'd never had the time and energy to expend on picking up an expensive new habit. She made a face at herself, and wished that she were beautiful. Paul's wife had been beautiful. She'd seen that from the wedding photograph. Probably, she told herself, Paul's wife had divorced him because he insisted on being *reasonable* all the time. There is nothing worse than trying to argue with a man who's being reasonable. You'd have to be a very unusual woman to put up with it.

She sighed again. She was not a very unusual woman. She was a nice, plain, sensible Scot, brighter than average, perhaps, and undoubtedly a decent person—but ordinary. Robert, too, was ordinary. Eventually, she would marry Robert or somebody like him, and they would have nice,

plain, sensible, ordinary children. There was nothing wrong
with that. Only she hungered still for the tangent which led
into the dark—and already that hunger was redefining itself
as love.

She told herself that she'd take Paul and Malcolm into
town the next morning, and in the evening she'd go out with
Robert. She would not invite Paul to lunch—not tomorrow,
anyway. He'd be tired, after his first trip into town and he'd
want to go home. Another day, perhaps. There were no big
decisions that needed to be made yet, and perhaps there
never would be. She had a horrible suspicion that falling in
love with Paul was something about which she had no
choice.

THE TRIP INTO TOWN WENT WELL. THE OTHERS WERE
ready when Sandra arrived to pick them up, and they were
able to find parking in the town centre—which was by no
means guaranteed on a Saturday. Sandra had suggested rent-
ing or borrowing a wheelchair, but Anderson insisted on
walking and was, in fact, finally becoming steadier on his
feet. They went to the insurance office, and then to the bank.
"If all your money's been wired to South America, we'll
know what to think, huh?" said Malcolm.

The money had not been wired to South America, however, and there turned out to be quite a lot of it scattered
about in various accounts and investments. The bank manager knew Anderson, and went out of his way to be helpful,
ordering fresh bank cards and credit cards to be signed when
he was able, and providing showers of cash and a draft for
Malcolm's salary for two weeks.

"Do you feel awkward about it?" asked Sandra, when
they were leaving again.

"No," said not-Anderson, surprised. "Why?"

"I was just worried that you might feel uncomfortable
taking Anderson's money if you think you're someone else."

He gave her a bewildered look. "I thought we agreed that

the balance of evidence still favours the proposition that I am Anderson."

Of course, she thought with resignation. *If the balance of probability inclines to a particular proposition, he would never adhere to a contrary proposition out of sentiment alone.* She grinned to herself, because this line of thinking was so entirely typical of the man, and she should have seen it coming.

They returned to the insurance office, and paid out for Malcolm's insurance cover. Sandra thought that Malcolm looked pretty pleased about it, for someone who wasn't sure whether or not he dared drive a real car. She suspected that not only did he dare, he was aching to tell his Royal College friends that he'd spent the summer driving about in a Jaguar XJS.

On the way back from town, they stopped at a supermarket and did the shopping. At first, not-Anderson stumbled down the aisles looking withdrawn, while Malcolm pushed the trolley and Sandra fetched items from the shelves. Not-Anderson found the displays of unintelligible items profoundly depressing. He could not remember what any of these objects were, let alone how they were prepared and what they tasted like. But after a while Malcolm and Sandra began suggesting items in competition, disagreeing over the merits of doughnuts and crumpets, TV dinners and frozen pizza, loudly disparaging each other's suggestions and laughing as they praised their own, until even not-Anderson stopped looking sober and smiled.

When they at last pulled back into the drive of 12 The Mays, it was about lunchtime, and they were in a noisy happy mood. Sandra parked, and Malcolm jumped out and opened the door for his employer. Not-Anderson got out of the car on his own and stood a moment with one hand on it, regaining his balance.

"Mr Anderson!" called a voice from the road.

From behind the yew hedge at the front hurried a tall

black-bearded man, followed by a shorter red-head with a camera on his shoulder.

"Mr Anderson!" repeated the tall man, closing in. "Could you tell me what your connection with the MoD is?"

"It's Rodney Jones," said Malcolm, torn between surprise, apprehension, and an uncomplicated glee at this unscripted television drama being enacted before him.

Not-Anderson became aware of how great his previous hope had been by the sudden magnitude of his disappointment. He leaned back against the car and watched resignedly as Rodney Jones bore down on him.

FIVE

RODNEY JONES STRODE ON, AND EXTENDED A MICRO-
phone under not-Anderson's nose. "You might as well answer me, Mr Anderson," he said, in a brusque matter-of-fact
Midlands voice. "Ms Gresham of Stellar has admitted that
you have some connection to the MoD. What is it?"

Not-Anderson reflected inwardly that Anderson would
never have been able to pass off Jones' corpse as his own.
The reporter was about his own height, true, but was much
bulkier: Anderson's clothes and shoes would have been too
small for him. Jones' own clothes weren't like any in Anderson's cupboard, and consisted of jeans and a black T-shirt
emblazoned with "REFUGEES: WHAT REFUGE?" in red. The
face above the black beard was set in an expression of wary
belligerence, and there was a fading bruise over the nose and
under one eye—undoubtedly a legacy of the pub incident.
Not-Anderson wondered if he should apologise for that, but
could not quite bring himself to admit the blow as his own.
If he set aside his disappointment, however, he was pleased
to see Jones, and glad that the reporter had managed to avoid
a meeting carefully managed by Stellar. He hoped to learn
something by talking to the man unsupervised.

"Mr Jones," not-Anderson said, picking his way carefully, "I'm glad you've come. Please, can we go inside the house?"

"Please could you answer my question first," said Jones. The "please" was evidently for the benefit of the whirring camera behind him, and it received no support from his tone of voice.

Not-Anderson shook his head. His situation seemed far too complicated to explain standing in the drive. Besides, the day was hot, the air thick and muggy, and the unaccustomed walking had left him tired and thirsty. "Mr Jones," he said, "you may have heard that I was involved in a car accident. I am not fully recovered yet, and I want to sit down. Please, can we continue this inside? I promise to answer your questions as well as I can."

Jones' pugnacious expression gave way to a look of astonishment. "You're inviting us in?" he demanded incredulously.

Not-Anderson nodded in reply.

Jones glanced over his shoulder at his cameraman, who shrugged his camera-free shoulder. Then he eyed Malcolm and Sandra, both now standing against the car, one on either side of not-Anderson, Sandra anxious and Malcolm delighted. "Who are they?" Jones asked not-Anderson, apparently deciding to forget the camera. "Your minders?"

Not-Anderson hesitated: he wasn't quite sure what a "minder" was. He decided to disregard it, and answered the first question. "This is Mr Malcolm Brown, a student at the Royal College of Fine Arts. He is presently acting as a care attendant for me while I recover. And this is Ms Sandra Murray. She saved my life in the accident, and has been kind enough to help me in innumerable ways since. The car is hers, and is full of food, much of it frozen. Would you object if we unloaded it before we talked?"

Jones let out a long breath in a noise that was half a snort and half a sigh. "What is this?" he demanded. "Has Lloyd threatened to get rid of you if you get the firm any more bad publicity?" His eyes fixed on Sandra again. "You work for Stellar?" he asked.

She shook her head. "I'm a research assistant at the Institute of Plant Pathology. Sir Philip Lloyd did want to arrange for you to interview Paul, but he wanted to be here when you did. It's nothing to do with him that Paul wants to talk to you now."

Jones rolled his eyes and made a chopping gesture at the cameraman, who lowered his instrument. "OK," he said disgustedly. "We can unload the car and go and sit down in the house. But remember, I've got it on record that you invited me in, so don't try claiming invasion of privacy or trespass, OK?"

They unloaded the car. Sandra, Malcolm, and, surprisingly, Rodney Jones, all took armloads of carrier bags to the front door. The cameraman pretended not to notice his associate's burden and confined his carrying to the camera. Not-Anderson was still too unsteady and clumsy to carry anything. Malcolm set his bags down by the front door and fished for the key. Jones edged up beside him, and watched closely, as though he expected his quarry to go to earth inside and lock him out.

"I really like your programmes, Mr Jones," Malcolm told him shyly as he turned the key. "I thought that thing on AIDS victims was brilliant. Do you go back and check on the people after your documentaries are screened?"

Jones blinked. "Yeah," he said gruffly. He slid sideways through the door as it opened.

"So that guy Pete, did he get his compensation?" Malcolm continued, following him.

"Nah," said Jones, going to the sitting room and looking around for a place to dump his groceries. "He died before the miserable bastards paid up. Where do you want these?"

"Shit," said Malcolm, with real anger and pity for Pete, whom he had seen on a television documentary a year before. "Through here."

The frozen goods were slapped into the freezer, but the

rest of the shopping was abandoned on the dining table. "You want some coffee?" Malcolm asked the company.

"What the fuck is this?" asked Jones. "This isn't going to be a cosy chat. Give Anderson coffee and he'll probably end up chucking it over my head."

His cameraman, however, was less scrupulous about accepting hospitality from enemies. "I'd love a cold drink," he interrupted. "We were standing around out there waiting for you for hours."

Malcolm took a freshly purchased bottle of Pepsi-cola from one of the shopping bags, then went to the kitchen cupboard for glasses. Sandra resignedly fetched more ice.

Not-Anderson picked up the cola bottle and studied the list of ingredients. He had no memory of the substance, and a mix of sugar, carbon dioxide, caramel, caffeine and phosphoric acid sounded improbable and rather unpleasant. Malcolm retrieved the bottle with a grin. He put ice in five glasses, emptied the Pepsi into them, and distributed them among the company before leading the way into the sitting room.

Not-Anderson sipped the drink cautiously. The bubbles felt odd and unpleasant at the back of his throat. But the wet sweetness was agreeable.

The cameraman drank his Pepsi quickly, smacked his lips appreciatively, and began to adjust the light setting on his camera. Jones took a few swallows of his own, then put the glass aside and picked up his microphone. "So," he said to not-Anderson, "if you're willing to cooperate now, what *is* your connection to the MoD?"

The cameraman hurriedly lifted his instrument to his shoulder and set it whirring again.

Not-Anderson pressed the glass in his hands. The slick coldness of it, sensed even through his bandages, was somehow comforting. "I don't know," he admitted. "I have amnesia, and I can remember nothing about myself. I'm sorry."

Jones stared for a moment. Then his face folded in anger and disgust. He chopped his hand at the cameraman, and the whirring again stopped. "Oh, fuck!" he exclaimed. "You don't expect me to believe that, do you?"

"It's true!" Sandra declared angrily. "You can ask the hospital."

"Try another one!" scoffed Jones. "Anderson's done everything he could to stop me from asking questions about Stellar—obstruction, avoidance, lies, D-notices, assault and threats. Now I've finally got him in a position where he looks bad if he doesn't provide a few answers, so he develops amnesia! It's too fucking convenient!"

"It is not convenient," said not-Anderson. He had not raised his voice, but Jones suddenly turned and looked at him as though he'd been struck. "It is terrifying and crippling. I would infinitely prefer to be lying to you. Mr Jones, I said outside that I would answer your questions as well as I can. I don't remember anything before the accident, but I have spoken to Sir Philip Lloyd and Denise Gresham of Stellar since, and I have no reservations about repeating what they told me. There is also a fair amount of information on the computer in the study upstairs. I haven't yet succeeded in extracting everything from the closed files, but you are welcome to all the information I do have. In return, I hope you will tell me what you know about Stellar Research and . . . *my* . . . part in it." It took him some effort to substitute "my" for "Anderson's" and, when he had finished, the personal pronoun still seemed to stick in his throat, a sour lump half-way down. He felt queasy, and swallowed in a vain attempt to dislodge it.

Sandra looked at him with concern. Now that she'd met Rodney Jones, she thought Paul should have as little as possible to do with the man. The reporter's hostility was only too obvious. He would take any information he was given, and have no scruples about employing it as a weapon against the man who'd given it to him. "Paul," she said, "those are private computer files. You don't know if . . . I mean, there could be all kinds of secrets on them! At the very least it would be a breach of confidence to show them to the media. Stellar would sack you—and you don't *know* that Stellar has done anything very wrong."

"If I am Paul Anderson," not-Anderson said flatly, "then I have changed so much that it would not be feasible to work for Stellar again. If I am not, then I never worked for them in the first place, and cannot be guilty of breach of confidence." The lump in his throat dissolved, and in relief and revulsion he finished, "If I am going insane, I will not need a job at all."

Jones was staring again. "What do you mean, 'if you aren't Paul Anderson?'" he demanded.

Not-Anderson decided that there would be no point in trying to fake a mental certainty that he did not possess. Jones was not Philip Lloyd, to be baffled in self-defence. Not-Anderson met the reporter's eyes with a calm implacable gaze. "I woke up in hospital certain that I was not Anderson. I accept that the evidence suggests I am."

"Jesus!" whispered Jones. "You're serious, aren't you?"

"He really is," put in Malcolm. "Last night he was even wondering if maybe somebody had given him plastic surgery."

Jones kept staring, his eyes narrowed. Sandra could almost see him weighing his natural suspicion of conversions against the apparent sincerity of the converted. Then a look of mixed resolution and cunning flickered over the heavy face, and she knew that he'd decided that he had nothing to lose by going along with the story. If his old adversary's mental confusion were genuine, there were advantages to be snatched. She bit her lip unhappily, wondering how she could stop the interview. She was not sure what Paul might have been like before the accident, but she knew she valued him now, and for this burly black-bearded rottweiler to savage him while he was crippled by amnesia was monstrous.

"And you don't want to work for Stellar Research any more?" asked Jones, with a wondering surprise that did not fool her for a minute.

"The position is as follows," not-Anderson replied, with oblivious precision. "My amnesia is apparently not caused by any serious damage to the brain. It must be essentially psychological, and probably caused by trauma. I was certain when I woke that I feared and distrusted Stellar Research. On first meeting Sir Philip Lloyd, I was very much afraid of him. I do not remember why: there may be no good reason. On the other hand, I would be a fool to disregard what amounts to a warning from the past, and what I have learned of Stellar's general conduct, and Ander . . . *my* own past activities, has not been reassuring. It is safest to assume that Stellar injured me in some fashion in the past, and may try to do so again in future. To protect myself I need to know what happened and why."

Jones blinked.

"Shit," said the cameraman. "Rod, the guy talks different now. And what happened to his accent?"

Jones shrugged. "It was always too posh to be natural."

"Do you want to see the computer?" asked not-Anderson quietly.

"Paul!" protested Sandra. "Please—you know you don't remember enough to have a real idea of what the situation is. You may be making a terrible mistake. Don't you think it would be better to wait until you have a clearer idea of what's going on?"

But he had already wavered to his feet, a tall thin figure with a face set in an expression of remote decisiveness, like a microbiologist determining the class of a debatable protozoan. "I do not know how long Stellar will continue to trust me," he told her coolly. "I may not have another opportunity to talk to Mr Jones unsupervised." Then their eyes met, and there was a sudden shock of communication, an almost physical connection between her concern and his underlying anxiety. Fear suddenly opened in his face, and he whispered, "If I am going insane then nothing I do matters, does it?"

"You're not going insane," she said, her voice shaking.

"Then I must follow my best judgement," he replied, in a more normal tone. "Mr Jones, the computer is upstairs."

It was not an invitation that an investigative reporter could turn down. Fascination warring with scepticism on his face, Jones followed his host up the stairs. The others trailed behind him. The cameraman, who appeared to be called Dave, was muttering to himself that it was impossible to make a fucking computer look good on television.

There was only one chair in the study. Not-Anderson took it, and switched the machine on. The others crowded round behind him, elbowing and nudging each other as they stared at the top level of the menu. Besides the usual software, the files were arranged in folders labelled "Investments," "Tax," "Personal" and so on. Not-Anderson clicked on "Stellar," and the list of file names leapt on to the screen. Half of them were in red.

"Those are the passworded files," not-Anderson said, indicating them with a clumsy jiggle of the cursor.

The red files were labelled "Astragen," "Patents," "Lloyd," "Jaeger," and "Jones."

Jones grinned and, reaching over not-Anderson's shoulder, grabbed the mouse and clicked on his own file. The screen went blank, then it asked politely, "Password?"

"So what's the password?" demanded Jones.

"I don't remember," replied not-Anderson patiently. "I have been reading the files directly from disc, where they are interspersed with other material. I saved what I retrieved, here." He pushed return, got the menu again, and clicked on the final black folder, which was identified simply with an asterisk. He sat back.

The screen filled with the jumble of different documents Sandra remembered. Jones, leaning over his host's shoulder, began scrolling down them, his heavy face greedily intent.

"You probably understand these better than I can," said not-Anderson, in a neutral tone. "I lack all memory of the context."

Jones shot him an oblique look, and Sandra once again

bit her lip. It was quite clear to her that Jones was planning to grab the info and run.

"You asked about my contact with the MoD," not-Anderson continued obliviously. "It strikes me that the letters addressed to Mark Jaeger are likely to deal with that. Can you tell me why I should have such a contact?"

Jones gave him another oblique look, then stopped the cursor at the beginning of a letter addressed to commander Mark Jaeger, Aldermaston. "Most big research companies have somebody in them who tells the MoD what they're up to," he said. "The military like to keep an eye on research, so that if something strategic comes up, they can classify it. The companies don't usually know who the spy is, though. Stellar may have two of you." On screen, the letter said:

> *Dear Mark,*
> *This is just to let you know that Astragen is thundering along with huge success. I'm still not certain whether it will be of much interest to you, but in commercial terms it'll be a winner. We had a trial on the 28th which was a hundred per cent successful and Sir Philip is already putting out feelers about contracts for the batteries. The only worry is about maintaining security, but Phil which we acquired from H.W. Clark three years ago for £100 . . .*

Sandra realised that the last phrase was from another document. The letter to Mark Jaeger was dated the 2nd of April.

"And do you think this Mark Jaeger is my contact for the MoD?" not-Anderson asked, undeterred.

"Pretty obvious he is, isn't it?" demanded Jones, eyes fixed greedily on the next fragment. "With an address like that."

"I do not recall its significance," not-Anderson told him patiently.

" 'You do not recall its significance,' " Jones repeated, in sarcastic mimicry. "Jesus!"

"Aldermaston," Malcolm supplied quietly. "Military research."

"Why would I have contact with the military?" asked not-Anderson.

Jones shrugged. "Old school chums. You don't remember your old school either, I take it?"

"Correct."

Jones' eyes remained fixed on the screen. "Beaulieu Academy. Veddy, veddy posh, and it has a cadet corps. Lot of boys go on to the army, the rest go into business. Or into politics, like your friend Henry Ellis. You've done well out of old chums in both directions. Stellar hired you for your contacts."

Not-Anderson frowned. "When?"

Jones dug a notebook from his trouser pocket, and made a note of something on the screen. "January this year," he said, scrolling on.

"Had they started the Astragen Project then?"

Jones put the notebook down and looked at not-Anderson with raised eyebrows. "That's my theory," he observed. "They'd started Astragen. They knew it was gonna be big, and they thought it might be tricky, so they looked for the slickest, best-connected, most unscrupulous marketing man they could find, and when they found you they offered you a directorship."

"Thank you," said not-Anderson evenly. "Why was Astragen likely to be tricky?"

Jones' eyebrows pulled down into a frown, and he stared hard at not-Anderson. "Astragen was likely to be tricky, *I* think, because they nicked the technology for it. They've done it before. They tell some poor bugger of a researcher that his pet project is no good, and they show him results of their trials that seem to prove it's useless, but they agree to pay him a pittance for his patent, in case it turns out to have some application later on. Then they conduct new trials, and lo and behold, his little invention turns out to work just fine after all! They make a mint, and the poor bastard who dreamed it up gets nothing. But when they've done it before, it's been legal—or close enough that they can make it look that way. But Astragen is different. I heard . . ." He stopped, and glared at not-Anderson suspiciously.

"You were looking into Stellar's acquisition of patents when you heard of something that happened at the Astragen trial in March," not-Anderson said calmly. Jones looked resentfully triumphant, as though he'd caught his opponent in a trick to discover his source, until not-Anderson explained, "It says so in one of the letters." He clicked the document to its end, and showed Jones the letter Sandra had seen before.

But he's got hold of some shit version of what happened at the trials in March, and he's going to keep digging until he finds out more.

It was now glaringly obvious that the "he" referred to was Jones. Sandra wondered when Paul had realised that. She suspected that he was miles ahead of everyone else; that he had two or three different connections for every fact, and several models of what was going on continuously under revision—and betrayal by Jones figured in none of them. He was so honest, she thought, that the calculated dishonesty of others would always catch him by surprise.

Jones snorted. "Shit version? Yeah. OK. I heard that when the first trial was successful, they got a message flashing up on every computer in the building: 'Remember that this technology was given to Stellar to develop, on the understanding that it was to be shared among all the people of the world,' or something like that. When Sir Philip Lloyd saw it, he hit the roof, and had all the software doctored for viruses. It shut the whole lab down for about three days. That's the story I heard. Lloyd has always been secretive, but on Astragen he's really gone to town: he won't let anyone even mention it off-site. Since he won't admit it even exists, there's no way you can ask him whether the idea for it was something that came up in-house, or whether Stellar's developing somebody else's baby. But I think that story shows that Astragen was somebody else's idea. Some idealist-genius type—in an ivory tower somewhere—who thought he could get Stellar to develop it as a public service. And he's being fucked worse than the poor buggers who only had their patents stolen. From the sound of his message, he isn't asking for just a share in the profits; he's asking Stellar to do the whole thing *non*-profit, and because of that they're determined to cut him out of the picture altogether. Sharing their trade secrets is against every habit that company ever formed, and Astragen is likely to be the most profitable enterprise they ever hit on."

"What is Astragen?" asked Sandra. It was clear from Jones' tone that, secret or not, he had a good idea, and the question had been itching in her mind since the name first flickered across the computer screen—or perhaps even before then; perhaps she'd begun to wonder when Sir Philip Lloyd first referred to Stellar's latest project in Anderson's room in the hospital.

"From the version I heard," said Jones, "it's a new type of battery. It lasts about three times as long as any battery around now, and it doesn't use any chemical nasties that pollute or cause problems for recycling plants. It's cheap and easy to make, and yeah, the guy who dreamed it up did the world a service. But a company that can sell it as a monopoly is gonna be rich beyond the proverbial dreams of avarice. Just think how many million batteries are sold worldwide in a year. Now imagine one company corners the market. Shit! Stellar would *kill* for that."

Not-Anderson sat silently, his eyes fixed unseeing on the screen before him. Jones reached for the mouse, and began to scroll back up through the document.

"You're wrong," not-Anderson said abruptly. "Astragen is not a type of battery. It's a method of confining magnetic fields."

Jones stopped. Sandra leaned forward and grasped the

arm of the chair. "You *remember* that?" she asked breathlessly.

He looked up at her and smiled, his whole face lighting with joy. "Yes," he agreed quietly. "Painlessly."

The lucid, elegant mathematical expression of it had glided into his mind as soon as Jones had started describing Astragen. He became whole in the equations, no longer divided into an island of turmoil-wracked consciousness and an inaccessible continent of memory, but one individual, and complete.

"I was told it was a battery," said Jones suspiciously.

Not-Anderson dismissed that with one clumsy hand. "Of course. It can be used that way. But the most important aspect of the idea lies in the ability to confine very powerful magnetic fields within a very small space. That has applications across a whole range of technologies. For example, it could be used to alter chemical reactions."

Jones looked blank. The cameraman Dave was listening with furrowed brow. "Y' mean the way magnetic fields can wreck film," he said.

"Of course," agreed not-Anderson. "Every electron has an intrinsic magnetic moment. If E is the energy in a given system . . ."

He explained it to them in the terms that came to him most naturally, and it wasn't until he was nearing the end of his explanation that he noticed they were all staring at him in glazed bewilderment.

"What's the matter?" he asked.

"I'm afraid we couldn't follow you," said Sandra weakly, still struggling in the haze of equations. "I did some physics in my first year at university, but what you were saying goes well beyond Natural Sciences Part I-A."

"It's quite simple," said not-Anderson, surprised. "You must have done basic electro-magnetism. If you assume a monopole in Maxwell's equations and allow for the quantum electrodynamic effect of—"

"The only Maxwell I've ever heard of is Robert," broke in Jones. "You were talking gibberish."

"It wasn't gibberish!" Sandra said angrily, glaring at him. "I could tell that much." She looked back at not-Anderson, who was staring at them all in genuine surprise. She was not surprised, not really. She'd known that he was brilliant, and it seemed somehow natural that he was brilliant at this kind of thing, this inhuman purity of abstract thought. But she was glad: Jones' gibe about slick unscrupulous marketing men had rankled. Stellar hadn't picked this one for slickness or contacts: the company undoubtedly employed a lot of good physicists, and it knew one when it found not-Anderson.

"It wasn't gibberish, Rod," Dave the cameraman agreed. He looked shaken. "I think it's probably revolutionary stuff, if you can understand it."

"What didn't you understand?" asked not-Anderson patiently.

He began his explanation again—then tried again in a still simpler form. Eventually he realised that, among his audience, only Sandra had any real knowledge of mathematics. Dave knew some chemistry and enough about electricity to distinguish between voltage and wattage, but Malcolm and Jones were utterly and helplessly innumerate. He gave up, and stared at them in astonished despair. He did not see how an intelligent person could possibly be ignorant of Maxwell's equations, and he could not conceive of explaining the concepts in anything as imprecise as words. Sandra stepped in.

"You know what magnetism is?" she asked Jones.

"I thought it was what made those little gadgets stick to the fridge," replied Jones sourly. "But I guess I was wrong."

"No, you were right, but that's just one kind of magnet, a ferromagnet. Magnetism itself is the other side of electricity. If you run an electrical current through anything, you get a magnetic field—you've heard of electromagnets?"

"Trains and cranes," said Jones succinctly. "They run

electricity through something or other, and it sticks; they switch it off, and it comes loose."

"Right! Some materials, like iron, react to a magnetic field by becoming magnetised themselves—but they're unusual. Most things don't respond at all, and a few are weakly resistant. The thing is, the field itself is produced whenever you have an electrical current, and it goes through nearly everything. It's like throwing a pebble in a pond: the ripples just go out and out until they fade away. If you think about it, that's a lot of wasted energy. What Paul is talking about is equivalent to tying a knot in the ripple and confining all its energy around the place where you tossed the pebble— and then picking that energy up, putting it back in your pocket, and carrying it off."

"Jesus," whispered Jones. He stared at not-Anderson in what was now a quite different way. "You know a lot of maths," he observed.

Sandra was grinning. "Paul, you *remember* it all!"

He blinked, realising with a thrill that she was right: he had all along reached into his knowledge of mathematics as effortlessly as if his memory had been whole. Even Astragen had come back to him without the least confusion, once he'd realised what the name referred to. But it had seemed so natural that he hadn't given it a moment's thought. It was, like talking, simply something one did—no, it was more natural than talking; he'd had trouble framing words. He began to smile: in this, at least, he was whole.

"Just what do you remember?" asked Jones. His manner had changed completely. Scepticism and oblique sneers had been replaced by a bright-eyed predatory eagerness. "Your scientific background, I mean. Start with physics—just tell me the areas, and don't try an' explain 'em."

Not-Anderson sat still for a moment, evaluating his knowledge—his wonderful, beautiful knowledge, gloriously complete in his divided mind. It was hard to resist the impulse to gloat as each fragment of universal law swooped obediently to his call. "Electromagnetism, of course," he said, forcing himself to answer the question. "Quantum mechanics, quantum electrodynamics, particle physics, field theory, relativity, chaos theory, thermodynamics, classical mechanics, statistical mechanics, astrophysics, physical chemistry . . ."

"Shit," interrupted Jones. "You got a PhD in Physics?"

Not-Anderson stopped smiling: memory again tilted to inaccessibility. "I don't know."

Jones turned on Sandra. "Would anybody know all that without a Physics PhD?" he demanded.

She hesitated. "Maybe," she said cautiously. "It would depend on how much detail you went into in any one field. You might get it in a good BSc."

"But you'd need a good university degree in Physics?" Jones demanded impatiently. His air of suppressed excitement was growing.

Puzzled, Sandra nodded.

"Right," said Jones. He stood grinning a minute, hands in pockets, thumbs waggling with excitement, gaze fixed voraciously on nothing. Then his eyes flicked back to Sandra. They reminded her abruptly of a dog's when it sights a rabbit. "Let's start this at the beginning," he said brusquely. "Can you tell me about the car accident you saved your friend from?—Davie, we'll want a record of this."

Dave's camera came back on to his shoulder. Then he shook his head. "We're gonna have to go back downstairs," he told Jones. His manner had changed, too, from grumbling hanger-on to terse professional. "There isn't space in here for a clear shot of anything."

"What is the point of all this, Mr Jones?" asked Sandra, as Jones pushed his way to the door.

"Oh, come on, darling, just come downstairs and tell me what happened!" urged Jones. He was grinning, rottweiler teeth white in the black fur of his face.

"No," said Sandra levelly. "Paul is my friend, and I don't like the way you've been taking advantage of him. He's unwell and confused and you've been planning to take every bit of information he offers and use it to crucify him. I want to know what you want me to tell you this *for*."

Jones was not offended. He only grinned wider. "OK then. Anderson had a second class degree in Business Studies from Warwick University. No Physics. When I asked around about him, several people told me they were surprised Stellar hired him, because he didn't have the scientific background they normally insist on. Your friend doesn't talk like him, doesn't act like him, and knows things he couldn't have known. His gut-feeling that he isn't Paul Anderson has got to be right. My guess is that he's the guy who invented Astragen, and the reason he docsn't like Stellar is because Stellar tried to kill him and pass his corpse off as Anderson's. Now, be a good girl and come and tell me about how you saved his life, OK?"

Sandra's eyes flew instinctively towards not-Anderson, and she saw his face go white even before he doubled up. She thrust the others aside, rushed over, and dropped to her knees beside him. He was making a choking noise, and she saw that he was trying not to be sick. He bent over, shaking, and covered his face with his hands. His body went rigid in a violent spasm, but his jaw was clenched.

Sandra put her arm protectively over his shoulders and glared up at Jones, who was staring in slack-jawed consternation. She was incandescent with anger—though when she evaluated the scene afterwards she realised that she'd believed Jones' theory instantly, and that it had relieved her mind of a dozen anxieties she had never admitted to herself.

"Look what you've done!" she shouted furiously.

"What the fuck did *I* do?" asked Jones stupidly.

"Can't you get it into your thick head that he's ill?" Sandra screamed back. "He's not playing some stupid game, he was nearly killed and he's lost his memory, and you're mucking about with him while he doesn't know what the hell is happening—all so that you can make some idiot television programme, so that everybody can watch it and say, God, that Rodney Jones, he's hard-hitting! The people who get hit hard are the ones you make your programmes *about*!"

"That is unjustified," mumbled not-Anderson. He pulled himself slowly upright in the chair. Her protective arm was drawn from across his shoulders, and dropped limply to the arm of the chair. Not-Anderson lowered his own bandaged hand on to her hand, and looked into her face. He was still pale with nausea, and his face was wet: sweat beading his forehead and upper lip, cheeks streaked with the tears of sickness. His expression, however, was more puzzled than pained. "This has happened every time I've started to re-member," he told her. "It is not the fault of Mr Jones. I in-vited Mr Jones in because I hoped that he could help, and he has provided information that is invaluable. Sandra, I don't understand why you're so angry."

"I don't like him capitalising on your being hurt," she said.

She could see that he understood that even less, but she did not want to explain. Besides, her anger had gone again. She got slowly to her feet. "I'm sorry Mr Jones; that was in-deed unjustified," she said stiffly.

Jones had gone very red. "I didn't know that was gonna happen," he said. "I didn't know he was that ill. Should he be in hospital?"

Malcolm was the one who answered. "Yeah," he said. "But he insisted on leaving." He had found a box of tissues, and had managed to worm his way over to not-Anderson and offer them.

Not-Anderson took one and wiped his face with it. Rod-ney Jones began asking for, and receiving, an account of not-Anderson's state of health. Not-Anderson took no inter-est in it. His mind was engaged instead with the luminous vindication of proposition (not-A). He was not Anderson. The nightmare of insanity had retreated: he was after all the person he felt himself to be, and not some intruder whom he could not even understand. As soon as Jones had voiced his theory, he had been sure it was right, and in that certainty he had almost remembered everything. The sickness had battered it back again—but that was secondary. He was not Anderson. The relief was so immense that even the physical distress of almost-remembering—the ribs aching as they hadn't done for days, the stabbing pains in the chest, the weakness and queasiness and exhaustion—seemed niggling and insignificant. He was not Anderson!

He re-checked the evidence. Rodney Jones had leapt to his conclusion quite shamelessly: the fact that Anderson had no degree in physics didn't mean that the man knew nothing about the subject. He could have pursued it as a hobby. Still, taken with everything else—not-Anderson's instinctive reaction to the identification, the differences in taste and expression between himself and Anderson, the puzzled reactions of everyone who'd known Anderson—it tilted the balance firmly towards proposition (not-A).

Of course, Jones had an even more flimsy basis for his conjecture that not-Anderson must be the originator of the Astragen Project. And his assumption that Stellar was corporately responsible for whatever had happened was hasty and mistaken. Not-Anderson felt a degree of pity for Jones: the man's ignorance of basic science had obviously left him handicapped in deduction.

The others were still on the topic of car accidents and post-traumatic stress and neurological damage. "Mr Jones," not-Anderson interrupted, "I've spoken to Sir Philip Lloyd and Denise Gresham since the accident. I'm quite certain that they believe I am Paul Anderson: I was surprised by it even when I had no evidence that they were wrong. If the theory that I am not Anderson is correct, then they cannot have had any part in the substitution."

There was a moment of silence as the others turned uncomfortably from the subject of his health and Jones absorbed what had been said. Then, "*If* the theory's correct?" Jones demanded. "I thought you said you felt you weren't Anderson. I thought you felt so sure of it that all the evidence that suggested you were him made you worry that you

were going crazy." He seemed affronted, as though not-
Anderson had spurned a gift.

"What I *feel* may be relevant, but it isn't proof of anything,"
not-Anderson explained, with a touch of irritation showing in
his tone. "If we do not follow strict principles of deduction, our
conclusions will be worthless. We have no evidence that I am
the inventor of Astragen or anything else."

Jones made a rude noise. "OK, Mr Sherlock Holmes,
who do you think you are?"

"Is that who invented Astragen?" not-Anderson asked eagerly.

"Who?" exclaimed Jones, astonished. "Sherlock
Holmes?"

"He's forgotten an awful lot," said Malcolm defensively,
and explained, to not-Anderson, "It's a character in a book.
An expert at deduction."

"Oh," said not-Anderson, disappointed. He had already
begun testing himself to see if it could possibly be his own
name.

He turned his attention to Jones' question, evaluating the
evidence about himself and cautiously analysing the disori-
enting moments when he had almost remembered. "I must
be either an employee of Stellar Research, or in some way
connected to them," he said, after a few seconds. "Otherwise
I wouldn't know about the Astragen Project. Stellar may
have been involved in some of the things that happened to
me, but it is not directly responsible. Paul Anderson, however, is definitely linked with what happened: I am either
one of his enemies whom he wished to eliminate, or an ally
who was involved in a scheme with him."

"How do you figure that last?" asked Jones sceptically.

"If I am not Anderson, then Anderson is missing," said
not-Anderson impatiently. "I would not have been substituted for him if he was likely to appear and denounce me as
an imposter."

"I saw that," said Jones, just as impatient. "How do you
figure you could have been his ally? Seems to me that he

must've arranged what happened to you. Maybe he's off now pretending to be you."

Not-Anderson would have considered that possibility the night before, but suddenly he doubted it. He remembered the strange sense he'd had of knowing how his hands had been injured. He had a similar sense now that Anderson was dead. There was no memory connected to the awareness, no image, no emotion. It was as though the death were something he had learned of in a newspaper, a fact that had lain all along at the bottom of his mind, inert and unobserved beneath the doubt and turmoil above. Yet the sense was now so strong that he said slowly, "No. I think he is dead."

There was a silence. "Do you remember that?" Sandra asked. Her voice seemed to come from somewhere else. The idea of Anderson dead seemed to make everything else real.

Some interior border fell away behind her. She believed now that the man she'd started to call Paul was not. He was someone else, a physics genius whom someone had disguised as Paul Anderson and left in a car to die. She looked at the man, who was still sitting enthroned in the chair before the computer, dark eyes regarding her quizzically. The bruises, from accident or plastic surgery, had faded now to yellow, and the thin, angular face beneath them had a look of ascetic nobility. She saw that her worry about Jones had been entirely misplaced: this man had dominated Jones from the moment the reporter walked in the door. He was dominating them all. From the beginning the rest of them had trailed along reacting to his decisions, and she herself was more subjugated than anyone. Suddenly she wanted to go home very badly, to go out with nice, ordinary Robert that evening, and forget all about this knot of unfathomable riddles.

"I seem to simply know that," not-Anderson said now, in a remote voice. "I think I did know it from the beginning, but I could not acknowledge it. They said I was Anderson, so I could not remember that he was dead."

There was another silence. Then Jones rebelled. "You

wouldn't 'simply know' anything else useful?" he asked, with a return of the sneer. "Like how he died or who killed him or what Stellar was doing while this was going on?"

Not-Anderson, as always, took the questions at face value. He shook his head. "It may be that I'm wrong," he said. "I may yet prove to be Anderson myself. But I think he is dead." He stopped, then continued even more slowly, "On examination I think I do 'simply know' one more thing now. I think my native language may not be English."

The continent of memory was *different*, its concepts set at angles to his present experiences, its recollections swollen with meanings to which he had somehow lost the key. Its proximity battered him because it was his and he could not interpret it. Only mathematics, whose sense was universal, flowed easily across the divide. What could that mean, except that his memories were shaped in another tongue?

He watched their reactions to that: surprise, thoughtfulness; uncertain acceptance. "You don't *sound* foreign," said Dave the cameraman. "You don't sound anything much. But you do talk funny."

Sandra remembered how his first hoarse whisper had grown steadily stronger and more fluent; remembered his ignorance of common words, of politics and laws, of food and fictional characters any English-speaker would know. It was true, he had no accent—but the accent-less precision with which he spoke was in itself more foreign than any accent.

She could imagine him as a child, learning English from tapes and books, and as an adult burying himself in scientific periodicals. That was indeed the way he spoke, as though his knowledge of English were something theoretical, as though each sentence had been carefully translated before it was uttered.

"I think you may be right," she said.

"Parlez-vous français?" asked Malcolm helpfully.

Not-Anderson did speak French. He also spoke German. But he did not think either of these was the language of his memories. He did not speak Italian, not even as much as Malcolm, who had learned most of his in Art History classes, nor as much Serbian or Hindi as Jones, who knew little more than, "Hello, we are making a film. Do you speak English?" That exhausted the languages known to the others.

"I'll tell you what," said Jones. "I know this Russian who's a hypnotist. She owes me a favour: what if I get her to come and see you? We can check if you know Russian, and we can see if she can't help you remember something."

Jones was still grinning with excitement. Sandra understood it: he had walked into the most riveting documentary of his career. It had everything: corporate corruption, official secrets, murder, and a cover-up which he could pick apart *on screen*, if . . . Paul . . . turned out to know Russian. She wouldn't be surprised if he did. He had, now she thought of it, an Eastern European air. Supermarkets and other manifestations of Western consumerism had baffled him, and his apprehensiveness towards authority, medical or industrial, was the common heritage of those accustomed to being governed by tyrants. She wondered where he was from. She wondered if he had a wife and children in his own country. She found she didn't want to see him hypnotised by any Russian. She didn't want to know any more secrets. She had plunged in out of her depth, and she was afraid.

"I'm going home," she announced abruptly.

They all looked at her. He—Paul—not-Paul—looked bewildered. "Is something distressing you?" he asked.

"Yes," she said shortly. "All this. It's too much for me. I'm going home."

He stared at her, and she could see by his growing look of shock that he realised "I'm going home" meant "I want out." She stared back without flinching. She told herself that she had done more than enough for him already: she owed him nothing. It was not as though there was anything between them. Perhaps she was a little in love with him, but he showed no sign of reciprocating. Why should she plunge

into the icy waters after him now? He had used her, dominated her enough.

Not-Anderson blinked stupidly, growing more profoundly disconcerted as he took in the finality of the
announcement. In all his calculations for the future, he had
assumed her presence. She had saved his life, understood
and advised him in the hospital, helped him escape it, and
assisted him to the point he had just reached. He acknowledged at once, ashamed, that he'd had no claim to her help,
and she possessed every right to go. But he did not want her
to. He wanted her long elegant red-haired shape somewhere
about; he wanted to know he would talk to her again. He
hadn't realised how important she had become to him. The
way she smiled and the sound of her voice steadied him, as
though a radio should pick up one clear signal in a storm of
static.

"I am sorry," he said humbly. He was not sure why he felt
he must apologise, except that she was distressed, and he
knew it was on his account. "Will you come back?"

She bit her lip, her cheeks going red. "There's nothing I
can do. This is all beyond me, very much beyond me."

"I thank you for all you have done," he said quietly. "For
my life, and more. I . . . hope that you will come back. If
not, I hope that when this is over I will see you again?"

His eyes, watching her, had the look of fear and loneli-
ness that had twice called from her offers of help. She made
no offer now. There did not seem to be any help she could
give. "I . . . need to think," she told him. "I'll . . . I'll ring
you later in the week, OK? Just to see how you are."

"Please do. Should I telephone you?"

"I'd rather you didn't."

She cut short the goodbyes and marched resolutely out of
the room and down the spiral of the stairs. She was aware
that he came out on to the landing to watch her go, but she
did not look back. She felt vaguely unreal, as she had when
she sat in the car after saving his life. But that had been because she had achieved something so enormous that every-

day things dwindled beside it, and this was . . . she didn't know what. Cowardice and treachery, said a part of her: but she denied it vehemently. She had trespassed in something strange and terrible. She was out of her depth. Nothing would be helped by staying there to drown, so she might as well thrash her way back to the shallows where she belonged.

SIX

SANDRA'S DESIRE TO STICK TO THE SHALLOWS MIGHT have lasted longer if Robert had not decided to talk about UFOs.

Their date was for dinner and a film. Sandra arrived at the restaurant meeting place silent and on edge, and Robert, forced to do most of the talking, unfortunately fixed on his favourite subject. His UFO group, which was called B-Seti—the title stood for "British Search for Extraterrestrial Intelligence"—was organising a trip to Northumbria, where strange lights had been sighted over a reservoir. B-Seti was fond of outings, and often arranged them, if the possible UFOs had been seen in interesting country near a good hotel that gave a reduction for group bookings. The UFO enthusiasts would have a good dinner, then go out to sit by a deserted highway or a darkened lake clutching binoculars and flasks of coffee and watching for lights in the sky. Sandra supposed it was fun, if you could even half-believe in it— but she did not half-believe in it, and it simply seemed a tedious waste of time, like fishing but with even less chance of catching anything. Robert rambled on about the delights of UFO-watching in Northumbria, and she knew that he

hoped she would express interest, and maybe come along—
but she said nothing.

"We're going to bring the new magnetometer," Robert
went on, after a disappointed pause. "And incidentally, I was
talking to my friend Alastair about your rescuee from Stellar, and he said it's really true about Sir Philip Lloyd being
interested in SETI. Apparently he's been keen for years. He
was particularly interested in what we were using the magnetometer for, of course. He . . ."

Magnetometers, thought Sandra. Confined magnetic
fields. She remembered the man who was not called Paul
sitting in his chair and reeling off electromagnetic formulae,
and she winced. "Of course he's interested in the magnetometer," she said out loud. "Stellar's latest research project
is to do with magnetic fields, and he probably wants to know
what sort of background readings are normal. Probably
your . . . *Beasties* are the only people who go about taking
random readings in open country. He's using you as unpaid
research assistants."

Robert gaped. "No!" he protested. "Apparently he's really interested. Alastair said he told our president that he'd
had an encounter himself. He didn't want to talk about it—
I suppose he was afraid of the press getting hold of it—but
he wanted to know if there were any unusual magnetic phe-
nomena associated with UFOs. He asked if we thought
extra-terrestrials would look magnetically different from humans."

"Oh, come on!" said Sandra in disgust. "If he'd acted
sceptical, would you have helped him?"

"Why shouldn't he be interested?" asked Robert, hurt.
"It's very likely that we're not alone in the universe. If only
one out of every hundred of the stars in this galaxy had hab-
itable planets going round them, and only one in a hundred
of those had intelligent life on them, that would still leave
about ten million stars in this galaxy alone with—"

"That's different from UFOs," Sandra replied sharply,
losing her temper unreasonably, aware that she was proba-

bly going to regret her words but unable to stop herself. "Extra-terrestrial intelligence makes sense: UFOs don't. If there are super-intelligent alien beings out there, why should they travel millions of miles through the depths of space just to do lightshows over Northumbria? If they want to contact us, why not call us on the radio? And if they don't want to contact us, why hang about flashing lights?"

"Why should we assume they speak any of our languages?" said Robert huffily.

"Because anyone with any sense could learn!" Sandra answered impatiently. "If Vietnamese peasants can learn English from the BBC World Service, why can't extra-terrestrials? We've been using radios for a hundred years: we must show up as a radio source light-years away. Don't UFOs have any radio receivers?"

"You're applying human common sense to something that isn't human," said Robert.

"Common sense has never been humanity's strong point," said Sandra, "but if we have more of it than your UFOs, good for us!"

Then the argument began in earnest, as she'd known all along that it would. Robert defended UFOs angrily, and she grew more and more sarcastic in reply. They missed the film. At last, late, they parted in hurt silence, and she went home and sat in the kitchen alone, drinking a cup of cocoa. She knew beforehand everything that would happen: the tentative phone call next day, the apologies, the uncomfortable skating round the quarrel, the inevitable drift apart. She felt now that she'd known all along that it would end like this. The only thing that shocked her was how little she minded. She did not, after all, regret her words. The thing she regretted, which burned in her now, as it had all along beneath the sarcasm and the anger—was the way the man who was not called Paul Anderson had looked at her, and she had walked away.

She telephoned 12 The Mays the following afternoon. Malcolm answered.

"It's me," she told him, "Sandra Murray." And because she did not know what else to say, she sat there with the cracked plastic of the telephone cradled against her cheek. She still did not want to return to the deep water. She had phoned because the questions had crawled about her mind like rats, keeping her awake at night and disturbing her during the day. She kept remembering the man who was not called Paul sitting in his chair before the computer and watching her. She was ashamed of her inability to give what his eyes had told her he needed. She did not want to talk to him and refuse again. But she did want to know that he was going to be all right.

"Oh, right!" exclaimed Malcolm easily. "You wanna talk to *him*?"

"No!" she said hastily. "I just want to know how he is— how you all are."

"I'm fine. He's OK," said Malcolm. "He's upstairs working on the computer. He got dressed by himself this morning, and he let me take most of the bandages off his hands. He's just got the splint on the broken finger still, and the wraparound bit on the wrist. Looks like a tennis player. Lemme tell him you've phoned. He'd love to talk to you."

"I'd rather not," she said. "He's still sorting out those files, is he?"

"Yeah."

"What's Rodney Jones going to do?"

Malcolm laughed. "Do you wanna know?"

She felt her face go hot. "Look," she said. "I do want to know. I do care still. It's just that I don't . . . it's just that there's nothing I can do to help, and it's all so . . ."

"OK, OK, look, I wasn't accusing you of anything! You don't need to get so upset."

"I *am* upset!" she declared uselessly; and felt ashamed, because it wasn't Malcolm's fault.

There was a silence, and then Malcolm said, "Look, can you just tell me straight what it is with you and *him*? Otherwise I'm gonna be saying the wrong thing all the time. Is it just that you saved his life, or what?"

Her face went even hotter. "I don't *know* what it is with me and him," she said.

"OK," said Malcolm, as though this had told him a lot. Probably it had: she could have hidden behind Robert, and said there was nothing between herself and . . . *him*.

"Look," Malcolm went on, "you know he isn't gonna phone you. You said you didn't want him to, and he takes things literally."

It was so true that she had to smile. "I know that."

"OK, just so you realise. He'd like to talk to you, I think—he started talking *about* you yesterday, after Rodney Jones went—but he won't phone."

What did he say about me? Sandra wondered. But she could not quite bring herself to ask it out loud, and Malcolm was going on, "OK, I'll fill you in on what's happening. Rodney Jones is in top gear to find out who *he* really is. He's really excited about the whole business—Rod is, I mean. He was here for hours yesterday. He stayed too long, really: *he*—you know who I mean—was not in good shape yesterday afternoon, but he would not lie down and rest and he would not send Rod away, and they hammered out a plan of action together. Rod wanted to get as much as possible on tape, so that nobody'll be tempted to hush things up with a murder or anything. He wants to go public as soon as possible. But *he*—Jesus, it's hard to make it clear who I mean! What's-his-name doesn't want to go public *at* all, or at least not until Stellar works out that he's not Anderson, and the shit hits the fan. He wants to lie low while he can, and sort things out. In the end, they agreed that Rod can tape as much as he likes, but he can't show the tapes to anyone or tell people what's going on until what's-his-name agrees. Rod is gonna try and find out what he can about people working in electromagnetism who might've gone missing, and he's gonna come back with this hypnotist as soon as she's free. She sounds OK. She's a qualified hypnotherapist, and she works in a clinic. Rod hopes we can get enough stuff by the middle of the week to prove that what's-his-name can't be Anderson, and maybe even sort out who he *is*. Then he wants to move on to Astragen, and prove that Stellar stole it. He says we may have to go to the police as soon as we prove what's-his-name isn't Anderson. He says he's gotta do that if he gets evidence of a serious crime, or he'll get charged with obstruction of justice or something, and he thinks we'll get evidence of abduction and attempted murder if we find out who what's-his-name really is.

"He thinks he can edit his material, and get a documentary out around the *sub judice* rules. If Stellar manages to get hold of him to arrange the official Anderson interview before we've got anything hard to go on with, he's gonna say he's busy this week, and set a date for next. If Stellar contacts what's-his-name again, *he's* gonna say that he's taking it easy and starting to get better, and hope they go away and let him get on with it.

"What's-his-name printed out all the secret files he's got, and gave Rod a copy. Then he tried to write up what he told us about Astragen—"

"He can't!" Sandra interrupted in shock. "It's an official secret! *He* said so himself!"

"Maybe," agreed Malcolm. "But Rod wants it anyway. He said it would make things harder to hush up if there were extra copies around, but I think mostly he just wants to make sure the whole thing is for real. He says he knows somebody who'll look at the equations and not talk. He knows a lot of people. And *he*—what's-his-name—was perfectly happy to give them to him. As far as he's concerned, confined magnetic fields are like washing machines: everybody oughta have one."

"But if he passes it on, he could get into terrible trouble!" Sandra protested. She wondered what the penalty was for telling official secrets to the media. Of course, if . . . *he* . . . wasn't English, presumably the official secrets act didn't apply to him. On the other hand, maybe that only meant he'd

be punished as a foreign spy. Or no, the most aggressive intelligence agency could hardly find a man guilty of spying
for passing his own discovery on to its own nationals—if he
was the one who'd invented Astragen. But perhaps his own
country would consider him a traitor. And maybe he hadn't
invented Astragen. Maybe he *was* Anderson, and everything
else was confabulation, dreamed up by a subconscious that
loathed its real past and longed for something better to replace it, and backed by a newsman greedy for a story. Nobody knew the truth. All they had was a tower of
conjectures, and she knew from scientific experience that it
needed only one error, one false assumption at the foot of
the tower, to bring the whole edifice tumbling down. It
seemed quite clear to her that in nearly all circumstances
publicising the theory would be a mistake. *He* was being
very, very reckless—and she still didn't trust Rodney Jones.

"Well, cool down, because he hasn't passed it on yet,"
said Malcolm. "He tried to write it out, but he couldn't, because he still can't use a pen. He tried to do it on the computer, but the computer didn't have any software for
equations. He couldn't believe that: Anderson went down
another five notches in his estimation, you could see, having
a computer that couldn't write out equations. Finally he
started to dictate the formulae into Rod's cassette recorder—
all E equals and lambda over H-bar. What is H-bar, anyway?
It sounds like a ranch."

"Planck's constant over 2pi," said Sandra, her heart sink-
ing. "It crops up in lots of things."

"OK, ask a stupid question . . . that got stopped when my
Mum turned up. It was about six by then. She'd come to see
if I needed anything. By that stage what's-his-name was
looking like he was gonna keel over any minute. He hadn't
had anything to eat since breakfast, 'cause of feeling sick,
and I think that shopping trip was harder on him than he
wanted to let on, and of course the afternoon was worse. But
that guy does not like to admit what's going on with him
physically. If he got stabbed in the back he'd pull a jacket on

over the knife and try to pretend it wasn't there. My Mum does not approve of that sorta thing, and when my Mum doesn't approve, you might as well roll over and die." He began to laugh. "Soon as she found out who Rod was, she laid into him: what did Mr Jones think he was doing, coming in to Mr Anderson's private house and upsetting Mr Anderson, and didn't he realise Mr Anderson should still be in hospital, and if Mr Anderson had a relapse, she'd testify in court it was because Mr Jones had gone in and harrassed him. So then what's-his-name tried to tell her it was all right, he'd invited Jones in—and she laid into him, too. Told him he ought to be in bed and she laid into me for letting Rod in and not looking after my patient properly. What's-his-name tried to reason with her, but it didn't do him any good. She had Rod out the door and him in bed in ten minutes. Neither of 'em knew what hit them. Shit, I love it!"

There was so much affection in his voice that Sandra had to smile. "Your mother's quite a character," she said.

"When she really gets going she makes the Iron Lady look like plasticine," agreed Malcolm proudly. "Rod phoned up later to ask if she was gonna spread it around that she'd seen him here. She'd scared him shitless. She won't spread it around, though. What's-his-name asked her not to. As far as she's concerned, patients are sacred."

"Rod," noted Sandra, had phoned to make sure of his own security, not to inquire after the health of his subject, despite her own rebuke earlier, and despite leaving his subject "looking like he was gonna keel over any minute." Again, she wished that "Rod" had not turned up. Malcolm seemed to like the man, but Malcolm was a student and an artist. She could remember from her own student days how events much less dramatic than this became Experiences, to be savoured as part of the great Real World outside university—and she'd only been a scientist, and not someone who would look at Experiences as the raw material for art.

"So," finished Malcolm, "today we have off, to recover from yesterday. Tomorrow morning we go back to the hospital for a check-up and physiotherapy. Rod was gonna phone in the afternoon to say if the hypnotist can come tomorrow evening. You want me to give you a ring to let you know how it goes?"

"Please," said Sandra.

"You sure you don't wanna talk to *him*?"

"Quite sure."

THE HYPNOTIST WAS FREE MONDAY EVENING. HER NAME was Natalya Semyonova Simpson. She was, as Malcolm had said, a qualified hypnotherapist who spent her working days assisting the paying public in its ambition to stop smoking, eat less, and otherwise give up its various noxious habits. Jones had once included a sequence on her work in a documentary on the evils of the tobacco trade, and she had been grateful enough for the boost in custom to promise to help him "any time." She had not expected this to mean being driven up the M-11 at twenty-four hours' notice and with very little in the way of explanation, but she took it in her stride. She was good at taking things in her stride: a marriage in Moscow at twenty to a visiting English businessman, divorce in St Alban's six years later, raising two children on her own, and dealing daily with all the squirming dishonest perseverance of the human psyche. Helping Rodney Jones' "misidentified amnesia victim, probably a Russian" was a minor perturbation, and rather fun.

She arrived at 12 The Mays, with Jones and his cameraman, at about half-past six. Not-Anderson was on the overstuffed sofa in the sitting room, labouriously writing out the equations for the Astragen theory. The physiotherapist that morning had recommended that he practise using his hands as much as possible, and he had found that if he used a felttip and made the characters large enough, he could after all succeed in writing. When he heard the car pull into the drive and its door slam, he put the papers down and eagerly went to the front door. The likelihood that he was not Anderson, which had at first been such delight, had over the past two days become an eroding pit in the back of his mind. He had no identity to replace the one he had lost. He was still living in Anderson's house, using Anderson's money to pay Malcolm and provide food. He had nowhere else to go—and he felt like a maggot, living on the corpse of the dead. He was desperate to take up his own life again, and the hypnotist seemed his first—and best—chance of finding it.

The front door needed two hands to open it—one to twist back the latch on the Yale and the other to turn the handle. He could not grip well enough to manage either one-handed. The door bell rang, and he went on struggling grimly, despising his own clumsiness. He had great hopes that the hypnotist would return his name to him and now he could not even let her in! After what seemed an eon of scrabbling, Malcolm came from the kitchen, where he'd been washing up the supper things, and put the Yale on the latch. The door opened at last, and the three visitors trooped in.

"*Zdrastvitye*," said the woman, smiling from not-Anderson to Malcolm. She was a large blonde in her mid-forties, dressed in a loose suit of brightly dyed cotton, and her voice was loud and booming.

"*Dobriy vyechyer*," not-Anderson replied politely, and continued in Russian, "I take it you are the hypnotist who has been good enough to offer to help me, *Gaspazha*?" The words felt flat in his mouth. They were as natural, and as foreign, as English.

The woman beamed at him. "My friend Rodney told me you spoke Russian," she said, still in that language. "That is, he said you had amnesia, but thought you spoke Russian. He said you thought you were a case of mistaken identity." She offered her hand; after a moment's hesitation, he held out his. She looked at the dark red marbling of scabs and torn nails, the splinted middle finger and bandaged wrist, and returned her hand to her side without touching him. "Rodney said you were in a car accident," she observed. "Poor man, how you must have suffered!"

Not-Anderson drew back his own hand uncomfortably.

Rodney Jones was looking very pleased. "Native language?" he asked.

"No," said not-Anderson wearily.

Jones' face crumpled with vexation. "Sure?" he asked.

Not-Anderson nodded. "Would you like a drink, or some coffee?"

Malcolm, Dave, and Natalya had drinks; Jones and not-Anderson had coffee. "Speak to me some more in Russian," said the hypnotist. "Maybe I can tell where you are from by your accent. The only people who know Russian, apart from poor fools of native speakers like myself, are the ones who had to learn it in school. You must be Soviet, or at least Warsaw Pact."

They spoke for a while in Russian about accidents and hypnotherapy. Dave filmed them. After a little while, Natalya rolled her eyes and said, "You speak my language so beautifully! All I can hear is a slight English accent. I don't believe you are English, but I can't tell where else you could be from. Your fluency has let you down: I'm sorry." Then she looked at Rodney Jones and shook her head. "I am sorry, Rodney," she said, in English. "He has a little bit an English accent, but that is all."

Jones shrugged. The experiment had not been as successful as he'd hoped, but it was not a failure. He doubted very much that Anderson had known Russian, though he would check. "Maybe the hypnosis will do better," he said.

Not-Anderson regarded the hypnotherapist without enthusiasm. Much as he'd looked forward to this meeting, this loud effusive woman did not inspire him with confidence. He found that he intensely disliked the thought of yielding his precise reasonable mind to her suggestions.

Natalya, however, had evaluated her subject with an experienced eye, and had seen that this one was desperately self-reliant and ferociously rational. She began her professional patter by stressing that they must cooperate to make the session successful. "I am not going to hypnotise you,"

she said. "I'm only going to help you to hypnotise yourself,
OK?" She was gratified to see him relax a bit. "In fact," she
went on, "if you do not want to be hypnotised, I cannot hypnotise you at all. With most people it takes me several ses-
sions to get them in any kind of trance. I am not Svengali or
the Mad Monk! So you must just relax and let me show you
how to hypnotise yourself."

His dark eyes fixed on her with abrupt determination, and
he nodded. She felt a glow of satisfaction. There was no
doubt that this one wanted the hypnosis to work. That made
it much more likely that it would.

She moved her subject to one of the armchairs, and sat
opposite him on the coffee table. She rummaged in her capacious handbag for one of her professional props—a photograph of a sailboat on a lake—and stood it up on the table
in front of him, propping it against her glass. "Relax," she
told him, taking his left hand in both of hers, and beginning
to stroke the forearm gently. "It is very important that you
relax. Nothing is going to hurt you. I am not going to do
anything against your will. Now, I want you to focus all your
attention on the boat. Imagine that you are in the boat on a
deep blue lake . . ."

"I do not remember ever being in a boat," protested not-
Anderson. "It is difficult to imagine it."

She hesitated. She generally used images of boats and
water in hypnosis, because she liked them and they usually
worked well for her patients, but she was not wedded to
them. "Think of something you find relaxing, then."

He thought, running back over the ten days that com-
prised his memory. For a moment he fixed on Sandra Murray's smile. But that was a signal ringed in tension—his
revulsion towards his alien appearance, her departure—and
he rejected it. He thought instead of the clouds he had seen
through the window on first waking, gliding steadily across
a sky glowing with diffuse light. Beyond them lay more
light, the background of the universe, a constant stream of
waves progressing through an infinity of space, their speed

defining time, their photons tracing the principles of eternal law.

"Light," he said.

"Sunlight?" smiled Natalya, thinking of beaches and holidays. "Fine." She put the picture of the boat away. "OK. Close your eyes. Imagine you are lying in the warm sunlight . . ."

He imagined it, sitting motionless in the chair, and allowing the small repetitive movements of her hands and the steadiness of her voice to lull him into a state of dreamy relaxation. Gradually his surroundings became insignificant, and what mattered was the constancy, the warmth, the eternity of the light. She told him that he could float up into the light and he did so. He was aware, at some other level, that she told him to raise his left hand and rest it on a shelf that had not been there—was not there—and he did as she asked. She pressed his arm gently, but it was resting on the non-existent shelf, and didn't dip. She smiled.

"Now," she said, "I want you to think of a time when you are lying in the sunshine. It is a time before the accident. You are not doing anything, you are just lying in the warm sunshine . . . you are thinking in your own language and you are lying in the sunshine . . ."

Pain.

He was trapped, he could not get out.

Pain.

Think, think, think, he could not *think*! Lunacy! The universe shattered around him in great bloody fragments: no, go back, get out!

He was trapped. Sense closed down like a star dying; he could not *think* and his mind fizzed with random emissions that formed no coherent sequence. He struggled to escape, and was tangled in the screaming of his nerves.

Pain, terrible pain. How could anyone endure it?

He was trapped, he was trapped, he could not get out!

Not-Anderson hurtled to his feet, mouth open in a scream that ended in a horrible drowning gurgle of agony. Then he folded and fell forward on to Natalya. She caught him, barely, and managed to keep him from striking his head against the coffee table as he came down. His body jerked rigid in her arms. Her feet scrabbled an instant, trying to brace against his weight, and then the table slipped backwards and tipped over, spilling her to the floor. The glass top shattered around her. She shouted frantically for help. Not-Anderson rolled off her lap on to the carpet, back arched, jaw clenched and heels drumming. His eyes were open, but had rolled up in his head so that only the whites showed; his face had gone crimson, and there was a bloody froth on his lips. His limbs thrashed uncontrollably.

"Jesus Christ!" exclaimed Jones, appalled.

Natalya scrambled back, kicking aside shards of broken glass. Dave, who had been filming, continued filming, as though he were a recorder someone had forgotten to turn off. Then Malcolm shoved Dave out of the way and hauled the thrashing form away from the pile of broken glass, pushing over an armchair in his haste. "Move that table!" he ordered Jones. "Try to get the glass away from him. Hurry, man!"

"Shouldn't we put something in his mouth?" asked Jones.

"No," said Malcolm firmly, going to move the table himself. The broken glass wasn't as bad as it had looked: it was in large pieces. He piled them on top of each other and moved them swiftly out of the way. Natalya, shaking, dragged the table clear.

"That has never happened before," she said tearfully. "Every day I hypnotise people, and never, never do I see anything like this. You should have told me he was an epileptic!"

"How the fuck could I know?" said Jones. "*He* didn't remember it."

Not-Anderson thrashed more feebly, and at last lay still. Malcolm hurried over to him. The face was a mottled purple now under the bruises, and the lips had gone blue. The jaw was slack, and blood dribbled from it on to the carpet. A smell made it evident that the casualty had soiled himself.

"Jesus Christ!" said Jones again.

The body gave a harsh, sobbing gasp.

"Thank God!" said Malcolm fervently. "He's starting to breathe again."

"Had he stopped?" asked Jones stupidly.

Malcolm gave him a look, and knelt to wipe the bloody froth away with a crumpled paper tissue.

"Jesus!" muttered Jones again, edging closer. "I thought you were supposed to put something into their mouths, to stop them biting their tongues."

"You can hurt them that way," said Malcolm, professionally pulling the body over on to its stomach and drawing up one of the limp knees. "And he'd already bitten his tongue." He pulled the matching arm up, and carefully drew back the head. More blood gushed out of the slack mouth. "Shit," said Malcolm, checking the source. "Badly, too." He got to his feet. "We better call the hospital."

Not-Anderson regained consciousness a few minutes later. He stared for a moment at the green carpet inches from his eyes. The fibres swirled away from him, arched and knotted into the backing beneath. Shadows crossed it, soft-edged, cast by the light from the window at the far side of the room, and there were sounds. He hurt very much. His right side ached more than it had since he first woke, and his tongue throbbed. His mouth was full of a salt metallic wetness, which his instincts associated with injury. The nausea was washing over him in hot clammy waves.

He did not ask what had happened. He was aware of it, up to the moment when consciousness had shattered, and he was aware—more aware than ever—of the tilted continent of his memory, as inaccessible as ever. He made an inarticulate noise of grief.

"It's OK," said Malcolm, appearing at his side and patting him on the shoulder. "You've had a fit. We're gonna get you to the hospital."

Not-Anderson tried to speak, and found his tongue crippled. He tried to shake his head, but it hurt too much. Helpless, he lay still.

"I am so sorry," said the hypnotist, from somewhere high above him. "But that has never happened before. I don't understand . . ."

"I wash trap,'" said not-Anderson, forcing his tongue to move despite the pain. The words came out slurred in a bubble of blood. "Coul'n ge' ou.'"

Somewhere to the left, Jones groaned. "The accident," he said. "He was trapped in a car during the accident." He came over and knelt, and his face appeared beside Malcolm's, square and black-bearded. To not-Anderson's racked senses it loomed horribly large, like a cliff collapsing on him. He looked up at it with terror, and it fell back a little.

"I'm sorry," Jones told Not-Anderson. "This was my idea, and it was crap. You are too ill to be fucked about with."

Not-Anderson understood, bitterly, that the illness Jones was referring to now was mental. In the past the reporter had treated him as physically weak, but intellectually an equal, to be fought or helped as circumstances required. Now, he could see, he would be surrounded always by a cushion of gentle distrust. And perhaps that was right. Perhaps he was beginning to go insane. Perhaps even the things he thought he knew, the elegant purity of mathematics, were delusions: gibberish in symbols.

"No!" he protested. His eyes moved about the sitting room, trying to make sense of the unfamiliar perspective. "Wrote theory," he said. "Coffee 'able."

The sheets had been scattered when the table overturned. Some of them had been crumpled and trodden on, and one was flecked with bloody saliva. The mathematical symbols wavered over them in a large unsteady black scrawl. Jones picked them up and smoothed them out. "You want me to take these?" he asked not-Anderson.

"Ye'h," not-Anderson whispered. "No' change ayyesthing. I don' go hosh'al."

"Yes you do," said Malcolm firmly. "You bit your tongue and it needs stitches. I already phoned the ambulance. Stop talking. Rod, I think you and your friends better go. Einstein, I'm gonna get you an ice-pack for your tongue, and then you're gonna get cleaned up before the ambulance comes."

"Einstein was a scientist," said Jones helpfully, gathering up his cassette-recorder.

Not-Anderson lay unmoving on the green carpet. He opened his mouth in a welter of blood. "I know," he said.

THE JONES DROVE MOST OF THE WAY BACK TO LONDON in silence. When they were approaching St Alban's on the M-25, Natalya said suddenly, "I'm very sorry. I should have asked about your friend's accident before I hypnotised him."

"I should have told you," replied Jones unhappily. "It was my fault. The guy's girlfriend was there before, and she told me I shouldn't fuck about. He was too ill. He's just so reasonable I thought it was OK."

" What were the papers he wanted you to take?"

"He thinks he's really a physicist," said Jones. He had long sailed close to the wind of the intelligence services and the libel laws, and knew better than to admit he was knowingly taking away an official secret, even to a friendly witness. "He's written out some equations and he wants me to check if they mean anything or not. He doesn't trust himself to judge. The hospital told him he was somebody different from who he thinks he is, and he's worried that he might be going crazy."

"Poor man!" said Natalya, with deep feeling. There was another moment's silence. Jones turned off the M-25 on to the St Alban's approach road, orange in the neon.

"You won't show me on your documentary, will you?" Natalya at last demanded nervously.

Jones laughed. He knew what she was afraid of: a sequence of her hypnotising a subject into an epileptic fit. Screen that, and bang would go her practice. "Shit, no," he said. "I told you, it wasn't your fault. And I was a lot more useless than you were."

Natalya sighed with relief and leaned back in her seat. "So your documentary is against hospitals, this time?" she asked.

"Not hospitals," said Jones at once. "Cuts in hospital funding. See, the man the hospital thought he was had private insurance cover. Treating him didn't come out of the hospital budget. So they *wanted* him to be the other guy and ignored it when he said he wasn't." He didn't feel that it was really lying to say this. He considered it the reason the hospital had gone along with the misidentification, and he was against cuts in funding and felt he *might* make a documentary on it one day.

Jones dropped Natalya off at her house in St Alban's, and drove back on to the M-25 and round towards his own place in Romford. Dave came too: the cameraman had been sharing the three-bedroom semi with him for the past eight months. Jones didn't conceal his homosexuality, but he didn't usually flaunt it, either. He hadn't slept with any of his cameramen before. Sex, he'd felt, was something that should be kept apart from important things like work. But Dave was different. With Dave everything fed into work, and filming seemed to kick into a fifth gear it had never reached before. He loved Dave, and loved the way Dave's shots looked: jolting, harsh, grainily alive. He felt that, given the subject and a bit of luck, he and Dave together could make something greater than anything he'd made before. It was the reason he had seized on this project so eagerly. He wanted to make a great documentary with Dave, something that would be shown and reshown, a classic of its kind, a monument to what was between them.

"It's a good thing she didn't use the boat," Dave said now, hanging over the seat.

Jones laughed. "Oh, shit! Can you imagine it if the poor fucker had thought he was drowning again, as well as trapped?"

Dave shook his head. "I didn't know what to do. I just stood there, whirr, whirr—God!"

"I wasn't any better. Shit, he scared me. Lucky that black kid kept his head straight. He's sharp, that kid."

"His mother's a nurse, isn't she? Probably made him learn how to help her."

"His mother's a terror. Do you think he's gay?"

"You fancy him, do you?"

"Eh, maybe a bit."

"Keep your mouth shut about it, then. He's straight," said Dave.

"How can you tell?"

Dave shrugged. "Dunno. Way he talks."

Dave always noticed the way people talked, and his guesses about them, which he based on their speech, were generally accurate. He had decided that the man they were dealing with was not Anderson even before the question of Physics had cropped up.

"Any more thoughts about Sherlock Holmes?" asked Jones.

"You realise that fucker is fluent in at least five languages?" said Dave. "I bet his English accent in Russian is just 'cause he's been speaking English so much. His French and German were much better than yours or mine."

"That's only four."

"Native tongue. Rod, think about it a minute. You can't tell from his English or Russian accent where he's from. Fuck it, you know how rare it is to speak *one* foreign language without an accent, let alone two! I mean, look at Natalya. She's been in Britain half her life and has raised kids here, but if *she* were knocked down on the street, the hospital would know she was foreign the minute she opened her mouth."

"That's true," said Jones, surprised by it.

They drove on for a minute. The headlights of the cars on the other carriageway flickered over them, and the red taillights ahead filled the car with mauve shadows.

"He must've learned the languages as a kid," said Jones. "You learn a language young enough, you don't have an accent."

Dave grunted. "He was a sharp kid, then. Tell you somethin' else. Sherlock Holmes never said he was a physicist. You're the one that said that. You asked him what he knew about physics, and he came out with a list a fucking mile long. If you'd asked him what he knew about maths, I betcha it would've been just the same."

"Shit, maths and physics, they *are* practically the same."

"They got two different degrees for them, don't they? And I dunno that you wouldn't have got another mile-long list if you'd asked him about chemistry."

"What're you trying to say?"

"That fucker isn't just *bright*," Dave said forcefully. "He's right off the scale. Anderson was normal-bright, and he was fuckin' you about like crazy. This guy is one helluva lot sharper than Anderson—or you, Rod. And there is something seriously weird about him. Right now he's cooperating because he wants to know who he really is and he thinks you can find out for him. But once he knows, I wouldn't trust him one fucking inch. And this is gonna be dangerous. Somebody tried to murder that fucker, and maybe somebody did murder Anderson. And we got D-notices and legal threats from Stellar and MI5 to work around. You gotta watch it."

Rod grinned. "Yeah, we got a mad genius and his secret formula! But he gave us the secret formula." He glanced down at it where it lay, dim in the mauve shadows, on the floor of the passenger seat.

"Yeah, well, you just be careful with him, OK?"

"You kidding? After tonight I'm hardly gonna dare breathe hard in his direction."

"Ha, ha, ha," said Dave resignedly. He knew his colleague: when it was a question of getting at the truth, Rod would spare no one. "Anyway, that's not what I meant."

"I know what you meant. And I say, fuck you."

"You wanna?" asked Dave, leering.

Their eyes met. Riven with an intense happiness, Rod wondered if this was what true love felt like. He reminded himself fiercely that he didn't believe in true love: nothing this good was ever going to last. "Yeah," he said casually. "Don't I always?"

SEVEN

NOT-ANDERSON SPENT MONDAY NIGHT IN HOSPITAL.
He had not intended to, but by the time Casualty had finished with him it was too late and he was too dazed with painkillers to do anything else. Malcolm, who'd followed the ambulance to the hospital in Anderson's Jaguar, waited with him a while, but eventually went home. There was a lot of waiting: after the first examination and the initial dose of morphine; after the local anaesthetic and the tongue stitching; after the X-ray which showed that the half-knitted ribs had been cracked afresh in the convulsions, and after the second injection to soothe them. At last the hospital formally re-admitted "Paul Anderson" and put him back in ward C-2, room 3, "for observation." There he dozed fitfully. Nurses came periodically and checked his pulse and blood pressure or shone lights in his eyes, just as they had in his earliest memories.

In the morning he got up and put on the socks and trousers someone had taken off him the night before. He left the shoes—he could not do up the laces—and padded slowly out into the corridor. His legs were unsteady, and he felt generally weak, stiff, sore and exhausted, but he was de-

termined that he would not return to the dazed impotence of
his first stay in this place.

Sylvia Brown had just arrived for her shift and was
checking the day's schedule at the nursing station. When
not-Anderson tottered down the corridor towards her, she
dropped her clipboard and hurried over to catch his elbow in
a grip like a vice. She drilled him with a close-quarters glare
of disapproval.

"Mr Anderson!" she exclaimed. "You should *not* be up
on your own. You might fall. You wanna walk, you call
somebody to help you, OK?"

"I ganh bwalkg," not-Anderson told her, his swollen
tongue slurring the words horribly. The local anaesthetic had
worn off, leaving an ache on the nerve and a metallic taste
throughout his mouth, and his tongue itself was horribly
painful. He swallowed and tried to enunciate. "I am going
home this morning." That was better: slow and laboured, but
at least clear. He frowned down at the nurse, who stood half
a head shorter than he. "Is your son Malcolm here?"

"My son Malcolm is at home," replied Mrs Brown
firmly, "and he's not gonna take you outta here. I know what
happened last night. Malcolm told me about it. You are a
whole lot sicker than we thought you were. This time, man,
you're gonna stay *here* until you're better. My Malcolm is a
good boy: he won't take you home just because you give
him money. You worried about the money you pay him
already, we pay it back."

Not-Anderson stared blankly. Tremors of a new fear rippled through him. He remembered Malcolm the night before, cleaning him up before the ambulance arrived. "Don'
worry," Malcolm had said, seeing not-Anderson's helpless
humiliation, "I'm used to shit." With a grin, "I'm black,
aren't I?" It was not just the competent gentleness that
moved him now, but the good humour. He himself was terrified of his body, of its alien appearance and its broken condition. Malcolm's relaxed acceptance of all things physical

had helped him more than he'd realised. Who could he trust to help if the horror and pain struck again?

Malcolm, not-Anderson realised, had moved instantly and effortlessly from the position of paid attendant to that of friend, trusted and relied upon. He had assumed Malcolm's help no less than he had assumed Sandra's. And he had lost Sandra. Now he was losing Malcolm. He was bitterly aware that he could not fend for himself. Without help, he was incapable even of getting himself back to Anderson's house. Without friends, he would be trapped here, and eventually Sir Philip Lloyd would discover that he was not Anderson, and then . . .

He staggered against the grip on his arm. "Please," he said to Sylvia Brown. "I can't stay here. Let me speak to Malcolm."

Her look softened into concern. "You sit down," she ordered, and guided him to a chair in the corridor. He collapsed into it and bent over double, shuddering with weakness. He was aware without looking up of the nurse leaning over him, capable hands braced against her thighs. "Look, man," she said, gently but firmly. "Pretending you aren't ill isn't gonna make you any better. You been pushing yourself just as hard as you can ever since you woke up. What you need to do is give your body a chance. It's doing its best. Give it a rest and it'll do fine."

He shook his head. "Not here," he whispered. "At home."

"You were home, and you didn't rest, did you? Besides, the doctors need to run some tests on you."

With an effort, he raised his head. "Why?"

She patted him on the shoulder. "You had a classic *grand mal* epileptic seizure last night. It can happen after injury to the brain. You got no history of epilepsy, and we gotta hope it was a one-off, but we need to check. You may need some medication to stop it happening again."

He stared at her for a moment as he evaluated that. If he was not Anderson, his medical history was unknown. Either Malcolm had not told his mother much, or she had decided to ignore what he had told her. Either way, communication between the Browns was imperfect. Sylvia Brown might have completely misjudged her son when she said he would not help not-Anderson leave the hospital again.

The relief of that deduction was so intense that he had to struggle to bring his mind to bear on the rest of what the nurse had said. He did not believe that he had a history of epilepsy: the condition struck him as unutterably foreign and frightening, and it seemed unlikely that he would feel that way about something he'd long had to live with. He knew a little about it now, from the books Sandra had loaned him. In an epileptic seizure the tissue of the brain produces an abnormally high voltage of electrical discharge. In sufferers who are not normally epileptic, a seizure is usually a symptom of some kind of stress or injury to the brain.

"I had tests before," he told Sylvia Brown. "They showed no significant brain damage."

"Man," replied the nurse, "you may not have anything that shows up on a CAT scan, but that accident obviously gave your poor old brain a hammering. You got amnesia, disturbance to fine motor coordination and balance, and now an epileptic fit. When we did the tests before, we obviously didn't find out what was going on with you. So we need to try again. And even before, we didn't do all the tests we wanted. You remember the EEG machine broke down. EEG is the first thing we need to look at."

EEG: electroencephalograph, a reading of the brain's electrical activity. Sourly, he remembered the abortive EEG test he'd had before. It had been early in his stay in the hospital, when he was still drowsy with painkillers and bewildered by most of what went on around him. They had wheeled the EEG machine—a thing like an old-fashioned computer printer with wires—into his room on a trolley, and they had covered a set of electrodes with conductive jelly and taped them over his scalp to pick up the minute electrical signals of the tissue below. Then they had plugged the machine in and switched it on—and nothing happened.

They'd fussed over it, and eventually taken off all the electrodes, and wheeled it out. A couple of hours later they wheeled it back in, saying that now it would work. More jelly, more tape; the machine was switched on and tested. The paper jammed in the trace. More fussing. Finally, they plugged in the knot of electrodes—and the machine blew a fuse, very dramatically, and produced clouds of black smoke and nurses with fire extinguishers. Not-Anderson had been left with his room full of smoke, his hair full of jelly, and no test.

"I do not want an EEG test," he said firmly.

"You wanna have another seizure?"

"The test itself does nothing to prevent seizures," he pointed out impatiently. "Even if it showed an irregularity in brain function, the doctors would surely wait to see if the problem continued before they took any action. No one would give me any medication if the seizure I had was a . . . 'one-off.' " He repeated her words carefully, with audible quotation marks: it was one he'd never heard before. "If I do not have another seizure, the EEG test is unnecessary. I have had only one seizure, and it occurred under exceptional circumstances. I see no point in having the test now."

"Good morning, Paul," said Sir Philip Lloyd.

Not-Anderson spun round in the chair. Stellar's chairman was standing only a metre away. He was immaculate and smiling in an elegant grey-green suit, but the sight of him sent a trickle of cold terror down not-Anderson's back. Not-Anderson reminded himself that Sir Philip had shown no sign of realising that they were enemies, and tried to breathe evenly despite the thudding of his heart. "Goog mlorning," he replied thickly—and despised himself for forgetting to enunciate.

"Good Lord!" exclaimed Sir Philip. "What happened to you?"

"I bit my tongue," said not-Anderson, making the effort to speak clearly.

Sir Philip looked concerned. "The hospital told me that

you'd had a seizure and had been readmitted," he said. "I thought I'd stop by on my way to work and see how you were. What's this about an EEG test?"

"Mr Anderson is scheduled to have one this morning," said Sylvia Brown. She stood back, retreating into blue-and-white professionalism, but not quite losing her look of personal disapproval. "He wants to go home instead."

Sir Philip shook his head. "Good God, Paul, what's got into you? Anyone would think you had a doting mistress waiting in that house of yours. You never used to be such a home-lover."

"I joined Stellar six months ago," said not-Anderson, slowly and coldly. "Do you really know me well enough to pronounce on my tastes . . . definitively?"

Their eyes met. Sir Philip's smile vanished, and his gaze was baffled, but assessing. "I suppose not," he said, after a moment. "I'm surprised, that's all. Didn't you have an EEG before?"

Not-Anderson shook his head.

"The machine broke down," said Sylvia Brown. "I understand why Mr Anderson is so reluctant now. Anybody'd get fed up with a machine that breaks down as soon as it's hooked up to him. But he ought to have it."

Sir Philip abruptly went rigid. The whites of his eyes showed in a ring around the irises, and the pupils contracted. For a long instant he fixed not-Anderson with a blind blue stare of shock. Then he licked his lips. He wiped his palms on his trousers, first one hand, then the other, and turned his head towards the nurse, with a quick false smile. "Really?" he asked. "What happened to the machine?"

His eyes were on the nurse, but not-Anderson felt that the other man's attention was still fixed on himself. The trickle of terror became a turbulent flood. Something about the EEG, or some idea associated with it, had triggered a conjecture in Sir Philip's mind.

"It blew a fuse," said the nurse resignedly. "It does that sometimes. It's old."

"But you have it fixed now?" asked Sir Philip. His tone was bright and interested, but not-Anderson felt still the other man's attention was far from the polite words, fixed fiercely upon himself, weighing him against that conjecture with steadily increasing alarm.

The nurse shook her head. "It had to go back to the manufacturers. But our other machine is working again. Mostly they take it in turns to break down."

Sir Philip tut-tutted, his eyes still on the nurse, his attention still on not-Anderson. "I'm sorry to hear you have such trouble with your equipment," he said. "Perhaps Stellar could make a donation for a new machine—we have a programme for investing in the local community, this might be a good cause . . . what's your worry about the machine, Paul? Afraid you'll blow it up again?"

The tone was playful, but under the playfulness the new alarm had grown. "I would simply prefer to go home," said not-Anderson, desperately casting about for some way to pinch off the conjecture before it flowered into certainty. "If I must have the test, I can have it as an outpatient. You said yourself, this hospital is a depressing place."

"You can go to The Oaks," said Sir Philip quickly.

"I don't want to," said not-Anderson; then, struggling for an unexceptional excuse, "I don't like Maureen."

"You seemed to get on well with her before," said Sir Philip. "You've been acting very strangely, Paul. Not at all like the man you were before."

There was a test in his voice. The blue eyes rested on not-Anderson again, doubtful and appalled.

"I was nearly killed," replied not-Anderson. "I have lost my memory. Can you reasonably expect me to be the same?"

"That's true," said Sir Philip thoughtfully.

There was a silence. Then, with visible effort, Sir Philip produced another smile. "I think you should listen to your doctors," he told not-Anderson. "They're the experts, after all. You should stay in the hospital until they think it's time to discharge you, and you should have whatever tests they recommend. If you do leave, you should go somewhere like The Oaks, where you'll have expert care. For you to stay alone in your own house, with just that extraordinary teenager in the T-shirt to look after you, would be gross stupidity and dangerous. Where on earth did you dig that boy up, anyway? I hope he doesn't steal anything." He glanced at his watch, and favoured his audience with another false smile. "I must go. The office awaits, eh? But I'll stop by here and see you again tonight, shall I?"

Not-Anderson nodded, and Stellar's chairman strode off down the grey hospital corridor.

Sylvia Brown watched him go with a glare of outrage. "Racist pig!" she muttered under her breath. "My boy's more honest than you are." She turned to not-Anderson with some further comment, then stopped in concern at the sight of his sick face and terrified dark stare. "What is the matter?" she asked.

He shook his head, then covered his face and sat still. He felt cold and queasy with terror. Sir Philip suspected. He would make checks, and then he would know. He would . . .

Sickness. He forced himself to calculate the probable current needed to blow the fuse on the EEG machine.

He was aware of the nurse leaning over him. "What is going on?" she demanded quietly. "You're so scared of him you're ready to vomit. And he was scared of you. The whole time he was pretending to talk to me he was watching you like you were gonna bite him."

Not-Anderson shook his head again.

"That won't do you any good," said the nurse. "You can't pretend there's nothing going on. That Rodney Jones wasn't at your house just for coffee, but when I asked Malcolm what he wanted, I couldn't get a straight answer. And before you left here last time, all the nurses on this station got instructions that he shouldn't be allowed to see you."

Not-Anderson dropped his hands and forced them down on to his knees, making himself look at the nurse. In a way it was a relief that she believed something was going on. If she thought he was paranoid, terrified only by fantasies bred in his own traumatised mind, it would be still harder for him to escape. The hospital might even commit him for treatment against his will, or hand him over to Sir Philip. "Please," he whispered. "You know this hospital. How could Sir Philip Lloyd give orders about who is allowed to see me? How much influence does he have here? Why has he been informed about me? Would he be able to dictate what treatment I receive?"

Her lips pursed in a soundless whistle. "So that's why you're so eager to get away."

He did not try to deny it. He simply looked at her and waited.

"Sir Philip Lloyd's only been told what happens to you because your insurance policy has Stellar Research down as your emergency contact," she answered reprovingly. "Nobody decides your treatment except your doctors." Yet there was something half-hearted about her reproof, and she went on, more slowly, "You're right that Stellar has some influence with Admin here. Sir Philip goes around saying things like maybe he'll buy us a new EEG machine, so naturally everybody's gonna bend over backwards not to offend him. And I think he's friendly with the general manager. He can certainly get people to sit up and take notice if he asks us to make sure nobody bothers you. But our priority is patient care. We would not do anything to you just because some company director asked us to."

He was silent for a moment, evaluating. "Hypothetical situation," he said. "Sir Philip telephones his manager friend and expresses concern about me. He says I seem to be in pain and in some mental confusion. He asks that I receive a higher dose of painkillers. The manager relays this to the doctors. The doctors, who respect the manager and the reasonable request of a friend of the hospital, oblige. In a sedated state, I do or say something foolish—like suggesting that Sir Philip is my enemy and means to harm me. Sir

Philip again expresses concern at my mental state, and suggests that I be moved to The Oaks, where I can receive closer attention in a more relaxed atmosphere. When I refuse to go, he says that I am too confused with pain and drugs to understand my situation, and has me sedated and removed for my own good. Is this impossible?"

The nurse was silent for a long moment. Then she straightened and looked down at him with a deep frown. "No," she said. "It wouldn't happen just like that. There's things you got wrong. But it's not impossible. Why are you so scared of The Oaks? It's nothing but a glorified hotel. What do you think they would do to you?"

Not-Anderson shook his head. "I don't know." His hands clenched until the broken finger ached. "I can't remember. I believe something terrible happened before, but I don't remember what. I know Stellar owns The Oaks, though, and Sir Philip has told me that the staff there will obey him. I am afraid to put myself in his hands. I can't explain, but I am afraid for my sanity and afraid for my life."

"Are you Paul Anderson?" asked Sylvia Brown.

He blinked at her in astonishment. "No," he whispered. "I believe not. But I don't know who I am."

"I wondered," she said under her breath. "The way you said you weren't, soon as you woke up, without thinking first. You only got panicky afterwards, when you realised you couldn't remember. And you're not the hysterical type. I don't know what type you *are*, but you're not the hysterical one. OK. You got a problem. You go back to bed, for now anyway. I'm gonna talk to Malcolm."

Sylvia Brown was unable to reach her son on the telephone: Malcolm was already on his way to the hospital when she called. He sauntered on to ward C-2 about fifteen minutes later, and was instantly collared by his mother, backed into a cupboard, and forced to provide an account of what was going on. He had avoided doing this before because he thought—correctly—that his mother would disapprove. However, a few minutes later Malcolm collected not-Anderson from room 3 and helped him out along the corridor.

"My Mum said, just take him and go," Malcolm explained in astonishment as they got into the lift. "If the hospital phones later to say you shouldn't have left, we just say sorry, we didn't realise. What's the rush? If you ask me, you shoulda stayed and had some tests. I was only coming in to check what you wanted me to do."

Not-Anderson slumped against the side of the lift. Between fear and relief, he was so exhausted that it was difficult to stand up. "Sir Philip Lloyd visited this morning," he whispered. "He's started to suspect I'm not Anderson."

"Shit!" said Malcolm. He stood a minute, brow furrowed. "My Mum must really believe it would be dangerous for you to stay here," he concluded, visibly shaken.

Not-Anderson nodded. The lift doors hushed open, showing the green-carpeted hospital foyer, and beyond it the bright outer air of freedom.

It was only mid-morning when they arrived back at 12 The Mays. Not-Anderson struggled out of the car and stood staring at the now-familiar house: the glassed-in spiral stairway, the brick porch with its ornamental wrought iron lamps and the blank white expanse of double garage. It seemed an unlikely refuge. But it was the best he could do, and for the time being it was his, an inviolate castle in a land full of enemies. He stumbled up the drive with a sense of coming, not home, but to safety. The storm would descend, of that he was now certain, but for the moment this place was secure.

Malcolm unlocked the door. "We must warn Rodney Jones," not-Anderson told him as he wavered into the house.

Malcolm nodded. "I'll give him a ring. He left his number. You wanna get some rest?"

Not-Anderson nodded in return. Leaving Malcolm to dial the number, he crawled up the stairs, collapsed into bed, and fell at once into a deep sleep.

When he woke, heavy horizontal sunlight was patching the wall with gold. He lifted his head with a frightened jerk, possessed by a sense that someone was watching him—and saw Sandra standing in the doorway. Caught in the rich light, her hair surrounded her pale face with a halo of lambent fire. He was flooded suddenly by a sense of redemption. After the horror and humiliation of the night before, after the frantic fear of the morning, he woke rested and in safety, and she was with him. He could say nothing: he knew no words for what he felt.

Sandra cleared her throat awkwardly, ashamed at the joy in his eyes. "Hello," she said. "I hope I didn't wake you."

She had telephoned the house as soon as she got back from work that evening, impatient for Malcolm's promised report. When she received it everything around her had seemed to freeze, as though even the dust on the wide leaves of her houseplants turned to a frosting of ice. Now she saw that her attempt to retreat had been doomed from the start. She liked deep water, even if it drowned her. If she could have been happy in the shallows, she would have fallen properly in love with Robert long ago.

"I did not think you would come back," he said, in a slow, laborious way that made her remember that he'd hurt his tongue. (Nine stitches, Malcolm had said, and she had seen the bloodstains on the carpet downstairs, still visible despite the surrounding dampness of Malcolm's attempt to wash them away.)

"I was worried," she admitted. "How are you feeling?"

He sat up cautiously, favouring his right side. "Much better. Has Malcolm told you what happened?"

She nodded. "I'm very sorry."

He interpreted that as an expression of simple regret and made no comment, but she meant more by it. She was sorry she had been absent when he was injured, sorry that she had abandoned him to the shadowy dangers of his past and to Rodney Jones.

"I am very glad you are here," he told her quietly, with another radiant smile. Then he stopped smiling and said earnestly, "I know that you are unwilling to be involved in whatever will happen next. I don't ask you to be involved."

"I am involved," she replied. "I became involved a long time ago."

"I meant, I don't ask you to involve yourself further. I agree that it is likely to be dangerous. I have no desire that you endanger yourself."

The spots of colour appeared on her cheeks. "It wasn't *danger* that bothered me," she told him sharply. "I'm not some timid little girl who has to be protected by big strong men all the time. I wanted to get out of this because the whole thing is so strange, and I couldn't see what to do."

He looked bewildered. "Do you see what to do now, then?"

She sighed and shook her head. "I was just worried. I wanted to see you."

He looked still more bewildered. "I don't understand."

She gazed at him resignedly. Either he was emotionally obtuse, or she was calling across a cultural gap, or both. Do I dare spell things out? she wondered. She remembered the way he had consistently withdrawn from her touch. And yet, when he woke and saw her, he had looked so happy.

Slowly, she crossed the room and sat down beside him on the bed. She cradled his face in one hand, leaned forward and kissed him—a light uncertain kiss that made no claims. Then she drew back and looked into the confusion on his face. The lines of it etched themselves into her eyes: the yellow remnants of the bruises, the irises defined by the strong light as merely brown, not the black they so often seemed; the dark sleep-tangled hair pressed against temple and cheek, the stubbled jaw. His hand came up and touched her own, as though uncertain whether to hold it or remove it.

"I was worried because I care for you," she told him.

He said nothing: again he could not speak. She had said "care," but he understood what she meant by it. He wondered, with shame, when this had begun, and for how long he had failed to understand her. It had never occurred to him that *he* could attract *her*, not with a body that was a battered and malfunctioning lump, and a face not his own. There was a roaring in his ears, and his heart battered his cracked ribs with terror and joy together. He felt as though he hovered on the boundary between two distinct states, like water vapour on the point of crystallising into frost. But he fought the transformation, afraid to be trapped in Anderson's image.

She felt the shiver go through him, and saw fear join the confusion in his eyes. Grief knotted her throat: she had made a mistake. Her declaration of interest was a threat, and she should have kept her distance. She pulled her hand back. But his hand followed it, and curled tentatively about her fingers on the crumpled coverlet between them.

"Please," he whispered. "I . . ." He stopped, looked away. He withdrew his scabbed hand and held it in the air before him; it was trembling. "I find you attractive," he told the air, "very attractive, but . . . I don't know how to respond. I am afraid . . ."

"Oh, leave it!" she cried, hurt and ashamed. "I shouldn't have said anything."

He registered the pain in her voice, and looked back at her quickly. She was not looking at him; she'd turned her head, and he saw only her ear, surrounded by clouds of ginger hair, and the hunch of her shoulders which told him that he'd hurt her. A flood of tenderness forced his unsteady hand back, this time to trace the pink edge of her ear, and she turned towards him, blinking. "Please," he repeated, then tried desperately to explain. "I didn't mean to distress you. What you said . . . should make me very glad. A part of me is glad, despite everything. But I am afraid of losing myself in *him*, in Anderson. I have nothing of my own."

She understood, better than he'd expected. "Do you really think it's the way you look that matters, that I would have fallen in love with you if you really had been Anderson?" she demanded contemptuously. "Everything I know about him convinces me that I wouldn't even have *liked* him. I know enough about what you're like to form an opinion. But leave the subject—I'm not begging for anything."

He was silent a moment, thinking that she would never need to beg. "That young man who was with you the night we came here," he asked hesitantly, "he wasn't your lover?"

"No. He wanted to be. But I've split with him. Not over you: it was coming for a long time. I said, leave it!"

He pulled his hand back. "I'm sorry," he said again, helplessly.

He didn't want to leave the subject. He could still feel her kiss, as though the nerves in his lips were tingling awake after an anaesthetic. He wanted to sweep aside the demons in his mind and obey his body's impulse to hold her, to kiss her back. But the roaring was still in his ears, and the fear still beat at his side—and anyway, she had forbidden it.

"I did not mean to offend you," he said anxiously instead. "I thought this morning that I had lost all my friends, and I was very frightened. I cannot say how glad it makes me to see you now."

She could feel her face going red. Her anger suddenly evaporated. It was not his fault he could not respond to her. He *wanted* to; she could believe that. He'd never tell flattering lies. He was so literal-minded that he wouldn't see the point of it. But he had been mauled by his experiences, and he needed time and space to recover. She pushed aside the fear that time and space were something he might not have. "I'm glad I came, then," she told him.

He smiled at her rather tentatively, and she smiled back. "Will you stay for lunch?" he asked her.

"It will have to be supper," she replied. "It's gone seven already."

They went downstairs together. Malcolm had put the Beatles disc on again, and was sitting at the dining table sketching. As they came up behind him, Sandra saw that he had abandoned the *Amnesia* picture and was drawing from a photograph. A fair-haired girl sitting on the edge of the fountain in Trafalgar Square became in his sketch pad a weird naiad-like creature at the focal point of an array of mirrors that reflected and distorted her image endlessly. Only her laughing, intimate smile remained the same. Sandra noted the shadow of a similar smile on Malcolm's face, and guessed that the naiad was Malcolm's girlfriend—or, more likely, one of his girlfriends, since it seemed unlikely that Malcolm's youth and exuberance had settled to a single long-term companion. He was at the experimental stage—going out with lots of people, falling in love, breaking up, moving on to someone new. And naturally he would go out with white girls as well as black ones. He had a strength and a natural resilience that allowed him to shrug off the confines of race with a good-natured grin. All his ex-girlfriends would look back on him with affection, she was sure. For the first time she wondered about his private life, which must have hung suspended since he took the job of home help. Her eyes stung suddenly, and her throat went tight with a surge of anger and grief. She realised how much she was afraid of the future. Her own involvement could not be helped, but Malcolm was too young, too talented, too *nice* to come to grief because he'd taken the wrong job.

She reminded herself fiercely that Stellar Research was only a company. It could not openly murder or imprison anyone, and for what it might have done in the past, it could be called to account.

Malcolm glanced up, then put down his pencil with an apologetic grin. "You staying for supper?" he asked.

They prepared a supper of scrambled eggs and baked beans—a soft, bland meal to spare not-Anderson's tongue. When they were about to start the meal, not-Anderson turned his telescope look on the CD player and asked what the music was.

"It's the Beatles disc we were playing the other night," said Malcolm.

Not-Anderson frowned. "What does it have to do with insects?"

Malcolm dropped his fork and stared. "Oh, come *on*!" he

protested. "You must know the Beatles. Even Russians know the Beatles. Everybody in the *world* knows the Beatles."

Not-Anderson looked bewildered. "Isn't a beetle a kind of insect?"

"This kind is a music group," said Sandra quietly. "Do you want it off?"

"Yes, please," said not-Anderson. "It's distracting." As she got up he asked anxiously, "Are they really so famous, these 'Beatles'?"

"Yes," said Sandra, stopping the CD player. "But I don't think that Malcolm's right that everybody in the world knows them." She hesitated, then said, "Tell you what. I'll get a tape of something else from my car."

"Mozart?" asked Malcolm, with a grin.

"I was thinking of Bach, actually," she said.

Malcolm kept grinning. "I *knew* you'd go for classical," he said. "*Early* classical. Nothing crass and emotional like Beethoven."

Sandra laughed and blushed. "And you," she said, "like sixties rock 'n' roll, reggae, and . . ."—she hesitated, looking at his expectant smile: he'd go for something highbrow as well, but it would have to be human and emotional—"opera?" she finished.

He tossed his head back and laughed. "Got it in one!" he crowed.

Not-Anderson was mystified. Opera, rock 'n' roll, classical early or late—what were they all, and how could Sandra and Malcolm guess which of them the other liked? He realised he remembered nothing about music beyond the fact of its existence. He had not liked the Beatles. The voices from the disc had been at once impersonal and disturbingly visceral, laden with emotions he had been unable to comprehend. He was not sure whether he wanted to hear any more music.

But the tape Sandra fetched from her car was completely different. No voices, no words to bewilder. A theme was out-

lined in cool sound; restated, then varied. It was as elegant
and as lucid as mathematics—and yet it was sensuous, delicious to the ear. He listened, entranced.

"You like it?" asked Sandra.

He nodded, unwilling to speak, afraid of disturbing the
complex pattern of the sound.

"It's called the Goldberg Variations," she said. "I listen to
it sometimes when I'm driving to work." She'd thought he'd
like it. It was the most cerebral thing she'd had in the car.

Over the rest of the meal Sandra considered how much it
meant that he didn't remember the Beatles. Malcolm was
right: the group was so much a part of modern Western culture that everybody who was part of that culture would
know them. You could escape hearing Bach, but the Beatles
were ubiquitous. Perhaps it was simply that Paul (she could
not stop calling him that) had forgotten them, but if he'd
never heard them at all, what did that say about him? From
what she'd heard, the songs were popular in Russia, but the
natives of some of the other Soviet Republics—Georgians,
Azeris, Kazakhs and the like—presumably listened to music
from a different tradition. Middle Easterners . . .

The cold possibility occurred to her that Paul might be
from the Middle East. He was dark enough. A Syrian or an
Iraqi scientist might well have trained in Moscow and speak
fluent Russian, while learning English as the international
language of science. Her heart sank. The Arab nations were
an alien world to her. She knew them only from the blaring
headlines, the clichés of popular fiction: the men all sexist
pigs, and the countries governed by tyrants under barbarous
laws. They flogged and beheaded their citizens, and sent out
assassins against their enemies . . .

Her mind snagged on that thought, *assassins*. She
watched Paul slowly manoeuvre a spoonful of baked beans
towards his mouth. Maybe Stellar Research was innocent of
what had been done to him. Maybe he had been kidnapped
and dumped in that car by his own countrymen, to prevent

him from passing on a secret they did not know he had already betrayed.

She pushed her plate away unfinished. She did not want to think about it.

After supper, Sandra and Malcolm did the washing up, and not-Anderson sat on the over-stuffed sofa, listening to the Goldberg Variations. All at once he felt happy. Sandra came into the room, brushing back her hair, and Malcolm followed, picking up his sketch pad on the way: his happiness increased. He was alive. He had friends—these two, who had come out of nowhere to help him, and who unreasonably cared for him. There was a world before him. There was music to learn, and perhaps art. There was health to regain, and perhaps love. The future held hope as well as fear. All he had to do was stay alive.

The doorbell rang. Malcolm went to open it, and Rodney Jones shambled in, trailed, inevitably, by Dave. Rod was grinning in a self-satisfied way. "Hello again!" he said cheerfully to Malcolm; then, less cheerfully, "Oh, Ms Murray. I thought you'd walked out."

"I walked back in again," said Sandra tartly, "after I heard what happened last night."

Rod gave her a dismissive waggle of the eyebrows and pushed into the sitting room. Sandra was reminded more than ever of a dog—not a rottweiler, this time, but a setter, panting and wagging its tail over a ball it had succeeded in retrieving. Rod flopped into an armchair. "Well, Sherlock Holmes," he said to not-Anderson. "I've proved it: you are not Anderson, and you are a physics genius. Jesus, I could do with a beer!"

Malcolm fetched beers for all who wanted, and Rod started talking.

He had taken the Astragen equations to an old university friend, now in the Physics department of Imperial College. "At first he was pretty casual about it," he reported. "Said it was an 'elegant little statement about magnetism,' and pushed it back at me. That's the way he talks, 'elegant little statement.' He was a wild animal on the mid-field—I used to play football with him—but he talks like a fucking schoolteacher. He doesn't do magnetism, apparently; he does semiconductors. But when I asked him if it said how to confine a magnetic field, he started getting interested. He looked at it again, and then he ran upstairs and showed it to a guy who does do magnetism, and the magnetism guy started jumping up and down and waving his arms about. He said it was major, major stuff, Nobel-prize stuff, and he wanted to call in the rest of the department to hear it on the spot. I had to tell them then that it was an official secret. At that they both hit the ceiling, and swore that nobody had any right to classify something so important. They said that if it worked it was the biggest thing since superconductivity, only more so. They both want it published. The magnetism man was so keen to start work on it he was practically dribbling. He says if you send him a copy of the work, he'll look after it, and he won't try to claim it's his own, and he thinks you should send a copy to *Nature* and D-notices be damned. And he wants to meet you, and he wants to get you a post at Imperial College, and he wants you and him to settle down to work on magnetism together, world without end amen. Jesus, that man is crazy about magnets."

"Does he know the names of people who were working in that field?" asked not-Anderson eagerly. He sat on the sofa opposite Rod, with his hands clasped together before his knees, smiling, like a Victorian picture of rapture. His reason had once again been vindicated.

Rod shook his head. "He seemed to know everybody in the world who does magnetism and what they've all been working on recently, but he didn't know of anybody who was working on anything like that. He thought you must have been somewhere classified. I didn't tell either of 'em anything about you, apart from the fact you'd been in a car crash, which I had to do to explain the handwriting—but if you wanted to go public, I think they'd help you. The magnetism guy was practically begging to help. I think you should go public. It's pretty clear that as a great physicist with a major discovery to your credit you could walk into a job. If you need asylum, you could get it, no trouble."

"We don't know that the theory was my discovery," said not-Anderson, losing his smile.

"Shit, man, how much proof do you want?" asked Rod impatiently. "We know that it's new and revolutionary and hasn't got anybody else's name on it. We know Stellar is trying to steal it, and we know you woke up scared of Stellar. We know you're a physicist, that you've got Anderson's face, and you were left for dead in his car. And we know you definitely are not Anderson. The other thing I did today was talk to Anderson's ex. She says he spoke good French, a bit of Italian, no German, definitely no Russian, and he never liked Maths or Science and gave up studying them as soon as his school let him. And she says that this Mark Jaeger character, who was one of her hubby's best friends, was an army spook and knew lots of really unsavoury characters. This is what I think happened," Rod hacked at the air with a big hand. "You were working in some classified establishment in Eastern Europe. You worked out this great new theory, and you didn't want to see it eaten by the military, so you looked for a Western company to develop it for you. You picked Stellar because it has a nice green image. You sent your theory to Lloyd on a computer disc, together with a request that Stellar develop it for the good of the world. You fixed up the disc with a virus, so that when the trials were completed, the company got a reminder about what they were to do with it. Then you sat back and waited for your theory to cause a stir in the scientific journals. But nothing happened. You got worried, and eventually you managed to get abroad, and came to Britain yourself to see what was going on. This happened to be after I'd started looking into Stellar's acquisition of patents. The company had just got Astragen classified, and it knew it was in deep shit, because you were gonna be furious when you saw they'd done with it exactly the opposite of what you'd asked them to do. The least you were gonna do was give the theory to somebody else, and at the worst, you were gonna sue them for compensation. They knew, too, that I was hanging around just waiting for somebody like you to come along. So Stellar decided to get rid of you. Sir Philip and his friends were squeamish, though: they wanted you out of the way, but they didn't want to know any details. Anderson was tougher, and volunteered to handle it himself. I can swear to it that he was a vindictive bastard, and imaginative as well. I think he probably had something in his own background he wanted to cover up, too: he really hated me investigating. Anyway, he had no objection to getting himself a new identity. He decided to kill you and give himself the perfect alibi by faking his own death. He picked up a few names from his friend Jaeger and hired some hit-men. They kidnapped you, you were doped up and given a nose-job at a discreet establishment, and then you were given Anderson's ID and dumped in a river in his car with the doors locked. But something went wrong. Maybe Anderson tried to cheat his hired thugs, or maybe he had a reaction to his own plastic surgery. Anyway, he died. Stellar didn't know what Anderson had been up to, and when you turned up and he didn't, they naturally accepted you as him. There. That's *my* theory. See anything wrong with it?"

Not-Anderson looked down at the bloodstains on the carpet. Carefully, he laid Jones' theory against the inaccessible continent in his mind. The world slipped, and he clenched his hands until they hurt, focusing on the pain to keep his mind from stumbling too far into the unendurable past. Knowledge he could not touch heaved and shuddered against Jones' conjecture. He looked at Sandra's feet, resting on the carpet before him. White leather sandals, scuffed grey at the sides; her toes were thin and bony, with long nails, and her ankles stood out in a knot of sinew at the end of long, elegant calves. He liked her feet. Did the conjecture fit, or not?

"The doors of the car weren't locked," said Sandra.

Rod frowned at her. "So he was half-drowned first, or so he managed to unlock it too late. I still think my theory's the best thing we have to go on. What I suggest we do is this. We go to the police, give them the evidence we've got, and ask them to investigate.

"That's the best way I can think of to fill in all the gaps. If we're right, they'll find the real Anderson's body lying around in a wood somewhere. Once we get a murder investigation under way, we can raise a big stink, and make sure the whole story is dragged out into the light of day."

"And you get a lot of free publicity for your documentary," said Sandra harshly. "Have you thought that maybe the reason Paul didn't publish was because he was afraid of what his government would do to him if he did?"

"Look," said Rod angrily. "Your friend is safer if lots of people know about him. Even if he is from some little tinpot ex-Soviet Republic, he's not there now, he's here. If he's a potential Nobel laureate, nobody's gonna deport him—and if he's a key witness in a murder investigation, he *can't* be deported. And if Stellar and Sir Philip fucking Lloyd have been breaking the law and bribing ministers and the MoD to get away with it, then the public has a right to know."

"It's none of the public's business!" Sandra exclaimed in disgust. "You're talking about setting Joe Blogg's sensational Sunday viewing against Paul's life. What if he's not Soviet, not from any country with even a slight respect for international law? What if he's Syrian or Iraqi? Maybe his own people didn't realise that he'd sent the secret to Stellar earlier, and when he came to Britain and they saw him talking to Anderson, they tried to kill them both. Maybe they substituted Paul for Anderson because Anderson had been shot, and they didn't want the police asking awkward questions about his body. My theory's as good as yours. And if I'm right, the last thing we should do is announce to the world that their attempt at murder failed. Publicity won't be any protection against a hit squad. And what if Paul has family in his own country who might suffer for what he's done?"

Rod's eyes widened and he stared at not-Anderson for a moment. Not-Anderson was still looking at the floor. He had gone pale and was starting to sweat.

"Oh, shit," said Rod. "Are you remembering any of this? Is that true?"

"It is a conjecture," said not-Anderson quietly, without looking up. "Your theory and hers both. I cannot remember, and we do not have enough facts to prove or disprove anything. What is a 'hit squad'?"

"A team sent out to assassinate their employer's enemies," said Sandra, keeping her voice even with an effort. From their first meeting he had turned to her for information. She might as well carry on supplying it.

Not-Anderson shook his head. He took a deep breath and lifted his eyes again. The twisted edge of memory receded, and the tide of nausea became fainter with each ebbing wave.

"Perhaps it would be better if we re-examined the facts," he said, in a tone of leaden calm. "I was found almost dead in a car eleven days ago. I match Paul Anderson in appearance, but feel that I am someone else. I speak at least two languages which Paul Anderson apparently did not, and I appear to know more mathematics and physics than he did. This is strong evidence that I am not Paul Anderson, and suggests that I may be a mathematician or physicist—although, Mr Jones, I must point out that it does not constitute proof. Anderson may have known more than his ex-wife was aware of. I have some memory of Stellar Research, and feel instinctively afraid of the company and its chairman. Further, I know a theory about magnetism which Stellar Research is developing as the Astragen Project. This theory struck two informed physicists as new and significant, and the project is potentially very profitable. Stellar maintains strict secrecy about it, and has persuaded the government to 'classify' it. Those are facts." Impatiently, he wiped an invisible scribble of conjecture from the air before him. "I must know more, but my memory is damaged and must be regarded as unreliable. However, this is what it can add. I believe I used to think in another language, which I cannot now recall, that Paul Anderson is dead, and that Stellar Research injured me in some fashion. I think it was forbidden in some way for me to pass on the Astragen theory . . ." he stumbled a little on that, his latest gleaning from the dizzying edge of his memory, ." . . but I was not concerned by the ban. I did not, for example, feel any anxiety about passing the theory on to Mr Jones. I remember no family, and the thought of 'hit squads' does not frighten me. The thought of falling into the hands of Stellar Research does, though. They would . . . they would . . ."

He stopped, choking. Sandra jumped up, then hovered over him uselessly, wanting to comfort him but not daring to.

"They'd kill you," said Rod harshly.

Not-Anderson shuddered and lowered his head into his hands. The terror rippled within him, and he struggled again to fix its shape, to plot its unintelligible juddering onto his reasoning mind. "I don't think that's what I'm afraid of at all," he whispered, hardly able to credit it.

"You don't think they'd kill you?" asked Rod disbelievingly.

Not-Anderson stared through his hands at the stains on the carpet. Blood from my tongue, he thought. Blood from my body's failure to accept what happened to my mind. And all at once the terror was swallowed up in outrage. Stellar had cost him his identity, had inflicted on him horror and pain such as he hadn't known existed, to gain . . . the nausea surged up again, blocking the thought, but the outrage continued to rise with it. "They would try to use me again," he said thickly. "They did before. They deceived me and betrayed me. I will . . ."

Pain.

The sickness leapt horribly into his head, and he felt again the awful sense that his consciousness was splintering.

Not another fit, oh no, please, no! The thought burned through his mind like a comet. "Sandra!" he called frantically, searching for his one clear signal in the storm.

She was beside him. He turned away from the void and buried his face against her shoulder. She smelled of green plants and chemicals and sweat, and her collarbone was hard against his cheek. He clung to the thread of sense. She was real and warm. He would not fall.

"It's all right," said Sandra stupidly, crouching against him, feeling his breath hot and uneven on her neck. "It's all right."

He shuddered violently, then was still.

"Did you remember something?" asked Rod, somewhere in the distance.

"Leave him alone!" snarled Sandra. "Paul, do you want to lie down?"

She helped him to stretch out on the overstuffed sofa, then stood over him unhappily. He lay with his head still and his forearm over his eyes, because he was afraid that if he looked at the room he would find it dancing giddily about him. It was his right forearm, the bandaged one; it smelt of adhesive and antiseptics, and when he pressed it against his face the stitches under the bandage stung in a neat double row.

"That was almost another fit, wasn't it?" asked Malcolm despairingly. "Oh, man, you should go back to the hospital."

"No," said not-Anderson. The word slurred—he had forgotten to enunciate—but it was determined nonetheless.

"So where do all your facts get us, Holmes?" Rod asked, after a silence.

Not-Anderson did not answer. The outrage was gone, and the burst of energy with it: he felt simply exhausted. It was too much effort to think, to construct the tower of conjecture afresh, rebalancing it on the more stable of its supports.

"If what you sort-of remember is right, then my theory's more likely to be right than Ms Murray's," Rod said. "If you were in danger from your own people, you'd be worried about them, not Stellar. You agree with me that it's best to go to the police?"

"No," said not-Anderson from behind his arm. "I dare not tell Stellar I am not Anderson."

"Why not? You think Ms Murray's right, after all?"

"*Leave . . . him . . . alone!*" Sandra said vehemently. "You know what remembering does to him. You keep saying you'll be careful of his health, and you keep pushing him too far anyway! Don't ask him to do any more of it!"

Rod stared at her for a minute, then made a face and sighed. "OK. I suppose it's not crucial yet. We can wait until we have a better idea who he is, provided that doesn't take too long. Any suggestions what to do next?"

"Stellar could tell us everything," suggested Dave diffidently, speaking for the first time that evening. "They think he's Anderson, so he could walk right in and ask for a complete account."

"Didn't you get my message?" asked Malcolm in astonishment.

Rod and Dave had received no messages: they hadn't checked the answering machine for days. When Malcolm informed them what the message was, Rod swore again.

"Sir Philip Lloyd guessed?" he asked not-Anderson incredulously. "How the fuck could he?"

"I don't know," said not-Anderson. He moved his arm away from his eyes, and blinked at the sudden dazzle of the light. To his relief, the room stayed steady.

"Are you *sure* he guessed?"

Not-Anderson thought back on the morning, on Sir Philip's blind blue stare. "Yes," he said flatly.

"Shit," said Rod. After a moment, he tried again. "Here, Holmes, you say Lloyd *guessed*, not that he *knows*, and you say you don't want Stellar told you're not Anderson. That mean he thinks you *could* still be Anderson, acting funny because of your amnesia?"

Not-Anderson nodded, eyes focusing on the journalist with surprise. Rod's jaw came forward pugnaciously. "Then maybe we can still use Dave's idea. If I'm right that Lloyd doesn't know any details of what happened, he won't have any way of checking who you are, apart from what you say to him. What I'd expect him to do now is to try to catch you out knowing something Anderson couldn't 've. Maybe you could play him along. He doesn't know you've seen me or that you've realised you're not Anderson. As far as he's concerned, you're still an innocent, sick as a parrot and half gaga. You could discover a lot from the kind of questions he asks you."

"No!" protested Sandra angrily. "It would be much too dangerous."

They both looked at her, and she bit her lip. She realised consciously what she must have known for some time: Paul would make even fewer concessions to health and safety than Rodney Jones. He was stubborn and proud and he hated his own weakness. Once he'd set his mind on something, all his formidable powers of reasoning would inevitably turn into reasons for doing exactly what he wanted, and an ordinary person trying to argue with him would get precisely nowhere. *She* would get precisely nowhere now, but she loved him, and she was certain that following Jones' plan would be disastrous, so she had to try. "What if Mr Jones is wrong, and Sir Philip does have some way of checking who you really are?" she asked not-Anderson, ploughing on despairingly. "If you see him you'll be handing him the chance to . . . to do whatever it is you're afraid of. And you're not much good at play-acting, Paul. I'm sorry, but you're not. You couldn't convince him that you really are Anderson after all. You couldn't convince *me*, and I didn't even know Anderson."

"I can't avoid him," he replied in a low voice. "If I try to, it will confirm all his suspicions. Once he knows, he will take action. I am certain of that. All I can do is try to prolong his doubt." He paused, and she was aware, with a pang, that the super-cooled CRAY was on-line again, evaluating, projecting, choosing among its alternatives. "I will meet him," not-Anderson decided, "if I can do so in a place of safety."

EIGHT

SIR PHILIP LLOYD TELEPHONED TO PROPOSE A MEET-
ing that same evening. Rodney Jones and his cameraman
were still in the house, engulfing a late supper of microwave
pizza, when Stellar's chairman phoned from the hospital and
asked to speak to "Paul."

"What on earth are you doing at home?" he demanded,
when not-Anderson came to the telephone. "I thought we
agreed that you'd have that test and I'd see you here this
evening."

"No," said not-Anderson. He called to mind Anderson's
letters, and all the crude, vigorous illogic of the mind they
displayed, and tried to reply as the man who wrote them
would have replied. "I told you I didn't want to stay in the
hospital. We agreed we'd meet this evening, but I've been
expecting you here." He had a feeling that Anderson would
probably have inserted a "shit" or "damn" somewhere, but
he doubted his ability to swear convincingly.

"Oh," said Sir Philip, taken aback. After a moment he
asked, "Aren't you going to have the test?"

"I'll have it when the doctors reschedule it for a convenient time," replied not-Anderson. "I haven't spoken to them

today. I've been asleep. I wanted to rest." Anderson, he
thought, would have put in a "Phil"—"I haven't spoken to
them today, Phil"—but again, it was better to avoid words
he could not say naturally.

There was a silence, and then Sir Philip said, "Look,
Paul, about that interview with Jones . . ."

"Yes?" not-Anderson looked at Jones, who had come into
the sitting room to listen with a piece of pizza.

"I was wondering if we should arrange to have it at the
lab," said Sir Philip.

Not-Anderson felt a sudden sick surge of terror. He
snatched the telephone receiver away from his mouth, so
that it would not relay his frightened gasp, and looked across
the room at Sandra, who was watching him anxiously from
the armchair. He focused his attention on the way the light
refracted in her hair. He did not dare wonder why the
thought of Stellar's lab frightened him: the answer was certainly in the inaccessible part of his mind, and to grope for
it now would only cause a distress that might betray him.

When he was certain he could speak normally, he asked,
"Have you spoken to Jones?" and held the receiver out
again, this time so that Jones could hear the answer.

"Not yet. We still haven't managed to get hold of him.
But we could leave a message on his answering machine
suggesting that he meet you in our offices, Thursday or Friday. It would look more natural than having him at your
house. How are you really feeling? Are you up to it?"

"I thought we agreed we'd have the interview here." Not-
Anderson questioned Jones with his eyes. Rod's lips silently
formed the words, "Go for it!"

"He might not come," said Sir Philip. "He certainly
knows by now that you were in an accident. He may guess
we're setting him up. But if we hold it at the lab, he'll have
to come. He's been aching to get on site for months."

It was perfectly clear to not-Anderson that the person Sir
Philip wanted at the lab was himself. And he had a cold
crystalline awareness that to go would be dangerous. He

looked again at Rodney Jones, who was now nodding vigorously and making stabbing gestures with his piece of pizza.

"I'll think about it," he temporised. "I don't know if I will be 'up to it.' I am much better this evening, but not fully recovered yet." Rod grimaced, and he added, "Arrange it with Jones, if you like. If I do not feel up to it, I can cancel."

"I'll tell Jones Thursday at four, then," said Sir Philip. "Or, failing that, same time Friday." He rang off.

"You've got to go," said Rod, as soon as not-Anderson had put the phone down. "He can't pull anything funny if I'm there as a witness. And maybe between us we can prod him into saying something revealing."

Not-Anderson frowned remotely at nothing. His instincts screamed at him that the lab was a trap, a pit full of the dead and dying, a fanged thing lurking in darkness. But the very intensity of his dread made him suspect that it was not rational. Did it spring from something that had happened at the lab in the past? Had he ever been there? He had no mental image of the place. Jones' insistence that they accept the offer was not unreasonable. Sir Philip could do nothing with a freelance documentarist and his cameraman there to record his actions.

Not-Anderson realised that he was once again staring at the bloodstains on the carpet. He felt a stab of revulsion and anger. He was tired of being an invalid. He wanted his memory to be his own, not something he skulked about the fringes of, like a thief. He wanted to be able to walk easily, to write, to climb stairs without thinking about each step, to move and think without constantly judging how much pain and nausea he could tolerate. He wanted—desperation of the longing!—to be whole again.

"Very well," he agreed. "Provided that he really does arrange for you to be there, I will go."

STELLAR DID TELEPHONE RODNEY JONES NEXT MORN-
ing, and politely suggested that he interview his long-time
quarry Paul Anderson on the following afternoon. Jones
agreed to the Friday afternoon, and virtuously informed not-
Anderson that the later date had been chosen to allow more
time for recovery. Sandra was unconvinced by this deference to health, but glad of any delay. She had tried to talk
Paul out of going to the meeting, with predictable results.
She ended up agreeing that it was unreasonable to be afraid,
that Stellar couldn't do anything in front of the media, and
that Stellar was only a company anyway—but she still felt
deeply unhappy about it. She was consumed with anger
against Rodney Jones, whose idea it had been, who still did
not see that Paul was too ill to play guessing games with
Stellar. But the only thing she could do was come as well, to
give Paul whatever frail shelter her presence could provide.

"I'm coming with you," she told not-Anderson Wednesday evening. "I'll take the afternoon off work."

Not-Anderson didn't argue. He felt that he ought to try to
dissuade her, but he was glad of her offer. The dread he felt
at the prospect of going to the lab only increased as the time
for the visit drew nearer.

THURSDAY WAS THE DAY HE ALWAYS REMEMBERED AF-
terwards. He woke early, full of a restless urgency, a desire
to act before his enemies did. He got up, pulled on a tennis
shirt and trousers, and padded down the corridor to the
study. But he stopped in the doorway, staring at the silent
computer. He had spent most of Wednesday working at it,
retrieving the passworded files, but he had learned nothing
useful, and he suspected that the work wasn't good for him.
The giddiness had been growing worse, there had been
headaches, and the previous evening he had passed out at
the computer, waking to find the screen full of unintelligible
letters written by the pressure of his unconscious head upon
the keyboard. He had not mentioned any of this to anyone,

just as he had avoided any return to the hospital for more tests. He told himself that the disturbances were nothing more than the approach of memory—a sign of recovery, yes! But he decided that perhaps it would be better to leave the computer alone for a while.

He descended the spiral of the stairs, his bare feet noiseless on the metal steps. Malcolm was still asleep, and the house was silent. He went into the empty kitchen. The morning sunlight fell in bright puddles on the tiled floor. Moved by some impulse he could not identify, he unlocked the previously untouched back door and went out into the garden.

It was about six o'clock, sunny and calm. The square of lawn lay green and smooth, enclosed by the darker hedge, and dappled with shade by the surrounding trees. A bird was singing nearby, its call rippling liquid through the stillness, and the air was full of sweet scents of things growing. He walked slowly to the centre of the lawn, discovering a strange delight in the moist roughness of grass under his feet. He stopped in a patch of sun, and turned his face towards the light. The sun dazzled over the treetops of the surrounding garden, and he closed his eyes at its brilliance. His eyelids glowed red, and he could feel the warmth upon his skin. He felt suddenly that something of infinite value had drifted into his empty hands—something delicate and transitory, but with a permanence that could crack stone. Was it happiness? Words only confused: he stood in a sunlit garden and listened to the song of a bird. That was the only definition which made sense.

When Malcolm came out a couple of hours later, he found not-Anderson sitting in the middle of the back lawn, watching the house and smiling.

Malcolm liked most people, but he had recently been growing aware that he respected only a few of them. That Spring he'd been jilted by a girl he'd thought himself in love with, and he'd been shocked to find that it didn't really hurt because she hadn't really mattered. She'd been fun, full of jokes and *joie de vivre*, but some impersonal part of his mind had always judged her unreliable and second-rate. Failures or betrayals could only wound deeply when they came from those who mattered, those who were not second-rate. Sandra Murray, Malcolm had recently concluded, was not second-rate, not at all. Now as he looked at his erstwhile employer, he recognised that not-Anderson was not second-rate, either. The man was happy now, and that had started to matter to Malcolm.

"Nice morning," said Malcolm, coming over.

Not-Anderson nodded. "There is a bird's nest under the roof," he commented, pointing. "There are three young in it. The parents have been feeding them."

Malcolm turned to look, and saw the mud nest tucked under the eaves. He grinned. "House martins," he said. "They're great, aren't they? I love the way they fly."

One of the adult house martins swooped up, a flash of white belly and black wings. Three gaping yellow beaks appeared at the entrance of the nest to greet it. The parent bird hooked its tiny feet about the rim of the nest, and pushed food into the peeping maws. The two men watched it, then looked at each other and smiled.

"You wanna have breakfast out here?" asked Malcolm.

They had breakfast in the garden—coffee and toast with strawberry jam and bananas—and watched the house martins. Malcolm talked about the birds, which were favourites of his—how they flew to Africa every winter, and returned each spring over the endless desert, and the sea, and the mountains, to find the nest where they were born. Not-Anderson stared at the tiny birds with renewed fascination, and was struck again by how little he remembered. He could not remember ever noticing a bird before. Perhaps its name was locked in another tongue and buried in the inaccessible continent of his mind?

"It's gonna be hot today," Malcolm said, when breakfast was over. "You wanna take a day off from the computer, and go to the beach?"

The rest of the day was one long sequence of delights.

They drove up to the Norfolk Coast in the Jaguar, speeding over wide fields and twisting through towns under the vast summer skies. Then there was the North Sea, exquisitely blue in the June sun; the feeling of cold salt water against hot sweaty skin; the taste of ice-cream; the flight of seagulls. Children built sandcastles against the incoming tide; couples lounged under parasols; shore crabs scuttled under rocks in tide pools. On the way back, they stopped to buy strawberries from a roadside stand, and there was the scent of the field in the sun, and the car radio playing music by Vivaldi as they continued on. Then there was a cold shower and cream on the beginning of a sunburn, the sweetness of a cold drink in a dry mouth. Pleasures which to the rest of the world might be familiar and tame, to not-Anderson reared up out of nothing, shocking in their unexpected intensity.

Sandra came over after work, a visit that had already become habitual and expected. Malcolm had found a barbecue in Anderson's garage, and the three of them went into the back garden and scorched sausages, which they ate with garlic bread and salad, followed by the strawberries and cream. Not-Anderson listened while his companions talked about beaches and holidays, comparing, deriding, laughing. He had no childhood memories to add to theirs, but it didn't matter. It had been a day like no other he could remember, a day sunlit and golden and without pain. A single unique day, and over far too soon.

Sandra next arrived at 12 The Mays about three on Friday—the afternoon off work had, as afternoons off will, dwindled to a couple of hours when she came to take it. It was still too early: she sat about drinking tea with not-Anderson and Malcolm for half an hour, talking stiffly about nothing in particular. Malcolm had arrayed not-Anderson in one of the expensive suits from the wardrobe upstairs. Not-Anderson contrived to look simultaneously distinguished by it and out of place in it. Sandra was ashamed of her own plain green summer dress in contrast—until she looked at Malcolm's T-shirt. It was a new T-shirt, black, white, grey and crimson; it was if anything even weirder than his previous efforts, and it was worn over the same black shorts and orange flip-flops. *Not* approved company clothing, thought Sandra, and was obscurely comforted.

At half-past three they at last went out and got into Sandra's car—it had been agreed that they would travel to Stellar in the red Sierra, to provide an excuse for Sandra's presence—and started off into the tree-shaded street.

Sandra drove silently along the ring-road and turned right on to the A-road that led to the southeast. She knew where Stellar was based; she'd driven past the headquarters often and always admired the building, which had won a number of architectural awards. On the road by the site entrance a black sign announced the company's identity in silver letters surmounted by the Stellar logo, and beyond it, across a large pond, reared a tent of black glass. The central section rose three or four stories high, and the elongated corners stretched to earth in a dark glitter. Sandra turned towards it, and followed a wide drive which swept about the pond before debouching in a car-park at the side. It would be screened one day, she saw: young flowering cherries and Japanese maples rose from cardboard tubes among beds of bright summer annuals. Stellar had planted with its own growth in mind. The parking spaces allotted to visitors were near the entrance to the building. Sandra pulled into the nearest and switched off the engine. It was still only ten to four, but several spaces along was a battered grey Metro which they all recognised as belonging to Rodney Jones. It looked out of place among the polished Rovers and BMWs. The Sierra, Sandra thought, must look equally incongruous. She climbed out of the car, waited for the others to do the same, and locked the doors.

They all three stood for a minute staring at the shining black fortress before them. The great double doors were silvered and reflected their images back at them: a tall man in a suit, a shorter, darker man in a gaudy T-shirt, a red-haired woman in a green summer dress.

Not-Anderson closed his eyes to avoid seeing his reflection and stood very still, waiting for his heart to stop pounding. It would not. He felt that there was a line in the air, a line that passed just before the door and encircled the building with a rope of invisible fire. He was afraid of what would happen to him if he crossed that line. He turned his face away from it and clenched his hands until the broken finger throbbed.

"You don't have to go in," said Sandra's voice beside him.

"I do," he replied heavily.

"No, you don't. You could go home and phone to say you felt ill. It's a valid excuse, Paul. Most people in your condition would be in hospital. Sir Philip himself has said you ought to be."

He hunched his shoulders and said nothing. He told himself that he was recovering well. His tongue had knitted quickly, as tongues do, and was now only a little sore. He could walk almost normally, and he could eat with a knife and fork, and type with all his fingers except the broken one. He now insisted fiercely to himself that he did not have the excuse of illness, that there was no reason he should not cross the invisible line and carry on as he had planned. He had to go in. It would look suspicious to turn about and go now. Rodney Jones was inside already.

Eyes still closed, he lurched forward. When he reached the invisible line in the air he thought he could feel it, as though the film of surface tension on a glass of water punctured to drop a suspended pin. He staggered, down, down, down into deep water, and bruised himself against the door. Sandra caught his arm.

"You don't have to!" she whispered fiercely in his ear.

"I must," he replied: and, passionately and irrationally, added what he knew was the real reason, "My name is inside."

Inside were dove-grey carpets, ash-coloured walls, and chairs upholstered in midnight blue. A receptionist sat at a desk of polished ebony. She had skin the colour of milky coffee and hair of the darkest imaginable shade of red, and she was dressed in charcoal and ivory. She looked so perfect and sat so still that she might have been a mannequin in a shop window, but when she saw them she greeted them with an icy smile. "Mr Anderson!" she said, in well-modulated tones that expressed nothing. "How nice to see you again!"

Not-Anderson walked slowly up to the ebony desk and braced himself against it. Sandra noticed the receptionist looking at his torn hands, and just caught that faultless upper lip's fastidious quiver of revulsion. "I've come for the interview with Rodney Jones," not-Anderson said faintly.

"*Of* course," replied the receptionist. "It's in the executive common room."

There was a silence. "I don't remember where that is," not-Anderson said. "I have amnesia."

The receptionist smiled mechanically, but her eyes were shocked and disgusted. She pushed a button under her desk. "I'll get someone to show you," she said. "Who are these people?"

Not-Anderson looked at Sandra, then at Malcolm. "Ms Murray," he murmured, "Mr Brown—they've come to help me. Ms Murray has been good enough to drive me. Mr Brown is my . . . medical assistant. I want them to come with me."

The receptionist pursed her lips. "I'd have to get clearance for that, Mr Anderson. Strangers aren't allowed into the lab without prior clearance, as you know, and nobody told me anything about them."

"Rodney Jones has been allowed into the lab," not-Anderson replied icily. "My friends surely will be allowed as far as he is. Cannot I, as a director of the company, give them clearance?"

The receptionist blinked, then turned her false cold smile on Sandra and Malcolm. "I suppose that's right," she said. "I'll issue some visitors' passes for you two, shall I?"

Visitors' passes were issued—yellow name-tags printed with their names and the Stellar logo surmounted by the word "VISITOR"—and a silent young man appeared from somewhere. "Mr Anderson's forgotten where the executive common room is, Gilbert," said the receptionist condescendingly. "Show him please."

Gilbert nodded, and set off along the dove-grey carpet at a trot, hesitating now and then to see if they were following.

They entered an ash-coloured lift at the back of the foyer, and Gilbert pressed the button for the first floor. The lift doors hushed shut, hushed open again on an ash-coloured landing, screened off by more silvered and reflective glass. Gilbert paused, then pushed through a firedoor and into a corridor carpeted in ivory, with walls of glacial blue. They followed him past three or four smoked glass doors, to the corridor's end in a door of frosted glass. The words "Executive Common Room" were engraved in black on a white panel fixed to it. Gilbert nodded, indicated the door, then turned and trotted silently back down the corridor.

"I don' like this place," Malcolm murmured, to no one in particular, and opened the door.

The room beyond stood at the apex of one of the building's extended corners, looking out over the landscaped surroundings. Picture windows flanked two şides of its triangular space, their tinted glass giving the bright outer light a shadowy look of imminent storm. Pale gold carpets washed about dark gold chairs. On the far side of a brass and smoked glass coffee table sat Sir Philip Lloyd and another man, a small thin man with a bald forehead and a small moustache. They were both examining a machine upon the coffee table. There was no trace of Rodney Jones.

The machine was about the size and shape of a suitcase, and smooth as one, except for a small liquid crystal display and some keys on the edge facing Sir Philip. Sandra recognised from the thick dull-grey casing that it was refrigerated, probably super-cooled, but she had no idea what it did. Sir Philip and his associate appeared to be reading the display, but when the door opened they both stopped and looked up. Sir Philip's blue eyes fixed on not-Anderson with a strange look of mingled triumph and horror. Then he noticed Sandra and Malcolm, and was dismayed.

"What are *you* doing here?" he demanded.

That one look had told not-Anderson that Sir Philip now *knew*, beyond doubt, who he was. He wanted to turn and run, but a wave of giddiness made him stagger. He grabbed the door frame for support and hung there. His mind went numb and blank, except for a great silent howl of terror. He had walked into a trap.

"You weren't supposed to be here," said Sir Philip, to Sandra and Malcolm. "That wasn't part of the arrangement."

"We came with Mr Anderson," said Malcolm, puzzled. "He's ill, ya know. He couldn't have got here by himself."

"Where's Rodney Jones?" asked Sandra.

Sir Philip blinked at her, either lost for an answer or simply too angry to speak.

Not-Anderson found his mind working again. Sir Philip had arranged for Jones to be elsewhere. He didn't want to spring the trap in front of witnesses.

The only hope of escape was to cling to his witnesses and leave at once.

"Mr Jones is touring the lab," Sir Philip said, recovering himself a little. He spoke abruptly, with none of his usual smoothness, but he tried to smile. "He arrived early, so Ms Gresham offered to show him around. Would you like a tour? If you want, you can have one while we conduct the interview."

"No interview," croaked not-Anderson.

Sir Philip looked at him without surprise. The other man was staring in horrified fascination. Not-Anderson knew the other man's name: Alan Boardman, Stellar's Research Director. He had neither time nor energy for wondering why he knew.

"I am ill," not-Anderson announced. "I want to go home. Now."

He felt Sandra and Malcolm looking at him with astonishment, but he could not tear his gaze from the two Stellars. What did the polished faces and bright hostile eyes tell him? Was that furrow of the brows frustration? Calculation? Fear?

"That's very disappointing, Paul," said Sir Philip. The smoothness was back now. "I'm very sorry to hear that. Mr Jones will be furious."

Not-Anderson forced himself to let go of the doorframe. His broken finger was throbbing, and he could taste bile in the back of his throat. He groped, and caught Sandra's arm. "Nonetheless," he whispered, "I am going now."

Sir Philip sighed. His eyelids drooped, masking whatever might have been in his eyes, and he glanced down at the machine before him. Boardman continued to stare at not-Anderson. "You owe it to the company, Paul, to speak to Jones," coaxed Sir Philip.

Not-Anderson shook his head and took a step backward into the corridor.

"Very well, then," sighed Sir Philip. "Will you at least tell Jones yourself that you're too ill to be interviewed? He won't believe it from me."

Not-Anderson shook his head again and took another step backward. He felt himself breaking into a sweat. Still the trap had not closed. Perhaps the presence of Sandra and Malcolm really was deterrent enough. Perhaps he would still escape.

"You're letting the company down, Paul," said Sir Philip, getting to his feet. "Letting us all down badly." He picked up the machine—it had a handle like a suitcase, too—and started after them. Boardman edged after him, still staring at not-Anderson.

"What's that?" asked Sandra, putting herself between not-Anderson and Sir Philip. She did not understand what was happening, but she understood that Paul wanted to get away, and she meant to help him do so. Malcolm, similarly

confused but equally falling in with the change of plan,
caught not-Anderson by the elbow and guided him back
along the corridor. He appeared to need help: he had gone a
ghastly grey colour and was wavering unsteadily like a
drunk.

"This?" asked Sir Philip, hefting the machine. It was
heavy, Sandra could see: the tendons in his wrist strained
free of the skin as he lifted it. "This is a portable magnetometer. We designed it, and Alan and I were just discussing
how to improve it. Ah, I didn't introduce you. This is Alan
Boardman, our director of research. This is Ms Sandra Murray. She *saved* Paul's life." His voice went harsh on the final
phrase, charged with a savage and incomprehensible anger.
Sandra blinked, but had no time to try and understand. They
had reached the ash-coloured landing.

Malcolm shoved open the firedoor and pushed the call
button for the lift. It was still standing at their floor, and the
doors opened at once. Not-Anderson lurched desperately
into it, and his two friends followed. Sir Philip and Alan
Boardman came after them. Sir Philip set the magnetometer
down on the floor and nodded to Boardman. Boardman
crouched down beside the device and began touching its
keys and checking its display. Sir Philip had ended up next
to the lift controls, and he pushed a button. Sandra looked at
him sharply, but the button had indeed been "G." "We'll see
you out," said Sir Philip, as the doors closed. "Perhaps we
can persuade you to change your mind, Paul."

Not-Anderson was leaning against the back of the lift,
shivering. He gave Sir Philip a sick look. The lift dropped.

The doors hushed open again on the dove-grey reception
hall. Sir Philip got out, and stood aside for the others. Boardman remained crouched by the magnetometer. "I'm taking
this back to the basement," he muttered. "The rest of you go
past."

He took up half the entrance. Sandra edged round him.
Not-Anderson, desperate to be away, started after her, and

bumped into Malcolm, who was in front of him. Malcolm grinned and got out of the way, into the foyer.

Instantly, Sir Philip pressed another button on the lift controls, and Boardman sprang out of the lift as though it were on fire. Not-Anderson gave a cry of terror and started to fling himself after the others—then stopped. There was something in the way. He could not see it, but he knew it was there. He hesitated in bewilderment, and the lift doors closed. He dropped downward, and the lights went out.

He screamed in panic and lashed out at the door. His hand struck whatever it was that was in the way, and for a horrible moment he felt as though his life rattled loosely in its socket. Then there was a blinding pain in his head, and the nausea heaved his stomach up into a ball. He fell to his knees and was sick, again and again, until his stomach was empty and he was shivering with exhaustion.

He crouched doubled up on the floor, resting his head against his arm. It was completely dark and totally silent, apart from his own gasping. The hand that had struck the something was numb.

After a while, his mind began to work again. Sir Philip must have switched off the power to the lift: that was why it was dark and silent. It had stopped, probably between floors. What was happening to Sandra and Malcolm? Would Stellar harm them, dispose of them, since they had witnessed this . . . would it be called a kidnapping? Surely that would be too risky even for Stellar—surely, it wouldn't dare? Sandra had friends, a place of work where she was expected; Malcolm had family. They must both have told people that they were coming here. They could not simply be made to disappear. Sir Philip was an intelligent man: he must have seen that. Oh please, let him have seen that, please!

Sandra, with the light refracted in her hair. Sandra hurt, crying; blood on the green dress, on the fair freckled skin of her shoulders . . .

Sir Philip was an intelligent man. He would not have done that.

What about Rodney Jones? He had to be at Stellar. He had been invited, and he must have come. His car was there. If Sir Philip knew nothing of the alliance between them, he would not have expected not-Anderson to have recognised the car, and would have had no reason to plant it. If.

Assume the contrary, that he had somehow found out about the alliance. Why, then, would he have invited Jones to Stellar? It was calculated to alert Jones instantly when not-Anderson failed to show up for the interview. No, it was more probable he did not know.

Unless he'd decided to destroy Jones as well.

Not-Anderson repeated to himself desperately that Sir Philip was a rational man. He would not destroy a hostile reporter in his own office. It was too certain to be discovered. It was much more likely that he had indeed had Jones taken on a tour of the lab, and expected Jones to see "Anderson's" failure to show up at the interview as just another example of Anderson's perversity. Sir Philip had clearly not expected Malcolm and Sandra to be present at all. Most likely he still thought that such casual acquaintances could be fobbed off with an excuse, and sent home without too much trouble.

The sickness and panic began to retreat a little. The last explanation really was much more probable than that Sir Philip intended mass murder.

It must be assumed, then, that Malcolm and Sandra were safe and at liberty, that they would raise the alarm, and that Rodney Jones would help them. Not-Anderson *would* assume that. He would assume that, somewhere above, Sandra was even now arguing with Sir Philip, her Scots accent growing more emphatic with fury and her cheeks burning with colour. Or else she had already gone storming out of the building with Malcolm, stalking out to the car with her eyes bright with tears, slamming the door of her red Sierra and driving off to summon help. He would believe that she was alive. If she were dead because of him, he was not sure he wanted to stay alive himself.

He picked his head up and sat back on his knees. His numbed hand had started to tingle.

What was the thing that was across the lift door?

His tormented stomach gave another lurch, and the headache stabbed again, like white spikes driven upwards behind his eyes. He knew what the thing was, but he dared not even *try* to remember. Work around it, skirting the edge of memory.

The thing that was across the lift door was behind him as well, and to each side of him, and above and below. It was an enclosing bubble in the metal of the lift under carpet and panelling. He could feel it vibrating there, centimetres below his feet. But in front of him it was not inside the metal. It had been fixed instead in the air. It felt different there: it fluctuated back and forth unsteadily, only holding its place because the field would not admit a gap any more than a soap bubble would admit a hole. The rest of the barrier was inside an electrically conductive material, and it was better that way. Why then had the barrier been forced to form in the air, rather than in the lift doors? So that the device which Boardman had placed by the lift doors would be outside it, and unreachable. Otherwise, not-Anderson would only need to switch it off to . . . How did one get out of a lift when the power failed?

One step at a time. He could think about how to get out of the lift if he succeeded in switching off the device. He could not reach through the barrier to touch the device. Could he bring the device inside the barrier, without touching it?

He forced himself to his feet. The pain in his head stabbed again when he moved, and his stomach gave another heave. He forced himself to stand still until it had subsided. Then, moving stiffly, he took off his jacket. Between the pain and the way his usual clumsiness with buttons was doubled by the dark, it was difficult, but he managed in the end. Holding the jacket by the collar, he swung it tentatively out towards the barrier, bracing himself against another shock of pain.

Nothing. He was as aware of the barrier's position as though it were a solid wall and brightly lit, and he was certain that the jacket must have touched it, but there was no jolt—not even a spark of static. He swung the jacket again, harder this time. The buttons clicked against the door of the lift, on the other side of the barrier. Very good!

The darkness and the pain had disoriented him. He was aware of the lift's shape only because of the barrier. The position of the device he did not know. He moved carefully to the nearest side wall and swung the jacket down, *shush-click* against the wall, then swish along the floor. Nothing there. He moved one step sideways and tried again.

On the fourth step sideways, one side of the jacket caught against a hard obstruction half a metre from the floor. His heart gave a lurch of triumph that sent another stab of pain into his skull. He stopped a minute, recovering, then moved one more step sideways, and swung the jacket down hard.

He felt it catch; felt the device rock. He swung again, harder, and the device toppled towards him. But the barrier came with it. It struck his hand, outstretched on the jacket. Life gave another agonising wobble, and then the pain impaled him so that his legs gave way and he folded to the floor. It was worse this time. He passed out; woke to find himself lying in the dark in a stinking puddle of his own vomit. The pain faded a little, then surged back; faded and surged back. He stayed motionless, clutching his numb hand. In a little while, he thought wearily, I will sit up and check if the device is now inside the barrier. From the way the barrier had moved, he did not expect it to be.

He was still thinking of sitting up when the lights came on and the lift sank downwards a little. The sudden brightness hurt his eyes and sent splinters of pain into his head. He rolled laboriously on to his knees and put his good hand over his face. The doors hushed open. He blinked through his fingers into the dazzle beyond; human shapes loomed darkly over him, but they were blurred, and he could not distinguish them.

Someone dropped towards him, then pulled away again dragging something. He felt the barrier move outwards again: someone was examining the device.

"It's got another ten minutes secure," said a vaguely familiar voice—Boardman, not-Anderson thought. "It's probably good for a while after that, but I can't be certain."

"Thank God for that!" Sir Philip's voice replied. "I was terrified it was going to fail before we could get rid of those people. *Damn* that reporter! We've got to move him."

"He looks like he's had another fit or something," another, unknown voice said hesitantly. "He's been sick."

"The illness was perfectly genuine," Sir Philip answered. "But I very much doubt that he feels real pain from it."

Not-Anderson said nothing. Best not to speak until he had to, and only after learning as much as he could about what his captors knew and what they intended. He slitted his eyes behind his fingers and was able to make out the numbers and features of the men facing him. Sir Philip Lloyd. Alan Boardman. Another man, unknown or unremembered, in a white coat. Sir Philip was holding a small black gun— holding it with a rather self-conscious, embarrassed air, but pointing it unwaveringly at not-Anderson. All three stood on a floor of polished tile, with a screen of the inevitable silvered glass behind them. The three backs were reflected in the glass, two in suits, one in a white coat. Not-Anderson's own reflection was mercifully concealed by the three pairs of legs. With an effort, he turned his head, and read the lift display. The button was lit for "B." Basement, singular: only one level below ground.

"He couldn't have got out anyway while the lift was stopped, could he?" White-coat asked Sir Philip, with an air of deference.

Sir Philip gave not-Anderson a glance of loathing. "I wouldn't bet on that."

Boardman was still examining the device. It might fail in

ten minutes, not-Anderson thought wearily, watching him, noting what keys he touched. Or it might last longer. Why would it fail?

Because some of the components were superconducting, and needed to be super-cooled to function. The device was inside a case of some coolant, probably liquid nitrogen. But it was small, with no refrigeration unit of its own. The liquid nitrogen would gradually boil off into a gas, the components would heat up to the point where they lost their superconductivity, and the device would fail. Not-Anderson could then spring out of the lift, snatch the gun from Sir Philip, and use it to force his way out of the building. Provided, of course, that he could stand up.

The precautions seemed entirely excessive for one sick and unarmed man.

There was a rattle, and then a door slitted open in the silvered glass. White-coat hurried to open it fully, then flung open its matching double. An immense box almost as high as a man juddered through. It was made of wire mesh, stretched over a frame of wooden posts strengthened with iron connecting rods; it had been balanced on two flat trolleys tied together. Another white-coated man, this one vaguely familiar, appeared behind it, pushing. Attached to the back was a block about the size of Anderson's television set. The two white-coats manoeuvred the box up to the lift. Not-Anderson watched with dismay. He was despairingly certain that the wire mesh had been put there to make the box conductive, and that the unit on the back was another barrier device. A larger one, this time, with its own refrigeration unit. He was looking at a hastily assembled high-tech prison cell.

One of the white-coats opened the screen door of the box and carefully set it against the metal inner door of the lift, so that the two conductive panels were in contact. The other adjusted something at the generator on back of the cell, and not-Anderson felt a new barrier go up in the metal of the wire. There was a painful stuttering of static where the two

barriers touched. Why all the rigmarole? not-Anderson wondered—Sandra's word, "rigmarole": "If you're going to
murder somebody, why all the rigmarole?"—Why not just
march him out of the lift at gun-point and lock him in a cupboard? The box wasn't much bigger than one.

Boardman called a few figures out and the device on the
prison cell was adjusted. Then the device on the lift was adjusted. Not-Anderson felt the invisible wall before the door
drop as the two barriers blended into one. There was now a
long tunnel of barrier stretching from the back of the lift to
the back of the cell.

"All right," said Sir Philip. Not-Anderson could see him
through the door of the cell, a stern blond figure holding a
gun, overlain by innumerable hexagons of wire. He spoke
directly to not-Anderson for the first time since the lift doors
opened. "Get into it." He gestured at the prison.

The floor of the box was made of hardboard covered with
the same wire mesh as the rest. Not-Anderson shook his
head in horror, and shuffled backwards on his knees.

"Get in!" repeated Sir Philip. "If you don't, I'll shoot you
in the foot and drag you into it myself. I'm willing to risk it.
Whatever you did to Paul, I don't think you can do it
quickly, and my friends here are watching."

Not-Anderson stared. Sir Philip's face was set, angry,
merciless—but not deceitful. He genuinely believed that
not-Anderson had done something to Paul Anderson.

Query: *had* not-Anderson done something to Paul Anderson?

Nausea and pain. There were memories, memories he
could not touch. Hands scrabbling at a locked door, a car's
headlights shining through water, then fading away. Not-
Anderson bent his head against his knees, shaking.

"Go on!" ordered Sir Philip.

Not-Anderson picked his head up again. "The floor isn't
insulated," he said unsteadily. "If I go into it, I will be touching the . . . the diamagnetic field. It would kill me."

The nausea was rising again. He knew that the barrier

was called a diamagnetic field. He tried not to remember any more about it, and frantically began calculating the number of hexagons in the mesh before him.

Sir Philip's eyes narrowed and he frowned at not-Anderson. His gun dropped, then lifted again. He glanced at the two white-coats. "Foster, McKenzie," he ordered. "Go fetch some insulators—cardboard, paper, carpet, whatever you can find quickly. Hurry!"

The two white-coats hurried off. Sir Philip glanced moodily at not-Anderson, then kicked the cell away from the lift. The tunnel split in half; again the invisible wall ran before the door. Sir Philip laid his hand against the cell and gave it an additional shove, getting the doorway clear for the insertion of insulators. Not-Anderson caught his breath with astonishment. He was quite certain that if *he* had touched that charged metal with his bare hand, he would have folded up on the floor. He was afraid to touch it even with his shoes, with his vomit-dampened and conductive clothing.

Sir Philip heard the gasp. He looked back at not-Anderson, and for a moment their eyes met and held. "What surprised you?" he demanded.

"I touched the diamagnetic field before," said not-Anderson. "That was why I was sick. I didn't have another seizure."

Sir Philip frowned. He came forward, then slowly crouched down until he was facing not-Anderson across the slotted opening of the lift. He put his hand out, directly into the invisible barrier. A red line like a bruise encircled his fingers where the field crossed them, but he did not flinch.

Don't think, not-Anderson told himself, don't think . . . Or think of Sandra. He remembered how she had kissed him; how his lips had tingled like his now-awakening hand.

"You were sick when you did that?" asked Sir Philip. He took his hand out of the field; the red line began to fade.

Not-Anderson said nothing. He knew that he was sweating, that his face showed all the strain of his effort not to think about what he had just seen.

"Why would it make him sick?" asked Boardman, coming over.

Sir Philip shook his head. "This isn't something I know about," he said. He leaned closer, eyes devouring and implacable. "Why did it make you sick?" he demanded.

Not-Anderson again shuffled uncomfortably backwards. "Why should you expect me to know?"

Sir Philip frowned. He seemed about to ask another question, but the two white-coats, Foster and McKenzie, came running back through the silvered doors with an immense cardboard box full of something white.

"From the shredder," panted Foster, picking up a handful of fragmented paper and letting it drop back through his fingers. He was quite a young man, tall, brown-haired, bearded. Not-Anderson knew he was Foster, because the slightly older, shorter, smooth-shaven one was McKenzie. Andrew McKenzie, divisional head of Electrical Storage Systems, Stellar Research. He remembered that.

"It will do," said Sir Philip. He began bundling the box through the narrow door of the cell. It was almost too wide to fit: it tore, and dropped fragments of shredded paper over the polished tiles. The white-coats helped him force it through. When the box was inside, Sir Philip ripped its sides open, flattened it, and scattered its contents in white drifts over the interior. Then he leapt out, shoved the cell back to the lift, and clanged the door back against the lift's metal frame. There was a *flick* of something, and the tunnel was back again.

"It's insulated," Sir Philip stated. "Get in or I shoot you and drag you in."

Not-Anderson drew himself unsteadily to his feet and swayed there. He looked down the tunnel into the cell, now floored with shredded paper. The image of himself being wheeled off inside was crushingly humiliating for him. Perhaps that was the point.

"You are being ridiculous," he told Sir Philip.

"*You* are trying to delay," replied Sir Philip. "If you're not in by the count of five, I'll shoot. One . . ."

Not-Anderson staggered forward. At the entrance he paused, baffled: he was afraid to touch either the metal inner door of the lift or the doorframe of the cell, but the door itself was low, and he needed to duck to get under it. He would have to duck and hop at the same time. He was terrified that he would stumble, and fall against the barrier. "Two . . . three . . ." said Sir Philip, and not-Anderson bowed his head and jumped blunderingly in, shoulders hunched and arms pressed against his sides so that they would not inadvertently brush the uninsulated sides of the cell. The roof was too low to let him stand up straight. Sir Philip slammed the door shut behind him; the tunnel broke again into two bubbles. Sir Philip slipped a padlock through the bolt that secured the door. He locked it and put the key in his pocket.

Boardman did something to the other device, and the field around the lift snapped and dissipated. "Seven minutes into extra time," he told Sir Philip. His voice shook a little. "Probably it was good for another twenty, but still . . ."

"Too close for comfort," agreed Sir Philip seriously.

Foster and McKenzie were grinning in triumph and relief.

Even through everything else, not-Anderson felt indignant. What right had they to act as though *he* had been threatening *them*? "You are being ridiculous," he repeated, more loudly this time. "What did you think I was going to do? Strangle you all, with these hands?" He held them up, trembling and scabbed and splinted.

Sir Philip came up to the cell and peered into it. "What did you do to Paul Anderson?" he asked in a low, fierce whisper.

They were all watching him again, fascinated, speculative, horrified. Not-Anderson shut his eyes, fighting the nausea, the terror, and particularly the question "What *did* I do to Paul Anderson?"

"Is he still . . . alive somewhere?" asked Sir Philip. "Or did you kill him?"

Not-Anderson opened his eyes again and shook his head. "You assume that I have been lying about my amnesia," he replied, in a voice equally low, but shaking. "I have not been. I do not remember. I was told that I was Paul Anderson. Now you imply that I murdered him. I have no way of knowing the truth."

"You are not Paul," Sir Philip said harshly. "We know that."

"Then you know more than I do," not-Anderson stated. "I do not *know* what happened to Paul Anderson. I do not know who I am. If you know, tell me."

They all continued to stare at him, assessingly now.

"It all fits," Sir Philip concluded at last. "He's telling the truth."

McKenzie made a noise of protest, and Sir Philip turned on him. "I told you I thought it must be true before, and now I'm certain of it. A week ago we all thought he was Paul, and he could have got any information he wanted just by walking into the lab. He could have set off every alarm in the building, and we wouldn't have twigged. He could have got stuck in one of the traps, and we would have switched it off and told him to stop fooling with our equipment. But he didn't come. I even encouraged him to come, as soon as he was up to it—and he acted like I was offering him poison. That Friday when I talked to him at Paul's house, he had no idea what was going on. He even asked me what Astragen is. On Monday he didn't know why the EEG test mattered. But today proves it conclusively. He knew I suspected, but he still came here."

"You made him think you didn't know," objected Boardman.

"Well, we weren't sure, were we? But he thought we couldn't find out." He turned back to not-Anderson, eyes narrowed. "What went wrong?" he asked. "Did the car crash upset your plans? Did Paul put up more of a fight than you

expected, and break something? Or did you just get tangled
in the strings when you tried to move the puppet?"

The words "I don't know" shrivelled in the back of not-
Anderson's throat, and choked anything he might have said.

Sir Philip let his fingers walk from hexagon to hexagon
down the side of the cell. "You don't know, do you? You
don't know who you are. You thought yourself so superior,
so wise, so much above us; you knew everything there was
to know—and now you don't know who you are. How are
the mighty fallen!" He smiled, but there was another look
entirely in his eyes.

Boardman coughed. "Phil," he said, "we've got to get
him out of sight before anyone comes."

Sir Philip nodded. He glanced round, noticed not-Anderson's jacket lying in a corner of the lift. He picked it up: one
sleeve was grey with vomit. He tossed it on top of the cell
with a disgusted wrinkle of the nose, then went to the still-
open reflective doors and stood with his hand on one, smiling. The others put their shoulders to the wire mesh and
started pushing.

Not-Anderson staggered as the cell juddered about, and
sat down hastily on the flattened cardboard box. The thought
of falling against the diamagnetic field terrified him, and he
did not entirely trust the shredded paper to insulate the floor.
He was painfully aware of the invisible enclosure all around
him. It was a kind of aching blur, just at the back of sense:
he could feel even the place on the roof where the dampness
of his jacket formed a conductive strip outside the cell and
made a small bulge in the field. The prospect of touching
any part of it made his stomach knot with dread. But it didn't
seem to bother the men who were pushing the mobile
prison. It was true that, unlike Sir Philip, they seemed reluctant to touch it without a layer of insulation—Foster and
McKenzie had both pulled the sleeves of their white coats
over their hands—but it was obviously not painful for them.

He could not think about that. He dared not. He was remembering too much, too fast, and his body was tormented

with it. He felt that soon he would remember his name, and he didn't think he could endure it in his present state. There was an unbalanced feeling in the centre of his mind, like the charge in a thundercloud before the formation of the lightning. Do not let me go insane! he thought, not sure who he was pleading with. Not that, please! Quick death, or another fit, if it has to be, but oh, sweet reason, let me not be corrupted away!

Behind the silvered doors, Stellar's basement was obviously used principally for storage. It was hived off into sections by partial walls, but there were no narrow corridors and no proper rooms, and the cell rumbled freely over a floor of smooth beige linoleum. Labelled supply cupboards flanked the building's outer wall; a refrigeration unit hummed by a white-lagged, ceiling-high tank of liquid nitrogen; screens and tubes and bits of equipment were stacked against dividers. An incinerator squatted by a chemical disposal unit. The paper-shredder was there, surrounded by tiny heaps and scuffs of white, where Foster and McKenzie must have spilled some of its waste as they hastily filled their box of insulators. There were no people about. Not-Anderson checked the watch on his wrist: to his surprise it was still working, and said 6:34. The working day had ended, and most of Stellar's minions were gone. Sir Philip did not want anyone to see what he did with his prisoner. Yet the kidnapping had taken place in the foyer. That was not significant: it had been a matter of seconds, and no one had seen except Sandra, Malcolm and possibly the receptionist. That receptionist would obviously not help him. What had become of Sandra and Malcolm?

Sir Philip was an intelligent man. He would have found some excuse to send them off. He would not have hurt them. *Let them be safe, only let them be safe* . . . It was improbable that he had hurt them.

The cell juddered round a corner, and rolled towards another set of doors, the first he'd seen in Stellar that were not made of glass. They were made of something far more substantial, black-painted and labelled "AUTHORISED PERSONNEL ONLY." Sir Philip hurried ahead and put a card in a slit beside them. A panel lit; he keyed in a code—not-Anderson strained to see what it was, and failed. The doors buzzed, and were pushed open. Not-Anderson closed his eyes and filled his mind with the equations which define the speed of light as the cell lumbered through.

NINE

HE FELT THE SECOND PRISON CELL BEFORE HE SENSED
anything else in the room beyond. There was another aching
blur at a moderate distance, and inside it was . . . someone
else. He gave a yelp of surprise, and his eyes flew open:
across a room stood another wire mesh box, this one no bigger than the generating device beside it. It was completely
surrounded by a tangle of scanners and consoles. He leapt to
his feet, forced into movement by horror—then stood
frozen, too horrified to move.

"Oh yes," said Sir Philip. His voice glowed with mock-
casual malice: he had been waiting for this. "We caught *that*
three weeks ago. I thought for a while it was you, but then
I . . ."

Not-Anderson did not hear the rest. The other prisoner
became aware of him and spoke, and his understanding of
English shut off like a door closing. The other's speech was
not a matter of sounds; it used no centres in the brain and
formed no syllables upon the tongue. It had more in common with mathematics than with any earthly language, and
no human translation of it could ever be better than a paraphrase. Concepts formed in an infinitely complex web of

symbols emerged in a pattern of electromagnetic variations, were perceived, and instantly comprehended.

Wavevector, came the wordless communication, *what have you done?*

Consciousness splintered explosively. He did not hear his own shriek of anguish, or feel himself falling. There was only pain. He struggled to get away from it, but he was trapped, hopelessly entangled in a whirling mass that clung to him with a thousand sticky tentacles, pulling him down and down into the pain . . . and then, out of what seemed a horror worse than anything he could imagine, a worse horror came: the trap itself was struck and pounded, and he felt himself shaken into the void. He began to scream, frantically and without sound.

Wavevector! someone was saying to him, urgently. *You are unreasoning. Become coherent.*

I can't! he screamed. *I am in pain!*

But the act of screaming forced him into the coherence he'd thought impossible. *Pain.* A technical term for the suffering of animals with a developed nervous system. He felt what he should not feel. Where was its origin?

You are inflicting the pain, said the other. *You are producing a higher electrical voltage than the brain of the entity you are entangled with can tolerate. Modulate or you will kill it.*

I can't, I can't, I can't think! He was being torn in two and the pieces pulverised, and his mind would not function properly: all his thoughts seemed to end in explosions of pain.

Listen to me! Oscillate in nanosecond cycles.

He modulated as he was told. One form of pain stopped abruptly, leaving him aware that there had been two. The other pain continued to tear through him in waves—waves that had direction, that ripped from one side to the other, but pounded him so hard that he could not track them. He knew he would soon disintegrate entirely.

You are in contact with the diamagnetic field, the other told him. *Withdraw from it.*

He became aware of the barrier again, and recognised that the waves of agony came from his contact with it. Contact where? Right arm. Move it. Can't. Must. No, it won't, it's gone dead, I've lost it . . .

Gravitational Constant, he pleaded, calling the other by name before he even remembered that he knew him, *I can't withdraw! Help me!*

I cannot help, said Gravitational Constant. *I am a prisoner myself. Remain coherent! The biological entities appear to be trying to help you.*

He could not sense them or anything but the pain. Gravitational Constant was evidently aware of this, because he began to project steadily the equations describing the theory of unified fields. The flow of pure concept through his mind kept him from lapsing completely into unreason, but he could not retain one term to connect with its successor. The pain forced him down towards a place where coherent thought became impossible, and identity would dissolve forever away.

Then, abruptly, the waves stopped pounding. Their aftereffects throbbed desperately, surge and ebb, surge and ebb, but the torture's source was gone. He became aware that he was lying face-down on the floor of the cell, and that Sir Philip was kneeling over him. His right arm was back by his side. He knew that he had had another seizure and had fallen against the barrier, and he was aware that he had stopped breathing. It troubled him that despite this he was conscious and able to see Sir Philip—and then he realised that he could not *see* Sir Philip, only scan him electromagnetically: that he was using his own perceptions, not Anderson's.

Are you still rational? asked Gravitational Constant, in a tone of deep concern.

Yes, he replied.

He was not sure how true that was. His consciousness hung straddled between the part of himself that had been using Anderson's brain and the previously inaccessible continent of his memories. The two parts had completely dif-

ferent methods of thought, and his self zig-zagged dizzy-
ingly between them. The knowledge that he was not human,
taken for granted by the original half-self, staggered the
newcomer. He fought blindly through a churning mass of incompatible perceptions, struggling for coherence. He was
still alive and self-aware, so he must conclude himself rational. He knew that his name was Wavevector . . .

The part of him that had been human suddenly grasped
the name, which was not a sound but a concept. It latched on
to the concept, to a thousand other concepts from mathematics and physics. His two halves meshed in a seam of ab-
stractions, and the churning began to subside.

He knew that his name was Wavevector; that his natural
form was a complex interweaving of energies; and that what
had just happened had almost killed him. No, was still
killing him! He was deeply entangled in Anderson's body,
and that body was still not breathing. He was not sure what
would happen to him if it died.

Sir Philip had been joined in the cell by Boardman and
McKenzie. Foster stood agitatedly in the door: there was no
room for him inside. The others turned Anderson's body
over and examined it, but they did not seem to know what to
do. They were emitting sounds—talking—but he'd always
found it difficult to perceive enough variation in the sounds
to understand what they were saying, and now he could not
concentrate. His human powers of hearing seemed to have
deserted him, but he felt, as though from a distance, their
hands buffeting him. His mouth was full of shredded paper:
that sensation was for some reason close and immediate. His
saliva had turned the outside of the mouthful into a gluey
pulp, and it pressed against the back of his throat, choking
him. The sensation of suffocation was less urgent than the
horrible texture of the paper against his tongue.

My body has ceased to respirate, he told Gravitational
Constant. *Please, advise me!*

Is respiratory failure fatal to entities of this type? asked
the other.

Wavevector remembered that Gravitational Constant had never had the slightest interest in biological intelligences. He had just time to wonder what Gravitational Constant had been doing to get himself caught by Stellar, before the physical awareness that he himself was dying of suffocation became so overwhelming that he had no attention left for anything else. His chest hurt. He tried to cough the paper out, and couldn't. He tried to raise his hands and dig the paper out, but his arms were numb, and would not obey.

Can you separate yourself from that biological entity? Gravitational Constant asked, doing his best to help.

Wavevector urgently explored the tangle of Anderson's nerves and his own electrical links to them. A thousand thousand twisting junctures bewildered him at every turn. Now, he remembered how he had forged those links and found them multiplying, as though each were a glue-covered string being pulled whirling down by a spindle, adhering as it spun to itself and everything it touched. *I don't think I can*, he said despairingly. *Certainly not in the time available to me before this body dies.*

But Sir Philip had finally opened the mouth of the body before him and seen the paper. He began digging it out in slimy lumps. Without any guiding volition, the body drew a deep breath of mixed air and paper, coughed agonisingly, then breathed again. Air. The universe wobbled back into place over the void of death. Wavevector felt, for the first time, a stab of affection for his body. It fought for its life so bravely, so tenaciously! And it had been healing itself so cunningly—he was aware now of the way the cracked ribs were gluing their own ends together and solidifying into bone; the bruises breaking down and being absorbed away by the blood; the stitched tongue seamlessly renewing itself. He had tormented it, he saw that now: the nausea, the headaches, the seizures—they had all been caused by his own burning presence in a structure that was never meant to hold him. But it had adapted itself, and allowed him to live.

I am respirating again, he told Gravitational Constant
joyfully.

For a moment there was no response, and Wavevector
understood why. *I am respirating*, he'd said. His kind did
not respirate any more than they felt physical pain. His
pleasure in his body gave way abruptly to a realisation of his
own degradation. He had reduced himself to a filthy lump of
flesh which lay on a heap of shredded paper and gasped for
air. As his human senses reconnected themselves to his consciousness, he was growing more aware of its condition. His
right side was numb and his left side hurt. During the fit he
had once again emptied his bowels and bladder, and there
was vomit over his shirt and in his hair. He had joined himself to this pain-ridden heap of organic matter; he had even
believed that he, Wavevector, was one of these short-lived,
violent, irrational human beings.

And yet, it *was* brave, this network of nerves and blood
and muscle, this heart which, for all its sufferings, would not
stop beating. He clung to it, confused by pride and shame together. The superiority of energy-based to organic intelligence had always been something he'd assumed, an axiom
which had underlain all his dealings with biological entities
in the past. For two weeks he'd been operating without it,
and he saw now that however much he wanted to, he would
never be able to assume it again.

Wavevector, what have you done? Gravitational Constant
asked at last—his first question, and most urgent one.

Wavevector could not answer. The pain of his injuries
surged and ebbed, surged and ebbed with the fragile tide of
his breath. Above him the humans spoke to one another. He
could hear their voices now with his human ears, but he was
thinking in his own language, and the sound washed over
him without meaning.

What I have done is self-evident, he said at last. *I interfered with these entities by teaching them the theory of magnetic confinement. They broke an agreement with me about
how the theory should be used, then attempted to trap me. I*

wanted to disguise myself as one of them to enforce the agreement, but manipulating a body proved more complicated than I had anticipated, and I became entangled.

What you have done is contrary to principle, stated Gravitational Constant.

There was no answer to that which was not also an admission of guilt. It was contrary to principle for his kind to interfere with biological entities. He had interfered recklessly and persistently, and ended up entangled with one.

Why did you come here? he responded finally.

To establish the extent and nature of your interference with the biological intelligences on this planet, said Gravitational Constant. Wavevector could not tell if he were sad, condemnatory, or simply bewildered. *There was discussion of you at a Gathering, and concern—*

He stopped abruptly: one of the humans had left Wavevector and was marching purposefully towards him. Wavevector opened his eyes: the light lanced into them painfully. He closed them again, and relied on scanning instead. Humans looked completely different electromagnetically, but he had seen most of them before, and recognised them. The one who was walking towards Gravitational Constant was Boardman; Sir Philip was still in the cell with Wavevector. McKenzie had left the room, and Foster was still standing agitatedly by the door.

What is happening? asked Gravitational Constant, with a touch of anxiety.

I do not know. I will listen to what they say. He struggled to make the mental adjustment to human speech.

Boardman touched one of the consoles around Gravitational Constant's cell, and appeared to read something off a screen. "It's been emitting bursts all over the spectrum," he called to Sir Philip. "Radio, infrared, microwaves, X-rays. It's all such low intensity, though, that I wouldn't have thought it could hurt anything."

"It obviously *did* hurt something," Sir Philip replied irritably. "Unless you can think of another reason why he folded up like that. Is it still emitting?"

Boardman shook his head. "It seems to have stopped now."

Gravitational Constant, have they been observing your emissions? Wavevector asked.

They have been observing me by various means since they entrapped me.

"Phil, it's started again!" shouted Boardman. "Radio and X-rays, varying frequencies—it's stopped."

They are aware of it when you speak, said Wavevector. *They theorise that this caused my lapse into unreason.*

"I think we'd better take him out, quick," said Philip. He sounded angry. "We can't risk losing him."

It is expedient that you understand them, said Gravitational Constant. *They have attempted to communicate with me, but I have so far failed to comprehend their system of semiotics. Why have they imprisoned us?*

"That was another burst!" yelled Boardman.

Sir Philip swore. "Foster!" he shouted. "Open the security doors. We'll take him out into the corridor." He jumped out of the cell.

Gravitational Constant, they are about to move me, Wavevector said urgently. *They do it to prevent damage to me. I . . .*

"Phil, I'm getting an echo," said Boardman.

If they are concerned for our safety, can you induce them to release us? Gravitational Constant asked eagerly. *They are rational beings, and their technology is more developed than I had expected. Can't you reason with them?*

"An echo?" repeated Sir Philip; and "There's another burst!" said Boardman, simultaneously.

They conjecture that they can benefit greatly from our superior knowledge, said Wavevector quickly. *They also fear us. I attach . . .*

"There's the echo."

. . . a very low probability to the chance that they will

*release us voluntarily. I will do what I can. I deeply re-
gret . . .*

"Where's it coming from?"

*. . . that you have been involved in the results of my
violation of principle. I will attempt to escape by any prin-
cipled means: if I succeed, I will release you.*

"Over by you."

"My God," said Sir Philip. "They're *talking*." There was
a moment's pause, and then Sir Philip shoved the mobile
cell violently towards the now-open security doors.

*What probability do you attach to your chance of es-
cape?* asked Gravitational Constant, as the cell rolled
through.

*I do not have enough information to do the calculation. I
will do what I can.*

The doors closed. Sir Philip stopped pushing the cell: he
was evidently confident that the walls of "AUTHORISED PER-
SONNEL ONLY" would block electromagnetic emissions. He
was right, too: Wavevector's anxious backward scan discovered only that the doors were steel under the black paint, and
the walls ferro-concrete. It ought to be possible to communicate through them by boosting the frequency of emissions—gamma rays would penetrate anything—but one
would need energy to do that. The most natural source of energy was the Earth's magnetic field, and that was unreachable through the diamagnetic barrier. Wavevector had a brief
glimpse of the room as Foster came out after them, but
Gravitational Constant might be screaming for help, and
Wavevector would not know.

Sir Philip stalked round to the door of the cell, jumped in,
and strode over. Wavevector made no attempt to move. Now
that he was out of Gravitational Constant's presence, the
physical exhaustion of his human half was sliding down like
an avalanche to overwhelm him. His right side was still
numb, the rest of him hurt, and he didn't think he could
speak, let alone stand. He lay on his back in the shredded
paper with his eyes closed. He thought that Sir Philip was

glaring, but he couldn't judge by scanning. Strange, how much he had understood from human faces, when he had had no experience with them. That understanding must have come from his body. It had done much, much more for him than he had realised.

"What were you saying to the other one?" demanded Sir Philip.

Wavevector did not respond. It took too much effort. Communicating in English would be very much harder than using his own language, and all he wanted was to go to sleep, to allow his battered mind to recompose itself and his abused body to heal.

"Don't try to pretend you're unconscious. You were talking to the other one. What did you say?"

McKenzie came up carrying a box of something. "What are you doing out here?" he asked.

"We had to get him away from the other one," said Foster. "It was emitting bursts of radiation. Sir Philip thinks they were talking."

"I thought you said the other one was just an artificial decoy," McKenzie said to Sir Philip, coming closer and peering into the cell.

"That's what I thought!" snarled Sir Philip. "It never responded to *us*." He crouched beside Wavevector and shook him violently. "Who's the other one?" he demanded. "How many more of you are there?"

"Phil, stop!" said McKenzie. "He's not conscious."

"Yes he is," said Sir Philip sharply. "Alan was getting an echo from him on the detector. He was talking to the other one." He grabbed Wavevector's limp right arm and held it out towards the wire mesh side of the cell. "Answer me, or I'll make you touch the diamagnetic field."

The touch of that field had almost destroyed him only minutes before: the thought of another brush with it now was unendurable. Wavevector gave an involuntary whimper of terror and opened his eyes. Sir Philip's face hung immediately above him, glaring down. The hatred on it was unexpectedly frightening. His arm was so numb that he could not feel Sir Philip's hand on it, but he could sense its proximity to the diamagnetic field clearly. "No!" he begged, in a slurred whisper. "Please!"

"You see?" said Sir Philip triumphantly, to McKenzie; then, to Wavevector, "Answer my question. Who's the other one?"

Wavevector stumbled in a haze of concepts which his exhausted mind refused to translate. His eyes started to sting. "Please!" he repeated. "I'm tired. I can't."

"You could talk to it, you can talk to me," insisted Sir Philip. "I'm going to count to five. One, two, three, four . . ."

"Gravitational Constant," said Wavevector. The name came out in a slurred mumble.

"What?"

"Gravitational Constant. His name."

"What sort of name is that?"

"Horse-lover," retorted Wavevector indistinctly. He looked at his arm, with Sir Philip's neat, clip-nailed hand gripping it around the stained bandage. He tried to move it away from the wire mesh. The fingers twitched a little.

"What did he say?" asked McKenzie.

"'Horse-lover'" replied Sir Philip with disgust. "It's what 'Philip' means. In Greek. The intended point being that Gravitational Constant is as good a name as Philip. I didn't know you knew Greek." The last was said in a tone of savage mockery.

"Etymologies . . ." slurred Wavevector. Sir Philip's visual image blurred: his eyes would not focus properly, and he thought he would faint.

Sir Philip shook his arm and slapped him across the face. "So, who is Gravitational Constant? You told me before that you were the only one of your kind on Earth."

He'd forgotten that he'd told Sir Philip that. "Was true," he mumbled.

"So, you remember that now! What is this other one doing here?"

Wavevector discovered that he was crying. His mind churned with concepts he could not translate—*gathering*, and *principle* and *interference*. He tried again to move his arm. Sir Philip jerked it back towards the charged mesh. "No!" gasped Wavevector. "He came on my account. I didn't know. Please, no!"

"Phil . . ." said McKenzie unhappily.

"What?"

McKenzie hefted the box he was carrying. "This is the first aid kit," he said. "I went to fetch it because we were afraid he was dying. I come back to find you torturing him."

"We need to know!" Sir Philip shouted furiously. "There may be an army of these creatures on Earth. They may have taken over dozens of people. We've got to know!"

The idea of an army of his own kind taking over humans was so ludicrous that Wavevector made a choking sound. "What?" demanded Sir Philip, whipping back towards him.

"Army of amnesiac cripples!" said Wavevector with deep contempt.

Sir Philip darted the hand towards the mesh. Wavevector screamed. He succeeded in bending his fingers so that they missed the wire, and Sir Philip held them, trembling, centimetres from the field.

"Phil!" protested McKenzie. "What if it kills him?"

"It won't kill *him*, and if Paul's body dies, it's probably a good thing," Sir Philip said fiercely. *"Requiescat in pace!"*

"Oh, fine!" shouted McKenzie, losing his temper. "What if Paul's still *in* the body somewhere? And how do you *know* it won't kill him?"

Sir Philip let go of Wavevector's wrist. Wavevector, sobbing with effort, reached over with his left hand, grasped his own right forearm, and drew it to safety.

Boardman came out through the security doors. "The other one's gone completely torpid again," he told Sir Philip. "You really think it's not just a decoy?"

"Its name is Gravitational Constant, and it was looking for our friend here," said Sir Philip. He got to his feet. "Our friend says he didn't know it was here, and that there aren't any others."

He sounded as though he did not believe it. His attitude struck Wavevector as profoundly irrational. If he would not believe the answers he received, why ask the questions?

McKenzie climbed into the cell. He knelt down beside Wavevector and opened the first aid box.

"You can forget that," said Sir Philip. "The emergency's over. We just need to work out where to put him."

"Phil, look at him!" said McKenzie in exasperation. "He's more than half dead and he stinks. Paul Anderson may still be in there somewhere. We've got to get him proper attention."

Sir Philip glared at Wavevector again. The hatred in his face was even more frightening now that Wavevector had some idea what it could lead to. The scene which had just passed echoed through his mind, Sir Philip's voice hammering at his own: "Answer my question . . . I'm tired, I can't . . . I'm going to count to five . . . No, please no!" He suddenly felt that he stood at the beginning of a long corridor of impenetrable metal, and that if he could not turn aside from it now he was doomed to walk down it over many years, until his sanity was broken, always with that voice beside him: "Go on, answer me, I'm going to count to five . . ." There would be diamagnetic fields, and then refinements on them, and Sir Philip would doubtless discover other instruments to humiliate and control. He was highly intelligent and inventive and he understood things very quickly. And he hated Wavevector. That was terrifying and bewildering. Wavevector had once expected Sir Philip to like him. He had given the man a beautiful and versatile theory, and Sir Philip had thanked him and expressed admiration for Wavevector's altruism. Yet the hatred was unmistakable: Sir Philip had been so eager to inflict pain that he had almost risked killing his prisoner.

Wavevector closed his eyes to blot it all out. He laboriously drew his right arm further away from the diamagnetic field, and lay with it across his chest, clutched tightly in his left. It was beginning to tingle.

"Is Paul Anderson still alive?" Sir Philip's voice demanded above him.

When there was no answer, McKenzie bent over Wavevector. "What would happen if Anderson's body died now?" he whispered.

Wavevector's eyes opened and focused slowly on the other man. He had met McKenzie before he acquired a human body, but did not know him well. He hadn't known any humans well, then—he hadn't been interested in them as individuals—but he'd known Sir Philip better than the others. McKenzie's smooth face was anxious and reasonable; his slight accent recalled Sandra's. "I don't know," he answered honestly.

"Would you die?"

"I don't know. Nobody ever . . . did this before. Please let me rest."

"Do you need a doctor?"

Wavevector closed his eyes and did not answer. The others began talking again, but he was no longer listening. His right side began to ache.

He drowsed, despite the pain, but woke when Foster bent over him and began unbuttoning his shirt. He struggled feebly, and Foster leapt back as if he were likely to be electrocuted.

"I—it's just to clean you up," Foster stammered nervously. "We've got to do that." He edged gingerly back and attacked the shirt again. Wavevector could not summon the energy to struggle this time, though the humiliation of being stripped and washed off by a frightened and hostile stranger with a bucket of lukewarm water and a handful of paper towels cut deep. Foster rolled the stinking clothes into a bundle and tossed them at the door, then covered Wavevector with a blanket and moved away. Wavevector went back to sleep.

There was a clang beside his head, and he woke. He did not think much time had elapsed since Foster woke him; certainly less than an hour. Sir Philip was standing by his head, just outside the cell, with the other three around him. He struck the side of the cell again, and Wavevector opened his eyes to show that he was aware.

"What would happen if we put your friend in a lead-lined box?" asked Sir Philip, without preamble.

Wavevector stared up at the wire-mesh ceiling and forced himself to understand, to think. He could see why they were considering this. Most electromagnetic radiation would be blocked by a lead box: Gravitational Constant would be incapable of communicating through it. But being screened off from electromagnetic contact would prevent him from doing more essential things, as well. The diamagnetic field must already have prevented some of them, and Gravitational Constant had been imprisoned in that, by Sir Philip's account, for three weeks. Wavevector's eyes stung with shame. Gravitational Constant had said nothing about his own state during their brief meeting, but it was evident now that he must be suffering.

"He would die," Wavevector whispered unsteadily. Short as his rest had been, it seemed to have helped him: it was much easier to speak. "He would die within hours."

"Why?" asked Sir Philip sceptically.

"He would be unable to absorb energy."

"You absorb energy, do you?"

There was a kind of greediness in his voice at the question. Wavevector turned his head and met the devouring blue gaze. He saw again the entrance to the impenetrable tunnel, and heard the whispers of the future in his ear: "How do you absorb energy? What are the formulae? Answer me. I'm going to count to five . . ."

"No," he said, with a flash of defiant sarcasm. "We create it."

There was a silence, and then Boardman exclaimed, "That's impossible!"

"Of course it is," said Sir Philip sharply. "He was being sarcastic. He probably guessed that we already knew the thing was absorbing radiation. Be careful, or I'll take you at your word, and lock your friend in a box to create energy for itself. How much energy does it need?"

"It would depend on what he's doing," Wavevector replied, and was ashamed at the way his voice trembled. "If Gravitational Constant has been torpid, it is probably because he is already starved for energy. You have cut him off from drawing on the Earth's magnetic field, and the walls of that room screen out most radiation. If you shut him up in a box, he will die." He expected no response to what he had to say next, but he said it anyway. "Please, Gravitational Constant is nothing to do with you. He never interfered with biological entities in any way, and he would continue to . . . to"—it was so hard to find a paraphrase of what he meant that he felt himself break into a sweat; words and concepts swirled turbulently through his mind without mixing—"he would continue to keep to principle if you released him. He would not harm you. And he is no use to you. He does not speak any Earth language: you cannot communicate with him. It is irrational to keep him imprisoned. You are already starving him in solitary confinement. To continue would be morally indefensible, and would not benefit you at all. Please, let him go."

He had expected no response, and he received none, apart from a derisive snort from Boardman. They did not trust Gravitational Constant's principles. They might kill him, but they would never let him go. The same was true for Wavevector himself, only more so: fear and greed together would make it impossible to release him, and Sir Philip wanted him to crush and control.

For the first time he was struck by the full measure of his stupidity. He had taught them how to imprison him, and was confined inside his own gift. The diamagnetic field genera-

tor now bolted to his cell had undoubtedly been built to confine magnetic fields for the Astragen batteries. The field was
impenetrable to magnetism but transparent to other forms of
electromagnetic radiation, and could tie an ordinary magnetic field in a knot. Wavevector produced a powerful magnetic field of his own: it was knotted already, in a way far
more complex than Stellar's technology could achieve, but
it could not pass through the diamagnetic barrier. He pon-
dered momentarily why touching that barrier should cause
his human body such pain, then abandoned his reflections
with a guilty jerk to listen to what the humans were saying.
He must pay attention and discover a way to escape. It was
essential to escape. Never in his existence had he had reason
to desire anything as much as he now desired to be outside
this cell.

The four Stellars were talking among themselves now—
or rather, Sir Philip, Boardman, and McKenzie were talking,
and Foster was listening with a tired, unhappy expression.
When Foster's eyes met Wavevector's as they both looked
at the same speaker, Foster looked away with a shudder. But
it did not seem to bother the others that Wavevector was listening. They didn't care if he knew their plans or not: they
were confident he couldn't do anything to hinder them. He
realised that they had not asked him his name. None of the
Stellars had ever asked that, even before, when he first came
to them with his offer of knowledge. He wondered if it was
because even then they had mentally assigned him the role
he had now, of a helpless commodity that could be used to
their own advantage.

The problem they were discussing was where they
should keep their prisoners. Most of Stellar's employees
were unaware of the existence of either Wavevector or
Gravitational Constant, and Sir Philip wanted to keep things
that way. "AUTHORISED PERSONNEL ONLY," which he called
"the Defence Lab," was the only area he felt was sufficiently
secure—but he was adamant that Wavevector and Gravitational Constant must not be allowed to speak to one another,

in case, as he put it, "they cook something up behind our backs." Putting one of them in a lead box would have been acceptable, but, to Wavevector's intense relief, this option appeared to have been scratched as wantonly destructive. Gravitational Constant, like himself, seemed to be regarded as potentially valuable, to be treated with care and not to be disposed of lightly. For all that, none of the men referred to him by name: he was always "the other one," "it," and "the other creature." Wavevector himself was "him" and "the thing" and "the first one."

Boardman recommended moving one or the other prisoner to some other part of the lab, and making that part off-limits to unauthorised personnel. Sir Philip vetoed this impatiently, with the air of a man who has done so several times already: it was not secure enough. "We'll have to take him out of here," he declared. "Foster, go get a van—take the new Toyota. The keys are in the cupboard in Automotive Stores. If there's junk in it, unload it, and wait for us at the loading bay. We'll take him to my house."

"Phil, that is crazy!" said McKenzie, as Foster trotted off. "You said yourself that that reporter is going to cause trouble. What if he goes prowling about your house, and finds what's apparently your missing marketing director locked in the wine cellar?"

"If he starts prowling about my house, he's trespassing," said Sir Philip. "And I don't have a cellar."

"Andrew's got a point," said Boardman. "Even if the reporter doesn't come prowling, the thing's only got to start shouting for help to make trouble. You'll have a string of milkmen and neighbourly ladies calling the police. You *can't*."

"Well, what do you suggest?" demanded Sir Philip angrily. "You can bet that that fellow Jaeger is going to be up here first thing tomorrow morning. Give him the slightest excuse and he'll whip them both off to Aldermaston before you can say 'Eyes Only.' We've got to have them both in *our* control."

The three men began discussing among themselves techniques for keeping the MoD and the security services at arm's length. Wavevector did not know whether to be dismayed or relieved. "That fellow Jaeger" was obviously Anderson's friend Mark Jaeger, the "army spook." Wavevector had met him once, he remembered now, in the days before he entangled himself with Anderson. It was perfectly clear from what Sir Philip and his friends were saying that the security services were fully aware of Wavevector's existence, and that the kidnapping had been authorised by them. It must be classified. D-noticed. Sandra and Malcolm would be unable to raise any alarm; Jones would be no help. On the other hand, Stellar would have had no reason to harm Sandra and Malcolm, since it could safely ignore them.

McKenzie's solution, which again seemed to have been suggested several times already, was that Wavevector should be taken to The Oaks. This was the plan which was eventually accepted. Sir Philip was not happy about it— "Maureen" apparently knew nothing about Wavevector, and Sir Philip did not trust her to keep quiet if she found out. But McKenzie thought that there was an isolated cottage in the grounds of the spa, and Sir Philip at last agreed that if they put Wavevector in this and told Maureen to keep all the staff away from it, it would be secure enough for a couple of days. In the meantime they could build a leaded screen across the Defence Lab. When this was complete, Wavevector could be returned there.

Despite his resolution to pay attention, Wavevector was falling asleep again by the time this conclusion was reached. He woke with a jerk when the cell began to move. McKenzie and Boardman were pushing him across the silent basement, but Sir Philip Lloyd had gone off somewhere. It seemed darker than it had been when they first brought him to the Defence Lab, eons before. Six thirty-four that had been. He raised his left arm to look at his watch, and saw that it was missing: Foster must have taken it with his clothes. He scanned for the clothes themselves, and could not find them. They had probably gone into the incinerator.

The cell rumbled across bare linoleum, through a door guarded by an iron screen, and up a concrete ramp into a garage. A van was waiting at a loading bay under the single light, a black delivery van with the Stellar logo emblazoned in silver on its side. When the cell appeared, Foster climbed from the van and opened the doors at its back. There was a brief struggle with ramps and trolley wheels, and then the cell was heaved off its trolleys and manhandled into the van. The doors slammed shut. Wavevector lay in the darkness, naked under the blanket, and listened to the indistinct voices of his captors until the engine started and drowned them out.

TEN

SANDRA MURRAY DID NOT SLEEP THAT FRIDAY NIGHT.
When the lift dropped, taking Paul with it, she did everything she could to get it back on the spot. She raged and insisted, pleaded and argued; she ran after Sir Philip when he tried to walk away, and was floored in a short, sharp tussle with Alan Boardman. She made a scene in the foyer, screaming furious accusations to the shock and distaste of the staff who went by, and she was eventually hustled from the building by a burly security guard. None of it did any good. At first Sir Philip told her that the man in the lift was not, unfortunately, Paul Anderson, but a dangerous lunatic who'd murdered Paul Anderson, and that Stellar was holding him until the police came. When the police did arrive—in response to Sandra's own phone call from a box outside—he coolly said that Sandra was hysterical and suffering from delusions, and that Anderson had gone off to avoid her.

Luckily, Rodney Jones and Dave appeared before the police did. Afterwards it emerged that they'd arrived at Stellar some five minutes before the others, and had at once been taken on a long tour of the duller parts of the lab, only to be

told at the end of it that Mr Anderson had phoned to say he
was too ill for the interview. Rod had cursed, but believed it.
Discovering that he'd been tricked gave him a blazing passionate eloquence that had the Stellars cringing—but for all
that, he achieved no more than Sandra, and he and Dave
were eventually also forced to leave the building and stand
helplessly with Sandra and Malcolm on the pavement outside.

When two policemen did finally pull up in a squad car,
they tended to believe that Sandra was indeed a hysterical
jilted female, aided and abetted by an individual who was
young, male, black and gaudily dressed, and therefore probably a criminal, and cynically supported by a left-wing television muck-raker on the lookout for any stick to beat his
chosen dog. They were willing, however, to go through the
motions of checking the indicated lift, and they went into
the building and spoke to Sir Philip. Sir Philip told them that
the lift was broken—they could see it was broken, they
could press the call button themselves—and he shook his
head in amused disbelief at the suggestion that there was a
kidnap victim inside. He suggested that they try to get hold
of Mr Anderson at home if they really thought Sandra's
story worth checking.

By this time it was five o'clock, and Stellar's workforce
was streaming out of the building, averting its eyes from the
little group on the pavement. The police came out, told the
little group that the lift was broken, and bluntly asked Sandra if she were taking any medication. It was clear from
their sideways glance at Malcolm that they suspected him of
supplying her with what she'd been taking, and that they
didn't think it was medicine.

"The lift is not broken!" cried Sandra. "Sir Philip simply
switched off the power to it. The panel's right beside the
controls. I could switch it on again myself."

"That's as may be," said the older of the two policemen.
"How long have you known this Mr Anderson, miss?"

"Look," said Rodney Jones, "we're not going to shut up

and go away until we know for sure that our friend isn't stuck in that lift. Maybe he isn't, but if he is, and if it comes out that something was happening to *him* while you wasted time harrassing *us*, you are gonna be in deep shit. All you gotta do to guard your backs is go back in there and check the lift. You can at least see whether the fucking thing's working or not."

The police rolled their eyes in exasperation, but one of them went back into the building. The other one stayed outside, questioning Sandra. She could hear the story he was assembling in his questions: unbalanced single woman saves man's life and becomes infatuated with him; when he doesn't respond to her advances she convinces herself that it's because his colleagues are conspiring to keep him away from her. She was miserably certain that it was only the presence of Rodney Jones, and the occasional whirring of Dave's camera, which prevented them from escorting her firmly home and advising her to seek psychiatric help—and perhaps searching her and Malcolm for drugs on the way. Meanwhile, Paul was trapped in the lift. She was certain he still was in the lift. Sir Philip had torn the panel open and switched the power off immediately after the lift had dropped, and she could see through the tinted glass windows that the little lights on the lift's control panel were still not shining. They couldn't have got him out without switching on the power again, could they? And there would have been no reason for them to have switched the power off again if they had taken him out, so he *must* still be there. She hoped the fact that he'd made no sound, apart from the one muffled scream she'd heard as the lift first dropped, meant only that the thick walls and doors dampened the noise, but she was terribly afraid. Something had prevented him from following Boardman out of the lift. She had seen him rush forward, then stop short with a look of horror; and then the doors had closed. Then he had screamed. The little sequence kept replaying itself in her mind, over and over—rush, look, doors, scream; rush, look, doors, scream—until she thought she really would become hysterical, and then the police would cart her off.

However, the policeman who'd gone into the building came out unhappy. He'd gone to the lift to check the power switch, and Sir Philip Lloyd, who'd just been going off, had come back at a run, shouting for him not to touch it. The explanation given was that there'd been a short circuit, and that some of the wiring might be live. The policeman had believed this at first. But he had a do-it-yourselfer's knowledge of wiring, and he'd noticed that the panel over the supposed shorted wiring was steel, and thus as likely to be live as the wiring. He'd reproached Sir Philip for not putting up a warning sign.

Something about the wit's-end look which Sir Philip had given him in return had made the policeman feel uneasy. He asked if he could check the wiring. He was told he could not. He asked if he could look at the lift's basement landing. He was told he could not—apparently, Stellar Research had to have very strict security procedures, and unauthorised personnel were not allowed in the basement. He asked to be allowed to telephone Mr Anderson's home address, to check whether he was well: he was allowed, but there was no answer. He asked Sir Philip to wait for him by the lift, and came out to consult his colleague.

It was at this point that Rodney Jones at last jettisoned the cautious silence Paul had imposed on him. He began telling truths, and Sandra could only cheer him on. He said that he'd secretly been in close contact with "Anderson" for a week, that "Anderson" had said he was afraid of Stellar Research and asked for Jones' help, that "Anderson" had only agreed to the meeting at the lab because he'd thought Jones' presence would protect him. What was involved, said Jones, was an extremely valuable industrial secret which the company had probably acquired by illegal means.

The policemen remained deeply suspicious of the story, but they were worried by it, and when the reporter finished one of them went back into the building to insist on being allowed to see the lift, while the other radioed for advice. Sandra's heart rose with hope—for a few minutes.

Through the shaded glass she saw the older policeman stride across the dove-grey carpet; saw him talk briefly with the slight trim figure of Sir Philip, who had remained by the lift, glancing impatiently at his watch. It was almost six o'-clock now, and the foyer was otherwise empty, apart from one security guard who waited impassively by the doors to lock up after the policeman left. Sir Philip shook his head; the policeman gestured. Sir Philip shook his head again, and indicated the door. The policeman hesitated, said something else, then began walking quietly back. A cleaner appeared with a sheet of white paper scrawled over with black. She taped it over the control panel of the lift, concealing all trace of those lights whose absence formed the only indication of Paul's security.

Sandra could just make those letters out: "DANGER. LIVE WIRING. DO NOT TOUCH." The policeman gave it a nod of satisfaction and continued towards the door.

"Where are you going?" Sandra demanded frantically, as the policeman stepped out into the bright June evening.

"I'm sorry," said the policeman. He sounded it now. "He says he can't allow us to search the lab. He told me to apply for a warrant, if I thought there was evidence enough to get one, and he asked me to leave. He said he'd wasted enough time on other people's hysteria."

Behind him, the security guard was locking the door, and Sir Philip was walking hurriedly off into the depths of the black fortress.

Sandra grabbed the policeman's jacket. "You can't leave! They'll *kill* him!" she screamed. "You must be allowed to go in there to protect a man's life!"

But the police still did not believe there was a danger to anyone's life. Rodney Jones, in their opinion, was the sort of man who'd make wild allegations for the sake of it, and Sir Philip Lloyd was a leading icon of British industry. Even his last refusal was understandable: they *had* wasted a lot of his

time. They were willing, however, to go back to the police
station and apply for the search warrant, and they asked the
little group to come too, so that the police could take down
their statements about what had happened.

Sandra was unable to drive the red Sierra to the police
station. She was crying too hard. She let Malcolm take it.

Sandra made a statement. Malcolm made a statement.
Rodney Jones made a long and eloquent statement, which
included a truthful account of everything that had happened—with the one omission of his cavalier treatment of
an official secret, the Astragen theory. The police stared and
shook their heads. However, somebody phoned the hospital,
and when it was confirmed that "Mr Anderson" was amnesiac, probably epileptic, possibly brain damaged and definitely out of hospital against the wishes of his doctors,
official incredulity at last began to yield—not so much to
belief, as to concern. A man in that condition should not be
wandering about uncared for. Perhaps Stellar *did* want to
bully the poor fellow, and extract something from him
which he was too confused to deny. A more senior police officer appeared, and the statements were checked, this time
as though their content being taken seriously. But it seemed
that the local police authority could not issue a search warrant against Stellar Research. Because of the company's defence work, this had to be done by the Home Secretary
himself. The local police applied for the warrant, urgently.

There followed hours of phone calls, of sitting on hard
benches in police waiting rooms hoping for replies, of
watching the black hands of wall clocks crawl across the
featureless night. Sandra waited in helpless silence for the
most part, getting up occasionally to check with secretaries
and clerks for news. For a long time Malcolm sat opposite
her, sketching with a police pencil on a stack of borrowed
computer paper; about three a.m. he lay down under his
bench and went to sleep. Sandra went over and looked at
what he'd been drawing, and saw her own image. It was not
one of Malcolm's tricks with mirrors and peculiar angles,

but a realistic sketch: she was drawn with her head leaning against the wall, her eyes fixed dazedly on nothing, and her body folded in a long curve across the hard lines of the bench. There was a peculiar tenderness to the drawing, and a warmth that penetrated even the sick chill that had been growing in her since the lift dropped. She looked down at Malcolm where he lay with his head pillowed on his arm. His face, unguarded in sleep, had a look of grief and pity. The harsh light flattened the wide planes of his cheekbones and filled his mouth with shadow. She was suddenly intensely glad that he was there.

She flipped a page back in the stack of paper, and found herself again, only recognisable this time by the long thin legs and cloud of hair, dwindling steadily under an immense clock in a room whose angles loomed overpoweringly inward. She hurriedly set the paper down again, and went back to her place.

Dave had been asleep for hours by then, lying asprawl on his own bench and snoring softly. Rodney Jones was out of the room most of the time, telephoning or standing by silent telephones and waiting for the loud jarring ring of a reply. The calls were to officials and newsmen and parliamentary researchers he knew, who might be able to help.

At about half past three, Rod came back into the waiting room with two cups of coffee in styrofoam cups. He sat down beside Sandra and held one out to her.

"What about Dave?" she asked.

Rod gave the recumbent form of his cameraman an affectionate look. "He's gone till morning," he said. "He always sleeps like he was fucking hibernating. Kick him and take away the blankets and he just rolls over." Sandra blinked, realising for the first time that the pair were gay. "Nah," finished Rod, "I got this for you."

She took the coffee and sipped it automatically. It was milky, not hot enough, and tasted like something that would be used to clean a sink.

"Fucking police coffee," said Rod, swigging his. "No wonder they all have ulcers."

"Any news?" asked Sandra, more for something to say than because she expected a positive answer. If there had been news, Rod would have told it to her already.

He shook his head. "Look, maybe we better think about what we do next. Even if we get the warrant in the next half hour, it's gonna be too late now to be any use. They'll have moved him, and they're gonna say he was never there at all."

Sandra set her coffee down carefully beside her feet and rubbed her hands under her eyes. The tears started again. They'd been angry tears before, they had been loud and she'd choked them off quickly. Now she shed the tears of despair. They were quiet, and half of them seemed to flow down behind her eyes into the back of her throat, where they left a bitter taste. "They'll have killed him by now," she said.

"No, they won't said Rod, with deep conviction. "They can't."

"We didn't think they could just grab him like that. But they did. He was afraid they would. He said that as soon as Sir Philip Lloyd was sure who he was, he'd take action. And they didn't want to do it in front of me and Malcolm, but they did, rather than let him walk out. They must be desperate. They'll kill him."

"They can't," Rod repeated. "I don't care how many defence contracts they've got or how many ministers they've bribed, it's not gonna be enough for them. They might have swung it if he hadn't been ill, but the way things are, nobody's going swallow any shit about him being dangerous. They touch him and we can *crucify* them." He emptied his coffee cup, crunched it up, and hurled it, angrily and accurately, across the room into the bin.

"What use is that?" Sandra asked, biting the question off through the tears. "If they *think* they can get away with it, they'll kill him. It doesn't matter if they're wrong. He'll be dead."

Rod reached over and caught her hands in his. "Look, he said he didn't think they were going to kill him, remember? He said he was afraid they were going to try to use him. Now, all the things he sort of remembered have turned out true. That one's so weird that it's *got* to be right. Maybe there's some other theory he was working on they want to see, or some other person, a colleague who helped him, that they want him to shut up for them—but there's something they want him alive for. So they won't kill him."

"Unless they panic at all the trouble we're making."

"They shown any signs of panicking? They are not a bunch of ignorant yobs. They got expensive legal advice. Kidnapping and false imprisonment: out in two years, with good behaviour. Murder: life. They won't risk it. They'll hang on to him for as long as they can, and then most likely they'll send him back to his own country. You'll get a phone call from Tashkent or Alma Ata or wherever, and he'll offer you marriage to get a British passport."

Sandra knew that at this point she was supposed to give a weak laugh, wipe away her tears, and say OK, I won't give up. But she could not laugh. She did not intend to give up— she couldn't have even if she'd wanted to, with her outrage at the sheer blatant arrogance of the kidnapping burning so hot in her stomach—but she remained uncomforted. She took her hands back and picked up her coffee again. "So what do you think we should do next?" she asked.

He let out his breath slowly through his nose and slumped back against the wall. "What we gotta do is keep the pressure on. Somebody's protecting Stellar. They wouldn't have been so blatant if there wasn't, and we know they're in bed with the security services. Probably MI5 or whoever else is in on this, too. Maybe they're afraid Sherlock Holmes's country will try to lay claim to Astragen, and they want him to swear that it was none of his invention. If that search warrant gets refused, we'll *know* it's because this Mark Jaeger—or whoever—pulled strings. So what we've got to do is make things so hot that the protectors get em-

barrassed and drop Stellar. We hit the papers with the story.
We play up the medical angle for all its worth. We get an MP
to ask questions in the house, and we throw up all the dirt
about Stellar's links with government. I try and get something on the box."

"We won't be able to. It will be D-noticed. Paul isn't
British, they'll come up with some business about spies
and—"

"You know the parable of the Unjust Judge?"

Sandra looked at Rod. His image, black-bearded and
large, was blurred by her tears, but she felt that she saw him
with the clarity that only exhaustion can bring. "No," she
said.

"It's in the Bible. I like the Bible. Jesus was a real revolutionary. Don't like the church, though. Anyway, it goes
something like this. There was once an unjust judge who
wasn't afraid of God or man, and he used to sell his judge-
ments to the highest bidder. And there was a poor widow
who hadn't a penny who went to him asking for justice
against her enemy. He didn't want to know, of course. No
bribe: no date set for her in court. But she kept turning up in
court all the same, shouting for justice, waiting outside till
she was wearing out the doorstep, and finally he said to himself, 'Although I am an unjust judge who isn't afraid of God
or man, I'm sick of the sound of that woman's voice. I'll
give her justice, just to get rid of her.' And so he did."

Rod paused. "The point that gets made at the end of the
story is that if you can get justice from a human being who's
a complete shit just by persisting long enough, you can certainly get it from God. But the thing I've always liked about
it is that old woman. She wouldn't give up, and in the end,
she won. You shout long enough and loud enough, and in the
end somebody has to listen to you. That's what I'm gonna
do now. I'm gonna shout for justice, and I'm not gonna shut
up until I get it."

And Sandra, with her three a.m. exhausted clarity, saw
that this was the mainspring of his nature. He had not cho-

sen his fierce combative career as she had thought, out of a desire to humiliate people more powerful than himself and to attract attention; even his habitual, almost reflexive indignation was secondary. He really did love justice, that beautiful stern abstraction, and he would stand up and shout for it in all the courts of the world, expecting no more reward than the joy of its appearance. She was astonished, and a little ashamed.

"Thank you," she said fervently. Then, "But if the whole business gets classified, how are you going to do that?"

"They can't classify *everything*," said Rod. "And so far, all that's classified is Astragen. That means we can talk about the kidnapping until we're ordered not to, which means we've got today and maybe tomorrow to yell about it good and loud—which means that by Monday it'll be common knowledge, and hard to classify, so we can go on yelling about it. Besides, if a documentary's good enough, it'll get shown. I'm gonna make a documentary so good that nobody's gonna dare *not* to show it." And his eyes lit with eagerness.

AT HALF-PAST EIGHT NEXT MORNING, THE POLICE FI-nally had a response to their request for a search warrant. It had been refused "on grounds of national security." "Right," said Rod. "We start shouting."

The first results of the shouting campaign became apparent to Wavevector that evening. The process of moving him to The Oaks had been accomplished without too much difficulty. He had seen little of it: his cell had been removed from the black van only when the other arrangements were completed, and he'd had little more than a glimpse of trees and an overgrown garden around a small cottage, before his cell was dragged inside. It would not fit into the cottage itself, which was old and had narrow doors in a solidly built brick frame, but at some point a conservatory had been added on the back, and this had a sliding glass door wide enough to admit his prison. The windows of the conservatory had all been covered with a greenhouse shading compound before he was moved in, so that no one could see in. He could not see out, either, which depressed him. He found himself longing for sunlight.

McKenzie and Foster were staying in the cottage to guard him. Foster appeared unhappy about this: he muttered to McKenzie about his wife wanting him home evenings at least, but McKenzie told him to stop whingeing. The two men had been up all night, and spent most of the day resting. There were two bedrooms on the upper floor of the cottage, but McKenzie made up a bed on the floor in the living room, immediately off the conservatory, so that he could keep an eye on Wavevector.

Wavevector spent the morning asleep, but woke with an urgent need to think. The prospect of a future as Stellar's prisoner was too horrible to contemplate: he must escape. And he must do it soon. Once they had him back in the Defence Lab, it would be almost impossible for him to get out. He realised now that the whole of Stellar's headquarters building had been ringed with defences against him. The invisible rope he'd crossed coming into the building had really been there: he could guess now that he'd disturbed some circuit when he went past it, triggering an alarm and confirming Sir Philip's suspicion about his identity. He would undoubtedly set off more alarms trying to get out, even if he didn't fall into another diamagnetic trap. Besides, in the thick-walled underground lab he'd soon become as desperate for energy as Gravitational Constant. Absorbing energy was something he normally did as naturally as his body breathed: he'd unconsciously been drawing power from the Earth's magnetic field the whole of the time he'd thought himself human. Now he was cut off from it, and he was aware that the fuzz of ever-present solar radiance was no real substitute, and the energy produced by the chemical processes of his body no use at all. But at least here there was some energy to draw on, some visible light that crept through the green-

shaded windows, some steady background radiation produced by the Earth and the Sun. In the Defence Lab there
would be none of that: he would have to depend on Sir Philip
if he were not to fall into a torpor, and he was certain that Sir
Philip would exploit his dependence to the full. No: he must
escape within the next two days. He began analysing his position and evaluating the obstacles he must overcome. There
were four categories of these: the prison cell itself; his captors; his own physical condition; and the wider situation.

The prison cell was in some ways the least of his worries,
though it presented at least two layers of difficulty: the diamagnetic field and the frame. The frame was fairly solid—
but he could probably damage it electromagnetically and
pry it apart, if he could get rid of the field. To get rid of the
field he would have either to switch off the generator or to
damage it in some way. The case was not easily penetrable
by electromagnetic emissions—but that was not significant.
It was reasonable to assume that if the device could be sabotaged by electromagnetic means alone, Gravitational Constant would have sabotaged it and escaped. Therefore,
Wavevector should concentrate on mechanical means,
which were unavailable to Gravitational Constant. He
shouldn't even try to disentangle himself from Anderson's
body. He wasn't sure that he could, in any event, but at the
moment it was essential to be human. He knew that he could
thrust an electrical insulator through the field without being
hurt: he'd done it with his jacket in the lift. It ought to be
possible to devise some sort of tool which he could stick
through the mesh when his captors weren't looking, and use
to tamper with the controls. The materials available were
cardboard, shredded paper, and a plastic bucket provided by
Foster and McKenzie as a toilet. His hands were clumsy, and
he wasn't used to thinking in mechanical terms, but he ought
to be able to manage something.

Second, his captors. There were only two of them in the
house, but in his present condition either of them would be
able to overpower him easily. They were keeping a careful

watch on him, too. The door between the sitting room and
the conservatory was kept open, and as he lay thinking he
could see McKenzie's face, turned towards him even in
sleep. Any noise, and McKenzie would wake. Was he
armed? Sir Phillip's gun was the only one Wavector had
seen, but even if McKenzie and Foster had no guns, still
they must have access to knives, clubs, hammers . . . he had
seen enough of Earth to know that its inhabitants were ingenious at finding weapons. Wavevector was still not sure
what would happen if Anderson's body were killed while he
was entangled in it, but the more he considered it, the more
likely it seemed that such an event would violently disorder
the forces of his true nature. He would be torn apart, and the
energies which he was composed of would explode blindly
outwards as he died. Had the Stellars reasoned that out?
Wouldn't they be reluctant to kill him, when his death might
kill them?

They would be reluctant to kill him even if they hadn't
seen this. He was valuable. They would try to wound or
cripple him: that was an advantage. And the two men did not
spend all their time staring at him, either: they slept and
went to the toilet and prepared food in the kitchen. He could
probably tamper with the cell without their noticing, if he
chose his moment. But he'd have to be careful: if they
caught him, they'd allow him no second chance. And he had
to assume that Stellar could find additional guards for him if
it needed to. In the days of innocence, when he'd given them
the Astragen theory, the only Stellars he'd met had been Sir
Philip Lloyd, Alan Boardman, and Andrew McKenzie—and
Anderson. Foster was evidently junior to the other three, and
had been drafted in to help. Others presumably had been or
could be brought in as well. Not many others, though, or Sir
Philip would not have been so insistent that no part of the
lab but the Defence section was secure. Wavevector remembered that Rodney Jones had had at least one informant at
Stellar.

Query: if Wavevector's kidnapping had been authorised

and classified by the security services, why was Sir Philip so concerned about secrecy?

Wavevector found himself skipping the third category of obstacles to escape, and getting lost in the fourth: the wider situation, where he had few facts, little experience, and far too many questions. The security services were not the government, that much he knew. Had they told the government about him? Would it be interested? Stellar had bribed the government minister responsible for energy—Anderson had loaned him a villa. Would the government, then, do as Stellar wished? No: it was a democratic government, subject to laws, and the minister would have to resign if it became known that he had accepted the bribe. Rodney Jones was not in the least afraid of the government or the security services: he seemed to seek out and publicise their misdeeds with relish. Could he do that, if he were restrained by a "D-notice"? How far would a "D-notice" stretch? Would the government support this business of "classifying" the kidnapping? Was it in fact illegal to kidnap and imprison Wavevector to begin with?

He recognised with growing despair that it could not be illegal. There were no human laws governing the treatment of beings of his kind. If the way the four Stellars looked at him was any guide, the world at large would view him as a *thing* that had invaded and taken control of a human, a dangerous monster that must be destroyed or held captive. Whatever Stellar's reasons for keeping his existence secret now, he had to assume that if he succeeded in escaping he would find the whole planet turning against him. Suddenly he found that he was no longer rationally evaluating the obstacles to escape, but thinking about Sandra Murray. Would she too regard him as a monster?

"Do you really think it's the way you look that matters, that I would have fallen in love with you if you really had been Anderson?" she'd said to him. "I know enough about what you're like to form an opinion."

But she hadn't known enough. She had kissed him. He

understood now why it had terrified him when he found himself attracted to her; why he had been afraid when he realised that she reciprocated. It was utterly foreign to his true nature. He had observed sexual reproduction, and found it odd and repellant. Like all his kind, he had come into being as a by-product of a violent event in the life of a particular class of star: matter was compressed to nothing, energy and space were twisted into a knot, and, sometimes, consciousness sprang up in a pattern of instabilities as linked and as complex as the neural networks of the human brain. He would endure unaging for a time: he would die—soon, perhaps, of the consequences of his own recklessness, but if not, eventually, in some accident, or when his reason corrupted under the long accumulation of memory. He had no parents, no lover, no offspring. It was only chance that the human body he had taken was male rather than female: both were equally alien to him. Yet he remembered how she had kissed him with profound longing, and great grief.

It was so different from how he had imagined it must be. His theoretical knowledge would not map on to his experience. The thought of sexual intercourse was still repellant, but the thought of holding Sandra was like a burst of light in the hungry dark. He had imagined that desire was impersonal, but it was so intensely personal that he could not separate it from the person he felt it for. His longing mixed her physical and intellectual qualities confusingly: he liked the colour of her hair and her common sense; the shape of her feet and her honesty and courage; the sound of her voice and her freckles and her generosity.

What if he did see her again, and she looked at him and shuddered?

He had never been able to understand biological intelligences. Even allowing for the burden of the instincts they carried from their animal inheritance—the territorial aggressiveness, the fierce urges to reproduce and defend young—even so, they were unpredictable creatures, apt to act irrationally when you least expected it. He could not begin to imagine how Sandra would feel about him.

Foster came downstairs and went into the kitchen to prepare some food; McKenzie woke and checked the generator for the diamagnetic field. They brought Wavevector a cheese and pickle sandwich and a glass of milk, unlocking the cell door and sliding the paper plate and cup in without entering the cell themselves. Wavevector ate quietly. He found he'd recovered considerably from his ordeal of the night before: he could move more-or-less normally, and he had an appetite for the food. But he still felt weak and tired.

When the June evening at last began to darken, three cars drew up outside the cottage. He heard—rather than saw or scanned—them: heard the engines stop and the doors slam and men get out, talking indistinctly. He pulled the blanket about his shoulders, and waited. He wished very much that someone would give him some clothes.

The light in the conservatory came on suddenly, and there was a crowd in the doorway that led to the house. He checked them carefully. Sir Philip Lloyd was there, and a man he had met once before, in the days of innocence: Anderson's friend Mark Jaeger. There were also two men he did not know, and Foster and McKenzie. They were all staring at him, the strangers jostling each other to see.

"My God!" whispered Jaeger. "Paul?"

"He's not," Sir Philip said sharply. "Have your men scan him, or put a magnetometer inside the cell, and you'll see it at once."

The other man moved forward as though Sir Philip had not spoken, still staring. Wavevector had only met him once. He had come to Stellar's lab with Anderson, and Sir Philip had introduced him, without explaining who he was or why he was there. Wavevector had never seen him visually. Jaeger was a tall man with short fair hair and a long nose; he was wearing a plain dark suit. His mouth was working with a mix of emotions Wavevector could not identify. He gave a curt nod to the two strangers, and they came forward with a large aluminium box. They squeezed into a corner of the conservatory, opened it, and began to connect bits to the machine inside: Wavevector relaxed as he recognised the new device as a broad spectrum radio detector. This was just another way for them to stare at him. At this range his natural form would register, though the signal would be confusing.

An electrical cord was fed back through to Foster, and the scanner was pointed at Wavevector and switched on. "*Jesus!*" breathed one of the newcomers. He glanced from the scanner to Wavevector, then back again. He began twiddling dials.

"Not Paul," concluded Jaeger. This time the emotion was clear: anger. He looked back at Sir Philip. "All right, how do we get Paul back?"

Sir Philip looked at Wavevector. He removed a pocket cassette recorder from his jacket, set it down carefully beside the cell, and switched it on. "Is Paul Anderson still alive?" he asked directly.

Wavevector was silent. McKenzie had wanted to move to The Oaks so that medical attention would be available—if Paul Anderson needed it. He had not wanted to torture Wavevector—in case Paul Anderson felt it. It seemed unwise to inform his captors that Paul Anderson had been dead before he himself ever touched Anderson's body.

"Answer the question," said Sir Philip. "If Paul Anderson is still alive, we want you to let him go." He moved round to the other end of the cell, squeezing between the mesh and the inner wall of the conservatory, and studied the controls of the diamagnetic field generator.

Wavevector nervously folded his extremities away from the walls of the cell and swivelled to watch Sir Philip. "You assume that I am able to disentangle myself from this body whenever I choose," he said. "That is not the case."

"Oh, Christ!" exclaimed Jaeger, the anger suddenly erupting and colouring his face red. "Lloyd, you've got to get that thing out of Paul at once. *Nobody* should have to suffer something like that."

Sir Philip looked into the cell with narrowed eyes, and Wavevector realised that he was even angrier than the other man. "You don't have to tell me that, Commander," he said. "It is very much in my own interest for me to produce Paul Anderson alive and well tomorrow morning. If he *is* alive." He made an adjustment to the controls, and the field at the far end of the cell began to fluctuate. "Your *friends* have been making a great deal of fuss about your disappearance," he told Wavevector, in a low voice. "That unfortunate young woman who thinks you're Paul, and that bloody man Jones. I didn't know you'd been speaking to *him*." The diamagnetic field abruptly jumped from the end of the cell and flickered unhappily in the air some fifteen centimetres from it. Wavevector sprang to his feet and moved hurriedly away from it. He could not move far.

"What are you doing?" asked Jaeger.

"Shifting the field towards him," said Sir Philip. "He doesn't like touching it."

"I thought you said the field was harmless. Paul told me it was harmless."

"It is—to humans." The field flickered invisibly nearer. "Answer my question, *thing*."

"Please," said Wavevector, breaking into a sweat, "I don't think you understand how much it hurts. Contact with it last night almost killed me. I can't produce Anderson for you. Torturing me won't change that."

"What did you *do* to Paul, you horror?" Jaeger roared suddenly.

"Please!" exclaimed Wavevector, watching the field flicker closer and closer. "Please, what you're doing is dangerous. I am trying to cooperate. You don't need . . ."

The edge of the field reached him. He twisted sideways to keep his head away from it, and it caught his left shoulder. There was the sense of something in the depths of his being jolting loose, and then the explosion of pain. He struggled desperately to stay on his feet, but couldn't. For an instant the field crossed his chest as he fell sideways into it, and he was aware of his heart stopping in mid-beat. Then the field flicked back to the far end of the cell, and he toppled on to the shredded paper. Terrible pain flooded up his side, and the world faded out into a grey distortion. Then his heart started beating again.

"That was for making trouble with Rodney Jones," said Sir Philip's satisfied voice above him.

Somehow he managed to drag himself to the plastic bucket before he was sick. He didn't want to vomit into the paper: the moisture might make it conductive, and then the field might bulge and touch him again.

"Good show!" said Jaeger savagely. "He didn't like that, did he? Why does it hurt him, Lloyd?"

"I think that touching the field must disturb his control of Paul's body," replied Sir Philip.

Wavevector was sick once more, then let himself drop into the paper. He put his right arm over his head: the left one was numb and would not move. Sir Philip's conjecture had echoed his own tentative theory about the pain. He made himself aware of the junctures between himself and the body. Yes, some of those myriad entanglements had been jarred loose. But already they were renewing themselves. The body wanted to live, and it held on to him with all its strength. The pain was its scream of anguish as he was forced out of it. It was both frightening and peculiarly touching to think that it was so reluctant to be parted from him.

Jaeger had been thinking hard. "So all we need to do to free Paul is drag him through the field," he said. "The thing won't be able to get through, and it will have to let him go."

"*If* Paul is alive," said Sir Philip coldly. "If he's not, we'll have his corpse on our hands. I don't think either of us wants that."

There was a short silence. Wavevector lay where he was, face down beside the pail of vomit with his arm over his head, trembling with reaction.

"You still haven't answered me, *thing*," Sir Philip pointed out, in a chilling voice. "Is Paul still alive?"

"My heart stopped," Wavevector said in a hoarse slur. "When the field touched it."

"Answer me!" At the end of the cell, the wall of the field once again began to fluctuate.

"You are being recklessly and dangerously irrational!" cried Wavevector, lifting his head. "I've told you that I can't produce Anderson for you. I've told you that any prolonged contact with the field might kill both this body and me. To ignore that is utter unreason. You know what I am. What do you think will happen if this body's death so disorganises the forces that I am composed of that they disintegrate on the spot?"

He could not see Sir Philip's face: the man stood behind him. But he could hear his shock in the sudden silence, scan it in his immobility. Then the field at the front of the cell fell back smoothly into the mesh. He lowered his head with a gasp of relief. Sir Philip had understood. He might be half blind with hatred, but he was not stupid.

"What would happen?" Jaeger asked Sir Philip.

"Sir," one of the men who'd been operating the radio detector volunteered hesitantly, when Sir Philip did not answer. "Sir, all the indications are that that thing contains quite a lot of energy. The readings are the most bizarre thing I've ever seen, but . . . well, I mean that if whatever holds that thing together disintegrated, there'd be a pretty big bang."

"You mean the thing is threatening to blow us up?" demanded the commander.

Sir Philip squeezed his way back past the side of the cage to the door. "There is a risk that the creature might explode if it died," he said reluctantly. "I don't believe that separating it from Paul's body *would* kill it—but I can't risk being wrong." Wavevector could feel that the blue glare had been turned on him again, but he did not look up. He was miserably certain that he'd purchased nothing more than a respite. Sir Philip would soon discover some way of inflicting pain on him which was less likely to be lethal to both of them.

Still, a respite he had: they would not torture him any more tonight.

"I think we must assume that Paul is dead," Sir Philip said slowly. "I think that otherwise the creature would have answered us. Probably you can't have two consciousnesses in the same body."

Jaeger began to swear, his voice soft and rough at first, then rising to a thunder of condemnation. He pressed his face against the side of the cell and roared, "What did you do to him, eh? What did you do? I want to know. Tell me!" His fingers knotted into the wire like grapples trying to hook out an answer. "Tell me, or I swear to God I'll go in there and beat the answer out of you!"

It had been no use, clinging to his silence, hoping their doubts would spare him an inch of mercy. The furious red face which pressed against the wire above him had already condemned him. "I did not kill him," he whispered, the only defense he had left. "He died in the car accident."

"It wasn't an accident, you horror! What did you do?"

"Nothing." He remembered the car lying in the water, the headlights fading, and the man inside struggling frantically to get out, tearing his hands upon the sealed windows, choking as his lungs flooded with the river. Nothing; he had done nothing to help. "It was an accident," he protested again, weakly. "He was driving too fast, and the car came off the road. I never contemplated manipulating this body until after he was dead. That is the truth."

"You foul thing," whispered Jaeger, in disgust. "You think I can't see that you fixed the car somehow and caused that accident? Then you crawled into his body, didn't you? Crawled in while it was still nice and warm."

"I did nothing until he was dead," whispered Wavevector, but Jaeger paid no attention, and began to swear again.

Wavevector despaired and let the words flow over him. Slowly the trembling in his muscles began to subside.

When he started paying attention again, Sir Philip and Commander Jaeger were arguing. The impossibility of producing a live Paul Anderson was apparently going to cause both of them grave problems. To counter these, Jaeger wanted to take Wavevector to Aldermaston and show him to some officials: Sir Philip furiously insisted that only Stellar had enough knowledge and experience to handle the situation.

"What am I supposed to tell the general?" Jaeger demanded. "To say nothing of that god-awful woman from MI5. The phone started ringing first thing this morning and hasn't stopped all day, and every time I answer it the person on the other end is higher up and more worried. Jones has set Liberty on to this, and Amnesty International, and the oversight committee! How am I supposed to tell my overseers that this poor, sick, defenceless, mentally impaired man you kidnapped in broad daylight with my approval is actually an alien bodysnatcher, unless I have something to show them?"

"The last thing you want to do is show them *him*!" snapped Sir Philip. "He looks human. *You* called him 'Paul' when you saw him, and you know the background. Your idiot overseers don't know physics from physical education: they're never going to believe magnetometers and broad spectrum radio detectors over the evidence of their eyes. If you have to tell them, you want to show them the data and leave him out. We've got some good computer-enhanced radiographs and X-ray pictures of the decoy, and we can probably get you some sort of image on an MRI, *him* on top of the body . . ."

"When?"

"When it's safe to move him back to the lab! I couldn't leave him there. We've had phone calls too, you know, and the press, and I didn't know if you'd be able to keep the police off."

"Look, Lloyd, I've been sticking my neck out for you. You said this was our only hope of saving Paul. But we haven't saved him, and we never could have: that thing killed him two weeks ago."

"You think we shouldn't have tried? You think we should have left that creature loose?"

There was a slight pause, and then Jaeger said, "Why the hell did you have to grab him in front of two witnesses and a rabid telejournalist?"

"I had no choice. He understood the situation the moment he walked into the office, and he'd never have given me another chance to get near him. Inviting the journalist made it look good, and anyway, I wasn't sure it was really him until he set off the alarms coming into the building. If it had really been Paul we could have let him do the interview. As for the other people, they weren't invited. I never expected him to have found some woman idiot enough to fall for him, even if she does think she saved his life."

Wavevector found himself smiling into the paper, his attention once again sliding away. Sandra. Sandra with her hair flaming around her face, kissing him. Idiot enough to fall for him; brave enough to fight for him. Safe all along, and trying now to raise the alarm.

What would she think if she knew the truth?

He dragged his attention back to the present with an effort: Jaeger was saying, "At least give me the decoy. It would be something to *show* them, something to make them take it seriously."

The "decoy" had to be Gravitational Constant: the Stellars had all referred to him by that word the previous night. Probably he had appeared so inert to them that no other explanation of him made sense, and Wavevector had had reason to try things like decoys. But Sir Philip and the Stellars now knew that Gravitational Constant was not a decoy, and they had chosen not to pass this information on to Jaeger. Sir Philip had also attributed his decision to remove Wavevector from Stellar Research to fear of a police search—something which had not even been mentioned the previous night. Sir Philip was keeping things back from his ally. And the ally, from the sound of it, had kept things back from his superiors—his worry now was how to convince his "overseers" that he was telling the truth about Wavevector. It had not been clear from Anderson's letters precisely what Jaeger's position was. He was in the army, and he was involved with military surveillance of industrial research, that much was evident, but from his comments his relations with the official security services were uneasy, and his connection to the government, tenuous. The number of people who knew what Wavevector was appeared astonishingly small. Again Wavevector queried the motive for such secrecy, and found himself unable to account for it.

Sir Philip evaded the request for Gravitational Constant by an oblique shift: with all the attention the lab was getting, he didn't want to start shipping large boxes off to Aldermaston. Jaeger accepted this reluctantly, and asked for the computer-enhanced radiographs instead.

"We can pick them up tonight," said Sir Philip. "Are your men recording the readings now, too? Fine, we'll run their results through the computer and do another, of *him*." There was a slight pause, and then he added, "In fact, we can do two copies. We need to shut Jones up. We'll tell him the truth."

Wavevector lifted his head.

"What the hell do you mean?" asked the commander. "We don't tell that bastard anything! We try to shut him up."

"Paul tried to shut him up before, and he just kept digging," said Sir Philip coolly. "We can get a D-notice that stops him publishing what we tell him, but we need to convince him to shut up, or he'll blow the whole thing wide open. If he knows the truth, he won't want to publish. He is a rabid fool, but he's not an enemy of the human race. He won't go on trying to defend *that*." He looked at Wavevector. Their eyes met.

Sir Philip frowned. "That bothers you, doesn't it?" he observed. He went closer and crouched down, staring through the mesh into Wavevector's face. "You'd assembled your little pack of human dupes, and you were relying on them to shield you. Well, you're going to lose them."

Wavevector licked his lips: his mouth seemed strangely dry. "You intend to speak to Ms Murray as well?" he asked hoarsely.

The blue eyes narrowed. "Why do you ask about her?"

There was a silence.

"Good Lord," whispered Sir Philip. "You enjoyed having her romantically attracted to you, didn't you? You liked that. Poor girl."

"That's obscene," said Jaeger. He spoke with real and passionate disgust.

"Were you trying out what it's like to be human?" asked Sir Philip. "Playing around with the sensations? Did you fuck her, just to see what it was like?"

Wavevector looked away. He felt intensely a mix of emotions he could not identify, some of which seemed to come from his body, and some from a part of his mind he had not encountered before. They were all extraordinarily painful, and bewilderingly strange. "No," he said unsteadily. "Will you . . . is it likely that what you say will distress her?"

"Yes," said Sir Philip. "I should think any woman would be distressed, to find that the attractive man she's fallen in love with is really a . . ." he hesitated, searching for the words, then continued with sudden vehemence, "a corpse with a thing from a black hole inside it."

"I regret causing her distress," said Wavevector faintly. "Please, if you have any . . . any human feeling for her, tell her that much. I never wished her distress."

ELEVEN

IT WAS UNDENIABLE THAT RODNEY JONES KNEW HOW to conduct a shouting campaign. What had on Friday night been a minor incident at Stellar Research, of little interest to a sceptical police force, was by Saturday night a breach of civil rights by an irresponsible and greedy company, frowned on by the press. And by Sunday night it became a violation of basic human rights by a security service out of control, deplored on television. On Saturday Rod phoned frantically about trying to get the story into the press; by Sunday, the press was phoning him, begging for more details.

The authorities had followed the first refusal of a search warrant with a terse statement that Paul Anderson was co-operating with an investigation into a breach of national security. Rod at once demanded to know what he was charged with, and applied for a writ of habeas corpus. The authorities responded by saying that the writ did not apply, because the individual known as Paul Anderson was in fact an imposter, name unknown, and that the case could not be discussed further on grounds of national security. Rod gleefully telephoned to London and produced his trump: Mrs Chris-

tine Anderson Barlow. Mrs Anderson Barlow was beautiful.
She had fair hair and immense aquamarine eyes and skin
like a soap advert; she was small and curvaceous. She
dressed in bright tight clothes, fashionable but not too wild,
and she had a sweet-toned Sloane voice. There was nothing
subversive or anti-establishment about her. She was genuinely upset that her ex-husband was missing and nobody
had bothered to inform her, and every television viewer in
the country could sympathise with her. Every television
viewer in the country saw her, too: Rod filmed her watching
Dave's video sequence of Paul speaking Russian, and the
clip of her bewildered response—"That man isn't my husband! What happened to my husband?"—appeared near the
end of the ten o'clock news on Saturday night.

By Sunday noon, Sandra was feeling battered. She had
given interviews on Saturday till she was hoarse, again and
again describing the kidnapping to newspaper reporters who
listened only with reluctance, and always asked how she
knew Paul. ("But if, as you say, his name isn't really Paul,
Ms Murray, why do you call him that?" "I don't know what
else to call him.") The stories they wrote had all referred to
her as "the girlfriend" of the missing man. She had half-
expected that; it seemed premature, but she didn't mind. She
did not like the way the man himself was distorted, though:
Rod had pushed the medical angle hard, as he'd promised,
and Paul came out sounding mentally handicapped. His
story changed too, after Mrs Anderson Barlow's appearance.
Before then, the few tentative newspaper stories had reported the story as Sandra and Rod told it, though without
committing themselves to believing it. Afterwards, they accepted that Paul really had had plastic surgery to make him
look like Anderson, but they speculated about why: had this
substitute for Mr Anderson been sent to Britain to steal state
secrets? Had he murdered the real Anderson, and planned to
take his place, before the car accident and his amnesia intervened? Who had sent him—a rival government, or just a
rival industry? Sandra found the tone threatening, though

Rod told her it was quite all right: the balance would shift back again if the authorities continued to stonewall. Sandra still didn't like it. She did not like Mrs Anderson Barlow, either—the woman seemed more concerned about what would happen to her ex-husband's estate than about what had happened to him. Admittedly, the marriage seemed to have ended very bitterly and Mrs Anderson clearly felt that she was owed a lot—but even so it seemed mercenary. The media loved Mrs Anderson, however, and at a press conference Sunday morning she played up to them, weeping on camera and making appeals to the government to "at least tell me whether my husband's still *alive*." Sandra was interviewed immediately afterwards: it was her first time before the television cameras, and she was only saved from terror by her disgust at Mrs Anderson's hypocrisy. Dave surprised her by coming up to her while she waited to go on and handing her a stick of mascara.

"I don't wear make-up," she told him.

"You gotta wear it now," said Rod, sweeping down on her. "Look, the public's an ass. People are quite capable of deciding that Anderson was murdered by Holmes because Anderson's wife is prettier than Holmes' girlfriend. You got good eyes, but they don't show up."

Sandra began putting on mascara. "Then that's what they're going to decide," she said, blinking her eyelashes unhappily into the brown goo. "Anderson's ex is much prettier than me."

"Yeah, but you're a bluestocking. Joe Bloggs doesn't expect intellectual women to be pretty, so when they are it counts more. You'll be OK: you're thinner than she is and you've got a prettier accent."

"She's got Pre-Raphaelite hair, too," put in Malcolm. Sandra looked at him in surprise, and he grinned. "You do. *Beata Beatrice*. Did none of your boyfriends ever tell you you had Pre-Raphaelite hair?"

"No," she said, and felt her cheeks going hot with the too-ready blush.

"Then they were a bunch of scientific philistines."

The Sunday morning press conference had been Rod's idea. He had been summoning up the storm like a demented wizard, orchestrating appearances, issuing press releases, and, in the middle of it all, shooting, cutting, splicing and editing for his own documentary. His hair and beard bristled like those of a cartoon pianist, and his voice scraped up and down with excitement like a police siren. Dave tagged behind him, shooting this, shooting that—"get a tracking shot"—"we want something here with the voice-over about the accident"—saying very little, wholly subsumed into the work.

Sunday afternoon found Rod and Dave in Sandra's sitting room, working on rushes with a digital film editor fetched from the car boot, as full of energy as if there had been no press conference and as if they had not had only about six hours sleep in the past two days. Mrs Anderson Barlow had established herself in 12 The Mays, to which the others had not dared return, and the two documentarists had established their local base at Sandra's. Sandra sat curled up at the kitchen table, numbly watching Malcolm sketch. Malcolm had had very little to say since the kidnapping. On the other hand, he had sketched almost constantly. Sandra had not asked to see what he was drawing: she was not sure she could bear an accurate reflection of what she felt.

"When do you go back to college?" she asked, after a long silence.

"September," said Malcolm, without looking up. "Got the whole summer for this, if we need it. But I don' think it's gonna take more than a week."

"Are you . . . I mean, you're not going to be earning any money from this, and student grants don't stretch far these days. Is it going to hurt you?"

He did look up at that, and smiled. "I got two weeks' salary from Anderson's bank account. I plan to hang on to that, and hope nobody remembers it. And maybe I can sell some pictures. Hey, there aren't many summer jobs going, particularly for art students, particularly for black ones. I expected to be unemployed all summer. Mum always says I should put on a suit and go and apply for everything, but I hate suits. I've survived two years at the Royal College on grants and loans and what I can sell at shows: I can finish the course."

"You're coming up to your last year?"

The smile became a grin. "You thought I was younger, didn't you? Everybody does."

"It's your boyish good looks."

"*Glad* you noticed 'em. I'm twenty-one in August. You aren't as much older than me as you thought, are you?"

The doorbell rang before she could decide how to answer that. Sandra went to open it, and found Sir Philip Lloyd standing on the doorstep.

"Ms Murray," he said, with a pleasant smile, as though he had not last seen her screaming accusations as she was forced out of his headquarters by a security guard. "I'd like to speak to you and to Mr Jones, if I may."

Sandra fell back, and Sir Philip slipped quickly in the door. He was alone: no legal adviser, no research director, nothing but a briefcase. Rodney Jones and Dave shot out of the sitting room and stopped, staring; Malcolm came out from the kitchen with his sketch pad under his arm.

"Mr Jones," smiled Sir Philip. "I've come this afternoon because you've been stirring up a campaign against Stellar Research which, quite frankly, I think you would not have begun if you'd known the facts of the situation."

Rod gave a volcanic snort of derision. "And you're going to tell us the facts?"

"Yes," said Sir Philip pleasantly, surprising him. "Off the record, of course. Most of what I have to say is classified. You will of course understand that if you repeat it, you can be prosecuted. But I am going to tell you the facts."

"What's happened to Paul?" Sandra demanded anxiously. "Is he still alive?"

Sir Philip looked at her, his pleasantness hardening into

something else. "Paul Anderson died two weeks ago," he replied quietly.

"So you know what happened to him now!" exclaimed Sandra. "Fine—I mean, I'm sorry he's dead. But he wasn't the one I was asking about, and you know it. Where's the man you kidnapped?"

"I'll discuss that in due course," said Sir Philip. "Shall we sit down?"

They all went into the leafy sitting room and found places on Sandra's battered sofa and mismatched wicker chairs. Sir Philip lifted the digital editor off the coffee table and set it on the floor. Then he opened his briefcase, took out a sheet of paper, and set it down in the editor's place.

It was, Sandra saw at once, a computer-enhanced image of something in false colours. She thought at first it might be a satellite picture of a mountain, and then she wondered if it were a telescopic image of an interstellar dust cloud. Then she decided it was neither, and that she had no idea what it was. Contours shading from yellow to blue enclosed a blur that seemed to be composed of innumerable intertwined strands of nothing. The central thing was out of focus, but the bits of it which were clear seemed to knot together at angles worse than anything in Malcolm's sketches.

"The colours are radio frequencies," said Sir Philip. "Micro to long wave: blue is highest. Scanning on any one frequency doesn't provide enough information: the pictures have to be layered and processed in false colour, as you see. The amount of radiation is very small. If *that* was in the room you wouldn't even get static on your radio unless the radio almost touched it. But you'll notice that the frequency goes down as it approaches the singularity."

"That's a *singularity*?!" exclaimed Sandra. She did not want to be awed and excited; she was still bitter with rage. Awe and excitement pushed through anyway. This was hot science.

"What's a singularity?" asked Rod.

"It's what you get in the middle of black holes," said Sandra. "It's a sort of hole in the space-time continuum, where the ordinary laws of physics don't apply. This thing isn't in a black hole, though, or you'd be getting much worse than radio distortion around it. Where is it?"

"Is this Stellar's latest?" asked Rod suspiciously.

Sir Philip smiled in a way Sandra instinctively disliked, evaded the second question and ignored the first. "In a way. We don't think these radio effects are emissions: as Ms Murray guessed, we think the singularity distorts radio waves near it. It also absorbs them. Incidentally, we believe this is a magnetic singularity, though we're not sure. Now," he pulled out another sheet of paper, "this is the X-ray image."

The X-ray was a photograph: the same deep black blur, even more out of focus, and this time smeared with a faint grey halo.

"You took that with an X-ray camera?" asked Rod. "I thought they only showed bones."

Sir Philip gave him a withering look. "This was taken on X-ray sensitive film, *without* an X-ray camera. The outline is X-ray emissions. Again, they're scarce—if this hadn't been taken in a screened room, the normal background radiation would have drowned it—but the fact that they exist at all is a pretty clear indication that the source is quite energetic."

"Make yourself clear, Lloyd," said Rod irritably. "I don't have a scientific background. I don't think 'energetic' means the same to you as it does to me, and I don't know what it has to do with X-rays."

Sir Philip's eyebrows gave a slight ironic jerk. "If you warm up a bar of iron, first it gets hot, then it glows—in other words, first it gives off infrared radiation, then visible light. It starts by glowing red, but if you carry on heating it, the glow gets paler until it's white-hot. This is because white light comes from a source that's hotter, or more energetic, than red light does. To get X-rays off your iron bar, you'd have to vaporise it completely. Think about that. This thing is producing X-rays: it must be as full of energy as a cloud of vaporised iron. But there's no heat coming off it. Even the X-rays are shed a few at a time, the way you or I might shed dry skin cells. The energy doesn't radiate. *All* electromagnetic energy travels in waves that move at three hundred thousand kilometres a second—except this. It sits still. It's the equivalent of sunbeam tied in a knot—a sunbeam that's gone dark."

Malcolm picked up the false-colour radiograph and looked at it with lips parted and eyes narrowed, a gaze of peculiar intensity that seemed to absorb completely what was before it.

"You said this was taken in a screened room," said Sandra, touching the X-ray picture. "Did you make this . . . magnetic singularity, using the Astragen theory?"

Sir Philip shook his head. "We did not make that thing. We don't know how it was made. Probably it was formed in space by some catastrophic force we can barely imagine. We have confined it, though—using the Astragen theory." He met her eyes and smiled, and again she felt that the smile was sinister, and could not say why. "He told you about Astragen, did he? I thought he didn't remember."

"He remembered physics and mathematics perfectly," said Sandra coldly. "But you don't need to worry. We didn't know enough to understand it. He invented the theory, didn't he? And he wanted you to use it to benefit the world, but you preferred to maximise your profits. What have you done to him?"

Sir Philip sighed. "I came here to explain the situation. Will you let me proceed? Or would you rather remain ignorant and prejudiced?"

"Oh, we want to hear your story," said Rod. "But I reserve the right to remain as prejudiced as I like."

There was another jerk of the eyebrows from Sir Philip. Silently he took another sheet from his briefcase and laid it on the table. It was another false-colour radiograph, similar to the first one. The dark shape in the centre of this one was even more blurred and out of focus. It seemed flattened, too: the first image had been a rough sphere, but this was a lopsided oblong. A few unclear dark tendrils bent at stomach-churning angles away from the main mass. The radio distortion around it was ragged.

"Looks like somebody stepped on that one," observed Rod.

"That is a radiographic image of the individual you were asking about," replied Sir Philip quietly. "It was taken last night."

There was a moment of silence—bewildered, doubting, chilled—which was broken by Dave. "Oh shit!" he said slowly. "Oh shit. I knew we shouldn't have got into this."

"What the fuck do you mean by that?" Rod demanded angrily. It wasn't clear whether he was addressing Dave or Sir Philip.

"That is an image of the individual who was pretending to be Paul Anderson," Sir Philip repeated calmly. "The body is Paul's, all right. Anyone can prove that. It has his fingerprints, his dental records—his DNA, too, no doubt, if we had any record of that. But the thing inside the body isn't human. Anyone can prove that, too. It will show up on X-rays, magnetometer readings, radiographs . . . we're hoping to catch it on an MRI scan, and see if we can tell how it penetrates its host. And of course, you yourselves have proven that the consciousness inside the body speaks at least one language Paul did not."

"This is the biggest load of crap I ever heard!" exclaimed Rod. "You're trying to pretend that all last week we were talking to a fucking *alien*?"

"Yes," said Sir Philip coolly. "Let me tell you how I was given the Astragen theory. About a year ago, I was working late in my office. I was alone, and I was going over some surveys, when the screen of the computer on my desk lit up suddenly and a message flashed up on it: 'Hello, Sir Philip Lloyd.' I thought someone was contacting me on the network and started to type in a query: it was only when the keyboard didn't respond that I remembered that the computer was switched off.

"Naturally, I thought it was some kind of trick. I looked around and tried to see how it was being done and who was doing it. At once the computer began flashing up more messages: 'The wires of this computer have not been tampered with. There is no remote control . . . ' whatever I was checking. So finally I switched it on and typed in, 'OK, how are you doing it?' And it replied that it was an extraplanetary intelligence, that it was manipulating the computer electromagnetically, and that it had chosen to communicate with me because it had a proposal of mutual interest.

"I didn't believe that of course, any more than you believe me now. I think I said something sarcastic—'Let's see your spaceship, then!' or something. But it kept on talking on the computer, explaining that it didn't have a spaceship, that it was composed of pure energy, that it had come to Earth to observe and so on. I started to get annoyed. It was a secure computer, and I thought somebody must have been tampering with it. I said, 'All right, if you're composed of pure energy, turn out the lights.'

"Instantly, all the lights on that floor went out. Only the computer screen kept glowing, but it flickered, and the light from it had turned a blue-violet colour—it was unspeakably eerie, that light. Another message came up on it, 'I have directed an excessive amount of power into the electrical system and blown the fuse.' I would have thought it was funny, if I hadn't started being frightened. It was dark, you see, and the office was suddenly very quiet, with all the power gone, and I was alone with that violet screen. I said, 'Where are you?' and it said, 'Here, in front of you. I do not emit in the visual frequency.'

"I asked it if it would mind coming down to the lab and letting me check whether I could see it on any of our equipment. It came, and I pointed most of the detectors in the lab at it. It registered most clearly on the magnetometer, but I could find it on radio as well, and it set off some of the other equipment deliberately so that I could be sure it was there. I have the original readings here."

Sir Philip took a sheaf of papers from his briefcase and spread them out. These held no images, only columns of figures, or graphs with sudden sharp peaks. They had been labelled by hand: "Low frequency radio," "Medium wave," "Magnetometer." "Geiger Counter" had scrawled across it, so hard that the pen had almost torn the paper, "*Help!*" Sir Philip brushed it with a finger. "It set that off deliberately," he said. "One burst of gamma rays out of apparently empty air, then complete radio silence. That was when I really started believing.

"I asked the creature what it wanted, and it repeated what it had said before, that it had a proposal for me. It spoke by flashing up words on another computer, you'll understand, not in sounds. It preferred it if I used the computer to communicate as well, though it could understand spoken English if it had to. We sat down and discussed its proposal. I asked the creature if I could get the computer to print up what it put on the screen: I was feeling very shaky, as you can imagine, and I wanted a record."

He took another sheet from his briefcase. The margins had translucent stains from handling, and there were three or four small tears in the edge: this paper had been looked at again and again. "This is the original print-out," Sir Philip told them. "The *thing's* own words."

I have been observing biological intelligences for some time and I am particularly interested in the way in which you process scientific theory into technology. I wish to give you a theory which is versatile and potentially of great benefit to your kind, and observe the ways in which you develop it. If you agree to this experiment I will communicate this theory to you and to Stellar Research—but you must agree to publish it and to allow all your fellow humans to explore its implications as well. I also would like you to agree to answer any questions I may have about why you proceed with the theory as you do. The theory concerns the confinement of magnetic fields.

For Sandra, it was as though gravity changed direction. Disbelief, which had been suspended, shot downward into what had been up and was gone and, though she tried to call it back, it would not come. Those were Paul's words. She could imagine him saying that. It was his tone, his precise way of setting things out. Everything she knew and felt about him rearranged itself. Yes, he was intelligent, he had a mind like a super-cooled CRAY. But he was ignorant of food, culture, music and politics and how to respond to her. Yes, he was ignorant of almost everything except physics and mathematics and yes, she'd felt all along that he was different. Yes, it was true. The shock was so huge that she was aware of it as a physical thing, an overpowering sensation of dizziness, a weakness in the bowels and a convulsive contraction in the stomach: her emotions registered nothing but a profound numbness.

"You'll have realised, of course, that I agreed to the thing's experiment," Sir Philip went on, into the shocked silence. "I was afraid to do anything else. I decided to call the theory *it* gave me the Astragen theory. Astragen means 'Star-born.' You may have thought the name referred to Stellar: it didn't. I kept its origin secret, however. The energy creature had come to me in secret, and there was nothing to be gained by advertising its presence, except, perhaps, a reputation as a crackpot.

"Now—Mr Jones. You say you have no scientific background: I must explain that what I was given was a theory. It wasn't a machine or a blueprint for a machine or even an idea for a machine. It was a mathematical expression of some ideas about magnetism. Turning those ideas into something people could *use* was the work of Stellar Research, and it was hard work. The energy creature gave us no help on that at all. I feel entirely justified in regarding the development as mine. Stellar funded all the development costs; Stellar should reap the rewards. But the creature didn't see things that way.

"I brought two of my researchers in on the secret, and we

started a programme of experiments to see how the theory could be applied. Once or twice a week we'd meet with the energy creature, and it would ask us why we were doing certain things. It was clear from its questions that it had been watching us, but of course we were never aware of it except when it chose to contact us. We started getting very nervous, those of us who knew about the thing. I had some idea, from the readings I'd taken the first night, that the creature was immensely powerful, and being studied by an invisible, powerful, and inscrutable alien is very uncomfortable, I can tell you. I started driving about with a portable magnetometer in the back of my car, and taking it in to the office, so that I could have some idea of when the thing was present. I tried to find out everything I could about it. I wasted time learning a lot of rubbish from UFO groups but, more usefully, I observed the thing while it was observing us. I didn't dare ask it many questions, and it wouldn't answer most of those I did ask: it pretty clearly thought of us as an inferior species, and had no intention of socialising. It was studying us as though we were rats. But I got the distinct impression that for the more violent of its electromagnetic manipulations, it needed to touch what it was manipulating—to bring the shorted electrical circuit or the sensor of the Geiger counter, for example, to the edge of the singularity. So it occurred to me that if we could confine it, it would be unable to harm us. That thought was a relief to me. I wanted desperately to know that there was *some* way I could escape it, if I had to. I was very much afraid of it, particularly as time wore on, and it started demanding to know why we hadn't published the Astragen theory.

"When we were preparing the first real application of the theory, I decided that it would be irresponsible of me to keep the energy creature's existence concealed from the authorities any longer. On the other hand, the theory was going to be vastly profitable, and I didn't want to be told to stop development because the source was so questionable. I compromised by giving a directorship to Paul Anderson. He had, as you discovered, Mr Jones, connections to the department of the MoD which monitors civilian research, as well as some good friends in parliament, and I hoped that he would make an effective go-between. I should not say this now—*de mortuis nil nisi bonum*—but I rather regretted the move afterwards: he was an impatient man with a terrible temper. I am sorry, Mr Jones, for his conduct towards you, in particular. Please accept my apologies.

"The rest of the story you can probably piece together yourselves. When you discovered Astragen, Mr Jones, you forced us to guard our valuable secret by turning to the MoD. When the energy creature understood that this meant the theory could not be published, *it* was furious."

Sir Philip laid yet another worn computer print-out on the table. Sandra read:

> *I remind you that when I gave you the theory you agreed that it would be published. Your actions have made it increasingly clear that you have no intention of keeping that agreement, and perhaps never did. It was irrational and immoral of you to have undertaken an obligation you had no intention of fulfilling. The agreement must be considered defunct. I consider myself at liberty to take whatever action seems reasonable.*

"By that stage, however, we were prepared for it," Sir Philip went on. "We'd invested in a number of precautions against it at the lab—we'd enclosed the building in a magnetically sensitive material so that we knew when it was present, and we'd been working on methods of confining it. It generates a powerful magnetic field, and the theory it had given us also gave us the technology to imprison it. It had underestimated human resourcefulness, or perhaps just human audacity. When we saw how angry it was, we set up a magnetic trap we'd devised, hoping that the next time it entered the building, we would catch it.

"Unfortunately, the trap wasn't strong enough. The creature was caught, but it broke the generator and vanished. That was nearly a month ago now. Quite frankly, we were terrified. We didn't know when the thing would come back or what it would do when it did. But we never for a moment dreamed that it would be able to *take over* one of us. That picture I just showed you, though, makes it clear what sort of action 'seemed reasonable' to a thing like that. It killed Paul on the night you, Ms Murray, thought you saved his life, and it's been manipulating his body ever since. It is only luck that either the accident or the struggle with Paul confused the creature, and made it forget whatever it had originally intended to do. Because of that, and because of a chance remark at the hospital, I had time to become suspicious. My colleagues thought I was imagining things, but when we invited the individual who was pretending to be Paul to the lab, our instruments instantly confirmed what he was. I very much regret the roughness we were forced to use against you when we apprehended him, but it was essential—*essential*—that that thing not be permitted to escape again. I believe it would have jettisoned its stolen body and attacked someone else.

"Now you know the truth, I hope that you will realise that Stellar Research has acted responsibly all along, and I would like to ask you to stop this campaign of vilification."

Rodney Jones' face had been growing darker and darker as Sir Philip spoke, and now it was beet-coloured. "Like hell," he announced. "If you think I believe that crap just because you show me a few weird pictures, you can think again."

Sir Philip silently took one more thing out of his briefcase. It was a pocket-sized cassette recorder. He set it on the table and pressed "play."

"You are being recklessly and dangerously irrational!" cried a voice they all recognised instantly. "I've told you that I can't produce Anderson for you. I've told you that any prolonged contact with the field might kill both this body and me. To ignore that is utter unreason. You know what I am.

What do you think will happen if this body's death so disorganises the forces that I am composed of that they disintegrate on the spot?"

Sir Philip smiled and stopped the tape. "The creature itself admits what it is," he commented smugly.

Sandra's numbness gave way suddenly to absolute rage. "What did you do to him?" she asked slowly, staring at Sir Philip. "What did you do to make him sound like that?"

Sir Philip stopped smiling. Sandra grabbed the cassette recorder and hit the "rewind" button. Sir Philip tried to snatch it back; Rodney Jones seized his arm, forced him down into his chair, and held him there. Sandra hit the "play" button.

." . . said the field was harmless," said an unfamiliar voice. "Paul told me it was harmless."

"It is—to humans." Sir Philip, cold but somehow glad as well. "Answer my question, *thing*."

"Please," the familiar voice, frightened but still beseechingly, desperately reasonable. "I don't think you understand how much it hurts . . ."

They played it through to the part they'd heard before. Then Sir Philip succeeded in kicking the cassette player out of Sandra's hand. It fell on the floor, and the voices dissolved into a whine of jammed tape.

"I came here in good faith!" exclaimed Sir Philip bitterly. "You have no right to manhandle me."

"Jesus!" exclaimed Rod. "You fucking torture a man into a heart attack, and then you complain about me grabbing your arm. Jesus!" He let go of Sir Philip's arm in disgust.

"Not a man!" said Sir Philip, angrily rubbing his arm. He picked his cassette recorder off the floor and switched it off. "We were trying to rescue the *man*, but it's fairly clear he died two weeks ago."

"What was this 'field' thing?" Rod demanded. "What were you doing to him?"

"We brought him into contact with a diamagnetic field," Sir Philip said sullenly. "It's impenetrable to magnetism, and it seems to interfere with his control of Paul's body. But it *is* harmless to humans. Didn't you understand any of that? The creature's making no effort to deny what it is. You have to believe it, because it confesses it and we can prove it. We can go before the public and prove it any day. But we don't want to cause a panic."

"Crap," said Jones. "You're scared of going public. You'd have to tell your little story in court, and explain *why* you didn't publish when you'd agreed to, and *why* you didn't tell anybody sooner and, whatever you say, people will know that it's because you wanted to keep all the profits from Astragen for yourself. Cover your development costs, my arse! You were gonna be market-leader in batteries and make millions in any case. But the theory had other applications as well, and you wanted a monopoly on those, too. If you went public, you'd show yourself up for a greedy little shit, you'd lose your monopoly on the theory, *and* you'd lose your prisoner. The military or the defence research establishments would take him, if nobody else did. You don't want that, do you? You want to hang on to him yourself, because you bet that he knows a lot more than Astragen, and you want to use it. He said you'd try to use him. He said that you'd deceived him and betrayed him, and that if you got hold of him you'd try to use him, and he was absolutely right."

"Weren't you listening to me?" Sir Philip asked in astonishment. "That thing is dangerous! It was experimenting on humans—on me! It murdered Paul and stole his body. How can anyone, even a professional bleeding heart like you, think we were anything but fully justified in defending ourselves?"

"He never threatened you," said Sandra quietly. Her cheeks were burning. "You said a lot about how frightened you were, but you never said he threatened you. He came up to you quite openly and offered you a priceless theory on the condition that you published it and let him watch you develop it: you agreed, and then broke your agreement. When he complained, you tried to trap him. If he did kill Anderson,

I bet it was in self-defence. You did deceive and betray him, and if he isn't human that only makes it worse. He was a complete innocent: he couldn't even understand a punch-up at a pub. You said he underestimated human resourcefulness and audacity: what he really underestimated were human treachery and greed. My God! He never hurt you. What right do you have to treat him like that?"

Sir Philip stared at her, absolutely flabbergasted. It had obviously never crossed his mind that anyone might believe him and still think he was in the wrong.

"I understood from the papers that you were romantically attached to him, Ms Murray," he said at last, recovering himself a little. "But don't you see that he was experimenting with you, too—toying with you, playing with the sensations of human sexual—"

Sandra jumped to her feet. "You filthy-minded, slimy, ignorant liar!" she shouted. "He did not!" She glared furiously down at Sir Philip, who cowered back in his chair. "You don't have the first idea about him—or about me! Where is he? What have you done with him?"

Sir Philip hastily pushed his chair away, then got out of it. He piled papers back into his briefcase. Rod reached over and grabbed his arm again before he could close it. "Answer the question," he said. "What have you done with him?"

Sir Philip looked up with a swift reptilian jerk of the head. "You can't expect me to tell you that," he said coldly. "Let go of me at once, or I'll charge you with assault. I risked coming here on my own, in good faith: I'm sorry to find you all so blindly prejudiced that you won't listen even to the truth."

"Fuckin' hell!" exclaimed Rod. "You expect me just to let you walk out that door so you can go back for another little torture session?"

Sir Philip put his hand in his pocket and brought it out holding a small black pistol. "Let go of me," he said distinctly.

Rod let go.

Sir Philip jammed his cassette player back in the briefcase. He took out the second radiograph, the one taken the night before, and dropped it in the middle of the now-bare coffee table. "Look at that after I'm gone," he said. "*That*'s what you're making such a fuss about. Not a man, not a person with *human rights*. You may defend it now that it's safely locked up, but I bet you'd change your tune if it were loose again." He slammed the briefcase shut one-handed, picked it up, and backed slowly out of the room. They heard the front door open, then slam closed, and he was gone.

Sandra wrapped her arms around herself. After a minute, she sat down and began to cry. Malcolm came over, sat down on the arm of her chair, and put his arm around her shoulders. She turned towards him blindly, and he put his other arm around her and made hushing noises.

"Do you believe it?" Rod asked, after a long silence.

"Yeah," said Dave. "I told you that fucker was seriously weird."

"Shit," said Rod. After another silence he bent over and picked up the film editor. He set it down on the coffee table and looked at it as though he had no idea what to do with it.

"What do we do now?" asked Dave.

"I don't know," said Rod. "If Lloyd does go public with this one, public sympathy for old Sherlock Holmes will go right down the plug-hole. He's *Invasion of the Bodysnatchers* come true. Stellar would lose custody of him, but we'd never get him free. If we carry on, the truth comes out, and we lose: if we shut up, they hush it up, and we still lose. Shit."

"He's completely innocent!" Sandra protested tearfully.

"Not completely. He killed Anderson," replied Rod. "I agree, maybe he was provoked. *Probably* he was provoked. But—shit! The thought . . ." He picked up the false-colour radiograph from the coffee table and stared at it numbly. "What did you call this? A singularity? The thought of it *going inside* somebody . . . oh, Jesus!"

"It's a fucking sensational story, though," said Dave slowly. "Fucking sensational. Jesus. Screen that, and the

whole country'd be glued to their sets. And if we carry on,
Lloyd loses. That's something. The military aren't gonna
treat Holmes any worse than Lloyd does, are they? I mean,
Lloyd hates him. That fucker scared him shitless, and he's
never gonna forgive him for that. I vote we carry on."

Rod hesitated, then sighed and nodded. "Yeah. OK. I vote
we carry on and make them admit it. Sandra?"

She shook her head against Malcolm's chest. "We've got
to get him out!"

"You think of a way to do that, you just tell us," said Rod
sourly. "We don't know where he is, and if we did he's probably under guard, and if we tried to break him out we'd be
guilty of assault and criminal damage, and if we did break
him out, the security services would have the whole country
on the alert and would get him again within a day."

"Maybe he could . . . could *disentangle* himself," sniffed
Sandra.

"Oh Christ! Then *we'd* be stuck with Anderson's corpse
and charged with murder. No, I'm sorry. We can't. Do you
want to carry on with the shouting campaign? I gotta warn
you, it's gonna get nasty if they do go public, and you'll get
the worst of it. Girlfriend of a body-snatching alien: it'll be
bad."

I wasn't," she said, pulling away from Malcolm and running her hands through her hair. "The idea scared him."

"You can't expect the tabloids to understand that," said
Rod, patiently now. "You'll have the *Star* offering you multi-
thousand-pound contracts for exclusives on your nights in
bed with an alien. Look, I think that if we carry on, it will
help him. Dave's right, that shit Lloyd hates him and is out to
break him. Even the military would treat him better, particularly if we managed to get his side of the story out. I'm gonna
carry on anyway, because I hate to let the bastards win. But
I'm a media person and this is my job and I wasn't in love
with him. You're not gonna be allowed to drop out of the
story altogether, but if you drop out now, it'll be a lot easier
on you."

Sandra held her hair against the back of her neck. In love with him. Yes, she had been. Was she still? That was less clear: her body was still so full of shock and rage that all other emotions were drowned. But she could remember clearly the joy on his face when he'd woken up after his fit and found her there. She could remember his voice, hesitant, hoarse and anxious. Her mind slipped from that into the well-worn track of the kidnapping: rush forward, look of horror, doors close, scream.

He was a friend. He was innocent: she was as certain of his innocence as of her own. He was being horribly abused.

"Will it help, if I stay in?" she asked Rod.

"Oh, yeah! A lot. You look good, and there's no dirt on you, and you come down like the wrath of God on the un-righteous. But it'll cost you."

She could foresee some of the cost. What would her parents, her family, her friends think, seeing her distorted in the news? What would happen to her job? Would she have to leave her house and go into hiding? She suspected that there were worse costs, too: that the repetition of the story would confuse things more, that after a while she would not be certain which had been her real feelings, and which the heated imaginations of other hearts cast backwards into her soul. She had hated the newspaper interviews, and hated the press conference even more. She was a private person: she felt mauled. She could not abandon him though. He had been betrayed by Stellar. She could not betray him too.

"OK," she said. "I'm in."

Rod grinned at her. Malcolm patted her shoulder. Rod switched the grin to Malcolm. "How about you?" he asked.

"I'll go along with Sandra," he said, looking down at her. "We carry on."

"Right," said Rod. "We're agreed. Davie, we'd better re-edit the car crash sequence. Nobody was trying to murder Holmes there, after all."

TWELVE

WAVEVECTOR HAD CHOSEN SUNDAY NIGHT FOR HIS escape. It seemed reasonable to wait until then. It was obviously better to try at night than in daytime: Foster and McKenzie slept during the night, though McKenzie did so on the sitting room floor, just beside the open door to the conservatory. It would have been impossible to leave on Saturday night: he had not had the strength. Sunday found him organically stronger, though the hunger for energy had grown. He did not dare wait any longer: the original plan had been to return him to the Defence Lab at Stellar within two days, and these were now over. Publicity had raised some problems, and Foster and McKenzie were now talking about leaving on Wednesday—but he'd be a fool to rely on that. Sunday night it had to be.

At seven in the evening, Foster brought him some food and emptied the toilet bucket. Neither of the men ever entered the cell: they unlocked the door and reached through the diamagnetic field to put things down and pick them up. They always locked the door again afterwards, though Wavevector could not have walked from the cell if they'd left it wide open. He ate his TV dinner of chicken Kiev, rice and green beans with his fingers—he was never given any cutlery—and meekly returned the dish once he'd finished. Foster said nothing to him. Foster did not like to speak to Wavevector, though he stared a lot. If Wavevector spoke to him, he always jumped nervously, and never replied. McKenzie did sometimes try to talk to the prisoner, but since his invariable topic of conversation was Wavevector's nature and history, Wavevector rarely responded. He could not afford to give his captors any information that could strengthen their hold on him.

After supper, Foster and McKenzie watched television. Wavevector moved into the corner of the cell closest to the door and watched too, with the blanket wedged carefully between himself and the charged mesh of the wall. He could not see the screen well, but the programmes fascinated him. They were so mysterious: characters were always doing irrational things for inexplicable reasons, and the other characters always seemed to understand motives which Wavevector found quite impenetrable. He wished he'd taken time to look at the television while he was at Anderson's house.

On the nine o'clock news there was an item about him. An announcer stated that "controversy has been growing about the disappearance of Paul Anderson, the marketing director of Stellar Research" (the ID photo flashed across the screen) "since it emerged that the man who was apprehended last Friday at Stellar's new headquarters" (shot of the black glass fortress) "was not in fact Paul Anderson, but his double. The situation is complicated by the fact that the man apprehended was injured in a car accident and suffers from amnesia; he is said to be cooperating with the authorities in an investigation into a breach of national security, but the police have no information as to his whereabouts. Nothing is known about the fate of the real Mr Anderson. Mr Anderson's former wife, Christine, appealed to the authorities to let her know what had become of her ex-husband."

Christine Anderson Barlow appeared, wiping away tears with a linen handkerchief and appealing to the authorities.

"Ms Sandra Murray, who befriended the man who was apprehended after he was injured, also appealed to the authorities."

Sandra appeared on screen, her cloud of red hair distinguishing her even at his oblique angle to the screen, and he heard her familiar soft accents again: "My friend has not been charged with anything. He is ill and needs medical attention. He can't even remember enough to know whether he did anything wrong or not, and it's intolerable that he should be treated this way without anyone having to say why, or what they think he's done. They should . . ."

The announcer cut her off, and the sequence proceeded with Sir Philip, looking harrassed outside Stellar and denying that his company had acted improperly. Wavevector found it hard to concentrate: the sound of Sandra's voice had affected him more than he'd thought possible. She had referred to him as her friend. Perhaps Sir Philip hadn't told her yet.

Foster and McKenzie watched until the sequence was over, then both looked at Wavevector accusingly. Behind them the presenter rambled on about redundancies at a car plant.

"The . . . interview with Ms Murray," Wavevector said, for once meeting their eyes. "When would that have occurred?"

"This morning," answered McKenzie, as Foster jumped and looked away. "Phil said he was going to talk to her this afternoon."

"Oh," said Wavevector.

"It's horrible," said Foster, to McKenzie. "I mean, she's a bright pretty woman, and she believes that . . . I mean, it's horrible."

"Why, 'horrible'?" asked Wavevector, rebelling at his dismissal.

Foster left the television and came over to the conservatory door. "I've seen the radiographs," he said, with an angry air of getting something off his chest. "I know what you really look like. And you're walking around inside poor Mr Anderson's dead body! It makes me sick. And if I think of you kissing that innocent girl—it's like a horror film come true. Looking at you when I know what you really are makes my skin crawl, and that's a normal human reaction. That's why 'horrible,' you horrible thing."

Wavevector sat still, trying to analyse this. It made no sense. He had always found the appearance of his own kind aesthetically pleasing, and he could see no reason why a human should find it horrible. But perhaps it *was* the normal human reaction: humans were often irrational. Would Sandra's skin crawl when she thought of what he was, and remembered how she had kissed him? The thought that it might was quite agonising.

Foster glared down at him a moment longer, then went back to the television and changed channels.

The two men switched the television off at eleven o'clock. Foster went upstairs; McKenzie emptied and rinsed the toilet bucket and checked that the generator for the diamagnetic field was working properly. Wavevector lay down on his shredded paper and pulled the blanket over himself. He listened to the sounds of McKenzie's own preparations for bed: the sofa cushions moved to the floor; the sheets going on; the trip to the toilet, the soft rustle of clothes being hung up; the grunt of a body lying down. Stillness, soft breathing.

He waited until midnight, then got stealthily to his knees and picked up the cardboard box. It gave out a hollow grating sound against the mesh at the bottom of the cell when he pulled it out from under the paper, and he froze. There was no change in McKenzie's breathing. Wavevector swept some more paper over the gap he had just made in the insulation, and ran his fingers along the box, tracing its folds. He started to tear a flap off. The noise was very loud in the stillness, and he stopped, afraid. McKenzie grunted in his sleep, and turned. Wavevector waited a minute to be sure he'd settled, then began folding the flap back and forth, back and forth, until it was worn and soft at the place where it bent. Then he tore it, forcing his clumsy hands to do the job in one long rip. It still made a noise, but not quite such a loud one. McKenzie stirred again, then settled again.

Sitting back on his heels, Wavevector rolled the cardboard flap into a tube: it was wide enough to make two and a half layers of card. He packed shredded paper into the end of the tube, moistening it with spit to glue it. Then he crawled to the bucket. The plastic handle was slotted through the sides of the bucket and secured by two small knobs. He wrapped the blanket around the bucket to muffle the noise, then wrenched the handle out. He unwrapped the bucket, wrapped the handle, pushed it into the paper on the floor, held it down with his foot, and pulled up on one end. The *snap*, as the handle broke in half, was reassuringly small.

Wavevector unwrapped his prize, and wedged the end of one half of the bucket handle into his crudely glued tube, so that it curled round a forty-five degree angle from the tube's end, with the small knob at the bottom. He picked it up and waggled it cautiously back and forth: it seemed secure. Good.

Picking up the blanket, he went over to the end of the cell by the generator. He folded the blanket into a pad, and with this for insulation, leaned, very, very, carefully, against the mesh. He carefully slipped the bucket handle through the mesh, then advanced the tube after it until the plastic knob was poised over the controls of the generator. The controls had a small clear plastic panel over them, to protect them from disturbance. Wavevector struggled to catch the edge of it with the plastic knob. His hands remained frustratingly clumsy, and they were trembling, too. He felt himself starting to sweat, though it was cold, standing there naked in the dark conservatory.

The plastic knob caught the edge of the little panel, flipping it up, but then slipped onwards and snagged against the mesh. The bucket handle slid out of the tube, rattled against the mesh, and fell to the floor with a clatter.

Wavevector froze, his heart thundering painfully. There was no change in McKenzie's breathing. Wavevector drew the cardboard tube back through the mesh. It should be all right: he still had another half bucket handle. He could not afford to lose this one, though. How could he make it more secure?

He had a memory of Malcolm tying his shoes for him. He visualised the strings crossing and knotting. He could probably make his hands do that. Very well. What to use for string? Blanket.

He unfolded the blanket. It was thick, and made of a harsh coarse dark-green felt. Foster had grabbed it from some storeroom at Stellar: probably it was meant for insulating equipment or putting out fires, not for sleeping under. Wavevector tried to tear a strip off, and couldn't. He felt along the edges: they were prevented from unravelling by a black cord. He broke the cord with his teeth, then unthreaded a section and bit it off. He put the second half bucket handle in his cardboard tube, and wrapped the cord around the tube several times, compressing the cardboard and the gluey paper about the plastic. For ten aching sweating minutes he struggled to tie a knot. The sense of triumph when he finally succeeded nearly made him sick. He folded up the blanket and braced himself against it once again, and again fed the cardboard tube out through the mesh. Try as he might, he could not see the controls clearly enough to know which keys to press. He closed his eyes and scanned, but they were close packed, and he could not distinguish them. The cardboard tube shuddered in his unsteady hands. What if he pushed the wrong button, and brought the field down on top of himself?

He fumbled the tube back and forth, back and forth, struggling to see what to do. He knocked a key, and the display flashed faintly, but he couldn't read it. Then he accidentally knocked the protective panel and brought it down again.

He opened his eyes and stared at the generator. Near the bottom a small green light shone from the side facing away from him, indicating that the refrigeration unit was working. He lowered his cardboard tube and eased the angled bucket handle towards the light. The knob on the end dropped into a small indentation just below that green glow. Not daring to breathe, he drew it back towards himself. Something rocked, and there was a small distinct *click*. The small green light turned red: he had switched the refrigeration unit off. Now the generator would gradually warm up and the superconducting components would fail, taking the diamagnetic field with them.

The trouble was, that failure would take time. Assuming that the components were made of ceramic superconductors, the case had to be chilled to about 70 degrees above absolute zero. It was well insulated. The portable unit which Stellar had used to trap him in the lift had taken about three hours to fail. This unit was larger: it was probably wise to calculate a failure time of at least four hours. What time was it now? Too late. Dawn would be early, and would probably arrive before the field failed. McKenzie would be sleeping more lightly, and might wake. Even if he didn't, Wavevector would have no chance to put any distance between his captors and himself. He could not risk the wait.

He turned his attention back to the controls for the generator and once more struggled to switch it off, but with no more success than before: he simply couldn't see what he was doing, and even where he could see, his hands would not coordinate with his eyes. At last he drew his crude tool back into the cell and set it down. He had done all he could by mechanical means: he was going to have to try electro-magnetic ones.

He was nervous of this. He could never have done any violent manipulations from inside the cell anyway: Sir Philip was quite right that he needed to touch what he was manip-

ulating for that. But there were gentler things that could be
done with emissions—only he was unsure whether he could
do them from inside a human body. The tissues were so delicate, so quick to feel pain: he was afraid of damaging himself before he hurt anything else. Still, he had no option but
to try.

After a few minutes' thought, he sat down in the shredded paper, facing the generator. Gingerly he held both palms
out towards it and concentrated. He was aware of himself as
a tangle of energies held in perpetual dance about a still centre; he was aware of his body as a thicket of nerves that
wound about the energies and held them firmly. The energies oscillated, shifting from one mode to another faster than
an eye could blink: if they remained constant, they would
overload the body, causing seizures and worse. He focused
them down into the branching nerve tendrils of his hands,
then emitted a beam of infrared radiation, through his hands
and the diamagnetic field into the casing of the generator, as
though he were humming a single low note.

His palms grew warm. He scanned the small spot of
warmth, which had formed on the casing of the generator,
and emitted more fiercely. At once his hands began to hurt:
he lowered the emission again. Slowly the warm spot
spread, glowing round the case, eating inwards to the super-
cooled fluid within. He kept emitting, steadily, steadily, not
too hard, and the glow brightened.

Even this moderate use of energy was draining, when
there was no way of absorbing more. After a few minutes,
he was fighting to keep his concentration: a weariness that
had nothing to do with his organic body kept tugging at his
head until he feared that he would faint. Gravitational Constant must have tried this, and exhausted himself setting heat
against the refrigeration unit's chill. Gravitational Constant
would have been unable to turn the unit off, of course. *What
probability do you attach to your chance of escape?* Gravitational Constant had asked him. He had been unable to calculate it. Could he calculate it now?

Abruptly the aching blur of the field around him flickered. He drew in his breath with a gasp and jerked back his hands. The diamagnetic field fluctuated again, like a film of oil on a puddle—and then, like a landscape concealed by a mist, he sensed the firm strength of the Earth's magnetic field beyond it. The film that separated him from it swirled madly for an instant longer, and then it was gone. He reached out gladly and drew on power. For a moment he drew so eagerly that his body protested, his stomach turning with familiar nausea—but he regained his balance, pulsed the draw, and renewed himself.

I calculate my chance of escape at greater than 90%! he emitted joyfully, as though there were anyone to hear him.

Then he sobered. He had yet to get out of the cell. Out of the cell, out of the house and into the world, where he must survive at least long enough to free Gravitational Constant. Put all those together, and the odds were less favourable.

He reached out and touched the wire mesh, cringing a little as he did so, despite his certain knowledge that its diamagnetic properties had gone. The mesh was thin and light: it was held to the wooden posts with thick iron staples. It would be no help to push it loose unless he could also shift at least one part of the cell's wood and metal frame. There were a couple of joints in the frame which his preliminary scans had shown to be weak, but his best hope was the door. This had a thick bolt, secured with a padlock—but weak brass hinges. He hurried over to it and pushed tentatively. Weak, but not that weak: he might be able to force them if he flung himself against the door with all his strength—but then he would crash through into the wall of the conservatory, and the shattering glass would undoubtedly wake Foster upstairs, let alone McKenzie two metres away. He had planned to try a little electromagnetic tampering here, and resort to brute force only if more subtle means failed. His earlier success only gave him confidence.

He scanned through the wooden door frame to find the exact location of the hinges, then carefully grasped the in-

side of the door directly over each. Not heat, this time: set
fire to the wood and he'd wake his guards. Cold. Leaning
against the door he once again concentrated himself down
into his hands. He pulled at the energy in the hinges, drawing it away with the power he himself drew from the Earth.
The wood beneath his hands chilled rapidly, and there was a
sudden crack as moisture in it became ice and split it open.
He scanned the hinges eagerly but the cracks were in the
wrong places, and he could not pull the hinges out. Impatiently, he drew harder, and suddenly his hands hurt. He tried
to let go of the door, and found that his palms were frozen
to the wood. He tried to drag them loose.

The door hinges, super-chilled and brittle with cold,
snapped. The door came off, still stuck to his hands, and the
bolt on its other side squealed as it twisted in its socket.
Wavevector struggled to balance it. His hands came loose
with a tearing sensation, and something wet ran down his
wrist. He succeeded in propping the door open against the
cell and scanned the twisted wood anxiously. Some of the
skin of his palms was frozen to the door frame. Stupid, stupid, stupid! Now his hands were bleeding, and would be less
use than ever. They didn't hurt much, though: they'd gone
numb. He wiped them on the shredded paper, then went
back to fetch the blanket before edging out the broken door
of the cell.

McKenzie was stirring, disturbed by the squealing of the
bolt. Heart pounding, hardly daring to breathe, Wavevector
crouched down with the blanket over his shoulders and
waited for the man to settle. The numbness in his hands
started to fade into an ache, and they were still bleeding: he
could feel a trickle running down his left forearm. McKenzie turned on to his side, and his breathing steadied.

Wavevector edged towards him. This was the hard part.
He had wanted all along just to slip out the nearest way,
through the conservatory door. But what use was it to escape
the house penniless and dressed in a blanket? Humans did
not wander about dressed in blankets: he would attract at-

tention even before Stellar started searching for him. He
needed clothing—clothing and money, and for those he had
to go inside. But to do that he had no choice but to step
across McKenzie, and he was terrified. If McKenzie woke,
he did not know what would happen. He would not go back
in the cell, of that he was certain. Somebody would die. He
did not know whether he was more frightened of the thought
that he might die himself, or of the thought that he might kill
McKenzie. It was contrary to principle to destroy a reasoning entity. He had violated principle before, but never as
drastically as that. And of his captors, McKenzie was the
one he found most sympathetic.

He stopped at the door that led into the sitting room and
looked down at McKenzie's sleeping form, for a minute unable to move. Then he drew a deep breath, grasped the door
frame with one bleeding hand, and stepped up and over and
down. He almost stumbled the other side, but caught himself. McKenzie slept on, peacefully oblivious, and
Wavevector blinked back tears of relief.

McKenzie had folded his clothing and draped it across
the sofa. Wavevector hurried over and grabbed it. He would
not put it on here: he might make a noise. He scanned the
clothes rapidly as he stumbled towards the front door: there
were coins and a wallet in the left hand trouser pocket.
Good—that was everything. No! Shoes. He went back for
them, then hurried to the door. It had a handle and a Yale: he
put the clothes down, twisted the Yale open with both hands,
then, as Malcolm had once shown him, put it on the latch
and turned the handle. It was wet and slippery, and his hands
hurt more when he touched it, but he got it open. McKenzie
stirred again at the cool night air, and muttered in his sleep.
Hurriedly Wavevector gathered up clothes, shoes, blanket,
stepped out into the night, and quietly closed the door behind him.

There were trees around the cottage, and a thick damp
smell of things growing. The air was moist and cold.
Wavevector staggered up the drive, the gravel hurting his

bare feet, and crouched down at the first bend. He was dizzy, shivering with cold and with the reaction to his escape, and he squatted with his head between his knees until it cleared a little. The ache in his hands was growing worse. He ignored it, and began putting on the clothes.

They did not fit. McKenzie was shorter and stouter than Wavevector. Wavevector managed to get his arms down the shirt sleeves only to find that the cuffs ended well above his wrists. The shirt was wide enough, but he could not do up the buttons: he had never been able to do up buttons, and now his fingers could barely feel them. The pants were all right, but the trousers were too short, and he could not do up the button at the waist of those, either, and the belt kept slipping. He had no idea what to do with the tie: in the end, he shoved it in the pocket of the jacket. The jacket sleeves were too short, though he welcomed the warmth when he got it on. But the worst problem was the shoes: they were at least two sizes too small.

He considered going back to the house and trying Foster's things instead: the younger man was nearer his size. But he could not face it. He was out, he was free, and he hadn't killed anyone. He could not go back. He must go on, and hope to find some other shoes. If he held the jacket closed, people might not notice how badly his clothes fitted him. How much did humans notice clothes, normally?

He abandoned the shoes and walked on up the drive, blanket over his shoulders, going on the grassy verge to spare his feet. The trees around him rustled in the night air. There were houses not far away: he could scan them, and sense the field produced by their electrical power. Could he go up to the people in their homes, and say—what? "I am sorry, I have been in an accident, can I telephone for transport to get me . . ." Where could he go?

The drive came out in a paved car park before a low, glass-fronted building. A light burned dimly behind the glass, outlining the frosted letters which spelled out in elegant italic script "*THE OAKS*," and, in smaller letters beneath,

"*Health and Hospitality.*" He stopped. It was of course quite impossible to ask for help here. It was too close, and too much in Stellar's control. And people might recognise him: his face—Anderson's face—had appeared on the television only hours before.

His heart began a slow sick thudding. In his earlier calculations he had made no allowance for the publicity. He realised now that he could not ask for help, not from anyone. Even before Stellar raised the alarm, he would be recognised, pinpointed, detained. And whatever mysterious reasons Stellar had had for keeping his existence secret before would surely not be strong enough to hold them silent now that he was free. He must assume that the search would begin as soon as he was known to be missing, and that it would intensify with each hour that passed. He must assume, too, that Stellar had told his handful of friends what he really was, and that they would now react as normal humans, and reject him. The whole planet would reject him. There was no help for him. He was on his own.

There was one thing which he must do. He had promised Gravitational Constant that he would try to free him. If he suffered because of his own stupidity, that was grievous but natural: it was intolerable to make Gravitational Constant suffer as well.

Gravitational Constant had never been exactly a friend. He was older than Wavevector, and he had always had other interests. Their kind was largely solitary anyway, pursuing individual interests for decades or centuries at a stretch, meeting together only occasionally. Yet they were aware of themselves as belonging to the same class, and to fail to show concern for one another would be contrary to principle. Whenever a star manifested the kind of conditions necessary to produce a new intelligence, there was always a crowd gathered in readiness, and any new entity found plenty of advisers to instruct him in language and in knowledge. Gravitational Constant had come to Earth because there was concern about Wavevector; Wavevector could not abandon him. That was a given which every plan of action had to accommodate.

And perhaps if Gravitational Constant were free, he would be able to help Wavevector disentangle himself from Anderson's body. Perhaps he could prevent the linkages from readhering after they were severed. Then they could both leave the Earth. That must be Wavevector's aim.

Something deep in the battered, exhausted body suddenly protested that it was *not* his aim, that he had never lived so intensely before, that he was in love—with Earth and with being human and with Ms Sandra Murray—and he did not want to go.

This desire is irrational, he told himself, astonished at the reaction. *If you remain upon Earth, the overwhelming probability is that you will be destroyed.* But he remembered the smell of strawberries, and a bird singing in a garden, and Sandra's smile, and the irrational desire grew stronger. He made himself insist. *This longing is incapable of fulfilment. The biological entities will reject you—except for those who wish to use you. You must escape.*

There could be no argument: the case was overwhelming. But the desire persisted. He felt himself begin to cry. He tried to ignore the tears, and scanned carefully in every direction. There was a concentration of power signals to the north-east: that would be the town. Where was Stellar in relation to the town centre? South-east, but not, he thought, as far south as he was now. He would have to walk east and north. He would walk as far as he could tonight, and then hide somewhere and rest. If he had an opportunity to acquire food—and shoes—without calling attention to himself, he must take it: otherwise he must do without.

He scanned, found that The Oaks' main drive led eastward, and started walking.

It was hard walking barefoot, and the ache in his hands was now a steady savage burning. He stumbled down to a country road, and found the path east blocked by a hedge. He had no idea how to get through a hedge, so he turned and

started to walk north along the verge of the road. Behind the
hedge, the sky was turning grey: the night was drawing to its
early summer end. The dew wet his feet, but the chill at least
numbed them a little to the prick of stone and stick, thistle
and nettle on the verge.

Lights glared before him. His heart gave an instantaneous
hammer of terror, and he turned and dropped against the
western hedge, pulling the blanket over himself for conceal-
ment. For a moment he was surprised at his own fear of
meeting a human, *any* human, but then he realised that his
fear was perfectly rational. Once his existence became common knowledge, any man was likely to be his enemy.

The headlights glared brighter, swept over him, and departed. He had not been seen.

Wavevector got to his feet and began walking again. The
grey in the east gave way to pink. The next time he hid from
a car, he found it difficult to get up again. His physical condition had always been one of the obstacles to his escape:
the body had been abused fearfully over the past two weeks,
by himself and by his enemies, and it was shaking with exhaustion. He forced it up with an effort, and continued walking. The first orange beams of sunlight struck the hedge,
criss-crossing him with a tangle of shadows. The part of
himself which had protested that it did not want to leave
Earth started protesting again. He found himself conducting
a long argument with it, an argument complicated by its insistence on thinking in English while he responded in his
own language, so that the concepts jarred against one another painfully in his divided mind.

"We've had so little time!" the English-speaker pleaded.
"Two weeks, and for all of those we've been ill. Most of the
time we've had amnesia and been in pain. If we like it despite that, what would it be like to be whole, to be well, to
be walking here in this translucent dawn with the birds
singing as they are now, to have shoes on, and no pain, and
Sandra beside us . . ."

It is senseless to imagine that, he replied. *She knows what we are. The biological entities were unanimous that the instinctive human reaction to our nature is one of horror and distress.*

"But not from Sandra! She knows us. Surely we could explain. I don't think Sir Philip told her that we regretted distressing her. He hates us. I don't know why, but he does. He would want her to hate us too. Surely we could explain. We could telephone. There are pay telephone boxes, we've seen them. We could telephone her, and explain. She would help us."

We would betray our escape and our location. I quote you, in your own language, what the biological entities have said: "That's obscene"; "Any woman would be distressed"; "Looking at you when I know what you really are makes my skin crawl, and that's a normal human reaction." It is unreasonable to presume we can predict a human's behaviour better than another human can.

"You say that, you—horrible thing. You just want to escape the pain, and get away from the indignity of being human, from clumsiness and sleep and eating and bodily functions. We're alive, don't you understand that? We never were before."

You—negatively valued lump of inert organic material! You are not me. I do not know what this has done to me. I must escape before I go insane.

"See? You are arrogant. You thought yourself so superior to biological intelligences. You thought you could run experiments on them. You even thought you could manipulate the body of one. Who's manipulating whom?"

Leave me alone! I don't want to be entangled with you.

"Yes you do. You want it more than anything else, and you know it."

I don't! You terrify me. I must, I must, escape!

There was the roar of another car engine, much too close. Day had arrived, and there had been no glare of headlights to warn him in advance. Wavevector flung himself away from the road. The western hedge had given way to woodland, and he crashed into the undergrowth and collapsed. He scanned the car slowing. It stopped. It reversed, and pulled over on to the verge. But it had missed its place: it was still a little distance away down the road. He lay face-down under the blanket, hoping that the dark green cloth would shelter him from the driver's eyes. Then the driver's door opened, and Sandra got out.

Wavevector recognised her at once, though his open eyes stared only into the dark ground beneath the blanket. All the time he consciously thought himself human, some sleeping part of his mind must have been scanning her shape, noting her temperature and the angles of her bones beneath her skin.

He almost jumped up. His human part began to scream at him that she'd come to look for him, to help him. But he held it in check: she might have come because she was angry with him and wanted to confront him. It seemed unlikely that Sir Philip would have told her where he was for any friendly purpose, and she had no cause to be on this road unless she were going to The Oaks. He could not risk speaking to her—and he was more afraid of her than of anyone else. He knew that if she shuddered when she looked at him, it would hurt him worse than any diamagnetic field.

But something inside him still cried helplessly, Sandra, Sandra, I'm here. Look at me and smile again, or I can't bear it.

SANDRA HAD WOKEN AT DAWN WITH THE THOUGHT, "What if he's at The Oaks?"

She had not been consciously thinking about where the man-whose-name-was-not-Paul was being kept. When she had fallen asleep her thoughts had been about Malcolm. Something had happened to the relationship between her and Malcolm. They had both been friends of the same man—whom she could not call Paul—but now that he had vanished, what was left between Malcolm and her was not the neutral companionship she'd somehow expected. She was fairly sure that Malcolm didn't want it to be, either. She wished that he did. She had been in love with—not Paul—but Sir Philip's revelation had left her feelings in turmoil. She could not claim that it made no difference to her to know that he wasn't human. It made an immense difference, but she wasn't sure what the difference was. And Malcolm—what was she supposed to do about him, at a time like this? She had even less attention to spare for him than she had for Robert, whose tentative peace-making phone call earlier in the week she had brusquely dismissed. A new emotional entanglement was impossible—she had no energy for it. She was in a turmoil and frightened of the future. How could he demand—? But that was unfair: he hadn't demanded anything. He had been rock-steady, reliably comforting; he had put his arms around her and let her cry against his chest. The last thing she wanted was to hurt him or quarrel with him. So what was she to do?

But despite falling asleep in the middle of this, she had woken early, fully alert, thinking, "What if Paul's at The Oaks?"

She lay motionless in her bed, looking at the dawn light brightening through the window. Her radio-alarm clock spelled the time in glowing red numerals: 4:27. They might have taken him to The Oaks. They'd wanted him to go there before, when they thought he was Anderson: he'd said that they owned it, and that he was afraid to go there. They couldn't have left him at Stellar, for fear of police searches. They wouldn't have dared put him in a hotel or one of their own houses, for fear of the press. Maybe the security service people involved had him in a house somewhere, or in some terrible research lab—but she'd had the impression that it was Sir Philip who had control, not the security service people. It was Sir Philip he had pleaded with, on that tape. (*Please, I don't think you understand how much it hurts . . .*) So where would Sir Philip put him, except The Oaks?

She got up and dressed. It was no use trying to go back to sleep now: she was much too wide awake. The only constructive thing to do was to go to The Oaks and look around. It was still early enough that she could do that without attracting too much attention.

She found the address in the yellow pages, under "Health Clubs and Fitness Centres," and consulted a map for the best way there. She thought about asking someone to go with her. Rod and Dave were sleeping in her second bedroom. But Rod had been so firmly opposed to the very idea of rescue that she rejected the notion at once. She thought of phoning Malcolm, who'd gone home for the night. But that was complicated, complicated: she didn't want to see Malcolm at all, right now. She left a note—"Gone to look at The Oaks"—on the dining room table, just in case, and started off alone.

There was no traffic, this early in the morning, and she negotiated the ring-road easily, and set off along the correct road leading south from the town. She drove several miles without incident, and she was beginning to think of slowing down to watch for the turn, when she saw a figure walking along the verge in the distance, a dark tramping shape that looked ragged against the new morning. She slowed, and it seemed to notice her. At once it darted off into the woods at the side of the road and vanished. The car's momentum carried her past the place, but she stopped. Her heart was beating rapidly, and the steering wheel under her hands was slippery with sweat. Afterwards she could not explain her certainty as to who it was, but she had known, instantly and beyond reason.

She backed the car up. There was no sign of the dark figure. The grass glistened with dew, the trees dappled the bracken at their feet with shadow. She told herself that if it was him, if he had somehow escaped, he would hide: any car might belong to a party sent out to seek and recapture him. She got out of the car and stood where he could see her.

There was no sound from the forest, no sound but the singing of the birds.

"Paul?" she shouted, her voice thin and frightened in the morning calm. "Paul, it's me! Sandra!"

No answer.

She waded into the undergrowth, and the bracken splashed her bare legs with dew. There was no trace of any man. Perhaps it had not been him: perhaps it had been some tramp or poacher who was now slipping out of this piece of woodland on the other side, hoping she was no relation of the farmer's. "Paul, it's me!" she called again, more tentatively than before. Then she wondered if that was reassurance enough. Humans had deceived and betrayed him, imprisoned and tortured him. She was human. Perhaps he didn't trust her.

"Paul!" she shouted. "I've come to help. If it's you, please, let me help!"

The silence and the birdsong endured a few moments longer—and then the dark shape rose out of the bracken about twenty metres away. She whirled towards him with a gasp of relief—then froze.

He was haggard and exhausted, with a three-day growth of beard and hollows under his eyes. His face was smeared with blood, and there was blood all over the front of the white shirt that hung open over the gaping, too-short trousers. He had blood on his chest and there was more blood in a thick bright stain around his right arm. He had a green blanket draped about his shoulders. When he took a step towards her, she saw that he was barefoot, and that there was blood on his feet as well.

His eyes met her appalled ones, and he stopped. A look of anguish crossed his face and he looked away. "I'm sorry," he said, in a tone of perfect clarity and absolute despair.

"Paul!" she exclaimed again, and ran towards him. For a moment she thought he was going to run away, but he evidently decided that he couldn't, and stood still. She slowed a few steps away, then stopped: part of her wanted to seize and hold him; part of her was afraid of hurting or alarming him; part of her was afraid of him, and part just scared of the blood. "What have they done to you?" she cried. "Oh, my God! You look awful!"

He looked back at her with surprise. "What do you mean?" he asked.

"You're covered in blood. Oh, my God, your hands!" She had seen now where the blood came from: the palms of both hands were a red ruin. The bright stain around his right arm was only the place where blood had soaked into the old bandage. At least, she hoped that that was all it was. "What happened to your poor hands?"

He looked at them in confusion, as though he hadn't noticed their condition before. "I hurt them. Getting out." He looked back at her. "Sandra, I . . . I never wanted you distressed. I did not know who I was: I never intended to decieve you."

"What are you talking about?" she asked, still staring in horror at his condition.

He looked even more confused. "Didn't Sir Philip Lloyd tell you? He said he would tell you."

She did not have to ask, "Tell me what?" "He told me," she said.

He gave her the telescope look—no, it was not that, it was a look of intense and bewildered analysis, of a powerful mind struggling to make sense of something completely outside its experience. "And it didn't . . . distress you?" he asked hesitantly.

She bit her lip. "Look," she said. "Maybe it did distress me. But what they were doing to you distressed me much, much more. I came here to help you, Paul. I suddenly thought that maybe you were at The Oaks, and I came to see if there was anything I could do to help. Please trust me."

He shook his head. "I'm sorry," he said. "I never meant to distress you."

She realised the head-shake had not been refusal, but postponement of the whole question of help and trust, in favour of the apology for distressing her. Stunned, she wondered why he thought that so important. "Please!" she said impatiently. "You're in an awful state, don't you realise that? Anyone who sees you is going to phone the hospital or the police. And you probably don't know: there's been a fuss about you on the television and in the newspapers. You don't dare go around openly, especially not while you look like that. Come with me. We can hide you, for a few days at least, while we think what to do."

He looked at her earnestly, then suddenly smiled—the same radiantly joyful smile he had used to greet her before she knew who he was. Her own heart leapt with joy in response, and she saw, with dread, that in some ways knowing he wasn't human had changed nothing.

"Thank you," he said quietly. "Thank you very much."

She took his arm, and he allowed her to guide him back through the undergrowth to the waiting car.

THIRTEEN

THEY DROVE IN SILENCE NORTHWARDS TOWARDS THE town. The passenger was too stunned with stress and exhaustion to speak, the driver too bemused by a sense of unreality. When they entered the narrower, house-lined streets, however, Sandra recovered herself sufficiently to warn her passenger to crouch down. "You mustn't be seen," she told him.

Wavevector kneeled down obediently on the floor of the car, resting his head and arms on the passenger seat and clumsily tugging up the blanket to conceal himself. He had to use the backs of his hands and his teeth to pull at it: it hurt now to touch anything with the palms. He turned his head so that he could see Sandra's face, profiled against the window and framed by the fall of her hair. His rescuer, his one clear signal in the static: just to look at her restored to him a fragile sense of hope. "Do you have any idea where I can hide?" he asked her.

She made a face without looking at him. Her eyes were fixed on the road. "I'd offer you my house," she said, "but you'd be found there. It's the first place they'll look." There was a pause, and then she said, "You did escape, didn't you? They will be looking for you?"

It reminded him again of how much had changed in the past few days, how little each of them knew of the other's mind.

"Yes," he said heavily. "They will look for me."

There was another pause, and then she said, "I think you'd be all right with Malcolm."

That must mean that Malcolm too accepted him for what he was. He smiled so that his face hurt. Then he remembered his situation. "Won't they look for me there, too?" he asked anxiously.

"I don't think they will," she said slowly. "Sir Philip Lloyd has never really noticed Malcolm at all. He's just the hired help, as far as Sir Philip's concerned. He's never spoken to him. Even when he came and told us about you, he barely even looked at Malcolm: it was all 'Mr Jones' this and 'Ms Murray' that. I don't think he even remembers Malcolm's name. When we get to my house, wait in the car. I'll go in and telephone Malcolm to check it's OK, and if it is, I'll drive you over there."

"Thank you."

He was silent for a few minutes, thinking. The clock on the car's dashboard said six thirty-two. McKenzie and Foster had usually risen at about eight. He had left them sleeping: there should be no reason for them to wake up early. When they did wake, though, the search would begin. "I hope this will not cause difficulties for you, or for Malcolm," he told Sandra uncomfortably.

"This is what I choose," she declared fiercely. "There is no other course I want to take. And I'm sure Malcolm will say the same."

No, he really did not understand humans. But it seemed that Foster and Sir Philip Lloyd didn't either.

"Thank you very much," he repeated humbly.

At her house she parked hurriedly and ran to the front door, keys jangling in her hand. She was aware of all the

windows on the street facing her: blank screens where her
presence, early and urgent, might register and be remembered. She unlocked the door and hurried in. It was not yet
seven o'clock, but when she opened the front door, Rod
erupted from the kitchen, barefoot in trousers and no shirt,
clutching her note. His chest was remarkably hairy.

"Thank God!" he exclaimed when he saw her. "You were
out of your fucking mind, going off on your own like that.
What if he *had* been there, and you ran into a fucking army
of Stellars with pistols?"

"He's in the car," she said. "I've got to call Malcolm."
She went to the telephone and glanced at the table beside it:
Malcolm's number was still new enough to be on the top of
the notepad. She began dialling.

"What the fuck do you mean?" asked Rod, in his police
siren voice. "You never broke him out?!"

"He escaped. I met him on the road," said Sandra. The
telephone rang, and she cradled it to her ear, counting the
rings impatiently: one, two . . .

"Jesus," whispered Rod. "Jesus Holy Christ!"

. . . three, four . . .

"Hello?" A woman's voice, strong, middle-aged and
West Indian. Malcolm's mother; she had almost forgotten
Malcolm's formidable mother. For a moment she almost
panicked. What would Malcolm's mother think of Paul? Did
Malcolm have a father too—a resident father, who might
object to having his house invaded by aliens? Malcolm had
never mentioned his father. She knew nothing about Malcolm, nothing—except that she trusted him as she trusted no
one else.

"Mrs Brown?" she gasped. "This is Sandra Murray. May
I speak to Malcolm, please?"

"You've got a fucking escaped alien sitting in the fucking
car?" wailed Rod, and Sandra shushed him impatiently with
one hand.

A pause, and then Malcolm's voice, familiar and glad:
"Sandra! What's up?"

She stifled the urge to burst into tears, and began telling him. Rod stood staring at her for a few moments, then shot off up the stairs. She heard him yelping at Dave to get up as they had an emergency.

"OK, OK," said Malcolm, as soon as he'd grasped the situation. "Bring him here. I'll explain things to my Mum; it'll be OK."

"Will it? I know it's her house—that is, it is her house, isn't it? I'm sorry, I don't know at all what your circumstances are, but I don't know where else to take him, and he's hurt . . ."

"It's OK," repeated Malcolm. "It is a house, and it does belong to my Mum. Hey, if he's hurt it makes things easier: my Mum'll drop the questions and come down on him in nurse mode. Bring him here."

"Where are you? I don't know your address."

"Bury Road, number eighty-two. See you in a few minutes."

She knew the road: it was only about a mile away, a road of drab Victorian terraces like her own. She and Malcolm must have bought things from the same shops, posted letters in the same letter boxes, cursed the same roadworks, for years, without meeting. Of all the wild and unreal things about that morning, this suddenly seemed the wildest and most unreal of all. She set the phone down slowly, once more fighting tears.

Rod pelted down the stairs with his shirt half off and half on, arms full of a camera and a black vinyl carry-all. Dave stumbled sleepily after him. His shirt was on, but he was holding his trousers in one hand and his shoes in the other. He stopped half-way down the stairs, put the shoes on the step below him, and slid his left leg through the trouser leg and into his left shoe. Then he put his right foot through the trousers into his right shoe, pulled the trousers up, and fastened them as he continued down. When he reached the foot of the stairs, he took the camera from Rod and did up his fly. He was ready to go.

Sandra had no desire whatsoever to traipse into Malcolm's house trailing a television camera team. It would shake up the neighbourhood like a brass band. But it was clearly no use telling the two men to stay behind, and the longer she delayed, the more people would be awake to notice them. She confined herself to a furious demand for secrecy and swished out the door. Rod and Dave at least had the sense not to peer through the windows of her car and not to maximise the disturbance by collecting their own. They climbed into the back of the red Sierra without comment, and Sandra got into the front and started the engine.

"It's OK with Malcolm," she told the blanket-covered shape beside her, and pulled out.

Wavevector was enormously relieved to see her again. As soon as she'd left the car, he had been possessed by doubts. What if he had mistaken her? What if the person she really meant to telephone was Sir Philip, to say, "It's all right, I've got him?" Her look of horror when she first saw him was seared into his memory. He had believed her explanation of it, that she was merely shocked at his condition; his human instincts had told him that yes, all the small signals her face and voice sent out were those of concern and affection—but how could he judge the honesty of humans? What if that horror were what she really felt, and the rest a pretence? Her return reassured him: in her actual presence he *knew* she would not betray him. But her companions made him anxious, despite the fact that he'd recognised them by scanning even before they got into the car. Their presence was unexpected, and he could not account for it. Rod and Dave should not be at Sandra's house: they lived in Romford. He lifted his head and peered under the blanket into the back seat. The two men were staring at him. It was not exactly the same stare as Foster's, but it was not very different. Knowledge, he thought, alters perception. When they looked at me before they saw a human; now they see . . . what? A corpse with a thing from a black hole inside it?

"Hello, Holmes," said Rod, and grinned nervously.

"Hello," Wavevector replied noncommittally. He scanned a small piece of electrical equipment being switched on somewhere out of sight, and grew more anxious still.

"So. You escaped," said Rod.

"Yes," said Wavevector, "Why are you taping this?"

Rod's nervous grin froze into a rictus of alarm. Then he bent over and pulled the cassette recorder out of the black vinyl bag beside him, and set it on his knees. He made no move to switch it off. "I want a record," he said defiantly. "Just to cover my back. We're probably gonna get into trouble for helping you, and I don't want to get into trouble for more than I've really done. That OK?"

He was frightened, Wavevector realised. Frightened by the situation, but also frightened of Wavevector. (*That's a normal human reaction . . .*) "Of course," said Wavevector wearily. "I don't want anyone to get into trouble on my behalf. You can tape what you like."

Sandra turned the corner into Bury Road. It was one of the main roads into town, and even this early in the morning there was traffic on it. That was good, in that the sound of one more car was less likely to attract attention: bad in that there were more chances of being seen. Number eighty-two was an end terrace. It was built of the same yellow-grey brick as her own house, and the garden was trim, but functional: a respectable householder's garden, not an enthusiast's. A familiar 2CV was parked by the kerb in front of it, and there was just space for the red Sierra behind it. She parked, then hurried her blanket-draped charge up to the house and rang the bell. Much to her relief, the door opened at once.

Malcolm and his mother were standing in a small, yellow-carpeted entrance hall, looking as though they'd been interrupted in the middle of an argument. Mrs Brown was frankly aghast. They were both in night dress, Malcolm in white boxer shorts and blue dressing gown, and Sylvia Brown in a magnificent bitter-orange robe over peach-

coloured cotton pyjamas. She gave the newcomers a resent-
ful glare. Then her eyes fixed on Wavevector, and her expression changed.

"Dear Lord!" she exclaimed in concern. "What have you
done to yourself?"

Wavevector stared at her stupidly, and she advanced on
him and caught his elbow, brushing Sandra aside like a cob-
web. "You better come into the kitchen and sit down," she
said. "Malcolm, fetch the first aid box."

Malcolm grinned at Sandra and gave her a "You see?"
flick of the eyebrows behind his mother's back, then ran up
the yellow-carpeted stairs to fetch the first-aid box.

Wavevector found himself marched into a tiled kitchen,
sat upon a chair, and examined. The others stood about and
watched. Rod and Dave were now looking at him with the
same horror that had been on Sandra's face when she first
saw him: the blanket had hidden the blood while he was in
the car. It was obvious that his appearance was shocking. So
much for his carefully thought-out decision to take McKenzie's clothes and money; so much for his hope that if he held
the jacket shut, humans might not notice the ill-fitting un-
buttonable clothes! He felt ashamed and acutely ridiculous,
and it was worse when Dave pulled a still camera out of the
black carrier bag and started taking pictures. He was relieved when Sylvia Brown ordered the cameraman to stop.

Sylvia Brown pronounced his injuries not as bad as they
looked—"hands bleed a lot"—and gave him a basin of
warm salt water and instructions to soak his hands in it while
she saw to his feet. He'd almost forgotten his feet, and he
peered down at them distantly: the walk seemed to have cut
them quite a bit.

"What did you do to your hands?" Mrs Brown asked, as
she heaved a washing-up bowl of warm water under his feet
and began attacking them with cotton wool.

"I had to break a door," he said vaguely. "It didn't hurt at
the time." The combination of exhaustion and anxiety left

him desperately alert, but in a painful uncoordinated fashion. It was hard to think.

"Why are you wearing those clothes?" asked Sandra.

"They belonged to one of the men guarding me. I didn't realise they wouldn't fit."

"What happened to your own clothes? They can't have kept you locked up naked like an animal . . ." She stopped, seeing from the look on his face that they had.

"Did you kill anybody?" asked Rod in a strange thin voice.

Wavevector looked at him, and saw in the expression on the other's face a vision of the cottage where he had been imprisoned—in ruins and littered with dead.

"When you escaped, I mean," Rod went on, into the sudden chill. "Was anybody killed?"

Wavevector shook his head, as much in protest as in denial. "I left when the men guarding me were asleep. If they haven't already woken, they will raise the alarm in about an hour. Mr Jones, I have never killed any reasoning entity."

"Malcolm says," Mrs Brown reported, rinsing her cotton wool, "that Sir Philip Lloyd says you're not human, that you're somethin' called a singularity, that you killed the real Mr Anderson and took him over. He says Sir Philip Lloyd can prove this."

"I didn't kill Anderson," Wavevector replied. "He died in the car accident. I was to blame in that I might have saved his life and didn't, but I didn't murder him. I only linked myself to his body after he was dead."

There was a thick silence, and he felt that he'd said something wrong. Perhaps it was simply the admission that he might have saved Anderson which shocked them, but more likely it was the acknowledgement of what he was. Did it make their skin crawl? He bowed his head so that he would not see their stares of horrified fascination, and looked instead at the reddened water in the bowl on his lap, salt and stinging around his hands.

"I'd been watching Anderson all that day," he explained

defensively. "He'd driven to Aldermaston to discuss Stellar's handling of the Astragen Project with his friend Mark Jaeger, and that was something that concerned me deeply. On the way home he stopped at a pub to eat, and got into an argument with another person there. When he left, he was angry and drove too fast. The car came off the road on a bend and went into the river. The central locking system jammed, and he could not open the doors. When the car went into the water, I wasn't sure at first what was happening. I didn't understand why he couldn't get out. Then I scanned the doors and understood, but I didn't think that I should interfere. It is contrary to principle for my kind to interfere with biological intelligences. I had interfered already, of course, but I was reluctant to violate principle again to save the life of an entity who had been instrumental in frustrating the experiment which I had violated principle to set up. I didn't understand, either, how much it must have hurt him to drown. I didn't know what pain was like: my kind's perceptual system is completely different from yours. For several minutes he struggled to get out, and I did nothing. It was distressing to watch, though, and in the end I intervened and unjammed the locking mechanism. But it was too late by then. He didn't notice, and he kept beating at the windows, until he drowned.

"He'd been dead only a few minutes when Sandra came and pulled his body out of the car. She tried to revive him, and I could perceive that his body wanted to respond, to live, but it had no coordinating intelligence which would allow it to. Until that moment, I hadn't thought of doing what I did. But suddenly it struck me that the situation offered me a wonderful opportunity. For weeks I'd had no access to Stellar Research—they'd broken an agreement with me, and then tried to trap me. I'd been caught once, and had only managed to escape with difficulty. It occurred to me that if I manipulated Anderson's body, I could use it to gain access. No one had ever conducted such a manipulation before, but I could see how it might be done. Only I had to act at once, while the body was still trying to live. So I went to it and forged some links between it and myself. It was an impulse, a stupid, ignorant, reckless impulse. I thought . . . I thought it would be the equivalent of using a computer, that I could programme it electrically. But I had misjudged. The body was not inert, like a machine. It was an organism that wanted to live, and it reacted by seizing me. Every link I made to it multiplied exponentially. I tried to sever them and get out, but they multiplied too rapidly. It became impossible to think, because my own thoughts and perceptions were incompatible with the body's organic brain. Everything I did hurt the body, and when it was hurt, I felt it. In the end I lapsed completely into unreason. When I woke I was thinking with the body's human brain and had no access to my real nature at all."

"After your seizure you said you were trapped, and couldn't get out," said Rod slowly. "It wasn't a car you were talking about, was it?"

Wavevector shook his head. "Natalya Semyonova had told me to think in my own language. It was trying to do that which caused the seizure."

Sandra remembered the night she had taken him from the car, with the layered blades of wheat translucent in the headlights, and the way the body she had been struggling to revive had given a long shudder as life returned to it. What she had done then was not what she'd thought. She had not saved a man's life. She had helped to force life upon an intelligence that had long done without it and hadn't wanted it. She looked at him now, sitting in his blood-smeared, too-small clothes, exhausted, injured, hunted and obviously afraid—and she bitterly regretted what she had done. But she couldn't have known.

"You've got your memory back now, though," she observed quietly.

He looked over at her with an eagerness to be understood that was painfully apparent. "Yes. I've altered my modality, and now I can interface the human perceptions with my own."

"So you are this . . . singularity-thing," said Mrs Brown.

He shrugged, splashing the water on his lap. "Saying that I am a singularity is equivalent to saying that you are an assemblage of carbon-based molecules. It is true, but not particularly informative."

"You really are not human," said Mrs Brown, looking up and meeting his eyes.

"No," agreed Wavevector. "I'm not."

There was another thick silence. Then the nurse's eyebrows lifted in an expressive facial shrug that for a moment gave her a striking resemblance to her son. "OOOK," she said, sounding exactly like Malcolm. "This's gonna be a bit hard to take in, but I think I can handle it. OK. Do you have a name we can pronounce?"

He relaxed slowly. The water about his hands began to shiver: he was trembling with relief. "Wavevector," he answered. "That's an exact translation of the concept."

"Except I for one don't know what it means," put in Rod sourly.

Wavevector looked at him: he'd forgotten the man's astonishing ignorance. "It's the phase gradient," he said.

Baffled silence.

"The direction of propagation of an electromagnetic wave proportional to its spatial frequency," said Wavevector, trying again.

More baffled silence. Then Sandra gave a weak laugh. "He is much the wiser," she observed.

"Well, what the fuck *is* a 'wavevector' then?" asked Rod, in a more natural tone than he had used all morning.

"Don't you use that language in my house!" commanded Mrs Brown warningly.

"It's a physics function," said Sandra. "I must have done it in part 1-A, but I forget. Is there any reason why you're called Wavevector? Or did your parents just like the sound of it?"

"I don't have any parents," he said helplessly. "I'm not biological. I'm called that because I'm very single-minded when I'm interested in something."

They did not understand the connection between wavevectors and single-mindedness; it was abundantly clear that they did not. And yet the atmosphere in the room had changed. The fear had gone. It was as though the fact that he possessed a name and had failings made him comprehensible, ruling out dozens of shadowy and sinister meanings that had hovered around him before.

"OK," said Rod, gathering himself together. "You haven't killed anybody. Can I take it that you didn't come to Earth with any hostile intention—that all this business about it being immoral for you to interfere with 'biological intelligences' means there's no army of singularities out there waiting to invade us? I'm asking this 'cause I want it on record that I asked and you answered."

"I didn't say that interfering with biological intelligences is *immoral*," said Wavevector. "I said that it's *contrary to principle*." He stopped at the puzzled expressions on the five faces around him. The mass of incompatible concepts churned again in his mind, and he wished that the humans would leave him alone and let him lie down and rest. Then he told himself that they were risking reprisals from their own kind for helping him, and he owed them this reassurance.

"Please, you must understand that I am using English words to represent concepts in my own language," he told them. "It is very, very hard to translate. Perhaps I used the wrong word. 'Principle,' I thought, means a fundamental truth or law which forms a basis for reasoning action. To say that I acted in a way which was contrary to principle is closer to saying that what I did was irrational, or even insane, rather than immoral. In fact, I did try to interfere in a moral way. The theory I gave to Stellar is one that will be of benefit to your planet. I chose it because of that: I wished to benefit you. But what I did was still contrary to principle:

any interference with biological entities is. No, of course there's no army of my kind bent on planetary domination. To begin with, we are not a biological species. We have never been subject to any principle of natural selection; we have never had to compete for resources and defend territories. Aggressive instincts which are necessary in your kind would be absurd in ours. Furthermore, planets offer us no resources which are not more easily available to us from stars: we would have nothing to gain by dominating one. Also there are not very many of us, and those there are, are dispersed over a wide area, and only gather together occasionally. We have nothing equivalent to a government, let alone an army. It would be impossible for us to dominate a race of biological intelligences even if the biological intelligences wanted us to. And most of my kind have no interest in planets at all, and regard organic life—I'm sorry—as mere corruption, and biological intelligence as dangerously irrational. That is the reason why it is contrary to principle to interfere with you. It is utterly inconceivable that we should try to dominate you."

"You mean," said Rod, "we're a bunch of dirty little rats breeding in the filth of some dirty little rubbish tip of a planet, and your kind steer well clear of us in case you get bitten. You were stupid enough to come down and set up an experiment, and you got bitten."

Wavevector could not look at him. "I don't think that," he said to the red water around his hands. "It's not how I think about you at all." Not now, he admitted silently to himself. Once, it was true, they had been rats to him. Interesting rats, fascinating rats, rats towards which he had felt a great deal of benevolence—but rats. Only the loss of memory had forced him to respect them.

"But it's how most of your people think about us?" insisted Rod.

Wavevector nodded shame-facedly.

"And there's no Mother Ship or whatever coming to rescue you."

Wavevector shook his head. "We don't use ships."

Rod sighed. "OK, so you're wronged innocence incarnate. You realise, though, that nobody's gonna believe that? If Stellar goes public on you, you are gonna be the object of the biggest manhunt in history."

Wavevector looked up and met Rod's eyes. There was none of the resentment he had feared to see in them, and the nervousness that had been there earlier was gone. Instead he met a look of pitying, probing evaluation.

"I was told," said Wavevector, "that the normal human reaction to what I am is one of horror and disgust. Obviously that cannot be the invariable human reaction. I am very grateful to you all that it is not. I must say that: I am very grateful. Would it be correct, though, to assume that horror would be the most common reaction among those who don't know me?"

Rod nodded. "As soon as the public grasps what's been going on, there's gonna be a howl like nothing on earth. They'll be busing in police from all over the country, and television crews from all over the world. So what are you gonna do? You got maybe two days before the shit hits the fan."

"That long?" asked Wavevector in surprise.

"Sure. Nobody's gonna want to admit they lost you. First of all, Stellar will be out beating the bushes round where you disappeared. When they don't find you, they'll talk to their friends in the security services. That'll probably be this afternoon. That's when the fuck . . ." he glanced warily at Mrs Brown and corrected himself, "I mean, that's when MI5 turn up on our doorstep and confiscate all the material I haven't managed to hide first, and we look innocent and surprised and demand to know what they're looking for. But MI5 are not gonna have a free hand. They don't have the cooperation of the police on this one—in fact, the local boys are pretty narked with them over the way nobody's told them what's going on. If MI5 don't find you—and I bet they won't—they'll have to go to the government and the police, explain the situation, and convince the great and good that you exist. They'll never do that in a hurry. I don't think things will really hot up until tomorrow night at the earliest. But they'll be very hot then."

Wavevector smiled. He had not expected to have two whole days. "I haven't been able to understand why Stellar has kept my existence a secret," he said. "If they had had the resources of your government behind them from the beginning, I would never have been able to escape."

"Jesus!" exclaimed Rod. "You are an innocent! If you can come up with another Astragen Project, you're worth billions. If the government knew about you, the government would take charge of you, and nobody else would get a look in. Stellar was going to hang on to you as long as it possibly could. But I'm surprised MI5 didn't step in sooner."

"They didn't know," replied Wavevector. "When I saw him on Saturday, Commander Jaeger was planning how to tell them."

"Huh!" Rod exclaimed in disgust. "No mystery why *he* kept his mouth shut."

"There is to me," said Wavevector, baffled.

Rod rolled his eyes. "Anderson bribed him, of course. Probably with shares in Stellar. That's what Stellar hired Anderson for in the first place: the perfect go-between. That was Jaeger on Saturday, was it? The one who thought it was a 'good show.' "

Wavevector jumped, and gave the other an incongruous look of acute embarrassment.

"Oh, come off it!" exclaimed Rod. "Jesus, the way you were talking about seeing Jaeger on Saturday, anyone would think you'd had a business meeting with him. But Lloyd played us a tape. He didn't mean to play us that bit, but we heard it. We know what you're running from. The thing is, if you want to stay ahead of them, you're gonna have to decide what to do *now*. Even this afternoon'll find your options reduced. To be perfectly honest, I think the best thing you could do would be to disentangle yourself, if that's the right word, and go back wherever it is you came from. Just don't leave the corpse where it'll get connected to us, that's all I ask. But maybe you can't do that."

"I can't," Wavevector told him unhappily. "Not on my own." He did not know how to admit that he didn't want to disentangle himself, either. He told himself that it was irrelevant at the moment, anyway: Rod was right, he must concentrate now on deciding what to do.

"There is one other of my kind on this planet who might be able to help," he said in a low voice. "But I need to free him first."

The others went still, and he saw that he'd shocked them again, but he went on relentlessly: "His name is Gravitational Constant. He was not interfering with your kind. He came here on my account, and fell into a trap Stellar had set for me. I didn't know he was here until I saw him imprisoned. I would have been destroyed when my memory returned if he hadn't helped. He talked to me and kept me coherent, and advised me how to alter my modality when I was in too much distress to think. My chief objective now must be to release him. However, I do not want the rest of you to get into trouble on my account. If you would let me rest here today, and if someone could drive me to a spot near Stellar tonight, that will be all the help I need, and more than I expected. After that—"

"You can't go to Stellar!" interrupted Sandra. "Look what they've done to you! You can't even dream of going back!"

Rod was nodding agreement. "They'll have staked your friend out by tonight. You'd never get near him."

Wavevector looked at Rod anxiously. "Staked your friend out" sounded sinister in the extreme. "What does that mean?" he asked fearfully.

"It means they'll have some fucking guards sitting down the corridor from him waiting for you to come along!" snapped Rod, forgetting his language. "You turn up, they grab you."

Wavevector considered a moment. "Then I should go now. It's still early enough that the building will be largely empty, and probably Stellar isn't yet aware that I've escaped."

"Oh, Christ!" exclaimed Rod. "You're not up to any fancy stuff, Holmes—Wavevector, I mean. You're not gonna be climbing in any windows and coshing the security guard, not with those hands you're not. From the look of you, a junior typist's five-year-old daughter could flatten you. And Stellar starts the day early. It'd be nearly eight by the time we got you over there, and the support staff would be arriving for work. You can't do it."

"I'm not driving you over there now," put in Sandra. The spots of red had appeared on her cheeks. "I'm not helping you back to Sir Philip Lloyd."

"I must try," said Wavevector earnestly. "Please understand. Gravitational Constant only came here because concern had been expressed about me. I cannot allow him to die because I acted recklessly. I promised him that I would try to escape and free him."

"Let's see your hands," said Mrs Brown neutrally.

He pulled his hands out of the water. The skin of the palms had been stripped off down to the muscles beneath, and the raw flesh glistened wetly. Seeing the results of his own incompetence depressed him.

Mrs Brown examined the injuries carefully. She cut the old bandage off his right forearm and threw it away, and looked at the right middle finger.

"Wasn't that splinted?" she asked.

He remembered that it had been. He must have left the splint frozen to the cell door.

"You've made a right mess of yourself," said Sylvia Brown, shaking her head. "I don' know how you did that just by forcing a door. What you need is a bandage of artificial skin, a course of antibiotics, that finger re-set, then bed rest and plenty of fluids. And I'm pretty sure you want some painkillers as well. I can provide bed rest and fluids, cotton bandages and paracetamol. It's not good enough. How are your cracked ribs?"

He shrugged. They were sore, but he was so accustomed to that that he'd almost forgotten them.

"How are you planning on breaking into Stellar?"

"I don't know," he admitted. "I will have to examine the building and see."

"You're not up to it," said Mrs Brown flatly.

Rod nodded. "Look, if you can't disentangle yourself, what I suggest you do is give yourself up to the police. Like I said, they're annoyed about the way they've been sidelined and stonewalled, and if you go to them, they'll keep Stellar and the security services off you, even when the whole story starts to come out. We've already started a shouting campaign for you, and we'll keep it up. We got lots of different strings to play on now. Horror may be the first reaction to you, but curiosity is gonna be a close second, and we can use that to get people to listen to the truth. I can promise you that if you go along with this, you definitely won't go back to Stellar and we can probably fix it so that you don't wind up in any government lab either. You might even end up getting offered a job with the government. But only if you give yourself up, only if people are sure you can't hurt them. If you're a bodysnatching alien at large, there's no way anybody's gonna listen to your side of the story."

"What would happen to Gravitational Constant?"

"You tell the police about him, they'll go seize him from Stellar."

"It seems likely to me," said Wavevector unsteadily, "that Stellar would kill him, rather than allow the police access to him. They were evidently afraid that if he escaped he would harm them, and I doubt that they would trust the police to hold him securely. If he were dead, they could safely deny that he was ever there."

There was a silence. "He's not entangled with any human body, obviously," said Sandra. Her voice shook a little. "So presumably if he was dead, he'd just . . . disappear? Or would he blow up?"

"He would disappear," said Wavevector, trying not to think of it: consciousness losing its balance as the dancing energies failed, and falling, imploding into the twist of reality, the singularity, which might be oblivion and might be a death endlessly prolonged. "He is probably critically weak already. They have been keeping him closely imprisoned, and he has been unable to absorb as much energy as he needs. I must try to free him—and from what you say, the longer I wait to do that, the more difficult it will become. Therefore, I must try to do it now. If I fail, then I can consider other options. But I must try."

"You can't do it now," said Sandra. "You can't just march into that building in broad daylight. You'd be caught at once. I won't take you."

Wavevector gave her the telescope look. She realised, with horror, that he was undoubtedly calculating whether he could reach Stellar on foot before the staff arrived for work. He evidently concluded that he couldn't, because he slumped heavily in his chair. "I must go tonight, then," he said. "I think that this 'staking out' may not be as thorough as you fear, Mr Jones. Stellar was keeping Gravitational Constant's existence a secret even from Jaeger. When they first trapped him and found that he didn't respond to them—he speaks no English—they concluded that he was an artificial decoy I had sent to distract them. On Saturday they were pretending to Jaeger that they still thought that, even though they knew otherwise. I don't think they'll want to admit to him that they lied, so it seems likely that any 'staking out' will be done by the handful of Stellars who know the truth. It ought to be possible to get them out of the room long enough for me to release Gravitational Constant. It would only take a minute."

The night would also give him time to reach Stellar on foot, Sandra thought grimly. If she refused to drive him again, he'd walk. He was stubborn and proud, would make no concessions to his own weakness, and would always discover a reasonable argument for doing exactly what he wanted. She shouldn't be surprised at it: she'd known he was like that. Why should she have expected *him* to be different, just because *she* had learned that he wasn't human?

"Your name ought to be Immovable Object," she said angrily. "Very well. You stay here, and I'll go."

Malcolm and Rod both opened their mouths to protest, but Wavevector got there first. "No!" he exclaimed in horror. "It is too dangerous."

"Much less dangerous for me than for you! Even if I get caught, I'll only be thrown out, and maybe charged with trespassing or breaking and entering or something. *You* would be locked up and tortured. Besides, Sir Philip said that the whole building is covered in a magnetically sensitive material. If you go in you'll set off all the alarms, and you've said yourself that there are traps. It makes much better sense for me to go than you. Are you going to 'adhere to a contrary proposition out of sentiment alone'? Tell me where Gravitational Constant is and how to free him, and I'll drive there now. Why's he called Gravitational Constant, anyway?"

"Because he is extremely powerful and extremely reliable, but often difficult to fathom. You . . ."

Sandra laughed weakly. "I got that," she said. Rod gave her a sour look, and she said, "Gravity *is* very mysterious and extremely powerful, but you can always count on it."

"You won't be able to reach him," said Wavevector. "He is being kept in a secure laboratory in the basement. The doors are steel, and controlled by a computer circuit. To open them you would need to insert a magnetic identity card and punch in a code. You don't have a card and I don't know the code: you couldn't get in."

"Oh, wonderful!" snapped Sandra. "How were you planning to get in, then?"

"I think I can send the correct electronic signal directly to the lock," he said at once.

There was another shocked silence. Then Rod asked uncomfortably, "You can do things like that?"

Wavevector nodded. He looked even more uncomfortable than Rod, as though he were admitting some disgraceful perversion. "The signal would only need a low voltage. I wouldn't have to damage the body to send it."

"Damage the body," repeated Rod in a flat tone. He looked at Wavevector's ruined hands. "Jesus! Did you vaporise that door or something?"

Wavevector looked away. "I could not have done anything that violent without killing myself. I chilled the door of my cell to make the hinges brittle. I was impatient, did it too fast, and froze my hands to the door. If I have to do something similar again, I will be more careful. But you see, I do have a few resources to help me into Stellar. I will go tonight."

There was another unhappy silence. Then Mrs Brown sighed. "Maybe we should talk about this this evening, after you've had a rest. You wanna have a shower before I bandage your hands?"

Wavevector realised that he did want to be clean, and to lie down to sleep in a bed between clean sheets. He nodded, confused by the intensity with which his body longed for this, and Mrs Brown jerked her head at Malcolm.

"C'mon," said Malcolm, helping Wavevector to his feet. "The shower's upstairs. You gotta get there before my little sister Shula gets up, or you aren't gonna see it for hours."

"You've got a sister called Shula?" Sandra asked, as Malcolm helped Wavevector to the door.

"Seventeen, just finished A levels," replied Malcolm with a grin. "And a dad, divorced, lives in London. You?"

"Two over-protective parents in Inverness, and an older brother at a bank in Glasgow."

Wavevector was aware as he left the room that this little exchange had been charged with a subtlety he could not comprehend. Mrs Brown shot Sandra a look of startled and disapproving conjecture, to which she returned a slight shake of the head and a glance of apology. But it was too much effort to think about. It was too much effort to do anything but sleep.

FOURTEEN

THAT MONDAY STUCK IN SANDRA'S MIND AFTERWARDS as the longest day she had ever had the misfortune to endure.

She left the Browns' house with Rod and Dave at about half-past eight. Wavevector was asleep by then, in Malcolm's bed. Sandra went upstairs quietly and looked at him before she went. Malcolm's room was small and full of clutter, with paintings stacked three deep along every wall under shelves overburdened with books, paints, and portfolio folders. Wavevector lay under the cotton print bedspread, frowning into the pillow. Even in sleep he looked as though he were engaged in analysis, but even in sleep it looked as though the subject he analysed was one that made him afraid. His hair was still damp from the shower and clung to the skin of his forehead. She wanted to go up to him and stroke it free, but she held back. She told herself that it was only that she didn't want to wake him, but her mind was full of the image in the false-colour radiographs: the stomach-churning dark blur that was a sunbeam tied in a knot. She had always hated the way people sometimes spoke of women "catching" men; she'd rejected the image of herself as a baited trap. And yet she felt that somehow she had indeed caught this one, ensnared him in a kind of love that was alien to him, that visibly baffled and perplexed him. What was she to do? Still she felt the tenderness, the longing to hold, to be part of him, but the radiographic image had been part of nothing she could comprehend, and how could anyone hold a beam of light?

She turned away and quietly closed the door—and found that Malcolm was standing on the landing behind her.

Malcolm had privately decided some time before that nothing about Sandra Murray was second-rate. He could imagine her committing murder, given enough provocation, but he could not imagine her doing anything shabby, sordid or mean. In a world of brass and tin, she was stainless steel. He had fallen asleep the previous night thinking of her, and the thought had made him alternately smile and frown.

He had been expecting to get his degree in the next year, and had hoped thereafter to scramble a Bohemian living in London from what he could sell, and the dole. He'd been looking forward to it—to being footloose and free, to high culture and little money, to parties fuelled by cheap wine and fancy talk, to the dizzying drug of creation and the circuit of galleries. He didn't know how Sandra would fit into that, but he already knew that, given the choice between a wild Bohemian life and her, he'd choose her. Only she was in love with a friend of his.

He might have shrugged and left it, but it had turned out that the friend wasn't human. Malcolm could evaluate as carefully as Wavevector when he needed to, and he could see no future for the other on Earth. If Wavevector couldn't disentangle himself, he'd spend the rest of his life as a prisoner. Even if he gave himself up and Rod's campaign worked and he was given some official position as a "government adviser" he'd still be a celebrity prisoner, trusting barred windows and guards to keep the public and the psychos away from him. And Sandra would hate that. Either she'd leave Wavevector and feel guilty, or stay with him and feel miserable. Malcolm was certain, without self-delusion or conceit, that she would be much happier with him. He wished he could convince her of that. He suspected that even if he could, it would make no difference. She would not abandon a friend in trouble, or slough off a commitment she had made. It was one of the things he loved about her.

"Don't pay any attention to the room," he told her, as though this were the important thing. "It's a mess."

Sandra gave a nervous snort, not quite laughter. She edged past Malcolm and started down the stairs. She had in fact noticed that the room was a student's summer room, full of the disorderly strata of outgrown tastes and too cramped to say much about its owner's present frame of mind. She liked the Browns' house, though: it was warm-coloured and orderly, with a definite idea of itself. It had one serious omission, though. "You don't have any houseplants," she said.

"We get 'em, and they die," Malcolm replied. "You gotta come round some time when this is over and tell us what we're doing wrong."

Sandra stopped, half-way down the stairs. Come round when this is over. Malcolm stopped behind her, very close, watching her intently. For once his easy smile was missing.

Sandra made a small gesture with one hand, a fending-off movement that stopped half-complete. "Probably you over-water them," she said. "Most houseplants are killed that way."

"So come and explain how much water we should give 'em," suggested Malcolm.

She shook her head; looked down, then up again. Their eyes met. "I don't think I can think about when this is over," she said. "It isn't over now." She turned away, an air of finality in her updrawn shoulders and the lift of her red head.

He watched her go down to the foot of the stairs. "It's not because I'm black, is it?" he asked quietly—the niggling uneasiness which could never be completely ignored.

"No," she said at once, and was shocked at the way that fact, which would have caused so much consternation in her family, had become completely irrelevant. "That doesn't make any difference. It's just . . . it isn't over now."

Rod and Dave came out from the Browns' kitchen, Rod delivering a final flood of advice on police and security procedures, and Sandra went with them back to the red Sierra. She was aware of Malcolm still standing on the stairs looking after her, but she did not look back.

She went out to breakfast with Rod and Dave. Rod had decided that they must do this, and keep the tab from the restaurant, in case anyone had noticed their early departure from the house and informed the inevitable questioners about it. Rod had also decided that they must carry on as though nothing had happened that morning. Sandra had been planning to take the day off work, to help in the shouting campaign: she must do it. Mrs Brown had been planning to go in to work the night shift at the hospital: she must do that. Sandra had been scheduled to give two newspaper interviews about the kidnapping that morning: she must give them, and try to pretend she knew nothing more than she had on Sunday—before Sir Philip had arrived to deliver his apocalypse. Public knowledge of Wavevector's real nature was a thing that must be postponed as long as possible. It was hard, it was bitterly hard. She felt by lunchtime that something inside her was compressed to the point where it was about to shatter. And then her parents phoned from Inverness: they had just heard about her appearance on the television news the previous night, and they were worried. She dared not explode or burst into tears, as that would worry them even more, and she told the same lies she'd told to the newspapers, her own voice brittle and unconvincing in her ears, and wished the day would end.

At about two that afternoon, two dark-suited individuals, a man and a woman, turned up on Sandra's doorstep, produced ID cards stamped with the winged sealion of MI5, and came in to inspect the property. Rod protested loudly, demanded to know what they wanted, and protested even more furiously when they carried off all his tapes "for examination." (The black vinyl carrier, however, had been left at the Browns'.) Apart from this cold-faced intrusion, there was no sign that the authorities were aware of Wavevector's escape.

"Told you," said Rod. "Nobody wants to admit they lost him. They hope they can get him back before the higher-ups find out he's missing. And they probably think he can't get far. He must have left blood everywhere."

After MI5 left, Rod disappeared as well. He did not tell Sandra where he was going, only arranged to meet her at the Browns' at half-past six, and advised her that the telephone had probably been tapped. For once Dave was left behind. Dave looked disgruntled, but put the television on and quietly sat down to watch a game of snooker.

"How *can* you?" demanded Sandra furiously.

"I like snooker," replied Dave mildly.

"Where's Rod gone?"

Dave shrugged, eyes glued to the screen. "See his source at Stellar. Hush-hush top secret no witnesses. Way the source likes it. Me, I think it's probably just a cleaning lady with delusions of grandeur, but he always goes along with what his sources want, Rod does."

"He's gone to talk to someone from Stellar?" Sandra demanded, appalled. "Oh, dear God! He won't tell them about . . ."

Dave looked away from the snooker table with a glare of outrage. "Fuckin' hell, no! Rod? He can't stand people gettin' hurt. It makes him so mad he can't sleep. He was scared shitless when we went to get in your car this morning, but he wanted to help anyway 'cause he was so worked up about what that prick Lloyd had been doin' to your friend. He'd go to prison sooner than give him up. He's a fuckin' saint, Rod is."

A very unlikely saint, thought Sandra: foul-mouthed, belligerent, and as ruthlessly single-minded in his devotion to his causes as . . . some hero of the church. Or Wavevector. Dave was still glaring at her.

"OK, I'm sorry," she said. "I'm just nervous, that's all."

Dave gave a grunt of mollification and returned his attention to the screen.

They set off for the Browns' at half-past five because Sandra could bear the wait no longer. They walked: Dave thought it would be easier to see if they were being tailed if they walked, and if they were tailed, easier to pretend that they were only going to a chip shop. The residential streets were empty, apart from the occasional returning commuter car and the odd child cycling home for tea. When they reached the parade of shops at the corner of Bury Road, Dave pronounced himself satisfied that no one was following them—but he stopped at the chip shop anyway, and watched the passersby suspiciously through the windows while they waited for their order. They wandered on up Bury Road carrying greasy paper packets, and arrived at number eighty-two at five-to-six in an aroma of vinegar and hot fat.

Malcolm opened the door for them and quickly ushered them in: he smiled as easily as though he and Sandra had parted friends. There was a sound of voices from the kitchen. Malcolm nodded at the kitchen door and grinned. "Wavevector and my Mum are talking religion," he said, with uncomplicated glee.

"What?" whispered Sandra incredulously.

Malcolm grinned wider and nodded. "They're talking about God. Mum's a Baptist. She asked Wavevector if he believed in God."

"Good Lord," said Sandra. "Does he?"

Malcolm laughed. "Apparently he has to translate 'God' into three completely different concepts. One is self-evident, one is hard to assess, and one is irrelevant. They've been trying to work out which's which."

"Which one's self-evident?" asked Dave, with great interest.

"That's one of the things they can't work out," replied Malcolm. "He can't express it, except in mathematics. I sorta suspect that whatever it is, it's something that's irrelevant to *us*. But the idea of God as personal saviour is the one that's irrelevant to *him*. Apparently if you're a singularity the last thing you want is for a universal law to be bent, even if it is in your favour. It would be contrary to principle, and if the universe goes contrary to principle, where are you? Shit, I love it!" Malcolm's eyes gleamed with joy. He was not laughing *at* anyone, Sandra saw, with a stab of affection. He was simply revelling in the way in which his mother and Wavevector were each behaving so exactly like his or her unmistakable self. She grinned at him.

He grinned back. "That fish and chips?" he asked, indicating the greasy packets. "That's good. We were in the middle of supper. Shula's gone out, incidentally. She's out most of the time these days: friends and boyfriends. We didn't tell her about Wavevector, and she doesn't know he's here. So that's one thing we don't have to worry about."

Wavevector and Sylvia Brown were sitting at the kitchen table over a dish of curried lentils and rice, talking animatedly. Wavevector was dressed in some clothes which were obviously Malcolm's: black shorts—shorter on him than on their original owner, but not incongruously so—and a black T-shirt emblazoned with some Monet water-lilies and the word "Giverny." It fitted him: Malcolm always wore his T-shirts too large. Wavevector looked younger in the new style of dress, dark and athletic and a bit dangerous. His hands, however, were swathed in bandages, and his bare feet were patched with sticking plasters. He turned from the table to greet Sandra with his radiant smile, but she found that she could not smile back, and the conflict between all the things she felt when she looked at him momentarily choked her. His smile vanished rapidly, and was replaced with a look of anxiety.

"How are you feeling?" she asked when she could speak again.

"Very much better," he replied. "I will be able to go to Stellar tonight."

Mrs Brown seated Sandra and Dave at the table and of-

fered them some lentils along with their fish and chips, but
Sandra's appetite was now quite gone.

"You're determined to go?" she asked.

He nodded. "It seems the best time. I would be grateful if
someone could drive me there as soon as it is dark. Otherwise, I can walk." He did not say the last in a challenging
fashion, but matter-of-factly. He had decided to go. The rest
of them might disagree with what he intended, but there was
nothing they could do about it, short of locking him up—and
that was unlikely to hold him.

Sandra was quiet for a minute. She wanted to urge him
not to go, to follow Rod's plan and hand himself over instead—but she could not. He had said that he must free his
friend; he had said, moreover, that his friend represented his
only chance of disentangling himself from his human body.
He must want that. It must be painful and unnatural for him
to be bound in flesh: he must hate it. She did not want to
think of him disentangling himself—did not want to imagine that athletic body a corpse, that beautiful smile reduced
to a skull's grin, while the stomach-churning blur vanished
into the infinite darkness it had come from. She told herself
that *he* must want that, and that he had no future on Earth.
So she could not urge him to stay.

"I'll drive you over," she said. "But you must let me
come with you."

"It would be pointless for you to take that risk. If it can
be done, I can do it on my own. If it can't be done, it
achieves nothing for you to suffer as well."

"Oh, stop being masculine and protective!" she snapped.
"I'm capable of deciding for myself whether a risk is worth
taking. Stellar isn't going to do anything drastic to me: I
have rights, and they have enough trouble without laying
themselves open to a charge of assault or murder. I want to
come so that I can telephone the police if Stellar's waiting
for you."

"I'll come too," said Malcolm quickly.

"Malcolm!" said Sylvia Brown warningly.

Malcolm and his mother looked at each other.

"You got one more year on that course," said Mrs Brown. "You don't want to get tangled up with the law!"

"I'm an artist. We're not supposed to be respectable," replied Malcolm mulishly. "Mum, if he gets caught, we're both gonna be in trouble anyway. They'll trace the clothes—unless you want to send him out in what he was wearing when he came, and even then they'll see that somebody with know-how did the bandages on his hands."

"You don't need to come," interrupted Sandra. "There's no point in you getting caught as well."

"Stop being feminine and protective," ordered Malcolm, with a grin.

Dave cleared his throat. "I'll come too," he said. "I think Rod was planning to come anyway. He wants to get a record of it."

Malcolm laughed. "You mean we're going to break into Stellar on national television?" he asked. "Oh shit! I love it!"

"Please!" said Wavevector desperately. "I don't want anyone to come. It is bad enough that Gravitational Constant has suffered because of my violation of principle. I don't want all of you to suffer as well. Please, it would be better if I went on my own—in McKenzie's clothes, without the bandages."

Sylvia Brown gave him a glare of disapproval. "No," she said flatly. "I may not understand just what you are, but I do understand that you didn't hurt anyone, and that that theory of yours was a gift to the whole planet. The way you've been treated is a disgrace to the human race. I know what's right, and I'm not ashamed to stand up and be counted. If the police come here and say, 'Did you hide him and look after him?' I'll be proud to say yes. I just don't want my Malcolm in trouble with the police if he can help it, that's all."

"But I gave the theory to Stellar as an experiment!" cried Wavevector guiltily. "It was curiosity, not altruism."

"What were you so curious about?" asked Sylvia Brown, her glare unabated.

Wavevector spread his bandaged hands awkwardly. He had been interested in technological development, interested to the point of obsession. It had always fascinated him that biological intelligences could recognise and describe the same physical principles as his own kind—and not only that, but apply those principles in so many unexpected ways. He had come to Earth when a friend told him that its inhabitants were in the process of developing an advanced technology. He had arrived near the beginning of the twentieth century, and for decades he had watched, enchanted, as these short-lived swarming creatures unravelled the secrets of the universe, then used them to fly aeroplanes or provide energy to boil eggs. Their penchant for inventing new ways to kill each other he found less enchanting, but he had put it down to their inherited aggressive instincts and tried to ignore the deaths. He had learned most Earth languages which had a substantial scientific literature, and slipped invisibly in and out of every major research lab. Others of his kind visited the planet, looked, recoiled, and left, but he stayed, watching avidly. In the end the temptation to interfere, to *give* the creatures a theory and try to understand why they did what they did with it, had been irresistible.

"I wanted to see how you applied the theory," he told Sylvia Brown.

"Did you think we were gonna do something terrible with it?"

"No. I chose one I thought you couldn't do anything terrible with," he admitted. "I chose one I thought would help you. I did want to benefit you. But my motives were mixed at best."

"Motives usually are," the nurse told him. "Far as I'm concerned, you gave planet Earth a present, and planet Earth turned around and mugged you. I don't want to leave that as planet Earth's only response. We can do better than that."

Wavevector stared at her in confusion, and she smiled

sweetly. "We're offering. Nobody made us. There's no shame in accepting help if you need it."

Wavevector looked away. "Then, thank you," he said in a low voice. "I am grateful to you all."

He did want help, even if it was only the reassurance of a friendly and intelligible presence behind him. What Stellar had done to him was like a raw wound in his mind. It had been not merely agonising and humiliating, but irrational. He had been very valuable to them, they had lied to their own people in order to secure him—but they had nearly killed him despite that. True, Sir Philip had believed that what he was doing posed no real danger to Wavevector—but he'd had no rational basis for such a belief. He apparently believed it because he wanted to. There was no reasoning with such insanity, no way to cope with it. Worse, Wavevector had seen a reflection of himself in Sir Philip's hatred, an image of a twisted demonic thing which felt no real pain, which must be bound and broken for survival's sake. The false reflection of himself he had seen in the hospital mirror had somehow come true. He was afraid that the mirror-image Sir Philip held up to him would also crawl into his soul, and he knew that if it did he would go mad. Madness was the usual end for his kind, if no accident intervened: when too many memories accumulated, consciousness found itself bewildered by the self's contradictions, and disintegrated. To Wavevector it had always seemed the most terrible of all ends. The prospect of walking back into Stellar, risking captivity and madness, was something he was unable to contemplate directly, and he wanted any protection his friends could give him. He hoped that the humans were right, and that they really did not need to fear injury or death for themselves if they helped him.

"OK, then," said Malcolm. "If we're all going to Stellar tonight, we'd better make some plans."

Plans were in fact drawn in the literal sense of the word. Dave had been taken on his tour of Stellar only three days before, and he had a good visual memory. He sketched the

lay-out of the ground floor of the lab. Wavevector was able
to calculate from it the lay-out of the basement and the position of the Defence Lab. He remembered the rest of the
building as well, but most of his memories dated from a time
before he was human, and were hard to map on to Dave's
sketch. He had no idea of rooms, stairs, walls and corridors,
but he remembered electrical lay-outs—any large area of
metal, various pieces of equipment, and telephone cables.
They managed to outline several routes to the Defence Lab,
however, which did not involve using a lift or entering any
boxes of conductive material which might have been rigged
as a diamagnetic trap. Wavevector was confident that there
could not be too many of these. The diamagnetic generators
had only just been developed, were valuable and enormously complicated, and it was unlikely that Stellar had
more than three or four of them in operation. One was being
used to imprison Gravitational Constant. If there was a
stake-out, one must be nearby (waiting for me, Wavevector
thought, then pushed the thought queasily aside). It seemed
probable that Sir Philip would keep the portable device
which had been used in the lift with him, in case Wavevector
tried to approach him directly. Therefore, there was likely to
be no more than one trap in the corridors of Stellar, and it
probably guarded access to the computers or files containing
the data from the Astragen Project, or to one of the building's
alarm centres. Dave shaded those areas on the map.

While they were finishing this, there was a knock on the
house door, and Malcolm opened it to admit Rodney Jones.

"Hello there, party-goers!" exclaimed Rod, bounding
into the kitchen like a large sheep-dog. "What you got there,
Davie?"

"Making a map," said Dave, turning it to let his friend
see.

"Yeah, well the security guard sits *here* when he's not pa-
trolling," said Rod, stabbing at a spot on the ground floor.
"And the control box for the burglar alarm is in with him.
But we aren't gonna set any alarms off, brothers and sisters,

because we have got the keys." He took a ring of keys from his pocket and dangled them before his audience, with a grin of triumph.

"Keys to Stellar!" exclaimed Malcolm.

Rod smirked and nodded.

"How did you get those?" asked Sandra.

Rod grinned again. "I got a source at Stellar. I told the source I really really wanted to have a look round to see if there were any traces of what happened to Holmes. The source was not happy, but was even less happy about the way Lloyd and his cronies have been fucking—'scuse me, Mrs Brown—*fooling* about over the past few days and keeping the rest of the company in the dark. I got the keys and a run-down on the security system. Soon as it's dark, my friends, in we fucking go. Jesus, I could do with a beer!"

It did not get dark until half-past ten. Mrs Brown left for work shortly after Rod's arrival, and the rest of the party sat about in the sitting room, first planning and assembling equipment, then talking. Sandra found that she did not have much to say. All that interminable day she had longed to be here, to see Wavevector and resolve some of what she felt for him—and now she wished herself anywhere else. She kept looking at him and thinking of the blur in the radiograph. She felt that she ought to be full of questions—what wouldn't Robert have asked a genuine extraterrestrial?—but she was afraid of what the answers might be. It was clear from some of the things Wavevector said that he had been on Earth for decades, and a couple of times she almost asked him, "How old are you?" but each time the question dried on her tongue. It was such a human question. But stars measured their years by the million, and to light, Time itself is relative.

Wavevector noticed her uneasy glances, guessed the cause, and found them increasingly painful. He wished he could be alone with her, talk just to her, analyse what it was that she found so distressing about him. He did not know, though, if anything he could do would set her at ease again.

He was sick of the planning and talking, and the dread of what he was about to do kept growing on him. He had been aware, ever since he woke that afternoon, that these might be his last hours as a human. That dish of curried lentils might be the last food he would ever taste, these voices around him the last he would ever hear—because it was not hearing, to analyse sound in the air and assign values to it: it was not like hearing. You could not read emotions in it, any more than you could read them by scanning the electromagnetic conformation of a face. He wondered whether Sandra would kiss him again if they were alone. He was miserably certain that she would not.

He still did not know what he would do if he succeeded in freeing Gravitational Constant, and the question gnawed at him steadily, even through the growing dread. The suggestion Rod had made, of handing himself over to the police and hoping that the humans would eventually decide to free him, kept recurring to him. He pointed out to himself that it would involve months, perhaps years, of captivity. There would be endless buffeting questions, tests, analyses—and always the stares, the fascinated horror in the eyes. It might drive him mad. He pointed out to himself that they would want more theories from him, and there were so few he dared to tell them, so many they could use for their own destruction. He pointed out, too, that he had made enough trouble for his friends, that the best thing he could do would be to vanish before the public at large was aware of him, and hope that the government would decide to suppress even the fact of his existence. And yet, the suggestion still kept recurring.

When it finally began to grow dark, everyone was relieved. Rod produced a pair of shoes for Wavevector—red and black trainers, his own, and a little too large—and Malcolm fetched a tracksuit jacket which would act as protection against the night chill. It was a very Malcolmesque tracksuit jacket, in green, purple and black, but it had pockets to hide bandaged hands in, and a hood which could com-

bine with the dusk to conceal a publicised face. They all
stepped out into the gathering dark.

The afternoon had become cloudy, and the dying light
had that close green stillness peculiar to June twilights.
House-lights—red, gold and emerald, like the windows of a
cathedral—radiated through the curtains of Bury Road. "I
left my car up the road a bit," said Rod. "Weren't any spaces
this end."

They walked up the road, Wavevector with his head
bowed, his shoulders hunched, and his hands thrust in his
pockets. Sandra, beside him, could sense that he was trembling, and wondered if it was from fear or from tension.

Rod's car was not, in fact, very far, and he hurried ahead
to unlock the doors. Sandra and Malcolm climbed into the
back, but Wavevector hesitated, staring at the car.

"What's the matter?" asked Rod.

"You car is transmitting a radio signal," said Wavevector.

There was a sharp, cold, stunned silence.

"What?" Rod demanded. His voice was shrill with alarm.
"A radio signal?"

Wavevector nodded. He could scan it clearly, a short
rapid repeated burst in the short wave band. "The source is
there," he said, and took one mittened paw from his pocket
to point at the area before the front right wheel of Rod's battered grey Metro.

"Oh Christ," breathed Rod. "Oh fuck. MI5. They must
have put a trace on it." There was a helpless pause, and then
he knelt and peered into the dimness in front of the wheel. It
was too dark to see anything, and he groped at the rusty
metal with his hand.

"Shit," he commented. "It's there all right. They must
have slapped it on when they came this afternoon. Oh shit, I
never thought . . ." He stopped, thinking hard. "OK, don't
panic. If they were sitting across the road watching us,
they'd have moved by now. They've had four hours to
gather the troops, they want Holmes, and they're not gonna
risk him getting smashed up in a car chase. So, nobody's

looking at us. They don't know we helped him, and they put
the tracer on just on the off-chance. Probably they have
traces on half a dozen cars, and they have somebody sitting
in a van somewhere monitoring them. Maybe they think I
just parked here to go to the pub. Sandra, your car's at your
house still, right? OK, we drive over there now and we take
the fucking trace off and leave it, so they think I've come
back to your place for the night. Then we go. Dave, you and
Holmes get in the fucking car! Hey, Holmes, have they
bugged this car as well?"

"I don't understand the term 'bugged,'" said Wavevector
unhappily.

"Slapped a fucking listening device on it! You can hear
them, can't you? You spotted my cassette recorder fast
enough this morning."

Wavevector scanned the car carefully. "There's no other
electrical equipment operating in it," he said. "Only the
radio transmitter."

"Right! Well, they haven't turned up yet: we gotta hope
we're lucky. Christ, we were lucky, too! If Sandra and
Davie'd taken her car over here, they would've known
something was up. They must've done her car as well. But
they're not geared up for pedestrians. Oh, Jesus, I hope they
don't catch my source! Go on Holmes, get in! We gotta
hurry."

Wavevector went round to the left side of the car and got in
the back, as far away from the transmitter as he could. He was
not certain how close he needed to be to it to distort the radio
signal. Probably a momentary distortion wouldn't be noticed,
but a whole car-ride's worth might trigger an alarm.

Rod drove the car off with a screech of tyres, and jolted
down the backstreets to Sandra's house. He parked behind
Sandra's red Sierra, and they all got out. Rod stared at the
Sierra, then shot a questioning look at Wavevector.
Wavevector nodded, and gestured at the right front wheel
again. The two signals overlapped each other in his percep-

tions, *bleep-blip* jarring against *blip-blip-blip* in a way that set his teeth on edge.

"They didn't think they needed to watch us," Rod said bitterly. "They thought that if they tapped the phones and traced the cars, it'd be enough. It nearly was, too. The dirty buggers!" He knelt and tried to pry the radio transmitter off his Metro. He dug at it gingerly at first, then furiously. It would not budge. "Fuck!" he muttered, glancing round furiously. "They've fucking araldited it!" His eye fell on Wavevector. "Do some black magic to it!" he ordered. "We need to get the fucking thing off."

Wavevector reached nervously for the Earth's magnetic field, hoping that it would minimise his effect on radio waves, and came over and inspected the transmitter. It was about the size of the last joint of his thumb, and was surrounded by a thick ooze of set glue. Should he chill the glue? He was nervous about chilling things, after what had happened last time, but presumably if he pulsed the draw he could avoid injuring himself. But no—chilling would probably break the transmitter. If its signal stopped, the people who had put it there would be alarmed, and might come to investigate. Better to try something else. The metal of the car's frame was rusty: Wavevector realised it was possible to peel off the layer the transmitter adhered to. He clasped the transmitter through his bandages, and concentrated. Iron had a different magnetic resonance from iron oxide, but both responded to magnetism. He magnetised the oxide around the transmitter, then magnetised the iron of the car panel, polarising the two so that the similar poles faced each other. The poles repelled each other, and the transmitter sprang off into his hand. He fumbled with it, managed not to drop it, and handed it to Rod.

Rod, too, nearly dropped it, then sat back on his heels and weighed it in his hand as though it might burn him. "Is it still working?" he asked breathlessly.

Wavevector nodded. He felt distinctly satisfied at the way he'd removed the transmitter: it had taken only seconds and it hadn't hurt at all. "I probably distorted the signal when I touched it," he said, "and there must have been some static when I took it off, but it's working normally now. The oxide on the back is magnetised. It will adhere to another ferromagnetic material if you want to attach it somewhere else."

"Jesus!" whispered Rod. He went over to the nearest car—a white van belonging to one of Sandra's neighbours—and set the transmitter against its underside. It stuck.

"Right!" exclaimed Rod. "Maybe that'll confuse them in the morning. For now, as far as MI5 is concerned, I've gone to bed, and Sandra's spent a quiet evening at home. Off we go."

Wavevector found himself sitting next to Sandra in the back of the Metro as it pulled out again, with Malcolm next to the window beyond. It was fully dark now, and the street lights they passed cast orange glows across their faces, shifting all colours towards brown. They were pressed together, thigh to thigh, and yet there was no communication. Sandra sat withdrawn into a private enclosure and did not look at him. Wavevector's satisfaction ebbed. He had yet again reminded them all of what he was, and it frightened them. Black magic, Rod had called it, and he had been half-serious. The human part of him began to whisper that he could not let these last hours, perhaps the last he had of liberty or life, end with this bitterness between himself and the ones he most cared for.

Irrational, he told himself. *They cannot have any such emotion. They have come to help me at risk to themselves. That is inconsistent with "bitterness."*

"Humans *are* inconsistent," said his human self. "Speak to them. Speak to Sandra. To her most of all."

"Did it distress you very much, what I did there?" he asked, after a silence.

"I'm not even sure what it was you did there," she replied.

He was quiet for a minute, then said hesitantly, "Please, I

don't want to offend you, but it is clear to me that you are distressed because of what I am. I was told that you would be. I never wanted to cause you distress, and I would like to help, if I can. I value your friendship and good-will. Can you explain to me what it is about me you find so disgusting? It may be that some of it isn't true."

Sandra turned her head and looked at him. In the shadow of the hood his eyes were two openings into darkness, his mouth a mere smudge of charcoal—and yet the angle of his neck and shoulders spoke wordlessly of fear.

"Who told you I would be distressed?" she asked in a brittle voice.

There was a brief pause: she had again the sense of a great computer whirring through an unwieldy mass of raw data. "Sir Philip Lloyd and the others from Stellar," he replied. "And Commander Jaeger. They all expressed pity for you, and disgust and horror that you had been deceived into thinking of me as a man you could care for. Sir Philip Lloyd said that any woman would be distressed to find that the attractive man she's fallen in love with is really a corpse with a thing from a black hole inside it." His voice shook only slightly on the final phrase.

Her throat felt swollen, and she did not know how to answer.

"Of course, I am not from a black hole," he added. "Nothing comes *from* one of those. I was formed by extremely energetic magnetic fluctuations in an unstable O-type star."

"Sir Philip wanted to hurt you," Sandra told him savagely. "Wavevector, he hates you. You shouldn't have listened to him." She felt her face go hot. Her subconscious had finally given up on calling him "Paul."

Wavevector was confused. "But you and Mr Jones also agreed that the normal human reaction to what I am is horror."

"But not from *us*! Sir Philip doesn't know anything about me, and understands less about you. He was frightened of you, and then he cheated you, so he's convinced himself that you're a monster and he's a hero. He wants to hurt you so that he doesn't have to be frightened. You shouldn't have listened to him. And I don't find you disgusting, only . . . only very, very difficult to . . ." She stopped, blinking. The whole compressed about-to-shatter feeling of the day came to a head, and she knew, with disgust, that in another moment she would cry.

"I don't understand," said Wavevector.

"Difficult to understand!" finished Sandra, with a burst of fury. "You don't react like a human being. You're not even angry at Sir Philip, after all he's done to you. You just think he's crazy and want to stay away from him. And you're probably thousands of years old and you have a mind like a mainframe computer and you're composed of forces that would vaporise me if I touched them, but you act as though you're frightened of what some ignorant twenty-four-year-old plant pathologist thinks of you."

"I am," Wavevector said, and wondered if he should have admitted it. "I wouldn't vaporise you. It doesn't—"

"Don't condescend!" exclaimed Sandra. The tears had started. "Yes, I was in love with you. Yes, I am still in love with you, though now I'm scared of you as well. But my feelings can't separate you from the body you're entangled with, and I know you want to disentangle yourself just as soon—"

"But I don't!" he protested. "I don't! I want to stay human if I can."

"What?" she asked incredulously. "Why?"

"It's as though I had discovered a new universe," he told her, with unmistakable passion. "All the time I spent on this planet before, I never looked beyond what I knew already. I never realised there were so many things of which I was ignorant. I had no interest in biology, in plants, in animals, or even in humans, other than what they knew of science. Then suddenly I woke up plunged in sensations. I had only one sense before—a very wide band of sense, but only one form of it. To acquire *five* more—you're used to these things, you don't realise. Just to eat, to taste, is a whole dimension I knew nothing about. And there's sound—music: I know nothing about music. I've barely begun to realise what there is in this new universe. Of course I desire it, more than anything else I have ever experienced. And I've fallen in love with you, and I barely know what that means: it's quite different from what I thought humans must feel. My kind have nothing like the depth of engagement with each other that yours does. I want to stay human if I can. I don't care if I do die with the body. I want to stay entangled with it. Only I know that my desire is contrary to principle, and likely to destroy me and perhaps injure my friends as well. And probably you would prefer it if I were gone, and this distress had ended."

Sandra swallowed a hot lump of tears. "No," she said. "That's not what I'd prefer."

They looked at each other. Sandra was aware, in some remote corner of her mind, that the car was slowing, that the orange glare of the neon lights was gone, leaving only the uncertain darkness of a midsummer night; and that the others in the car had been silent for a long time. It did not matter: she was concentrated on the face opposite her, the large awkward body squashed against her side, the dark eyes focused so absolutely upon her own.

"You want me to try to stay?" repeated Wavevector in hope and disbelief.

"Yes," replied Sandra, without hesitation.

He gave a long shudder, as his body had when he first went into it: relief or horror, she could not say. He lifted one bandaged hand and tremulously, as though he were dusting diamonds, brushed the tears from her face. "It doesn't . . ." he hesitated, then went on, "it doesn't make your skin crawl to think that you kissed me?"

She laid her own hand over his, holding it against her cheek. She thought of the blur in the radiographs, but it did not seem real, not nearly as real as his human flesh. She leaned towards him, and found his mouth, and kissed him, and felt him relax, finally, and kiss her back.

"I love you," she whispered. She felt him shiver again, and knew this time that it was with joy.

"We've arrived," said Rod flatly, from the seat in front.

FIFTEEN

ROD HAD TAKEN THEM, NOT TO THE MAIN ENTRANCE of Stellar, but to a lay-by on a hedge-lined backroad. It was very dark: the moon was simply a blur of brightness in the curtain of cloud. When she got out of the car, Sandra was not even certain in which direction the black glass fortress lay. Rod, though, trotted confidently up the road and vanished. She followed him and found a gap in the hedge. A grey ribbon of drive trailed across an expanse of charcoal black, and at its end, the great tent pitched itself against the sky in a dark sheen of glass.

"We're behind the trade entrance," said Rod, with satisfaction. "This is the gate they use for deliveries. Holmes, which way do you want to go in?"

Wavevector had followed them. He now stood still, scanning the building. The joy of discovering that Sandra loved him anaesthetised even his dread. He felt an unreasoning confidence that the night would go well, that he would succeed in freeing Gravitational Constant and in escaping unharmed from the pit of horrors before him. His scan found no sign of life in the building. No lights shone from its windows, no radiation from its labs. Its underground electrical supply cables, over to his left, resonated steadily, with none of the fluctuations caused by equipment in use.

The nearest entrance was the garage which they'd brought him out through before, and it was to all appearances empty of life. It had the advantage of leading directly to the basement, and providing the shortest route to the Defence Lab. But their plans now included the setting up of a distraction, to lure from the Defence Lab any Stellars who might be staking it out. It was better to go in through the main door.

"I'd prefer to use the main door, if it's free," he told Rod. "But it might be better to leave through the trade entrance."

"Right," said Rod, hitching the black bag higher up his shoulder. "Can we agree that if we get separated, we meet back here? If we can't make it back here, we go up to the main road and turn right, and whoever has got back here will try and make a pick-up in the car. Here." He took from his pocket two keys, and handed one each to Sandra and Malcolm. "That's the key to the Metro," he said. "If you need to take it and go, do it. Now, I got two mobile telephones for calling the police with. One's in this bag, the other's in the car. If there's an emergency, first person back here calls the cops. OK?"

"OK," whispered Sandra. Her mouth had gone dry.

"I love it," said Malcolm admiringly, as he put the car key in his anorak pocket. "Burglars calling the cops."

Sandra felt a sudden stab of affection for him. Only Malcolm was ingenious enough to find something to love about breaking into Stellar.

"Davie, you got the camera?" asked Rod, and Malcolm laughed.

The field around Stellar was part of its landscaped grounds: the grass was short and smooth, easy to cross, even in the dark. They circled the building to the right, and came out at last on the pavement by the main entrance. The foyer was dimly illuminated, and its tinted glass panels coloured the room beyond sepia and black. The other windows were empty and silent, and the reflective doors gave back no more than a dark silhouette. Rod dug the borrowed keys from his pocket and unlocked the door. When it was open, he hurried to the receptionist's desk and fumbled behind it: there was a switch which had to be pressed within forty-five seconds or the burglar alarm would go off. Dave silently joined him with a small torch; the switch was found, and the stillness remained unbroken.

Wavevector stood before the doorway after the others had gone in, contemplating the invisible rope which he had broken before. It was clear now that he knew to look out for it that the glass had been treated with a spray of some weakly ferromagnetic chemical: when it came in contact with a magnetic field, its response would send a signal to an electrical receptor. The doorframe was similarly sensitive. He had told himself beforehand that he must be prepared to set off the alarms when he went in, but now that it had come to the point, he was afraid to. Perhaps if he did not touch the glass or the doorframe, he could slip in undetected?

"Could you hold the door open, please?" he said breathlessly to Sandra, who had paused inside, waiting for him.

Puzzled, she held it open, and he moved back, then ran towards the dark opening and hurled himself in a desperate leap across it. He felt something flicker as he passed it, and he stumbled to a stop and looked back.

"Did you set it off?" asked Rod.

"I'm not sure," replied Wavevector. "We must hurry."

During the planning session it had been agreed that two of the party would set up the diversion while the rest made directly for the Defence Lab. At Wavevector's suggestion, Sandra had made a crude electromagnet from a spool of copper wire and an old portable radio-cassette player. The hope was that the magnetic field from this would set off alarms elsewhere in the building, and perhaps spring the diamagnetic trap, and bring Stellars running to see what they'd caught. Rod and Malcolm had volunteered to take it to the areas where the traps and alarms were most likely to be. Rod now switched the electromagnet on. He paused a moment, then slapped Wavevector roughly on the back. "Good luck!" he said, and strode off into the dark lab.

"Good luck!" said Malcolm more quietly. He started after Rod, then turned, ran back, flung his arms about Sandra, and kissed her. "And good luck to you, too!" he said, grinning, and ran after Rod.

"No fucking kisses for me!" grumbled Dave, picking up his camera.

"You're not in any danger," said Sandra, a trifle unsteadily. There had been nothing brotherly about Malcolm's kiss, and her lips were tingling. Touched but annoyed, she started walking quickly to the left, in the direction where the maps they had drawn marked the stairs.

"Nor are you," Dave retorted, following her, "but you got kissed—twice."

Wavevector hurried after them, frowning. Most of his attention was taken up with anxious scanning of his surroundings, but the part that wasn't found itself engaged with an alarmingly large set of new questions. "Is Malcolm . . ." he began hesitantly, then stopped.

"What?" asked Sandra. They had reached another set of reflective glass doors, and she held one open. Beyond, stairs of grey marble led downwards into darkness.

"Is there an . . . is Malcolm in love with you?" asked Wavevector, stopping at the door and scanning it. There was another alarm circuit, and he moved back.

Sandra sighed. "I love *you*, OK?"

Wavevector ran, then hurled himself through the open door. Sandra caught his arm, afraid that he would trip and fall down the stairs. His weight rocked her on her feet, and they both staggered. He met her eyes and smiled the radiantly glad smile that had been the first thing she loved in him. "OK," he said.

Her eyes stung. A part of her wondered if Anderson had ever smiled like that. Somehow she was certain he never had: the mouth might have belonged to him, but the smile was Wavevector's.

They descended the stairs in silence. There were no lights at the bottom, and half-way down Dave flicked on his pen-torch so they could see where they were putting their feet. The faint glow did little to illuminate the darkness, and at the bottom its gleam reflected in another glass screen, showing them their own images suspended ghost-like against the black. Sandra opened the next door, and Wavevector made his hurried dash through. In the cavern of the basement he stood still, scanning it all: the linoleum floor, the shelves, the closed doors last seen from inside his mobile prison. It was silent, apart from the sounds of their own breathing, the creak and clunk of the plumbing, and the humming of the ventilator fans. Wavevector began walking towards the Defence Lab.

They were passing the landing for the lift when the lights came on. For one icy moment, they were all unable to move. Then all three of them ran to the nearest storage bay. A tank of liquid nitrogen squatted at the back: Sandra and Dave slid behind it, and Wavevector crouched in its shadow, behind a line of insulated containers.

Footsteps flapped against the linoleum: two men, hurry-ing. Wavevector, scanning over the top of the containers, recognised Sir Philip and Foster, and crouched lower. Foster started to go through the doors to the lift, but Sir Philip caught his arm.

"Stairs!" said Sir Philip, his voice carrying sharp and clear through the silence. "Can't risk anything happening to the power."

The footsteps flapped on, past the storage bay and through the fire-doors that led to the stairs. The doors closed, but for a moment longer the rush of feet climbing carried back, muffled and urgent. Then there was silence.

Wavevector swayed to his feet. Malcolm and Rod had ev-idently triggered an alarm: if he were to free Gravitational Constant, now was the time to do it. But he could not force himself to move. The sight of his enemies rushing to imprison him again had left him sick and shaking with terror. Sandra slid from behind the tank of nitrogen and caught his arm. "We've got to hurry!" she whispered.

He nodded numbly and set off for the Defence Lab at a panicky run.

The black doors marked "AUTHORISED PERSONNEL ONLY" were just as he had last seen them, closed and impenetrable under the dim night-time illumination. He halted himself against the control panel, then nodded to Sandra and Dave to go to the doors and get ready to push. He set both hands on the panel and scanned it carefully. The coded controls were a spiderweb of checks, but the pathway for the signal to unlock the door was clear. He closed his eyes and followed it with his hands to the lock. One signal, one small electronic adjustment—there.

The door buzzed and slid smoothly open. Dave set his back against it and lifted his camera to his shoulder.

Wavevector stood before the threshhold, still scanning with closed eyes. There was no trace of Gravitational Constant. His eyes flew open, and the bright strip lighting showed him that the much-discussed lead screen was in place, blocking off the far end of the room. Next to the door stood a familiar box of wood, iron, and wire that sent a jolt of sickness through him as he recognised it. The shredded paper still covered its floor, and beside the clumsily propped-up door were two brown smears where he had tried to wipe the blood from his hands.

He made himself look away from the cell, and scanned carefully around the entrance to the Defence Lab. No conductive box was set to flick shut around him. He edged cautiously through.

"There's nothing here," said Dave resentfully. He had panned the lab with one long sweep of his camera, and was looking at it now in disgust: white floors, white counters, white and aluminium machinery that might have been refrigerators or washing machines; one incongruous affair like a giant rabbit hutch.

"He must be behind there," said Wavevector, pointing at the screen. "I think they will have set a trap there."

He edged closer to the lead screen, scanning, scanning. There was a door in the middle of it. He reached out with a bandaged hand and lifted the latch, then stepped back, afraid to open it. "I am sure they have a trap there," he said, in a low, frightened voice.

Sandra pushed past him and opened the door.

The inside of the screen was lined with wire mesh. Against one wall, surrounded by a tangle of machinery, sat a box about the size of a television set. It had a dull-grey insulated casing and a green light on its front. Next to it was a wire box of the same size. Sandra's eyes examined it eagerly, and found it completely empty. Frowning in disbelief, she walked towards it. It still looked empty. She turned back to Wavevector with a look of shock and pity.

Wavevector was standing on the other side of the doorway. His face was turned towards the mesh box as though he were looking at it, but his eyes were unfocused, and he did not seem to see it or her.

"Wavevector!" she said in alarm. "Have they moved him?"

Wavevector's eyes focused on the empty box and widened in surprise. Gravitational Constant stood out to his scan like a bright light: it was bewildering to find that what was so clear to one sense was completely invisible to another. But Gravitational Constant was torpid—more than that, sunk into the dreamless unreasoning sleep of Travel, all thought suspended, all use of energy stilled. And Wavevector did not dare approach him. The wire that lined the inside of the screen also encircled the whole area about Gravitational Constant's cell, and the generator that imprisoned him was attached to it. Wavevector was certain that if he stepped through the door, the field would flick suddenly outward to enclose him. Those who had set this trap, though, had not expected a human to help him.

"He's there," Wavevector told Sandra. "Can you switch

off the generator? It's there, next to the cell. The controls are on top."

Sandra went to the insulated television-set-affair, found and flipped up the little plastic lid, and gazed down at the keyboard. "What do I do?" she asked.

"Type in the security code first. I think it's five-seven-six-six: that was the code on both the other generators I saw."

Sandra typed in the numbers. The liquid crystal display formed the black word "ready."

"OK," she said. "Now what?"

"Type 'Power Off.' "

She did as she was told, and a hum she had been unaware of hearing died. She looked into the empty wire box. It remained obstinately empty.

Gravitational Constant woke, and reached instantly and desperately for the Earth's magnetic field. He drew on it: to Wavevector it was as though the whole scene began a rapid monochrome flicker, such was the depth of the draw. *Thank you*, he told Wavevector.

We must go quickly, Wavevector warned him. *The entities who imprisoned you will return shortly.*

Are they not present? the other replied, scanning Sandra and Dave.

No. These are other entities, who are helping me out of motives of morality and affection . . .

"Is anything gonna happen?" asked Dave impatiently. "I've been shooting the whole fucking thing, and there's nothing that would make a clip for *Horizon*, let alone *Panorama*."

Do we have time to disentangle you here? asked Gravitational Constant. He drifted from the cell and out the open door in the screen, stopping beside Wavevector. He passed through Sandra's arm on the way, but she did not notice, and kept staring at the wire box. Wavevector found that he had turned to follow the other's progress, and that he was now looking into a presence his human eyes could not see. It was an odd sensation.

I do not want to be disentangled, he said, *but even if I did, there is not time for it now.*

He could tell that Gravitational Constant was deeply shocked. *That is contrary to principle,* he said, *but I will not argue it now, if there is not time. I suggest, though, that we destroy the diamagnetic field generators before we go.*

I admire the suggestion, and agree. I cannot do it, though: any violent manipulation would damage this body. He turned to Sandra, who was now staring at him in bewilderment.

"Is he still in there?" she asked, before he could say anything.

Wavevector shook his head. "Can you move away from the generator?" he asked. "Gravitational Constant wants to destroy it."

Dave at once jostled Wavevector aside and pointed his camera at the generator, and Sandra hurried away from it.

What is the electrical equipment which the entity further from me is operating? asked Gravitational Constant, drifting back to the generator and settling himself on top of it.

It is a device for making a visual record of these events upon a photosensitive film, said Wavevector. *When you destroy the generator, please remember that biological entities are extremely fragile, and take precautions so that your manipulation does not damage us.*

Gravitational Constant hesitated at that telling *"us,"* but said only, *I understand.* Wavevector felt him draw hard on the Earth's magnetic field. Then the insulating casing of the generator lit for a moment with an unholy violet light, and vanished, leaving only a cloud of nitrogen, white and visible as it boiled, and a burst of hot and cold together. Then there was nothing—no generator, no fragments of generator, only a few white wisps of vapour and a scorch mark on the floor.

Dave lowered his camera. "Christ!" he whispered.

There is another generator attached to a conductive en-

closure by the north-west wall of this room, said Wavevector.

Gravitational Constant went instantly to the generator that had driven the field around Wavevector's prison. Again there was the burst of light, the cloud, the scorch mark. Some of the paper on the floor of the cell caught fire, and was instantly put out.

Dave had whirled at the burst of light, and was in time to film only the cloud and the fire going out. "Shit!" he said, in the same shaken whisper. "How did that thing get past me? Why didn't you warn me?"

Wavevector shrugged. Dave and Sandra were both looking at him in a way that made him uneasy. "We had better go now," he said. He started towards the black doors.

Are there more generators? asked Gravitational Constant.

Yes, but they are probably attached to traps, replied Wavevector. *It would be dangerous to approach them. Better to go at once. This building is dangerous for our kind. It is encircled and riddled with substances that sound alarms when we cross them, and there may be a trap in any conductive enclosure. You should leave now. I will also leave, as fast as is consistent with the limitations of this body. I will speak with you later.*

Agreed. On the word, Gravitational Constant was gone. Wavevector was aware of him penetrating the ferro-concrete wall by a boost to his frequency, then departing upwards at the speed of light. There was no need to arrange where to meet: Gravitational Constant would find him by looking for a dimple in the Earth's magnetic field.

Wavevector hurried on to the doors. Dave had left these ajar, with the bolt of the lock resting against the edge of the opposite door. Wavevector tried to catch hold of the edge and pry it open, but his mittened hands were clumsy and couldn't grip. Sandra hurried over, hauled the dark metal aside, and Wavevector stepped out into the dim light of the basement.

He found himself face to face with Sir Philip Lloyd.

He stopped dead. Sir Philip's hand was clutching his small black gun, his eyes were wide with alarm, and his face was pale. The gun jerked up and pointed at Wavevector's chest. The knuckle of the trigger-finger whitened.

"No!" protested Wavevector. He spread his arms to shield Sandra and Dave behind him, and took a step back. For an instant a nightmare vision lurched through his mind: the gun firing, his own chest exploding in a mass of blood and blood-sodden flesh, and the thousand thousand links that bound him to that flesh ripping him apart, so that the forces of his true nature disintegrated—not silently into his centre, but catastrophically outwards. If that happened, his death would kill Sandra—and Dave, and Sir Philip, and probably everyone else in the building as well.

For an endless two seconds Sir Philip stood there with the trigger half-drawn. The gun trembled in his hand. Then he took a quick step forward and shoved the muzzle against Wavevector's chest. "Down on the floor!" he screamed. His voice was shrill almost to hysteria. "Down on the floor and put your hands behind your head!"

Wavevector dropped to his knees and put his hands behind his head. Sir Philip pressed the barrel of the gun against his forehead and glared over his head at Sandra and Dave. "You!" he shouted. "How could you? You've betrayed the whole human race!"

"What the fuck do you mean?" asked Dave. He had his camera on his shoulder, and it was whirring as he spoke.

"Switch that thing off!" screamed Sir Philip. "Switch it off, or I shoot! Both of you, get down and put your hands in the air!"

Sandra dropped to her knees behind Wavevector. Dave went on filming. The gun lifted from Wavevector's forehead, then ground back against it. "I told you to stop it!" shouted Sir Philip. "I shoot him if you don't stop it. First in the shoulder, then in the head. Stop it!"

Dave stopped. He took a step back, cradling the camera in both arms.

"You must not kill me," said Wavevector earnestly. "I've told you before, I don't know what will happen to me if this body dies. If the forces that compose me become violently disordered, it may be catastrophic. Please, there are innocent people all around us. You see, I am down, I am not resisting. There is no need to kill me."

Sir Philip struck him across the face with his free hand, a single frantic blow that nearly knocked its recipient over. Wavevector flung out one hand to catch himself, and Sir Philip brought an elegant black leather heel down hard on his bandaged fingers. The pain, as the raw wound ground against the floor, was beyond screaming.

"Put that hand back behind your head!" ordered Sir Philip.

Wavevector obeyed, breathing in short whimpering gasps.

"How *can* you?" demanded Sandra, alight with helpless rage. "You're not human!"

Sir Philip looked at her as though she were a drunk in a shopping centre. "*He*'s not human," he said. "Why did you forget that? Get back into the room and lie down on the floor, both of you. Put your hands together behind your heads. Go on!"

Dave and Sandra reluctantly retreated back into the Defence Lab and lay down on the floor with their hands behind their heads. Dave clutched his camera against his side with one elbow.

"Now," said Sir Philip, addressing Wavevector, "I want you to turn around, and then get up, very slowly. One false move and I shoot."

Wavevector did as he was told. The gun trailed round the side of his head, then dropped and ground against his back. "Now walk slowly into the lab," Sir Philip commanded. "That's right. Go up to your cell. That's right. Take your hands down, slowly, and open the door. Good. Now go in . . ." The voice stopped, and Wavevector could sense the other's frozen stare at the place where the generator had been minutes before. The gun drove into his back, and he understood that Sir Philip was utterly terrified, perhaps even more terrified than Wavevector himself. He was so frightened that he might shoot out of panic.

"I am not resisting," said Wavevector urgently. "You do not need the generator to hold me. I cannot disentangle myself from this body, and I cannot do any violent manipulations while I am inside it. That is true."

"What happened to the generator?" demanded Sir Philip shrilly.

"Gravitational Constant destroyed it. Please, I meant to give myself up next anyway. You can call the police. I will not resist."

"The other one!" shrieked Sir Philip, glancing frantically about. "Oh God, where is it?"

"He left, just before you came. You have equipment. You can see that I am telling the truth."

"I don't dare touch it," muttered Sir Philip. "Oh Christ, what am I going to do?—The other generator, the one by the other creature's cage—is that still there?"

"No. Please, you don't need to be afraid. I can't harm you."

The gun trembled against his back. Then Sir Philip glanced at Dave. "All right," he said. "You with the camera. Get up. Put the camera down. There's some electrical tape under the counter to your right—in the second cupboard. That's right. Bring it over here and tie this creature up."

Reluctantly, Dave got up and looked in the cupboard. The electrical tape was a fat black spool of the heavy-duty variety reinforced with nylon. Dave came over with it and stood in front of Wavevector, jiggling the tape helplessly in his hand. He met Wavevector's eyes and shrugged apologetically.

"He's not a creature," said Sandra in a voice that shook with rage. "He's a person. He has a name. You stupid idiot,

don't you realise that he could have vaporised you a thousand times over before now, if he'd wanted to? You can reason that out for yourself: you know he was able to follow
Anderson, and you've seen what happened to the generator.
He didn't do it because he didn't *want* to do it. You're trying to fight a war with someone who thinks fighting is a
mental aberration."

"Shut up!" shrieked Sir Philip. "You whore, you sold out
your own race! You, thing! Turn around, slowly. Kneel.
Keep your hands behind your head and your face against the
wall. Now, you—tape his hands together."

Dave reluctantly taped Wavevector's hands together behind his head. "Is it true what you told him?" he asked in a
low voice. "Would you really blow up if he shot you?"

"I don't know," said Wavevector shakily. "I might. I
don't have enough information to do the calculation. I
would try not to, of course." That sounded ridiculous, even
to him.

Dave finished with the tape. "I can't cut it," he pointed
out to Sir Philip.

"Go back and lie down on the floor again."

When Dave was down, Sir Philip grabbed a pair of scissors from a drawer without looking away from Wavevector.
He cut the end of the tape, then ordered Sandra to get up and
told her to tape Dave's feet together. Then Dave was forced
to tape Sandra's feet; then Sandra secured Dave's hands. Sir
Philip obviously considered securing Sandra's hands himself, but he didn't dare risk taking his attention from
Wavevector. He jammed the gun between Wavevector's
shoulders and ordered him to get to his feet.

"Are the generators upstairs still there?" he demanded.

"I don't know," whispered Wavevector. "Probably."

"Then we're going upstairs. You are going to walk in
front, and I am going to be right behind with this gun. You
two others will stay here. I don't want any interfer—"

There was a sudden buzz, and the black doors opened. Sir
Philip jumped violently, whirled towards them, then whirled

back again and shoved the gun harder into Wavevector's back. Foster came in, followed by McKenzie and an indistinct crowd of others.

"Thank God!" cried Sir Philip. "Foster, Andrew, I need help!"

"Davie!" came Rod's unmistakable voice, raised in a howl. There was a commotion, and his large form forced through the crowd and into the room, shaking off restraining hands like a dog shaking off water. He bellowed at Sir Philip, "What have you done to Davie?"

Wavevector felt the gun jerk against his back. There was an impression of brute impact against his left shoulder, and a deafening noise. Somebody screamed. The blow knocked him sideways against the wall, twisting him round, so that his stunned eyes faced back into the room. People, crowds of people: Sir Philip standing over him with the gun smoking in his hand; Dave on the floor; Sandra sitting up, her feet taped, her mouth open; Rod looming half-way from the doors; Foster holding Malcolm by the elbow; Andrew McKenzie looking as though he wanted to run away; others he did not know. Crowds of people, all staring in horror at him. The impact came again. He felt a pounding against his back and chest. It was more numbing than it was painful, but it made it difficult to breathe. His mind, creeping remotely along the trail of sensation, acknowledged at last that he had been shot.

"Look what you've done!" McKenzie shouted at Sir Philip. "Christ, look what you've done!"

"I—I didn't mean to!" stammered Sir Philip. "He startled me. It went off."

Malcolm wrestled his arm free of Foster and ran over. Wavevector opened his mouth with some vague idea of speaking, and found that his throat and mouth were full of blood. Malcolm's eyes focused on the blood with a look of recognition. "Oh, shit," he whispered. He pushed Wavevector's legs straight, eased him down, and jerked open the tracksuit top. The blue water lilies of the T-shirt

had turned crimson. Malcolm hauled it up, and his hands
reddened.

"It's gone through his lung," said Malcolm, his clear un-
panicked voice carrying through the confusion. "I think it
may have hit a major blood vessel, too. Somebody call an
ambulance at once."

Sandra screamed again: "You murderer! Wavevector!"

Wavevector scanned frantically, to the limit of his sense,
and found, not far away, a dimple in the Earth's magnetic
field. He directed a burst of radiation at it, boosting its frequency with all the energy at his disposal so that it would
carry through the thick walls: *Gravitational Constant! Help!*

Instantly the other was there. *What has happened?*

"Rod!" shouted Malcolm, his forced calm fraying at the
edges. "Get your phone and call an ambulance! Now!"

*The entities who imprisoned us returned and this body
has been injured. I think it will die. I am afraid its death may
disorder me catastrophically.*

"They took it away!" Rod was shouting. "Oh Jesus!"

"You have a phone here?" someone asked Sir Philip icily.
It was one of the strangers, a grey-haired woman in a grey
jacket and skirt.

You must disentangle yourself from the body at once, said
Gravitational Constant. *I will help you.*

"Send that thing to a hospital?" Sir Philip shrieked. "Let
the public in? We don't dare!"

The woman had spotted a phone and was striding over to
it. "What's the code for an outside line?" she asked briskly.

The linkages renew themselves as they are severed,
Wavevector said. He could not argue with Gravitational
Constant's decision. Not now. Bad enough to suffer for his
own stupidity: he would not inflict death on others.

*Then you sever them, and I will try to prevent their re-
newal*, replied Gravitational Constant. *Proceed.*

Wavevector forced himself to concentrate, and became
aware of his dual nature, of the thousand thousand links that
held him to the body that was now once again fighting for

its life. With a sense of unspeakable cruelty, he reached for the furthest of those links, and severed it. He worked slowly at first, one link, then another; then more rapidly, cutting them by fives and sevens. Like a tangle of strings they hung, spinning and trying to re-adhere, but Gravitational Constant drew them away, up and out of the body's desperate grasp.

The others still roared and buffeted around him. He was aware of Malcolm cutting the tape around his hands with the scissors, then taking off his tracksuit top and T-shirt, and wadding them up against the wounds—the two wounds, one below his left shoulderblade, the other below his collarbone. Something had broken between them. There was pain from it now. But already his feet were numb. The human part of himself pleaded desperately—"They might save you; they're trying to save you; you don't know that you'll die!"—but he did not listen to it. He could not risk bringing the others to destruction. He severed another set of linkages. His legs went numb. Another and another and another: the pain in his hands finally stopped.

Sandra's face appeared above him. She was crying. "Wavevector!" she said. He thought that she had caught his hand, but he could not feel it. He hesitated, looking at her with longing.

You must proceed! urged Gravitational Constant. *You cannot stop now: it is evident even to me that this body is weakening.*

I know, he replied, and severed another set of linkages. His body went numb below the waist. Best to leave the vital organs until last. He reached, with infinite regret, to the links which gave him the sense of taste, and cut them. The metallic saltiness of injury left his mouth. He cut his sense of smell, and the scent of blood and sweat vanished. He severed hearing, and the voices went. He looked one last time at Sandra's face, and moved his lips around her name.

In the silence, her lips answered. Her hand brushed against his forehead. "Kiss me," he whispered, soundlessly, and she lowered her lips to his. He cut sight as she touched

him, cut sense as her lips left his own, and then he had no
perceptions left but the single seamless awareness with
which he had been formed. The body's resistance to his part-
ing was feeble now, and its hold was slipping even from the
links he had not cut. It was dying. It had fought to live, as
bravely as ever, but its struggle was doomed. He severed the
rest quickly—speech, thought, organic memory; nerves,
heart, brain-stem—and he was free. He hovered on top of
the body, scanning Sandra stumbling back and sitting down
on the floor with her hands over her face; scanning Malcolm
closing the sightless eyes which had been his own.

We must go now, said Gravitational Constant.

No, said Wavevector.

*You said this place was dangerous. The biological enti-
ties are able to detect us, and there are still two diamagnetic
generators intact.*

I don't care. I wish I had died with the body.

You might have killed them all if you had.

*I would not have left it otherwise! I would have stayed. I
have lost a universe. You have no conception what it is like.
I was in love with that one, the female. She wanted me to
stay with her. I wanted to stay.*

*You are behaving irrationally. To remain now aids noth-
ing. You have been disentangled, and the body is dead.*

*I will stay to tell my friends I survived. I will tell them
that, at least.*

*Then I suggest you tell them somewhere else. If we re-
main here any longer, I foresee that we will come into conflict with the entities who imprisoned us.*

Wavevector hovered a moment, assessing. The human
voices around him had become only vibrations in the air: he
would have to concentrate hard to understand them, and his
concentration was shattered. His English-speaking self was
gone: it had vanished with the speech centres of his brain. To
have lost that, that as well! He had a sudden incongruous desire to weep. It was like the impossible pain of an amputated
limb. But Gravitational Constant was right. Sir Philip would

undoubtedly think of the equipment ranged around them—
the X-ray detectors and radio detectors, the magnetometers
and infrared scanners—and he would use it to determine
whether Wavevector had survived. And there were, as Gravitational Constant had pointed out, two diamagnetic generators still intact.

I will leave now, then, he agreed wearily, *and I will speak
to my friends later, elsewhere.*

The black doors were still open. He did not even have to
boost his frequency to go.

SIXTEEN

AT HALF-PAST SIX ON TUESDAY MORNING, AFTER twenty-seven hours without sleep, Sandra found herself being interviewed by the head of MI5.

Wavevector's body had been taken away by the ambulance long before then. She had cried to see it go. She had cried so much by then that her head was aching and her eyes burned at the fresh tears, but she cried anyway. She knew she would have no chance to weep at any funeral: if the body ever received burial, it would be in Paul Anderson's name. Fair enough: the body had been his. Mrs Anderson Barlow would shed false tears into a linen hankie, and the remains would be interred in some garden of repose under a marble stone engraved with the name of a man Sandra had never met and wouldn't have liked.

It was clear, though, that there would be no funeral at all for some time. MI5 sent a representative in the ambulance, and it was plain that as soon as the body was certified dead, it would be taken away "for examination." MI5 was eager to examine lots of things, including all of Stellar's archives and all of Rodney Jones' tapes. The organisation had arrived at Stellar while the final encounter in the Defence Lab was being played out. Foster had been in the foyer, throwing Rod and Malcolm out, when a dozen cars and three vans had drawn up in the visitors' parking lot, and the flower of British intelligence got out, ready to take charge.

It emerged afterwards that the organisation had been able to arrive at Stellar when it did because of Denise Gresham. Stellar's legal adviser had been Rodney Jones' hush-hush top-secret no-witnesses source. Sandra suspected that the lawyer had resented her exclusion from the company's secretive inner circle, and had been talking to the press principally to get her own back—though the woman had also clearly been worried that Sir Philip Lloyd was breaking the law in the Anderson affair, and that her legal reputation would end up smirched by his doings. At any rate, MI5 had found her by tracing Rod's car, and had approached her to ask what Rod had wanted. She'd told them at once—with, of course, the best possible gloss on her own motives, and much talk of her concern about the course that events had been taking. MI5 had not been overly interested in the notion that Rodney Jones wanted a private tour of Stellar's lab that night. They were looking for Wavevector, and they were confident that Rod knew nothing about him. Still, they'd upgraded Rod's status slightly, enough so that an agent was assigned to trail him. Not a very senior agent, though, and not one who had any real idea what the operation was about. Her radioed report that five people had got into Jones' car on Bury Road, and that one of them was a tall man who appeared to have bandaged hands, had taken some time to filter up to someone who understood that this was significant. Nor had the agent been following Rod closely: she had believed the trace which told her that his car was at Sandra's house, until she arrived at Sandra's house and found the trace stuck—magnetically!—to the bottom of a van. After that, however, the muddle and inefficiency ended. MI5 had descended on Rod's goal, Stellar, like a pack of starving wolves on a wounded elk.

Andrew McKenzie had let them in. He had been giving

the security service his full cooperation since he was first interviewed, at noon on Monday. He had been increasingly
unhappy about the way Stellar had treated Wavevector, and
Monday morning had flung him into open opposition. He
had woken up at the cottage and found Wavevector's cell
broken, with blood and torn skin on the door, blood on the
floor, and a trail of blood leading to the front door of
the house. A track of red droplets across his bed and on the
sleeve of his pyjamas bore witness to how close Wavevector
had come to him—but he had not been touched. Before that,
he'd believed Sir Philip's assessment that Wavevector was a
danger to humanity, though doubt had been growing in him
since Wavevector was captured. That bloody trail had confirmed every doubt. Wavevector was not a danger to anyone.
Stellar had been brutal in its treatment of him, and McKenzie was ashamed. He had repeated this conclusion to MI5,
where it had found a ready audience.

That, Sandra thought, was the crowning irony. MI5 opposed Stellar's treatment of Wavevector. MI5 would have
handled him with kid gloves, warm baths, feather pillows
and generous advances of cash. Here had been a genuine extraterrestrial, with a knowledge of physics far in advance of
anything on Earth and a willingness to share that knowledge. What couldn't he have done for the defence of the
realm? MI5 had fully believed that he'd killed Anderson,
and MI5 hadn't cared in the least. Andersons were a penny
a pound, but Wavevectors . . . well, the cousins over at the
CIA would have been sick, sick with envy. And Stellar had
thrown him away.

When it was clear that Wavevector's body was definitely
dead, and when scans on the Defence Lab equipment had
failed to discover any trace of the rest of him, MI5 took over
Stellar's headquarters and began the over-familiar business
of ascertaining What Went Wrong. All the people who'd
been in the basement were taken off into separate rooms and
questioned. Sandra answered her interrogator truthfully,
then sat alone for a while in the ash-coloured office she'd

been taken to, staring numbly at the blank screen of a computer.

By the time they came to tell her that the director wished to speak with her, it was day—a cloudy day, whose threatening light shone through the tinted windows with a look of imminent storm. A grey-suited MI5 woman showed her up to a room she had seen once before, on the day of the kidnapping—Stellar's Executive Common Room. It was unclear where Sir Philip was now, but Rod was standing with his own minder just outside the door. He gave her a tired smile and they went in together.

The head of MI5 was a grey woman—grey hair, grey suit, grey eyes. Her name was Mrs Matthews. Sandra remembered her calling the ambulance after Wavevector was shot, and beating the Stellars off to let Malcolm try first aid. Mrs Matthews had also personally cut the electrical tape around Sandra's legs, and around Dave's hands and feet, using a pair of nail scissors plucked from her capacious handbag. Sandra had a certain fondness for Mrs Matthews because of that, but she still looked at the woman bleakly.

"Please sit down," said Mrs Matthews, smiling at them in a motherly fashion. "Would you like some coffee?"

Sandra and Rod accepted coffee, and the head of MI5 sent one of the minders to fetch some. "I wanted to talk to you about the energy creature," she said matter-of-factly, when the brew was supplied. "I gather you knew it as well as anyone did."

"He wasn't a creature," said Sandra. She felt as though she'd been saying this all night. "He was a person, an individual. His name was Wavevector."

"And you knew him."

"I knew him fairly well, yes," said Sandra wearily. "I could tell you about him, but I don't think you'll be interested in the sorts of things I could say."

"On the contrary, I'd be very interested. I never had the privilege of meeting him."

Sandra shrugged and sipped her coffee. She felt grubby

and exhausted and all the tears had given her a headache. It was hard to think clearly. She was aware of Rod watching her silently.

"He was very reasonable," she said at last—and realised that she wanted to talk about him, to make him real in words so that people would understand. "He kept trying to work things out by reasoning about them, even when it was perfectly clear to everyone else that it was no use, and he believed what his reason told him. He said that if the balance of probability inclined to a particular proposition, he would never believe a contrary proposition out of sentiment alone. He tried to believe he was Anderson at first, even though Anderson horrified him, and it made him think he was going crazy."

"Why did Anderson horrify him?" asked the intelligence chief quietly.

"Because Anderson was *un*reasonable, and dishonest. He lied and cheated, and he did crooked deals and gave bribes. He lost his temper and he got into fights. Wavevector would never have done any of that. He was perfectly straightforward. He was also proud and impulsive and terrifically stubborn, and once he'd set his mind on something you couldn't argue with him. He'd reason you into the ground every time. He was incredibly intelligent—I think everyone sensed that. I know I did, from the first time I met him. It could be rather frightening. He was so far ahead of you that it made you feel subjugated—I felt like that sometimes, anyway. But it wasn't like that, really: he didn't have the first idea about dominating people. Aggression terrified him, because he couldn't reason with it. He was terrified of Stellar, and of Sir Philip. And he was very concerned about other people, earnest and anxious and bothered by what they thought. He was highly responsible and easily alarmed. That's what he was like. I told you it would be of no use to you."

"On the contrary," said Mrs Matthews, as she had said before, "it's very interesting. You're certain he had no hostile intention towards the people of this country?"

"I asked him that," said Rod. "Point blank. He said it was utterly inconceivable, and explained why. I'm sure you've listened to that tape already."

"Mmm," said Mrs Matthews noncommittally. "What was your impression of him, Mr Jones?"

"Like Sandra said," stated Rod. "Absolutely brilliant and a complete innocent."

"Do you know what he wanted to come back to Stellar for?" Mrs Matthews asked coolly. "I don't mean tonight. I mean the thing he took over Mr Anderson's body to do."

"No," said Sandra, as Rod shook his head, "but I'm sure it was something reasonable."

"You didn't ask him?" said Mrs Matthews, with a surprised tilt of her thick grey eyebrows.

"We didn't have much time," said Sandra. "This morning—I mean, yesterday morning, Monday—he was exhausted and injured and only wanted to go to bed. Last night we were too busy. We didn't have a lot of time for questions."

We didn't have a lot of time full stop, she thought bitterly. Barely enough even to agree that we loved each other. One kiss in the car, and one when he was dying.

She rubbed angrily at her chin. She had gone all night with the taste of his blood on her lips. There had been blood everywhere when she gave him the last kiss. There were probably traces of it still on her face, marked by her own tears.

"I see," said Mrs Matthews. She was silent for a moment, then said, "Tell me, in your opinion and on the record, how would he have responded to the offer of a confidential job with us?"

"What do you mean, confidential?" asked Rod sharply. "And who's 'us'?"

Mrs Matthews tilted her eyebrows at him. "Confidential in that it would not be given out to the likes of you, Mr Jones. 'Us' is Her Majesty's Government."

"You couldn't have given him a confidential job," replied

Rod. "The likes of me has made too much noise about his disappearance."

"Oh, if he'd accepted our offer, we could have arranged something," said Mrs Matthews comfortably. "One supervised press conference, and then a disappearance. Plastic surgery and a few forged documents. Would he have accepted that?"

"He'd have accepted like a shot," said Rod harshly. "Whether it would have been a good thing is another matter."

Sandra made a noise of protest, and Rod gave her a glare. "The offer would have been in exchange for information," he said. "And the information would have been theories the military could use. Do we really need a new lot of super weapons?"

Mrs Matthews sighed. "I know you don't like us, Mr Jones, but we don't start wars. Yes, I'd have been very happy if . . . Wavevector . . . could have given Britain an edge, technologically. I don't just mean in weapons, though. I don't think weapons are as important these days as the army likes to think. The nations that count are the ones with the big economies. Commander Jaeger and his ilk are the left-overs of the past. It's incredibly persistent, this old-boy culture—but it's not the way important things are done these days. To tell the truth, I probably feel as angry about what's happened as you do. We had this wonderful chance of advancement—and we let a crooked, secretive company director and a jealous military surveillance officer throw it away. Jaeger didn't tell us anything, you know, until Saturday. Even then he twisted half of it around, and we had to go back to source to get at the truth. He was a friend of Anderson's, of course, and furious about Anderson's death, which may excuse some things—but not everything. He was a stupid, conservative, old-fashioned male army officer who thought in terms of us and them. He didn't like a lot of civilians in MI5 telling him what to do, particularly when they were female—and you know that more than half our em-

ployees are. He discovered one important thing in the whole
of his miserable career, and he kept it from us. The whole
country's paid for it."

"I think Anderson bribed him," said Rod. "If I were you
I'd check to see if he's recently acquired a lot of shares in
Stellar."

The eyebrows tilted, and the eyes under them gleamed.
"I'll look into that, Mr Jones," said Mrs Matthews.

Sandra had a sudden vision of Commander Mark Jaeger
before a court martial. This woman, she was sure, would put
him there, see him broken, and get the responsibilities of his
department, whatever those had been, transferred to her own
hands. She was glad of it, though Jaeger had been no more
than a willing accessory to the real criminal. "What's going
to happen to Sir Philip Lloyd?" she asked bluntly.

Mrs Matthews sighed and shook her head. "I'm afraid I
don't know the answer to that. I understand that you must
feel very bitterly towards him, but I don't think there's anything he can be charged with—apart, perhaps, from corruption, if we can find evidence that he was giving bribes.
Obviously, we can't make the whole truth public . . ."

"Why not?" demanded Rod.

"It would undermine public confidence," replied Mrs
Matthews smoothly.

"You mean, you don't want the public to know how
badly everything was bungled."

"Mr Jones, you're a newsman. What do you think the
public's reaction would be if we announced that an invisible
energy creature from outer space had arrived, engaged in secret dealings with a power company, fallen out with them,
taken over a human body, and had been killed by the company director?"

There was a silence. "The public would praise the company director," said Sandra sourly.

Mrs Matthews nodded. "The public would also be very
alarmed about invading energy creatures from outer space. I
still hope that perhaps one of these creatures may decide to

contact us again, someday. I don't want the public mood
poisoned in advance. As for Sir Philip Lloyd—well, he
couldn't be convicted of murder, you know, even if the en—
Wavevector were able to claim human rights. It's quite clear
that he didn't mean to pull the trigger of that gun when he
did. The most you could hope for would be a conviction for
manslaughter, and a jury would undoubtedly accept that
he'd had real cause to fear for his life, and treat him sympa-
thetically. We can't punish Sir Philip Lloyd—except inas-
much as we can let it be known that we do not think him a
reliable person. Oh, but we are rescinding the classification
of the Astragen Project." The head of MI5 fixed Rod with an
innocent grey-eyed gaze. "The theory could be published.
There are probably some copies of it around."

Rod blushed.

"Now, you've been very helpful," Mrs Matthews concluded. "I have just one further question. In your opinions,
is there any chance that the energy crea— that Wavevector
could have survived the shooting last night? I understand
that he wasn't sure himself what would happen to him in
such circumstances."

"He thought he would die catastrophically," said Sandra
in a harsh flat tone. "That means, explode. He told Dave he
would try not to. I think he was trying not to while we were
trying to save him. His eyes weren't focusing: they did that
when he was doing things . . . doing something that didn't
belong to his human side. Maybe he was trying to disentangle himself. Maybe he succeeded: I hope he did. But if you
think he's likely to come back and talk to humans again—
would you, in his place? He's probably at the outer edges of
the solar system by now."

"What about the other one?" asked Mrs Matthews. "The
one he came to Stellar to free."

"He said that Gravitational Constant didn't speak any
Earth language and had no interest in planets. I should think
he's even less likely to come back than Wavevector."

Mrs Matthews sighed. "That's what I thought," she said

resignedly. "Well, thank you for your help. Now, for yourselves—neither of you are charged with anything, of course, and you are free to leave as and when you please, though you will need to advise us if you plan to leave the country in the foreseeable future. You may be subject to some surveillance for a time, under the terms of the Official Secrets Act." Rodney Jones opened his mouth, and the head of MI5 lifted one wearily restraining hand. "Mr Jones, you must see that one cannot simply drop people flat after events as extraordinary as these! You will get some of your tapes back, though I have to say that the energy creature's existence is now an official secret, and will be D-noticed. But you can feel quite free to discuss Stellar Research as much as you like. May I ask you both, though—if . . . Wavevector . . . ever contacts you again, will you please get in touch with us, *at once*? We could offer him any help he wanted if he chose to return. You would be doing him a service, and also doing a great service to the realm."

She spoke with unquestionable sincerity. But Sandra, looking in the limpid grey eyes, saw there another set of traps, a whole other range of betrayals. They would offer him help, undoubtedly. They would give him anything he wanted. They would locate another body for him, even— some coma victim somewhere, whose life-support system was about to be switched off. And then they would try to use him. Weapons or economics, in the end it wouldn't have made much difference. He would have been too valuable ever to be given real freedom. Oh yes, they would say, just do this, and we will give you—what do you want? A house? A lab? A top research job for your wife? And she saw that she herself would have become a trap, a thing they could manipulate to control Wavevector. And if he failed to be deceived—as he would have—then the doors would have closed on him once again. With a sense of profound treachery, Sandra realised that death had been the best option Wavevector had.

"Of course," she told the head of MI5. "If he contacts me again, I'll get in touch with you. But I don't think he will."

SHE WAS RELEASED AFTER THAT, AND WALKED DOWN to the dove-grey foyer. Rod squeezed her shoulder and went off to see if he could find Dave. A sign had been posted by the great double-doors: "BRITISH GAS REGRETS THIS BUILDING IS CLOSED UNTIL FURTHER NOTICE," and a number to contact for inquiries. But it was still too early for Stellar's workforce to arrive and question where the gas leak was. Sick of the way the glass dimmed the day, she pushed through the doors and out into the cloudy morning. There was mist on the fields, and the young cherries and Japanese maples in their cardboard tubes were dripping with dew. Too weary to think, she sat down on the edge of a kerb, and stared blindly at the beds of greenhouse flowers. After a little while, someone came up and squatted behind her, and she looked up and saw that it was Malcolm.

She began to cry again. He did not say anything, merely put his arms around her, and kissed the top of her head, and cried too. After a time, they looked at each other, and he brushed her hair back from her face, and said, "C'mon. I'll take you home."

They walked together across the wet field and down the drive to the lay-by where Rod's car was parked. Rod and Dave were already there, talking in low voices. Their arms were around each other, but they put their hands hurriedly back at their sides when Sandra and Malcolm appeared. Sandra thought it must be hard to be homosexual, unable to comfort one another in public.

"Hey," Rod remarked. "I didn't say. I was the one who startled Lloyd into letting that gun off. I was a complete idiot. For what it's worth—which isn't much—I'm sorry." His voice grated with pain.

Sandra shook her head. She might blame Rodney Jones for many things, but not for reacting with shock and rage at the sight of his lover lying supine on the floor while his enemy flourished a gun. "It was Lloyd's fault," she said. "He'd almost fired that gun at least twenty times, and it was *always* pointing at Wavevector. Don't blame yourself, and don't talk about it. I want to go home."

They dropped Malcolm off at his house and returned to Sandra's in the grey Metro. Sandra spent the rest of that day asleep, waking at suppertime with a headache, feeling dirty and thirsty. She got up and wandered into the bathroom. She filled the tooth mug with water, and drank it off, then caught sight of her reflection in the mirror. It was like a mask from a Greek tragedy. Her hair stood out from her head in a mass of tangles, caked here and there with clots of something dark. Her face was runnelled still with tears. On one cheek there was a smear of deep red, dried into flaking patches. She touched it hesitantly, and remembered again the way his blood had bubbled on his lips at the end, and the way those lips had felt against her own. She scrubbed at the bloodstain with her finger, then began to cry again. She took a shower and a paracetamol.

When she was clean and changed, she had an overwhelming desire to talk to the others. She went downstairs, and found Rod and Dave in the sitting room.

"We were just waiting for you to wake up to say goodbye," Rod told her. "We packed already, and the things are in the car. We oughta go home. Thanks for the house-room."

"Why don't we go out for supper first?" said Sandra hesitantly. "And why don't we phone Malcolm?"

Malcolm suggested that they get a takeaway and eat it at his house. "I don't want to go out," he told Sandra on the phone. "I mean—people might recognise you, or Rod, and ask about it, and I don't want to tell lies. Not so soon."

So they arrived at the Browns' with a Chinese takeaway, and sat down to eat it in the kitchen. Mrs Brown had already left for her evening shift, and Shula was out ("friends and boyfriends"). The four of them talked in a desultory fashion—about what Rod and Dave would do next; about what would happen to the Astragen theory ("I left the copy with the magnetism man at Imperial. I just need to phone him and tell him it's OK to publish. I don't know how that witch guessed it."); about Sandra's job and Malcolm's painting. When the food was gone, Rod and Dave remained in a huddle over the table, talking about how they could rearrange all their film to make a scathing exposé of Stellar.

Sandra and Malcolm drifted into the sitting room. A large painting adorned the wall there of Mrs Brown, Malcolm and a pretty girl—who had to be Shula—in clothing even more garish than Malcolm's. The portrait was almost too straightforward to be Malcolm's, but Sandra had seen one other drawing in that tender, affectionate style, and had no trouble identifying the hand.

"I know what you're gonna say," remarked Malcolm. "This room needs some houseplants. Well, you just tell us how not to kill 'em, and we'll get some."

Sandra gave a tired smile. He didn't give up easily. She was too battered to feel much but some part of her was glad of it.

"I don't think your mum will want any advice from me," she said. Mrs Brown had, in fact, treated her with stern disapproval.

"She just doesn't like me going out with white girls," said Malcolm. "She'll be fine once she gets to know you. She'll like you, in fact: you're a pathologist, even if your patients are green. She always wanted me and Shula to be doctors."

"I can see your mum's really disappointed in you," she said, smiling.

Malcolm grinned. "She's got used to me doing Art. But she'd like it better if I was a doctor."

"What does Shula do?"

"Computing. She's bright, but not the studious type. She wants to get a good job with some nice people and have a good time and maybe travel a bit."

"And marry and settle down and have babies?"

"In due course. Not yet. Life's got a lot of other things to try out first."

Sandra looked at him. His eyes were a lighter shade of brown than Wavevector's, almost the same colour as his skin. His face, always mobile and expressive, now held a look between hope and apprehension. So many things he had said, with his eyes and his smile, and she had not wanted to hear them. But she was sure that face had never, could never, express cruelty. A part of her had recognised long before that cruelty had no part in his nature.

Life still had a lot of things to try. "What sort of house-plants does your mum plan to buy?" she asked.

His face lit slowly in a smile almost as wonderful as Wavevector's. "Tell us where to start," he said. And he sat down beside her on the sofa, and kissed her until she felt some comfort even in the deep blood-stained hollow left by Wavevector's death.

"Show me some of your paintings," she told him. "I want to see how you're going to support yourself next term."

They went upstairs, and Malcolm began showing her paintings in earnest—which she hadn't quite expected—hauling canvases out on to the landing so that she could see them properly. He commented on their subjects, angles, colours, pigments and perspectives. Rod and Dave came up to see what was going on when one of the paintings was rescued from falling down the stairs.

"This is fucking brilliant!" said Dave, enthusiastically inspecting a canvas which seemed to be an operating theatre crossed with the *Book of Kells*. Malcolm beamed, and redoubled his commentary.

There were a few paintings in Shula's room as well, and Malcolm went to get them, then gave a yelp. The screen of the small computer on the desk lit with a violet glow, then went dark, lit and went dark.

Sandra rushed forward. "Wavevector!" she cried joyfully. Then she stared at the dark screen with a sense of utter fu-

tility, realising that even if it were him, she would not see
him again. "Is it you?" she asked, her eyes stinging.

The violet light came on again, and a single word flashed
up against the blankness: *Yes*.

He had been watching her for most of the day. He had
followed the car from Stellar Research to her house, and
hovered in her room, watching her sleep. There were manipulations he could have done to attract her attention, but
they were showy and extreme, and he had been afraid that
they would alarm her. He was not sure, now it had come to
it, whether he was wise to speak to her at all. What he felt
for her now was only the memory of a longing, not the thing
itself. He had lost all instinct to join with another, to form a
unit in a society such as his own kind did not possess. He regretted the loss bitterly, but regret would not restore what
was gone. It seemed to him now that this contact would only
lacerate them both.

"You're alive!" she said, and looked about the room,
knowing even as she did so that it was useless, that she
would not be able to see him any more than she had seen
Gravitational Constant.

Not alive, came the reply on the computer. *But I survived.
Gravitational Constant helped me disentangle myself. I am
sorry if you have been distressed by the supposition that I
had been destroyed.*

"I hoped you'd survived," she told him. "I didn't know,
but I hoped." She clasped her hands together, wishing they
could touch his—then remembered that his hands were in a
morgue somewhere, being examined by MI5.

I wanted you to know that I would have stayed, he told
her. *If it had been possible, I would have stayed. I regret how
it ended. I regret that very much.*

She said nothing for a moment, staring at the screen with
bowed head and remembering the limpid grey eyes of the
head of MI5. From the beginning he had turned to her for
facts, not reassurances, and she had never lied to him. She
would not lie now. "I grieve for it," she said slowly. "But I

think that if you had stayed, we would both have come to regret it, more than you now regret the way it ended. Before I left Stellar this morning, the head of MI5 asked me to tell her if you ever made contact again. They want to offer you a job and their cooperation if you stay. I am telling you this because I don't want to hide it from you, but I think it's the last thing in the world you should do. They would never leave you free. They want to use you, and they would use me, too, to imprison you. They'd destroy us both."

The screen went dark, and remained dark for a moment. She remembered him evaluating a new piece of information: the slight frown and the lowering of the dark eyes, the sense of a great computer whirring silently. The real computer on the desk before her might have been a toaster, for all the expression it conveyed.

The light flickered on again. *It would have been contrary to principle for me to stay*, he said. *I knew that from the beginning. If I had been able to remain undetected, it might have been feasible, but that option was ruled out. It is advantageous that circumstances prevented me from fulfilling my intention. I violated principle once on impulse and in ignorance. I will not do so again coldly and deliberately.*

And yet, the bitter regret still burned him. He found himself reflecting on MI5's offer, and knew that he must leave Earth at once, before the idea took hold.

"What are you going to do now?" asked Malcolm, coming in to stand beside Sandra and stare in fascination at the screen. "Are you going to stay on Earth?"

No.

He scanned them, standing so close to each other, their hands almost touching. He had seen them kiss downstairs. Jealousy was something he'd never had an instinct for, and it was a complete irrelevancy now, but the sight of their closeness had sharpened the torment. He could not stay on Earth any longer. It was too painful. He would be filled with contradictory longings and desires for the impossible, and that was the way to insanity.

"What are you going to do, then?" asked Malcolm.

Go away. Far away, somewhere I will have to travel for a long time to reach. He longed, desperately, for Travel—for the total unthinking unity with the principles of creation, when Time has slowed to one infinite moment. He knew, though, that he could never explain to them what it was like to move at the speed of light, and he did not try.

Rod cleared his throat. "Are you—that is, is there anything we can do for you?"

Unfinished scraps of a business he should never have begun. *Publish the Astragen theory*, he said succinctly.

"It's already in hand," said Rod, putting his own hands up. "Can you just tell me—is that the reason you wanted to borrow Anderson's body to begin with? To publish your theory?"

In part. I also intended to remove all the Astragen trial data from Stellar, including the blueprints for the prototype batteries, and post them to Stellar's six major rivals in alternative power.

Rod laughed. "Fucking A!"

I was stupid.

He scanned them again. He could read nothing from their tones of voice, any more than they could know his mind from the bare words he set upon the screen. He was concentrating hard to understand them at all, and studying the way they stood for clues to their emotions. His body no longer interpreted for him. But he thought that Sandra wanted him, from the way she bent towards the screen, from the way her hand touched it. He remembered Sir Philip's words, spoken to wound: "Did you fuck her, just to see what it was like?" He had not, and he would never know, just as he would never know the names and habits of the plants and animals that filled the Earth so abundantly, or learn music, or understand those paintings of Malcolm's that now littered the landing. He had read the table of contents, and then the book had been snatched away. The grief of that denial beat at him, and suddenly he wanted the goodbyes to be over, to be out

in the depths of space, travelling, sunk deep into dreamless-
ness while the years flowed past.

I am going, he told them. *I only came to reassure you that
I had survived, and to say goodbye.* The screen went dark.

"Wait!" called Malcolm urgently.

The screen lit. *What is it?*

"I want to see what you really look like," said Malcolm.
"I think we need to see what you look like. We've never
seen you, except in Anderson's body."

Sandra stepped back with an involuntary shake of the
head. She remembered the blurred black thing in the radiographs. She did not want to see it. She wanted to remember
instead how Wavevector had looked when he was alive. But
Malcolm had caught the gesture and quickly turned towards
her.

"You need it most," he told her. "You're why I'm asking.
You may not think so now, but if you don't have some idea
of *him*, something you can put in the back of your head and
take out when you think of him travelling the universe, it's
going to hurt you."

He was completely serious. They looked at each other for
a moment.

"Trust me," said Malcolm. "I did two summers working
as an orderly in hospital: I learned a lot from medical emergencies. What you imagine is *always* worse than what you
can see."

"OK," said Sandra shakily, and looked back at the computer screen.

I don't really look like anything, appeared printed on the
screen. *I don't emit in the visual frequency.*

Malcolm left the room, then came back with the radiograph Sir Philip had given them. He laid it flat in front of the
computer. "Sir Philip Lloyd gave us this," he said, addressing his words to the screen. "It looks like a bit of black wool
coming apart in an oil puddle. It's no good for anything but
nightmares. We humans are not very good with invisible
things. I think the fact that he couldn't see you was what

made Sir Philip so afraid of you in the first place. Can't you try to emit in the visual frequency, just to set our minds at rest? Sir Philip said you emitted X-rays. Can't you just sort of downgrade them a bit?"

Wavevector scanned the radiograph with horror. He didn't mind so much that his form was a mere silhouette, but it was the wrong shape. That tendril of energy should not be trailing like that. The frequencies distorted in a way that was painfully unnatural. He reviewed himself anxiously: the gradients all seemed normal now. The entanglement must have deforming him. Why hadn't Gravitational Constant mentioned it?

Gravitational Constant would certainly have mentioned it, he realised, if Wavevector hadn't disentangled himself. The other was concerned at Wavevector's state of mind, however. He had not wanted to disturb him further. He was waiting still, in Earth's neighbourhood, to make sure that all was well.

Wavevector scanned the radiograph again. Anderson's body had been tormenting him just as much as he had tormented it. Staying entangled had never been a real option at all.

"It's a pretty ugly portrait, huh?" said Malcolm, as the screen remained blank.

Yes, Wavevector agreed, with a bitterness they would never have guess.

So can you show us what you really look like?"

I will try. He focused on the dance of energies which he was composed of, and carefully reduced the frequency of their accidental emissions.

There was a sudden dark purple flicker in the air about the computer, and everything white in the room fluoresced glaringly. Sandra's eyes stung, and she put up her hands to shield them. But the dark purple softened into violet, then into blue—and then the computer was surrounded by a web of light that bent and curled and refracted about itself, shading through every colour in the spectrum. Space folded itself among the light with a shimmer like heat-haze on a mountain, and the beams glittered and shifted, dancing together in forms that defied geometry. It was fireworks and fountains of pure colour, a dream of flying and a symphony by Mozart written in light; it was the heart of a diamond and a butterfly's wing scaled in fire. It was beautiful beyond the limit of the human imagination.

"Oh, God!" cried Malcolm, in a tone of agonised joy. "Oh, God!"

Sandra felt something break inside her, and began to weep. *That* was what had fallen in love with her; *that* was what had been tortured and imprisoned. Perhaps it should have made no difference to her feelings about Wavevector that he was as inhumanly beautiful as Isaiah's vision of the glory of God, but it did make a difference, and it hurt.

The light vanished, except for the violet glow in the computer screen. *Did it distress you?* flashed up on the screen: Sandra could almost hear the anxiety, and the thought of that human-like anxiety coming from what she had just seen was incongruous.

"Oh, God!" said Malcolm again. He was crying too. "I can't, I can't. Nobody could. Oh Christ, paints don't *come* in those colours."

Sandra, looking at him through her own tears, understood that despite his denial, he was struggling to think how to paint what he had just seen. He might spend the rest of his life trying to paint it.

You seem distressed, said Wavevector unhappily. *I am sorry*. He could scan their tears. He wondered fleetingly what he would have seen if he had looked at himself with his human eyes. He had always found the appearance of his own kind aesthetically pleasing, but he had not forgotten that odd sensation of finding Gravitational Constant invisible. The visual frequency was not a natural way to emit. Perhaps he would look terrifying to a human.

"We're not distressed, OK?" said Malcolm. "Seeing

something like you shakes us up, that's all. You're very beautiful, but in a way we're not used to. OK?"

Wavevector was unconvinced. *Will it help you to remember me without fear?* he asked.

Sandra knew, and could not tell him, that if she had seen him like that at first, she would never have fallen in love with him. One regarded beauty like that with awe, with wonder, with admiration: one did not kiss it and put one's arms about it, laugh at it and snuggle up to it at night. But she did not need to lie to him. She could answer him with truth, as always.

"I will remember you with love," she promised him, "with love, and with regret."

He knew then that he had been right, after all, in his decision to come back to say goodbye. He twisted the systems of the computer, and sent one last message flashing on to the screen. *As I shall you, Sandra. And you, Malcolm, Rodney, Dave—I will remember you with gratitude. I wish you all good fortune, and all joy.*

And for the last time, the screen went dark.